THE
BUTTERFLY
CODE

SUE WYSHYNSKI

WB

WHITMAN
BOOKS

ACKNOWLEDGMENTS

So much goes into making a book, and I'm grateful to all the people who have put their time and hearts into The Butterfly Code.

Thank you to my insightful, fantastic writing buddies, Sharon Brown, Ellie Crowe, and Adria Estribou, who lived inside this story with me and helped me find my way. And to my long distance writer friend, Amanda Budde Sung, for her smart, helpful critiques.

Thank you to my husband, Scott, who's always there to root for me and continues to believe in me. What more could a girl want?

Thank you to my professional dream-team: story editor, Julie Scheina, whose in depth questions blew me away and forced me to dig deeper than I ever thought possible; jacket designer, Liz Casal, who deserves an award for her brilliant design that grabbed me and wouldn't let go; and copy editor Christine Ma, whose incredible eye for detail makes a writer look good. Hurrah! And thanks to my proofreader Christine Sackey for her incredible kindness and generosity.

Thanks to my cheerleader and sounding board, Claire Elizabeth Terry, and to my friends—old, new, and FB/Goodreads/Twitter pals—who have kept me going with their words of encouragement.

And a huge thank you to my family, Mom, Dad, Jill, Sarah, Raine, Alden, Olivia, Glenn, and Joan. Your support means more to me than you'll ever know. I love you!

Whitman Books

Cover design by Elizabeth Casal
Cover © Sue Wyshynski
Cover & interior images © Shutterstock/Nadya Lukic & SofiaWorld
Story editor, Julie Scheina
Copy editor, Christine Ma

ISBN-13: 978-0-9859852-4-0
ISBN-10: 0-9859852-4-0

For Scott
Who fills my world with sunshine

ONE

I STUMBLE THROUGH THE RED-TINGED NIGHTCLUB haze and wonder if this is what purgatory looks like. Ella and Gage are nowhere to be seen. *Did they leave?* I hurry out the club door and cold air engulfs me. A gasp bursts from my lips, half relief, half shudder, as the night's damp fingers creep through my fluttering dress.

Shivering, I wind my arms around my ribs.

That's when I see him. Dr. Hunter Cayman.

The man the town has been whispering about. The man no one really seems to know. The man my father despises.

He's across the street, leaning against a steel monster—a low-slung black car, its curves somehow wicked in the night. Rain sparkles like fire on the front hood under the glow of the orange streetlamps. His startling, magnetic intensity pulls at me so hard that I can't seem to look away.

For a doctor in charge of a research facility, he's young. Late twenties, maybe. His dark gray T-shirt stretches across his muscular chest. His thumbs are hooked into the pockets of his well-fitting jeans, and his strong forearms are bare to the relentless drizzle. In fact, he seems to enjoy the misty wetness. Like he's in his element. The way I would be on a beach in Hawaii, a million miles away from this tiny, nowhere town.

Despite the midnight sky, he's wearing dark glasses. Like the car, they, too, sparkle with rain. His face is rugged, more handsome than beautiful. His strong jaw is shadowed faintly with stubble. I wonder what he looks like when he smiles. If he does smile.

Why is he here? Is he debating whether to go in? Or is he waiting for someone? For one dizzy, strange moment, I wish he were waiting for me. Aeris Thorne.

Where did that come from?

He has no idea who I am. And even if he was interested, he's certainly not my type. From here I can tell he's hardheaded and probably used to getting his way.

I break off my gaze and stare at the glistening pavement. After a pause, I shift my chin and peek sideways. My eyes drift slowly up his body. What is it about him? The authoritative air? The mysterious aura that almost crackles around him?

Despite the suggestion of a sharp wit residing behind those dark shades, there's a wildness to him. It's as though his long, powerful legs and sturdy shoulders possess some superhuman strength. I imagine that if an army of foes descended right now, he'd happily take them on as a way to pass the time.

What am I doing? Ogling some guy on a street corner? This is ridiculous. I feel like I'm sneaking a glance at a demigod. Or maybe a devil.

Because as his stubbled jaw faces me dead-on and makes it clear I'm not the only one who's been staring, I realize he's one or the other.

Of that, I'm sure.

I stand frozen, caught in his crosshairs.

Music drifts from his car softly, but I hear it over the muffled noise of the Zenith Club. Mozart's Sinfonia Concertante in E-Flat Major, K. 364: II Andante. It's unexpected. I'm strangely delighted. That was my very first solo violin performance. I remember the nerves. The stage fright. The terror and the exhilaration. I'm like that now, with him studying me. The music blends with the sensation. It's in my fingers, which know every chord; in my wrist, which knows every pull of the bow. Every note soulful and yearning and spilling into this moment, so heightened and real as if time is standing still.

And I imagine he knows what I'm experiencing, can see the music in me, even though that's silly; he can't read my mind, my emotions, a stranger across an empty street. But then Mr. Olympian reaches into the car and turns up the volume. He smiles into me and I smile back into him. We're caught like two souls in a tiny eddy of reality.

The song ends. I wait for the next piece, but nothing comes on.

My gaze falters and I glance away.

He's a stranger and I have no idea what I'm doing.

Muffled dance music vibrates the slick wall behind me. The rhythm grips the air with unspent tension that's unleashed when the Zenith Club door flies open. Ella pushes outside onto the curb, all shimmery eye shadow and smudged mascara. She looks from Hunter to me. Then Gage strides out after his sister, his heavy-duty GORE-TEX jacket gripped under one arm.

"What a scene," Gage says, shaking his bright blond head. "Too much."

Ella laughs. Her cheeks are flushed. "Tourist season, gotta love it."

"Yeah, intense," I say. I hadn't expected the crush way out here in Deep Cove. I'm too embarrassed to admit that even after four years of New York crowds and subways, the fear of being trapped in a cramped place with no way out sends my heart into overdrive.

From across the street, I sense Dr. Cayman still watching me through his dark glasses. My skin prickles.

"How can he see through those?" Ella hisses, so quiet I can barely hear.

Maybe Dr. Cayman—Hunter—can read lips, because as soon as she turns away his mouth curves up in a grin. He's grinning—at me. Then he slides the shades from his face. His eyes, dark beneath strong brows, meet mine. They're the kind of eyes that can convey a whole world in just one glance.

My legs go off balance; it's these teetery heels—they're way too high. I reach for the wall. I'm suddenly aware of the dress sticking to my skin, which is damp despite the rusty awning overhead. I feel as if he can see right through the fabric.

I wind my arms tighter around myself.

A car thunders around the corner. The headlights shoot blades of light, pinning him in their beams. His pupils flash—it's as if they're mirrored.

Or a wild animal's whose eyes light up when it's caught on the road. I breathe in sharply, astonished.

The car passes.

What was that? What just happened?

His attention takes in my startled mouth, and he freezes.

I feel my chest rising and falling too fast under the thin white fabric of the dress Ella insisted I borrow.

Because you'd be pretty if you just dressed up once in a while, Ella said.

To which I'd replied, *What's wrong with my sweater? I love it and it's vintage. And these are my favorite oxfords.*

We're going to a dance club. Pretty please?

Which is how I ended up in heels so high I have to hold on to the wall, and a few flimsy strips of fabric held together with plastic wrap.

It's not my dress Hunter's examining, however. It's me. He holds his shades halfway to his face, yet he doesn't replace them. His hand practically crushes the frames, as he looks at me the way you look at someone you've seen before. Like he's certain he knows me. Knows me well.

But he doesn't. I would've remembered. Of that I'm sure.

Ella staggers a little, and I loosen one arm to steady her. She smells of Stoli and cranberry juice. Personally, I downed more than my share in an attempt to be less of a claustrophobic nerd. And now I'm hallucinating because, for a moment, I really thought Hunter's eyes actually flashed.

Eyes don't flash.

She jostles me with her elbow as she digs in her purse.

"Do you have to smoke those damn things?" Gage asks.

She clicks her lighter and takes a deep drag. "Maybe I should ask the good doctor over there to help me quit."

Gage glowers. "Sure. Head on up to his castle. You can be his first female Franken-girl."

Ella laughs. "It's not a castle, it's his research lab."

"Yeah," he growls. "There's what we need."

Why is everyone so down on Hunter and his research?

Quietly, I murmur, "I don't see anything wrong with trying to save people's lives."

Thunder rumbles in the distance. A salty breeze tugs at my hair. I picture his facility, the Phoenix Research Lab for Highly Contagious Diseases, several miles up the road out of town. I imagine the ocean, dark and choppy against the bluffs. High above, the secured compound's vast estate stretches along a jutting finger of land. From a distance, the old buildings, once home to a wealthy family, look both foreboding and beautiful.

The place is well protected—like an island with only one road in. Maybe that's why the researchers chose it. The hard-to-reach promontory provides a natural barrier against accidental infection of the surrounding population. Given people's reactions, it's still too close for comfort. Gage turns quiet and brooding whenever the lab is mentioned.

Just like Dad.

Yes, he's been touchy lately, which makes me wonder if he's back on the trail of Mom's death again. We both desperately want the truth, even though the case has been cold for twenty years. But this business with Cayman is different. The one time his name came up in passing, Dad made his feelings more than clear. *That doctor's a menace.* I'd rarely heard him speak in such a grim tone. It was strange, because under his gruff exterior, Dad is a softy.

What had Hunter done to deserve Dad's animosity?

Now, standing a hundred paces from Hunter on this cold, two-lane street, I long to know.

We've never exchanged a single word, me and this man with his fancy car and brash grin who's making me nervous and attracted all at once. He looks like trouble. According to Dad, he is trouble. Yet no one has ever caught my attention with such electrifying power.

A fresh gust of wind tears at my dress and sends sparks flying from the ember of Ella's half-smoked cigarette.

"Done yet?" Gage asks. He won't let her smoke in his truck.

"No. I'm not," she snaps.

Gage groans and leans back against the wall.

Clouds roll across the sky, revealing a partial moon. The light is gray and eerie and cold. In the murky flower shop window behind Hunter's car, streetlight reflections twinkle.

The club door opens once again, and a young woman strides out. Her long, dark legs jut from a micromini, and her high, rounded cheekbones are tinted an electric shade of peach. On anyone else the color would look bizarre. On her mocha skin, it's stunning. Hers is the kind of face you can't stop looking at. She was easily the most beautiful person in the club tonight. Maybe the most beautiful person I've ever seen.

Then I realize—she's why Hunter's here. She's the one he's waiting for. My heart sinks.

What is the matter with me? Am I crazy? He doesn't even know me.

The woman's eyes are as baleful as a cat's. I detect something else, though, something almost world-weary beneath her shield of glamour. She crosses in front of Ella, Gage, and me as if we don't exist. In this moment, I want to go home and forget this night. I want to forget the Zenith Club and its crushing crowd. I don't fit in. I never should have come.

Across the street, Hunter straightens at the young woman's approach. One corner of his mouth tips up. "I have no idea why you'd voluntarily go in there."

"It's called fun. You should try it sometime."

He lets out a short laugh. "I'll take your word for it."

"Let's go."

"As you wish." His tone is amused.

The car door releases a few inches, rimmed with cold sapphire light. Instead of opening out, the door slowly hinges upward. Butterfly doors— that's what they're called—but they don't look like the wings of a butterfly to me. Instead, this looks like a bird of prey. A raptor.

He guides her around to the passenger door. "Have a good time?"

"Not good enough," she replies.

"It never will be, Vic." It's said in a strangely gentle way, her name spoken as if he's known her forever.

"Don't get all poetic on me," she snaps, pouting up at him like an irritated angel who's unhappy about being stuck on earth.

6

I strain to hear his reply.

"Me? Poetic? Never." He laughs. It's a low rumble. A kindhearted noise that somehow surprises me. He makes me want to hear it again. Makes me wonder what it would feel like to have him laugh with me like that.

I watch him help her into the low seat. He bends and speaks quietly to her. As he does, the girl turns and stares at me through the driver's window. It's brief and piercing. Then she leans back against the seat.

They couldn't have been talking about me, could they? But then why else had she given me that quick, sharp study?

Two

"Do you know that girl?" I murmur to Ella.

"Victoria," Ella replies in a tight voice.

"Does she live here?"

"Yep. Nice, right?" Ella says, and hiccups. "A *scientist*. What kind of scientist acts like that? Prancing around like some high-fashion model. I mean, go back to New York or whatever!"

"Aeris lives in New York," Gage reminds his sister.

"Oh yeah. Sorry," Ella says to me. "But you don't count."

"Nice, Ella," Gage says. "That's insulting."

"I was joking."

"It's okay," I say, and laugh. She's right, though. I could never be that stunning. That full of life. Not many girls could. She'd danced all night—wild and powerful and nonstop, without exerting a single drop of sweat. She was like a doll that didn't need winding. Add to that the pull she had on others and she seemed almost inhuman.

If she's a coworker, did Cayman simply come to give her a ride? Or was there something between them?

He slides into the driver's seat. I imagine the scent of hand-stitched leather and wait for the throaty rumble that's sure to come. But he doesn't start the engine. What are they waiting for?

Ella lights a second cigarette from the butt of the first one.

"Put that thing out. Let's go," Gage says. "Aeris is freezing."

"She's fine. Aren't you fine?" Ella looks at me.

I'm too preoccupied to notice the cold. "I'm good," I agree.

"Anyway, if you'd let me smoke in the truck, we wouldn't be standing here in front of the club, would we?"

"How about I pick you up in the morning?" Gage says.

"Very funny. I'm smoking as fast as I can, okay?"

Gage rolls his eyes, his thick lashes catching light from an old-fashioned street-lamp. He takes his jacket, the one with NORTH COAST LOBSTER stitched across the back, and wraps it around my shoulders. Given that he's built like a Viking, it comes to my knees.

"I don't need it," I say, and shake it off.

"Your lips are blue." He tries to wrap it around me again.

"Look at you two, getting all cozy," Ella says.

"Ella," Gage says in a warning voice.

"What? It's like when you guys were little." She sighs. "So romantic."

"We were never romantic," I say. To my dismay, I see a tiny hurt in Gage's blue eyes. "We were friends. Best friends. Right?" I wait for his nod, which is a moment too long in coming.

All I can think is, *Don't do this, please don't do this, Gage. I can't bear to think of losing you.*

Four gleeful childhood summers, he and I were two rambunctious peas in a pod, all skinned knees and dirty noses, with an even littler Ella tagging along behind. He'd been a boisterous, happy, carefree kid with bright hair and kind blue eyes, and he'd pulled me out of my shell. We spent long, lazy days and cool, dusky evenings in our tumbledown fort, collecting lightning bugs and marveling at them after the sun went down. We shared our fear of the diving rock and finally climbed to the dizzy top and jumped off together.

Then Dad rented out the summerhouse, and we stopped coming to Deep Cove.

"Best friends?" Ella says. "Yeah, best friends who carved their initials in a tree!"

"We were seven," I say. "And Gage only did it on a dare. Right?"

He mumbles something I don't catch.

I know it's been a long time. Still, I miss the easy way we were together. I miss my old Gage, before he turned brooding and serious and hard to reach. Before the incident that left his baby brother dead.

Ella teeters a little, and I take her elbow.

"Seriously," she says, "that's all I've heard. 'Oh, I can't wait for Aeris to get back' and 'Do you think Aeris will stay now that she's graduated from Juilliard?'"

I sense color rising in my cheeks. I let out a nervous laugh. "Well, I missed you guys, too!"

"I think you two are adorable." Ella speaks in a loud, conspiratorial whisper, no doubt spurred on by all those vodka-fueled cosmos. "Look at you, blushing!" She punches her brother's broad shoulder. He doesn't even move. It's like he's made of stone. "Come on, tell me you don't want to marry this girl."

"Ella!" I cry.

"What?"

"I'm never getting married!" It bursts out of me with such force even I'm shocked.

She, for once, seems to have no words.

I feel panicked. Silly. They're staring as if I've gone raging mad. I realize I actually shouted it.

Ella takes a long drag of her cigarette and frowns. "Never?"

Gage laughs. "I think we explored that topic. Let's leave Aeris alone, okay?" He makes a final attempt with his jacket, trying to fasten it around me. "You must be freezing in that dress."

The heavy, too-warm fabric smells of the ocean and diesel oil.

Suddenly I want to escape. Which is awful. These are dear friends, friends I've cared about since childhood.

Footsteps sound on the pavement.

I realize Hunter's no longer sitting in his parked car. He's crossing the street, headed straight for us. His jeans and T-shirt are loose, except where they pull against his muscles. He could pass for a Navy SEAL, or a special ops guy out of a movie.

When he gets halfway across the street, Gage drapes an arm over my shoulders.

"What, hey, Gage?" I say.

He has the nerve to pull me closer. His arm grows tense as if expecting a confrontation. I'm so shocked I stand there, frozen.

Hunter reaches the curb like he's come specifically to say something. He steps onto the sidewalk, directly in front of me, so close an electrical current seems to grip the four of us. Gage bristles. The men are matched in size. But where Gage's hair is blond like Ella's, Hunter's is black as Cerberus's mane.

In the car, Victoria leans across the driver's seat and shouts, "Hurry up!"

Hunter doesn't respond. For one crazy moment, I think he's going to step in and save me from this awkward moment. His eyes meet mine in a fast, frank assessment. They seem to read things about me that even I don't know. After a moment, he turns from me, opens the club door, and disappears inside. I stare after him, confused. What was that about? And why on earth, after his earlier comment about the club, did he just go in?

"Freak," Gage mutters.

"Looks like Mr. Big Shot is the designated threesome finder," Ella snorts.

"The what?" I say.

Ella rolls her eyes. "You know. Going to find a second girl, for their little party?" She makes a lewd expression and shoots a glance at the car.

"Are you serious? No."

"Oh yeah."

I feel a faint flicker of disbelief.

"Come on," Gage says. "Stub out that disgusting thing. I'm taking Aeris home."

I step away from him, remove his heavy jacket, and shove it into his hands.

"Sorry. I need to go to the ladies' room."

Ella glances at the club entrance and back at me. She quirks an eyebrow. "Seriously? What are you doing?"

"She's heading to bathroom," Gage says. "Wait, aren't you?"

I chew on my lower lip. I'm not even sure of the answer. I feel my face growing warm as I say, "I'll be right back."

Then I whirl around, hurry to the door, yank it open, and step into the glittering lights.

I CAN'T STAND IT. I CAN'T stand the suffocating air, the press of sweaty bodies moving as one. The feel of them touching me, crushing me, their wet skin leaving a trail of foreign sweat on my own. I push through them anyway. I don't know which is worse: the crowd or the wedge growing between Gage and me, a painful wedge spurred on by Ella's well-meaning but misguided prods.

I scan the bobbing heads, hoping to catch sight of Hunter.

And I recognize he's the real reason I came in.

I have to know.

Know what? Why he stared so intently at me? Why he left his car and walked up to me? Why he disappeared into this place? Or am I trying to prove that Dad's right, that he's a troublemaker best ignored? I feel like I'm falling down some twisting hole, a hole I didn't even realize existed twenty minutes ago. I should leave. Now.

I should go home and—

"Hello," a low voice says.

I spin and he's there.

In the nightclub haze, half his face is in shadow. He's so close I can smell his clean, masculine scent, can feel his warmth.

"Hello," I manage. My heart is in my throat.

"Having a good evening?" The smoky lenses of his glasses hide his eyes, reflecting my own wide ones.

"Yes . . . I . . . I am. Thank you."

Someone bangs into me from behind. Hunter curses at him as I lurch forward, his arms catching me. Body sheltering me from the crowd, he turns me so that I'm against a high table. The heat of his powerful hands sends warmth shooting along my bare skin. I can feel each of his fingertips, the slightly rough texture, the strong tendons that are sensitive enough to

12

not squeeze me too hard. His thumb moves gently along my collarbone, and I nearly close my eyes with pleasure.

As if belatedly realizing what he's doing, he quickly releases me. My skin continues to vibrate. I sense him searching my features—my eyes, my cheeks, my lips. But for what? To dispel his sense of recognition?

Lights twist and splay through the fog, catching his jaw and the strong planes of his face. He looks strangely out of place among the thrashing, slumped-shouldered people gyrating behind him. Like a lion, wild and dangerous in a room of unsuspecting sheep.

The pounding music throbs in time with my heart. An inexplicable connection seems to pulse between us.

But I followed him to prove Dad's right.

"Why did you come in here?" I blurt.

He's not put off by the forwardness of my question. Instead, he says, "I was hoping you could tell me that."

"Me?" Then Ella's blunt words tumble through my mind. I step back a foot. "Right. Well, just so you know, I didn't come in here to be part of some threesome—"

"A threesome?" His brow wrinkles. He lets out a short, sharp laugh.

"Yes, with you and—"

"Stop right there." Now it's his turn to step back. Recoil, to be exact. "I am sorry if I gave you that impression." His voice is cool and polite. Despite his distant tone, his broad shoulders drop a little.

His reaction makes my stomach clench.

He says, "Excuse me, I've made a mistake." Then he bows—a formal bow—turns, and disappears through the crowd.

But I'm the one who's made the horrible mistake. What was I trying to prove? Rather than waiting to hear more of what he had to say, I blatantly insulted him. Who knows what he actually wanted to talk about? Part of me wants to blame it on those stupid cosmos I drank, but that would be a pathetic cop-out.

"Wait!" I shout, and run after him, desperate to apologize.

People jostle me. A guy tries to pull me onto the dance floor.

"Let go!" I twist away, and he slurs something I don't catch.

When I stumble out onto the curb, Hunter's car is gone. The air feels dead. It's as if magic has been spinning around me, wrapping me in a cocoon, in a dreamy realm beyond this everyday world. Now it's all come crashing down in mortifying pieces.

What did Hunter mean when he said 'I was hoping you could tell me that'?

"You okay?" Gage asks, catching my elbow.

I nod.

Ella gives me a searching look.

It's a moment before I can speak. "I'm good . . . fine," I say. "Yep, perfect."

A fat drop of rain lands on my cheek.

"Oh god," Ella says, glancing skyward. "Here it comes. Run!"

We race for the dirt lot behind the club. The three of us squeeze into the truck's front seat. My legs are drenched as I pull them in and slam the passenger door while Gage turns the key. The engine knocks and then roars to life. Gasoline fumes seep into the heavy air. He wipes a hole in the foggy windshield and I do the same to the passenger side.

Soon he's gunning away from Main Street. The lights rapidly diminish. A lightning flash reflects in the high, round window of the weather-beaten stone church. The elementary school squats like a brick bunker, preparing for the worst. On the outskirts, wires swing wildly over the closed gas station, threatening to break loose.

We rattle through the blackness, guided only by the glow of the winding dotted line.

I watch the rain crash down in waves. It's like the sky has opened up and plans to crush us with water.

Lightning explodes to our left.

"Holy crap!" Ella screeches, grabbing my arm.

"Calm down," Gage says.

"Watch out!" she cries as a tree branch smashes onto the road in front of us, thrashing in the headlights.

Gage careens around it. "Would you let me drive? You'll get us killed!"

Ella is white-knuckling my arm, and suddenly I feel sick. Sensations are flooding back to me, half-forgotten memories from long ago. The sound of crashing glass. The metallic scent of blood. I close my eyes, trying to push them down.

"Stop the car," I gasp.

"Or at least slow down!" Ella says, furious.

"Relax. We're almost there." Still, Gage slows.

I start breathing deeply. Careful and steady. Five counts in, five counts out. Five counts in, five counts out. Clammy sweat breaks out over my face and neck. My slamming heart begins to decelerate. My mind cuts away from the stormy view and veers back to Hunter, to that moment we shared alone on the street, drifting together in the sounds of Mozart.

That piece was a turning point for my heartsick, ten-year-old self. Had my violin teacher known it when she told me that some music scholars believed Mozart wrote that piece after his mother's death? Could I not hear it in the music? she'd asked. The awful cry of the violin and the answering comfort of the viola? I listened, and I no longer felt alone in my mourning. Mozart had suffered misfortune, too.

Did Hunter know the meaning of that piece? It's ironic that two people sharing the sound of loss were drawn together as if in that moment we were found.

"Here we are," Gage says, pulling into Dad's driveway.

I realize I've swallowed my panic.

"Good night," Ella says as I give her a one-armed hug.

"Thanks, be safe. Talk to you tomorrow," I say, glad our awkward discourse seems temporarily forgotten. Then I jump into the rain and run up the gravel path. The groan of the giant oak tree guarding the yard blends with the gale. Rain, slanting sideways, slicks the front hall as I tear open the door. I struggle to close it and stand dripping on the mat.

The hall light is on. Otherwise the house is quiet.

Thunder booms. A faint rattle of dishes comes from the kitchen, the plates drumming inside the cupboard's closed doors.

Dad's shaggy mutt, Sammy, gets up off the coffee-brown leather couch and pads over to me.

"Hey, you," I whisper.

He leans against me, almost knocking me over. I scratch his ears. He's so big I swear he's part horse. Which is somehow fitting, given that Dad grew up on a horse ranch.

I suspect Dad is waiting up. I picture him breathing a sigh of relief, and I grin. He won't come out and actually check in with me—he's way too gruff. Funny how a person can sense things like that. Or maybe I'm simply imagining it.

I doubt it.

My grin widens.

Dad's place might not be home to me, yet it's good to be here. Away from the city in this place where I can wander along the shore, stare at the waves, and feel the cold water on my bare toes.

If I could stay in Deep Cove, I would, in a heartbeat. But life doesn't work like that. Not when the New York Philharmonic offers you the position of first violinist and expects you to start in the fall. It's an honor.

And I'll face anything—including cramped subways and crowded streets—for as long as it takes to reach my dream. Someday I'll have saved up enough to get by without an employer, to have my own home in the country, one with a horse out back and a music room where I can turn all my scraps of composition into something real. When I have that, I'll allow myself to think about the rest: a man, maybe a family, but on my own terms. Even if it takes ten hard years to get there.

Quietly, I bolt the door, glancing through the thick glass panel at the obscured road. It's the only way to reach the research lab from town. Hunter must have driven by moments ago. Flown past in his steely black bird. Fat tires skimming the road, wicked lights piercing the darkness, engine growling like a beast. I wouldn't be surprised if that car was bulletproof. So solid, he probably barely noticed the storm.

No—he probably enjoyed it.

He strikes me as someone who likes danger.

Could Hunter truly be as bad as Dad makes him out to be? There was his laugh, a sound so unexpected and kind. I wonder what it would be like to have him laugh like that with me.

I really blew it. Why did I say such a stupid thing?

I give myself a mental kick.

At the very least, I wish I'd been quick enough to apologize.

It's obvious Ella had been dead wrong. Hunter had made that perfectly clear. So had he only come to pick up his coworker? And then he saw me and . . . *Stop. Just stop.* I'm not doing this. He's completely not my type. Worse, he's a distraction I can't afford.

Slipping into the guest bathroom, I switch on the light. I can still feel his intense gaze. The butterflies it sent churning through me return. We'd felt so oddly connected. And he'd seemed so curious. What did he see in me that made him stare?

My wet shoulder-length hair is plastered to my neck and forehead. The white dress, drenched, clings to me like crushed dragonfly wings. Not exactly a pretty picture.

Still, he'd looked at me like I was someone he wanted to know.

THREE

I WAKE WITH MY HAND CLAMPED over my mouth, as if I could stuff down something I said. Unease curls around me, like the twisting sheets that bind my bare legs. I untangle myself and sit up. It's morning.

The whine of a chain saw filters through the closed window in the guest room.

I go to the blinds and peer out.

That was one awful storm. The big, shady oak looks as if it were ravaged by a giant. Its leafy limbs, still pulsing with life, lie scattered across the lawn. My fingers tighten on the sill. It's a horrible sight. Who knows how long that old guardian stood rooted on this property?

Now it is gone.

Dad's over on the driveway—what's visible of it under the chaos. He's clearing a path, working steadily with his chain saw. Sawdust swirls skyward, disappearing in the blue.

He makes life seem easy, simple, straightforward. Part of me wants to burrow down in his solid, comforting house and stay here forever.

Another part of me, a part that flutters in my chest, wishes I could turn back the clock to last night and do things differently. Find out what Hunter wanted, why he'd come up to me in the club and said what he'd said.

I thought you could tell me that.

What had he meant? What had he wanted to talk to me about?

It was like he'd wanted me to follow him into the Zenith Club. Like he'd been waiting for me inside. Like he'd had something important to ask.

I watch Dad cut another fallen limb.

Condensation drips down the cold window and onto my fingers.

Yesterday Dad's hostility toward the controversial research lab and Hunter didn't matter.

Today I need to know what's behind it.

DROPPING THE CURTAIN, I SQUIRM into sweats and my favorite navy-blue Juilliard School T-shirt. I dig around in my suitcase for my sweater. Half a dozen sheets covered with my neatly penciled music compositions spill from the top pocket. I bunch them together and stash them carefully in the dresser's bottom drawer. Then I find the cable-knit pullover I was looking for and tug it over my head.

In the living room, the baby grand piano shines in the morning light. I swear it takes up a third of the space, and I feel guilty every time I see it. Especially against the backdrop of Dad-land—a rugged, comfortable, sports-viewing lounge in leather and dark wood with conveniently placed tables. One whole wall consists of a hunting lodge-style stone fireplace. Another holds a poster-sized photo of horses galloping across Grandpa's Montana ranch, which looks amazing framed against the room's amber paint.

I pad across the wood floor and rag carpet. When Dad had the contractor renovate two years ago, I begged him not to get the piano. He's not a music kind of guy. The only sound system he owns is the one that came with his car, and it's always tuned to the news.

I've got my violin, I said.

I want you to feel welcome, Peanut.

I do, I said, and gave him an awkward hug.

Good.

I go and lift the fallboard. My fingers test out the first bars of my work in progress. It's different from my usual work. I'm not sure if I like the sound. It's spacious and moody, almost ominous. In my mind's eye, I see Deep Cove beneath a sky of rolling thunderheads. People peer through their windows, wondering what's to come. To compose is to build a story.

To reveal it, layer by layer. I reach my stuck point and pause. I can't find my way through. Maybe it's because I'm afraid that I won't like how the song ends.

A dawning realization that the piano is in perfect tune sends my fingers running up and down in a grand finale. I glance at the front door, and a smile spreads across my face. That's so completely Dad to get someone in to tune it.

Standing, I close the fallboard and hurry outside.

The sun warms my shoulders through my clothes, but cold seeps up from the ground.

DAD TURNS, A SMILE LIGHTING his face.

In that instant, my decision to ask about his animosity toward Hunter and the Phoenix Research Lab leaves me. I don't want to stir him up. I don't want to spoil our time.

I push away the unsatisfying memory of last night. So I was rude. It happens. So he was curious about me—he probably thought I was someone else. I've never gotten so worked up over a guy, and I don't plan to keep doing it. That's for someone like Ella, who revels in her obsessions.

"I waited till nine," Dad shouts, nodding at his chain saw. "Wanted to let you sleep in."

"Thanks. You didn't have to," I call back.

Sammy gallops through the downed foliage with his ears flapping, sniffing at all the destruction. It's like he's making note of the changes. Shingles have been flung far beyond the yard. They're scattered all the way to Dad's feed store's parking lot in the distance. The store's rectangular sign, THORNE COUNTRY SUPPLY, WHOLESALE FEED AND SEED, hangs at a dangerous angle.

The strange feeling that someone's staring at me makes me spin toward the abandoned field across the road. A faint breeze tugs at the tall grasses and gnarled fruit trees. My eyes comb the swaying weeds and then squint at the knobby branches. One moves and I catch my breath, then laugh when a bird flies into the air.

Of course no one's watching. Why would they be?

Still, I can't shake the prickling sensation. I'm about to go investigate when Sammy darts over and checks in with me, pushing his wet nose against my elbow.

"Hey, you." I scratch his favorite spot under his chin.

"I think it's time for some coffee," Dad says. "What do you say?"

"Sure, but can I carry some of that firewood to the barn first?"

"Now, that wouldn't be much of a welcome home."

"I don't mind."

He cracks a smile at me. "No. But I do."

"What time do you have to open the store?"

"In a few minutes, but Thomas Creedy's coming in. I'll head over later."

Just then, a beat-up Buick pulls into the store's deserted lot. Mr. Creedy climbs out, looking more spindly than ever. He must be at least a hundred years old. He waves a thin arm at us. His hands look giant compared with his bony limbs.

"Hey there, Aeris," he calls in his familiar, thready voice. "Welcome home."

"Thanks," I call back, grinning. "I'm looking forward to catching up."

"Your dad gave me one of your concerts on CD. I play it all the time in my car."

"Really? Wow, I'm so glad you like it."

He shoots me a huge smile that's all dentures and then shuffles through the shop door.

To Dad I say, "He's awesome. But how does he manage all those heavy feed bags and hay bales? Should he really be working alone?"

"He's pretty spry. And he worked years in the shop before I showed up and took over. Besides, I like the guy."

That's Dad. His loyalty is both fierce and legendary. I know, because he's always been there for me. Even in the darkest of times. Even when we were both crushed by grief.

I was five when Mom died. Dad was fighting his own battles, yet he knew I needed a place to put my churning energy. One day he brought home a violin teacher who auditioned me for a musical "ear" and agreed to take me on. I'd never lived with Dad, and because of his work managing investment funds, we soon left her—and many teachers after her—as we moved from city to city. Changing schools made friendships difficult, but the violin has been my constant. That and my growing scraps of music compositions.

I slip my arm into his. "How about that coffee?"

Our feet crunch through the chaos. Before we head around back, I glance again at the abandoned field.

"Everything all right?" Dad asks.

"Oh yeah. It's nothing."

Sammy gallops ahead. We slam through the screen door and kick off our boots, tossing them under the mudroom bench.

The kitchen is big and bright. Modern fixtures and soft-yellow walls. Rugged, distressed pine cabinets and sanded wood ceiling beams give it a warm, rustic feel. Sammy's chocolate suede dog bed fills one corner. I found some wild purple hyacinths yesterday and put them in a jug. Their heady perfume is soft as velvet.

Through the kitchen windows, the gray ocean is visible, churning below the bluff. A powerful boat I recognize as Gage's bobs among some debris—the remains of a broken fishing vessel destroyed in the storm, perhaps? I hope no one was hurt.

Gage will be out on deck, investigating.

Last night, I caught at least three girls checking him out. He's sweet and deserves a wonderful girl, one who really loves him.

"You kids have a good time at the Zenith Club?" Dad asks, cutting into my thoughts.

I flash to Hunter holding my shoulders, pressing my back to the table, his body warm and his expression intense. I blink and push the heady memory away.

"It was all right. How about you? How was your card game?"

"Oh, fine." He opens the cupboard and finds the pancake mix. "The usual."

I skirt around him to start a fresh pot of coffee brewing.

"I got it. You relax, Peanut."

"Dad." A grin breaks my tension. "I am relaxed. I'm just making coffee. And the pancakes." I take the mix from him. "I'm a big girl. You don't have to spoil me. If you do, you might never get rid of me."

He wears a look of mock seriousness. "And that would be a bad thing?"

"Yes! I have no intention of coming between you and your card-shark buddies, and all the other stuff you've got going on. Seriously. You paid your dues."

He chuckles. "A parent never finishes paying his dues." But there's something wistful in his expression. "You're welcome to stay as long as you want. You know that."

"I know." I busy myself cracking eggs into a bowl.

AT NOON I INSIST ON joining Dad in the store.

"You sure you don't need to get your hours in on the violin?"

"I'm fine. Can't I hang out with my dad for a little bit?"

The truth is, I'm feeling oddly antsy. What I'm in the mood for is a powerful horse and a good, long ride to clear my head.

Twenty minutes later, I'm doing the next best thing. I'm polishing the consignment horse tack in the back of Dad's store. He says customers don't notice that sort of thing, it's a waste of my time, if they need it, they buy it. Let him grump. It's a pleasure turning the leather supple and making those buckles shine. There's workmanship in these pieces, beauty and plenty of life. I would be happy smelling saddle soap all day. It brings me right back to summers at Grandpa's ranch, spent almost entirely on horseback.

I'm standing there reminiscing when the shop door jangles. I glance over the heads of milling customers and freeze. There he is. Taller than the rest by half a foot. Hunter.

My pulse quickens, firing at my throat, in my fingertips, everywhere as he steps inside. He's only partially visible past the rack of seed packets. He seems larger than life, out of place, starkly handsome in his worn leather jacket and wind-tousled hair.

What is he doing in Dad's shop?

Last night I would have thought this the perfect opportunity to set things straight. Apparently, however, that's not going to work. Because I've been struck by an all-consuming nervousness that's locked my legs in place and is making my tongue stick in my mouth.

Get a grip!

Fortunately, he's too preoccupied to notice me.

To my shock, he heads straight for Dad with urgency clear in his booted footsteps. I bend forward, riveted at this surprising turn of events, and try to catch their low interchange. It's clipped and terse. For all of Dad's harsh words about Hunter, they certainly seem to know each other pretty well.

I begin to realize I'm not the only one watching. The store regulars are fixated on Hunter. Their stares hold suspicion, mistrust, although he doesn't seem to notice.

The only customer who appears uninterested is a burly man browsing the horse tack. His back is turned to the shop and he's studying the buckles intently. He's wearing brand-new buckskin gloves and his forest-green flannel shirt is too crisp, making him look like a tourist trying to play local. It's clear he's unfamiliar with the equipment.

"Can I help you?" I force myself to ask in a quiet voice.

His baseball cap is pulled low. He's older than I first thought. Crow's-feet. Hair turning steely at the temples. Strange eyes like a pair of gray marbles jammed into narrow sockets. About as much warmth as an android's.

"Possibly," he replies, matching my low tone.

At that moment, I hear Dad say, "I told you, it's not time. Not yet."

I can't help it. I turn to see Hunter standing there, one big hand kneading the back of his neck. He blows out a sigh, turns, and makes for the exit.

I duck my head.

The door opens and closes. And then he's gone. It's as though a dizzy whir of energy was vibrating all around and has suddenly been switched off. Like we're all floundering in his wake. I release the reins I'd been clutching and realize my fingers have gone almost numb.

I'd forgotten about the customer and see him moving away.

"Sir," I say, finding my voice. "I'm sorry, what can I do for you?"

He pauses. "I think I'll leave it for now."

"Did you have a question about the equipment?"

"My Nessa's always wanted a horse." His pupils are cool, hawk-like. "Unfortunately, it's not practical."

"Horses are a big responsibility," I agree.

"Yes."

"Maybe you two could go out for some lessons," I suggest. "There's a place not far that offers them. I'm sure she'd love it."

"That won't be possible."

"Next time you're in town, then," I say, making to leave.

"No. She's dying."

"I'm . . . so sorry."

"Yes, well. It's not condolences I'm after." He runs his callused fingers along one shelf as if testing for dust and then nods at me. "Good day."

I watch him leave, baffled. Grief has its own agenda. Still, his coldness is somehow chilling. I suspect there's a sea of roiling emotion beneath that impassive mask. I rub my arms as he looms briefly in the open door, his shadow slanting across the room. Then he's gone.

FOUR

When I'm able to pull Dad aside, I say, "Why was Dr. Cayman here?"

He doesn't reply. I'm surprised to see him wearing that old stony look of his. The one I used to see regularly before he left the investment firm and moved out here to "slow down."

"What did he want?" I ask.

"It's not important."

"It seemed important. Is everything all right?"

His gaze drills into me. Quietly, he says, "Promise me something, Aeris. Don't take an interest in Cayman. People like him are what's wrong with the world."

The bustle of the store drones in my ears. "I'm not. But if you really feel that way—I mean, he's a customer, right?"

"Now and then, yes."

"So—"

"So nothing."

"Are you sure everything is—"

"Yes. I am."

It's clear the conversation is over.

If before I was curious, now I'm downright interested.

Dad is acting beyond strange.

What is going on?

I go help a rancher who's waiting at the register. He pays in cash, two hundred-dollar bills. I lift the cash drawer, stow them away, and spot something strange. It's a carbon-fiber clearance key of some kind. Glancing at Dad to make sure he's not watching, I carefully lift it out.

Etched on the card pass is the Phoenix Research Lab's logo—a black Labrador chasing a phoenix, with the initials *PRL* underneath.

Dad, what are you up to? Hunter's obviously more than a casual customer. Why else would you have a card key if you don't go there often? And why are you being so strange about it?

Quietly, I replace the clearance pass. I'm not sure I want to know.

THE NIGHTMARE COMES TO ME, the fire, white-hot and blinding. I scream, my small legs and arms pinned to the thorny bushes, and watch the car burn. *Move!* I urge myself. It's not too late; she's in there. *Move!*

I lunge upright and my eyes fly open. Sunshine burns my face. It's wet.

The sheet is soft against my skin as I wipe away the tears. I climb out of bed and dress quickly. Then I snap open the closures on my violin case. The act of tightening my bow and prepping it with rosin calms me. I pull out my favorite composition and begin to play.

The fire was a long time ago. I can't make what happened change. I can't make myself save her. Even if I succeed in my dream, there's nothing I can do to bring Mom back.

I play through the morning, losing myself in the soulful sound of the strings.

It's noon when I finally set down the instrument.

I can partially see the feed store through the window. Because it's Sunday, the store's closed and the lot is empty. I have a sudden urge to borrow Dad's truck and drive past the research lab's gates on the off chance Hunter might drive through. And then . . . what? Wave him down? Start asking questions? No. Stop. Just stop.

Dad's landline rings. It's Ella.

"Lunch," she says, "I'm picking you up, and don't even think about saying no."

"But I . . ."

"No excuses. I'm hungover and bored, and I need company. And french fries. Besides, my dad's headed to your place to drink beer and watch the game. You seriously don't want to stick around for *that*, do you?"

As if on cue, I hear Dad switch on the TV.

A sports announcer blares.

Maybe if I go into town I'll run into Hunter.

"You're right," I say. "Lunch sounds good."

Why can't I stop thinking about him? This is not like me. Our whole relationship consisted of maybe five minutes of staring across the road at each other and ten spoken words.

And yet . . . Hunter.

Who are you?

You're certainly more than your powerful, handsome features. There's an energy around you. Something primal. Yet also otherworldly.

My fingers tighten on the phone, and I stare into space, seeing his eyes across that damp night street again. They shimmered like mirrors. Or so it seemed. And when he caught me in his gaze, I could hardly move. His name, Hunter, suits him. Because in that moment, when his whole focus centered on me, I'd felt hunted.

And what's very wrong, very upsetting, is that despite my resolve, I long to feel that way again.

"Shoot, I can't find my keys," Ella says, and I hear what sounds like a purse being upended. "Should I pick you up?"

"Okay, sure," I tell her.

"There they are, got them. See you in thirty."

THE LIGHTHOUSE CAFÉ IS PACKED with Sunday regulars.

"It'll be at least an hour," the girl in the blue-and-white uniform tells us.

"An hour, really?" Ella scans the packed restaurant.

"Let's just sit outside," I say.

"Outside?" Ella scrunches up her nose. "It's too cold."

It is cold. It may be June in Deep Cove, but chilly Maine air pours in from the ocean. The outdoor tables look like they've never been used.

"It's not that bad."

"All right," Ella says with a groan.

We choose one next to the window, hunching down in our respective sweaters.

Ella fishes out her cigarettes, lights one, and takes a long drag. "So what's all this about you never getting married?"

I'm caught off guard.

"Everyone needs someone, don't they?"

I scrunch lower and pull my sleeves down over my fingers. "Do you remember Trey Shields? I told you about him last summer."

"Mr. Lawyer-in-Training?"

"He asked me to marry him."

Ella jolts into focus. "He what?"

I stare at the menu, not reading it. "I liked him. No, I loved him. But . . . I guess not enough to move to Nebraska."

"Nebraska?"

"He's from there."

"And you didn't want to go?"

"It's like he didn't even see me—who I am. I've been invited to join the New York Philharmonic in the fall. The New York Philharmonic! How could he not realize how big that is?"

"So? Long-distance relationship. People do it."

"Not Trey. You should have seen his face when I told him I had to stay."

"Lawyers make pretty good money."

"Ella! Seriously?"

"What?" She grins at me.

"Very funny. One minute you think you're in love and the next you're being asked to change and follow their rules, and pretty soon you're living a life so far from what you intended you don't recognize yourself anymore."

"That's reality. We all give in at some point."

"Not me." *I'm one to talk as I sit here scanning the street for signs of Hunter.*

I'm not even sure what's driving this desire to see him again. Is it because I'm curious about what he and Dad are involved in? Because I'm dying to know what he'd wanted to ask me? Or simply because I can't stop thinking of his thumb dragging softly across my collarbone and sending electric sparks through my body?

Maybe all three.

The door bangs open, emitting steamy pancake-and-sausage-scented clouds. A harried guy with a pierced lip approaches, rag in hand. He throws the rag down and makes quick swipes across the damp enamel. An ant scuttles out of reach and escapes off the far side.

With his free hand, the guy plunks down a set of salt and pepper shakers.

Ella gives his bent, gel-spiked head an appreciative gaze.

When he glances at her, she offers up a flirtatious giggle.

"Your server will be out in a minute," he says, and shoves the rag in his back pocket. He disappears inside.

Ella sinks back in her plastic seat, watching him go.

"Speaking of guys, what happened with Finn?" I say. "You split up?"

She picks at a chip in the enamel. "Yeah."

I remember how she'd worshipped him. "Sorry. Well, it's his loss."

Softly, she says, "I really liked him. Sometimes I look at my parents and I wonder if I'll ever have that. You know?"

From above, misty rays struggle to work their way through the cloud cover. My muscles are clenched with cold. I nod. The door bangs open.

Our server takes our order and disappears back inside.

"Anyway!" Ella says brightly. "What's up with you? How long are you staying?"

"I'm not sure," I reply when a black SUV pulls into view. It slows. My heart starts racing. Could it be him? The passenger window buzzes down. A girl around our age with brown hair and freckles sticks her head out. I'm actually relieved.

"Ella!" she yells. "What are you doing out there? Don't you know it's freezing?"

Ella snorts and goes to talk to her. The rear window rolls down. All three girls in the car crane to look at me.

I wave, self-conscious, wondering what it must be like to have the comfort of lifelong neighbors and school friends.

Across the street, a touristy couple browses the postcard rack at the Whaler's Gift Shop. Mismatched layers of clothing make me think they're wearing everything in their suitcase at once. The woman shivers and tucks her hands into her armpits. The guy circles his arm around her. A minute later, they disappear into the used bookstore.

Ella's question burns through me. Is it normal I don't want to get married? Am I becoming my parents, mimicking Mom's refusal to marry Dad, or even live in the same town? Why couldn't Mom fit him into her life? I know she loved him.

So then why? What kept them apart? Had growing up in the foster system made her a loner? Or was it her genetic research? Could she have found her lab work so important that she didn't want the distractions of a full-time family? She made time for me.

If she were alive, I could ask her. Along with so many unanswered questions. Such as: What was she working on that was so important that people chased her down and killed her for it?

Hunter's a researcher. He may enjoy his work, but he couldn't be like Mom. There's no way I could imagine a guy like him dying for his job.

Ella returns as our server brings out our food. Heaps of crispy fries in a paper-lined basket. Grilled turkey club sandwiches with ruffled leaves of lettuce. I wasn't all that hungry, but now my stomach rumbles.

"Hello, hangover cure." Ella dives in.

I spread mustard on my sandwich and take a bite. Between the salty bacon, turkey, lettuce, and tomato, it's delicious.

Ella gestures with a french fry at the spot where the SUV had been. "It's like high school never ended. So anyway, I never got to hear what's up with you."

We chat happily until the food is gone and a breeze rattles our table, sending paper napkins cartwheeling into the air. They fly away so fast I can't catch them.

Ella says, "Let's go. You ready?"

"Sure. Thanks for dragging me out, by the way."

"You're like Gage. Way too focused on your projects. Someone has to pull you into the real world once in a while." She shoots me a grin. "Even if it means eating lunch on the sidewalk like a pair of outcasts."

"I'll be your outcast buddy anytime."

We pay and head for Ella's Honda coupe. She fishes in her deep shoulder bag for her keys. This is not New York. No yellow cabs idle on corners, no crowds jostle their way onto buses, no pedestrians fight up and downstream. There's no traffic at all. I'm in Deep Cove, that's for sure.

It's wonderful.

Overhead, the thunderheads have rolled inland. They loom like hunchback ogres, brooding in the distance.

With a pop, the doors unlock. I climb in. Stale cigarette air blends with Ella's familiar sweet perfume and clings to my face as she pulls onto the two-lane street. I crank down the window to let the breeze in.

That's when I hear it. The throaty roar of a powerful engine.

I can't see the car making it, but I hear it coming. The rumble grows, snarling as the driver downshifts. My pulse jumps, begins to pound. My eyes fasten on the vehicle in the distance, expectant. My mouth is open, my lips dry.

Ella leans forward and snaps on the radio. A country crooner bursts through the speakers.

It's all wrong. It doesn't match the car I can see clearly now, growing larger in the distance. The music should be dark and low, powerful and gripping. A deep bass, pounding in time to my slamming heart.

The light at the one main intersection turns from yellow to red. Ella rolls to a stop as Hunter does the same on the far side. I suck in my breath, holding it, trying to keep Ella from noticing my agitation.

He's alone in the driver's seat. Sunglasses cover his eyes, so I trace the shape of his jaw. His neck. His shoulders. His left hand on the steering wheel.

My hand clutches the door, so hard my fingers hurt.

I'm not sure what I expect him to do. Acknowledge me somehow? Acknowledge that he sees me? Because I know he does. His head is turned a fraction toward me. And I know he's aware of me here, staring, as clearly as I know the sky is blue.

The light changes.

Hunter's car purrs to life and slowly crosses the intersection, just as Ella's does the same. We're no more than ten feet apart, despite the metal and glass that separate us. Through my open window, wind pulses against my face, smelling faintly of motor fuel. I grip tighter to the door handle and turn to watch him pass.

My stomach sinks as he keeps his gaze fastened straight ahead. And even from here, from the distance, with the metal and road between us, I sense his dislike. His speed increases and he drives past.

I think I must be getting sick. Because I want to press my hands to my face.

FIVE

"So," ELLA SAYS, CUTTING INTO my thoughts as she guides the car toward Dad's. "I never did ask you what happened last night when you went back into the club."

"What do you mean?" I say with feigned brightness. "I went to the bathroom."

"Oh, come on, Aeris." She shoots me a look.

I don't really want to admit my awkward conversation. I bite my lip, searching for something to say.

"There's no point in it," she says. "You're not his type."

I pause. "I never said I was."

She ignores this. "Oh, he's hot, no question. I'd do him in a second. But that's all he's after."

I slip my cold hands under my knees and clasp them tight together.

On a laugh, Ella says, "I'm serious. Don't waste your time. The girls he's interested in are here for a weekend or two, and then they're gone."

"Ouch. How on earth do you know that?"

"Girls are always falling all over him, trying to get his attention. Like, everywhere he goes. I'm sure he takes advantage of it. What guy in his position wouldn't? He's got looks, money—he can do whatever he wants. But I know you. One-night-stands aren't your style."

"Like I said, I'm really not interested."

After what I sensed from him, it's true.

"Good. I'd hate to see you get hurt." She accelerates out of town. Her phone beeps once, and she paws it free from her purse. "Gage," she says, glancing at the screen.

The car weaves over the rumble strip, making the tires clatter a warning. "Watch the road," I say.

"I got it," she replies, adjusting course as she reads.

"Maybe you should pull over?"

"I'm done, okay?" She drops the phone in her lap. "Gage wants to know if you want to come to his place for a boat ride tomorrow."

"Ella, right now, me and Gage . . ."

"Yes?"

"It's complicated. I don't want to give him the wrong idea."

"Good enough. So are we on for a boat ride or what?"

I pause, and then a laugh escapes me. "Maybe, but not tomorrow." Ella can drill her way through anything.

"Good enough. You won't believe what he's done to his place since last summer."

I picture Gage's secluded bay slanting down to the rocky shore. There are half a dozen log cabins positioned in a semicircle around a stone lodge house. The place used to be a popular vacation spot for weekly out-of-towners, but that was fifty years ago. The owners abandoned the buildings and left them to rot. Gage bought them last August and moved into the central lodge.

"He's really fixed it up. Some of his buddies have taken over the cabins. You've met a few—Troy, Carter."

"Sounds like they've got a compound going on down there."

"That's funny. It kind of is."

A thought strikes. You can actually see part of the Phoenix Research Lab from Gage's private cove. If you peer up at the jutting finger of land rising from the beach, it's there, stretched out high above. He and I looked at it together when the lab opened last summer.

Gage and Hunter are neighbors, even though you'd need wings to travel between them.

"What's up with the research lab?" I blurt. "Everyone's acting so strange about it."

Ella laughs. "What do you expect? This is a small town, we need something to gossip about."

"It's more than gossip."

"Aeris, it's a lab that researches highly contagious diseases. Of course people are going to gossip."

"I can see being curious. This goes beyond that."

"You've seen them, Hunter, Victoria. They're strange. They don't fit in. They're gorgeous, they're rich, and they're working on some dangerous project right in our backyards." Now her voice holds an edge. "Who wants that in their neighborhood?"

"No one, but I'm guessing it has safeguards." I frown. "Why is Gage so against them?"

She sighs. "I'm not completely clear on this—you know how he can be. From what I can tell, Gage is convinced Hunter has connections with the experimental military project that—" Her voice catches and she falls silent. "God, you wonder why he hates people like that? Gage practically died. And my brother—"

Worry for Gage bubbles up inside me. "Your brother's sick?"

"No," she whispers. "My other brother. My baby brother."

Softly, I say, "You mean, Max?" I try to grasp what she's saying.

"Yes."

"You mean it was this project that—so Gage and Max were together when Max died?" Is this the awful tragedy they'd refused to talk about?

She nods.

"I'm sorry. I'm really sorry you lost him."

A stretch of trees pass us by. Dad's house comes up on the right. She pulls into the drive.

"We don't talk about it much." Ella puts the car in park and slumps back. "Max and Gage were exposed to some experimental research in the military. I don't know a whole lot. He keeps silent. The government shut the whole thing down after Max . . . died."

I'm stunned. I can't believe Dad never told me about this.

"What kind of research was it?"

She shrugs, turns away, and speaks out her window. "The whole thing was covered up. The soldiers were only released after interest groups put pressure on the military. The families tried to hold the government accountable, but Gage, Max, and the other guys had signed consent waivers. Supposedly they knew the dangers. I've given up asking. And now they're all living down in Gage's cove."

"Who? You mean Troy and Carter—they were part of this?"

"Yep. Them and the other six soldiers who were released."

"All of them?"

"It's good for them, I think. To be together."

I'm not exactly sure I agree, although I don't know why.

"Anyway," Ella says, "whatever those people did to Gage, he's different now. Physically. Mentally. Worse, he's never forgiven himself. For being the survivor."

My heart stutters. I know exactly how he feels.

"It's not his fault," Ella says. "I've told him a million times. But then he says Max looked up to him. He promised Max everything would be all right. Max died believing him."

My heart aches for my old friend. So many things make sense. His attitude. His bleak silences. We have more than our youthful memories in common. He lost his brother, and I lost my mom.

"So now you know why Gage gets all broody. I don't know if it's guilt or rage or . . ." She stops.

"Maybe he's just sad?"

"Yeah." Her voice is a hoarse whisper. "Max was special. I miss him. Sometimes I still can't believe he's gone."

Not knowing what to say, I reach across and give her an awkward hug.

When she pulls away, she wipes her face on her sleeve. "Seriously!" She lets out a gravelly laugh. "I have no idea where that came from. I mean, it's been three years. We're moving on. Max would want us to. Right?"

Before I can reply, she twists the radio knob, turning up the volume. Country music pours out. Digging in her purse, she fishes for a cigarette and lights it.

I know now that Gage went through a terrible tragedy during our lost years. But it didn't happen here. Not in Dad's sleepy coastal town.

Whatever happened was an accident, a horrible accident.

The Phoenix Research Lab couldn't have anything to do with it. It isn't the military. Their mission is to cure sick people. Much as I love and respect Gage like a brother, I'm not sure how he thinks the two could be connected. It sounds to me more like a general distrust of anything research related.

"Thanks for taking me to lunch," I say.

"Yep. Later, kiddo."

"WE'RE OUT OF COFFEE. Do you mind if I borrow the Range Rover?" I ask Dad over the phone as I search the kitchen cupboards one last time.

It's Monday afternoon and I need a caffeine boost.

In the background, the shop sounds busy. "Sure. You know where the keys are?"

"Yep, I found the extra set. Thanks, Dad."

"Drive safe."

My manuscript lies open on the table. Blank staves stare back at me. I'm working on my new composition, but I can't make headway. The song could be good. Possibly my best. But it won't be anything if I don't finish it.

Worrying a lock of hair, I wonder if it's time to step out of my comfort zone. Try writing in a coffee shop. Other people swear by it. I close the manuscript and stuff it into my book bag.

After filling Sammy's bowls, I detour to the guest bedroom and change into a white eyelet blouse, jeans, and chocolate oxfords. Then I grab the keys, climb into the Range Rover, and back out of the driveway.

White-knuckling the steering wheel with one hand, I lurch through the gears with the other. It always takes a while to get the hang of driving again. The road twists and turns. Potholes and buckled pavement rattle the car. My feet are tense against the pedals.

Fifteen minutes later, I reach the gas station on the outskirts of town, and then I'm cruising slowly down Main Street. My muscles relax. At this speed, driving is almost fun.

Half a dozen people poke along the street. There's a lone white car at the traffic light. Plenty of available parking spots on either side. This is what life should be like. Easy, unharried, uncrowded.

I park in front of the Foggy Joe.

The smell of fresh-brewed coffee greets me as I push inside.

It's empty, except for one customer. A guy with headphones hunches over his computer in such deep concentration he's either cracking genetic code or hacking into the White House.

At the counter, the barista rouses himself from his texting just long enough to fill my order.

I cart the coffee and my laptop to the battered window seat.

Sitting, I take a sip of the hottest liquid I have ever consumed. Reflexes send the scalding liquid shooting back out. As I jerk forward, I'm clutching the cup so hard the plastic lid squeezes off. Coffee splatters across the table, my bare arms, and my chest.

I shriek.

"You okay?" the barista calls.

"Yep," I lie as coffee trails down my front like flaming lava.

He comes over with a bunch of napkins.

Hacker Guy shoots me a clinical glance. He stands, carries his cup of ice water over, sets it on my table and goes back to his work.

I dab ice water over my scorched skin. "Thanks," I say, glancing down at the brown stain spreading across my white eyelet blouse. My bra is showing through. I look for my sweater and realize I left it in the Range Rover.

I clamp my arms over myself.

"Can I get you a refill?" the barista asks.

"Uh, no. No, thanks. I'm—I'm just going to go."

Before I can escape, the door jangles open.

I almost die.

Hunter, wide shoulders outlined under a carbon-gray T-shirt, steps inside.

Six

I SHRINK BACK DOWN AND TRY to disappear against the wall.

Hunter has to show up now? When I'm covered in coffee? For god's sake . . . why?

His black hair is rumpled, and a lock has fallen across his forehead. Despite his serious, weighty aura, it softens his intensity. For an instant, he looks almost approachable. Then he rakes the hair off his face, and I change my mind.

He scans the place, as if searching for someone. His eyes settle on me—warm amber irises meeting mine. His brow flickers as if in surprise. I read something else there, too. Unease? Frustration? Annoyance?

To my dismay, he turns to leave.

Just because I'm in here, he can't stay?

Before he reaches the door, however, he pauses. Then, with deliberate steps, he turns and approaches the counter. His broad, tapered back is taut. He rolls his shoulders as if to ease the tension and stands reading the menu drilled to the wall.

The barista says, "Can I get a drink started for you?"

It's a moment before he replies. "I'll take some coffee."

"Dark or blond?"

"I'm sorry?"

"Light or dark roast?"

"Whatever you recommend."

"I'm a blond fan myself. Size?"

"What's the choice?"

The guy wrinkles his forehead and laughs. "Uh, small, medium, and large? What, are you from the land where coffee shops don't exist?"

"Medium will be fine."

The barista dispenses it with a chuckle.

Hunter takes the coffee and stuffs some extra bills in the tip jar. "Have a good day."

"Likewise, my man."

And then he's turning to go. I'd wanted to question him about Dad. I'd wanted a chance to apologize for my rudeness in the bar. I'd wanted to ask why he sought me out with such interest in the first place. Well, this is it. Now is the time.

I brace myself as he starts walking, trying to work up the courage. My fingers grab at the table edge, causing it to rock slightly. Here I go.

I'll simply stand up and . . .

He's slowing down. He's stopped. He's fingering the lid of his coffee. His big hands are blunt-tipped, and the cup looks small in his grasp. His eyes meet mine. They twinkle like amber in sunlight. Not aggressive or angry. But intelligent. Searching. Curious. Earnest, even. His mouth is well shaped, not too large, not too small. It opens to speak and then closes again. Then it opens a second time. He's going to speak. Which is great, because I literally can't. My pulse is racing.

Suddenly, the coffee shop door bursts open.

My head whips around. It's Gage. His blond hair gleams in the entrance, and he wears an expectant grin. He must have seen Dad's car outside and guessed I was here. Sure enough, he catches sight of me and his grin widens. He doesn't even notice Hunter until he nearly runs into him.

"What the—" Gage's grin turns stony. "What are you doing here?"

Hunter clears his throat and salutes him with his paper cup. "Hello, Gage."

"Only my friends call me that."

"Sounds limiting."

Gage steps closer so they're eye-to-eye, until mere inches separate them.

Every part of Hunter is chiseled for action. Life force hovers around him, almost visible in its strength. I swear he's radiating an otherworldly glow. His forearms and hands are honed in a way that's primal, animalistic even. Tigers have that same nonchalance, one that masks a deadly speed. Gage, with all his Viking height, is clearly no pushover, either. I hadn't realized how strong he looks until this very moment.

Hunter isn't looking for a fight, though. Instead, he takes a sip of coffee and winces at the heat. His eyes flash to mine. "Ouch. That could cause an accident."

Is he referring to my shirt? Is he teasing me?

I stare, oddly offended, feeling ugly in my wet, see-through top. My crossed arms tighten.

"Like I said," Gage snarls. "I'm surprised to see you in here."

Hunter takes a second sip and grimaces. "Nope, still don't like coffee." He sets the cup down and says, "I hate to cut this fine conversation short, but I'm out of time."

"Then go."

"First, I must return the lady's coat." He raises his jacket as if to cover me, yet only comes halfway. "I believe you dropped this?"

"I—"

He bends closer. "I thought you might need it." His voice is so quiet I'm sure only I catch it.

My hands come up and our fingers touch under the buttery-soft black leather. His are warm and our fingertips lock briefly as if in some spontaneous, private handshake. A thrill shoots to my toes, making me almost dizzy.

"Thank you," I whisper. Feeling Gage's eyes drilling into me, I repeat myself, louder. "Yes, thank you." I pull it to myself, covering my stained eyelet blouse with its welcome heft. Instantly, I'm wrapped in his masculine scent—faint hints of cedar and leather and something spicy.

"Are you done playing gentleman?" Gage asks.

"Why? Did you need some assistance, too?"

"Very funny. I thought you were leaving."

"I am. You're in my way."

Gage's fists tighten and his shoulders expand.

What is with him? I know he was hurt in a military accident. But I don't see what that has to do with Hunter. Does Gage hate all medical researchers now? Would he have hated Mom and her work in human genetics, if she were alive?

They stand nose-to-nose, neither backing down.

"Hey," snaps the barista. "Wanna clear my doorway so people can get in?"

Reluctantly, Gage steps aside.

Before Hunter leaves, he shoots me a look. Brief though it is, it's like those powerful, sensitive hands are gripping my shoulders, like he's looking right into me. Goose bumps rush along my skin under the cover of his jacket. When his eyes release me, my heart is slamming.

Then he's gone.

"Freak," Gage mutters. He lets out a big breath and smiles. "Hey, Aeris!"

"Hey," I manage back. *I can't believe he gave me his coat.*

"I saw your dad's car out there. I figured it was you."

"Yeah."

"Shove over. I'll grab some coffee. Want anything?"

My numbness is giving way. For some reason I'm furious with Gage. I stand abruptly. "I'm leaving."

His eyes widen. "W-what?"

I angle my face away, bending over to gather my things. Frustrated tears prick my eyes. I can't understand why I'm so upset, but I really am. And I know banging out of here is no way to treat a friend, but I can't help it.

Why did I accept Hunter's jacket? I have to give it back. Which means tracking him down. I swore I'd stop thinking of him and yet he's everywhere.

"Aeris," Gage says, his face like a wounded puppy as he follows me outside. "You're not mad at me, are you?"

His blue eyes are pleading. Under that big-guy muscle and grown-up bravado is the same kid who always had my back. My guilt turns into a knot. Despite his attitude toward Hunter, I know he means well.

"Are you?" he repeats, standing under the stop sign, the afternoon light catching gold strands in his hair.

"Sorry, it's just . . ." I motion at my shirt. Even though I'm gripping Hunter's coat like a shield, the stain is up to my collar. "I spilled coffee all over myself. I have to go."

"Oh. I didn't notice."

"Talk to you later?"

He walks me around to the driver-side door. "Definitely."

I TAKE MY TIME DRIVING TO Dad's, pausing at the ocean lookout to calm down.

When I get back, Sammy almost knocks me over with his greeting.

I bend to bury my face in his fur. "Good to see you, too."

He wags his back half, his big front paws stepping on my toes.

I sniff the air and frown. "Is something burning?" Standing, I head for the kitchen. "Dad?"

The hook where his keys hang is empty.

I open the oven. Cold.

The smell wafts from outside. I pad into the backyard with Sammy on my heels. There are two barbecues out here. The old one and one I've never seen before. And smoke is billowing from it. Sammy leads me to it, but I get hold of his collar.

"Come on, boy." He's so heavy I can hardly budge him. "Come on, over here."

This is so completely unlike Dad. To leave something that could start a fire?

I head to the side of the house for the hose to spray it down.

The rumble of an engine stops me cold. A car is rolling into the driveway. From the sound of it, a muscle-bound racing car. A car I'm particularly attuned to. I edge up to the corner and peek around as Hunter's glossy black vehicle purrs to a halt.

The passenger door glides upward.

Dad's work boot is recognizable as he sticks one leg out and plants it on the drive. His hands reach up to grab the doorframe, and he levers himself out. His face is grim.

My mouth drops open.

What is this?

Dad's jaw is tight. I'm suddenly reminded of those horrible years when he tried to track down Mom's killers while the whole world insisted it was an accident. Grade school passed me by in a distracted dream, because I also was desperate to know the truth. I don't know when my obsession turned to a dull ache, a buried hope that I rarely allow myself to consider; I only know it happened somewhere along the way. The realization makes my stomach clench.

When Dad's clear of the car, the door reseals itself.

Hunter backs out of the driveway. With a roar, he accelerates down the country road.

What were they up to?

It can't have been more than an hour ago that Hunter gave me his jacket. I recall how he'd burst into the coffee shop. Now I know who he was searching for.

Dad.

Like Gage, Hunter must have seen Dad's Range Rover parked outside.

The smell of smoke wafts to me, and I put my questions on hold.

"Dad!" I cry, hurrying to meet him. "Something's on fire."

He covers his surprise at seeing me by walking swiftly toward the front door. "Where?"

"Not inside, out back. The new barbecue."

"New barbecue?" His hand goes to his beard, and he takes on a puzzled expression. "Oh! My smoker."

"Smoker?"

"Grandpa sent it out." His voice is artificially bright. "I'm smoking some salmon. Come on, I'll show you."

"Oh my gosh, I almost hosed the thing down."

"Good thing I got here."

There's a beat of tension.

He clears his throat. Obviously, he wishes he hadn't mentioned arriving in Hunter's car.

In the distance, the ocean is a vast plane of hammered steel, curving at the horizon. Far off, barely visible mist swirls around Hunter's verdant peninsula. It's a place that promises secrets undiscovered. Birds wheel above it and then dive into the waiting arms of trees. A foghorn blows.

Chewing on my lip, I stand there in Hunter's big leather coat, holding it tight around me. This is my chance, and I'm not going to let it slip away.

"Why were you with Hu—Dr. Cayman? I'm surprised, after what you said about him."

"Yeah, well. It's just work."

I have to tread carefully. When he's pushed, he turns silent as an old bear.

"I met him." I keep my voice light and stroke Sammy's glossy ears. "He seems nice."

"Cayman? Where?"

"At the club, with Ella and Gage."

Closing his eyes under his thick brows, he mutters a curse.

"Dad, what is up? You were in his car. He can't be all bad."

"Peanut," he growls, "you have everything going for you. Cayman is not worth your time."

"It's not that. I'm only trying to understand this whole double standard. I don't even get what you could possibly be doing for him."

"Yeah, well, sometimes I wonder the same thing. It was a mistake and I don't want to talk about it." He's stony as a mountain. "End of discussion."

I cross my arms over my chest. "All right. Fine."

"I haven't seen that jacket before, have I?" he asks, his gaze honing in.

"It's a loaner. From the coffee shop. I had an accident."

He stares at the coat a moment too long.

Sammy bumps between Dad and me, his doggy brows alive with worry. I loosen one hand and pat his big, furry back.

"I thought you were going to show me your smoker."

He blows out a sigh, as ready to drop our conversation as I am. "Right you are."

We turn and to my surprise he reaches around my shoulders and gives me a one-armed hug. "Did I tell you how good it is to have you home?"

I lean my head against him. "Yes."

"Well, I'm telling you again."

I SPEND THE AFTERNOON PLAYING VIOLIN and staring out the guest room window. Whatever's going on in this town is none of my business. I'll be back in New York soon enough, and it will all be forgotten.

After dinner, I help Dad light a fire in the living room. He claims his armchair, book in hand. I sink onto the couch.

"You weigh a ton," I tell Sammy. "You're not sitting on my lap."

"He thinks he's still a puppy," Dad says.

"Yeah, more like a pony." I rub his nose. "Aren't you, Sammy?" After a while, I crawl out from under his comforting warmth and go sit at the piano.

To my chagrin, the old fear creeps up and chokes me like a weed. After playing countless concerts in front of thousands of people, you'd think I'd have conquered it. I haven't. When the fear comes, my fingers freeze and I'm certain I've lost every hard-earned shred of my musical ability.

It's ridiculous.

I breathe in slowly through my nose and out through my mouth.

Bending forward, I depress the first note to my mother's lullaby. Then the second. *Hello, old friend.* It's been so long. The tune is beautiful and simple and lovely. I hum quietly, and everything is all right. Then I'm softly singing the words.

> *There, where my true heart lies*
> *I'll set my igloo*
> *Close to the twilight edge*
> *Silent and still . . .*

When did I stop playing this treasure? Why did I ever decide I'd outgrown it? Funny how we leave behind such wonderful things.

Hearing it again brings me back to the one vacation I remember Mom and I shared.

We were in a seaside hotel, an ancient place of wood timbers and creaky doors. She wore a white woven belt; I could see it clearly because that's how tall I was. A white woven belt over a pretty navy-blue dress. It's the only outfit I recall that wasn't a lab coat.

We discovered the piano under the stairs at the end of a deserted hallway. An upright with yellowed keys, the sort that makes *plink-plunk* noises when you press them with your finger.

Together we sat side by side, neither of us with any clue how to play. Then as if by magic, or so it seemed to me then, we carefully picked our way through the song she always sang when she tucked me in. We were both delighted as the tune emerged right enough to be known. We were no longer mom and daughter but two souls connected in piecing together a musical puzzle, two souls building an eternal moment through our joint discovery.

In that instant, I knew her. Knew everything there was to know about her. And I loved her more than anyone should safely be allowed to love someone.

I glance at Dad.

His eyes are on the James Patterson novel in his hands. There's a small smile on his face, so I'm pretty sure he's not actually reading. He might not be a music fan, but he likes listening to me play.

Even Sammy seems content, lolling on the spot where I'd been. Every now and then, he chimes in with a howl, which makes me giggle.

How I go from this perfect moment to thinking about Dad in Hunter's car, I can't imagine.

My fingers hit a discordant note. I stop abruptly and stand.

Dad glances at me, surprised. "Oh, is that the end?"

"Er, yeah." I manage a smile. "I'm beat. I'm going to hit the sack."

"Good idea. I think I'll do the same."

"Night, Dad."

I head to my room.

My Macbook whirs as it boots up. The first place I check is Facebook. Then LinkedIn. No Hunter Cayman. I come across a few references to the construction of the Phoenix Research Lab in old copies of the local paper. The reporters have nothing bad to say. There's no scandal to justify Dad's attitude, or Gage's for that matter.

I finger Hunter's jacket and recall his face before Gage walked into the coffee shop. What was he going to say? What's he holding in those amber depths?

Two people I care about act like I should stay far away from him.

Yet Hunter was nice to me. He offered me his coat. He didn't have to do that. And when we spoke, when our fingers touched, I saw someone likeable. Someone kind and good under his mysterious facade.

I recall his parting look in the café that momentarily caught my breath.

The clearheaded me wants to make it all stop.

A stronger, irrational force, however, is winning out.

SEVEN

THE NEXT MORNING, I'M STANDING in the kitchen, rubbing my eyes and yawning and willing the coffeemaker to hurry up, when Dad appears. He's wearing a suit, which strikes me as odd. Sure, he wore one every day when I was growing up, but here in Deep Cove, it's totally out of place. And his beard has been trimmed back.

"Wow, Dad," is about all I can manage.

He laughs. "I got a call. Sorry, Peanut, but I'm booked on a commuter flight into the city."

"Uh-oh, something urgent?"

Although the brew cycle is still under way, I pour him a coffee and hand it over.

"In the investment community, everything is urgent. I'll be away until tomorrow."

"Want me to man the store?"

"No. You have things to do. Mr. Creedy's coming in."

Sammy and I follow him to the garage.

Wind whistles from outside. Last year's leaves cartwheel under the electric door as it rises. He starts the Range Rover and rolls down the window.

"Thanks for the coffee. See you tomorrow."

I stand in the wan light from the overhead bulb as he backs into the predawn darkness. His headlights swing around. Dense, pooling mist swallows him whole.

In the living room, cold rattles down the chimney. I find a blanket and go into the kitchen. The house feels lonely. Empty.

My phone rings, echoing down the hall from the guest bedroom. I frown at the clock.

Six a.m.

It's still ringing when I pick it up. UNKNOWN comes up on the caller ID.

"Hello?" I say.

The line is silent.

"Hello? Who's this?"

"I'm looking for Jack Thorne." The man's voice is raspy and official-sounding, yet vaguely familiar.

"He's not here. This is his daughter's phone."

"We have a certified delivery scheduled for this morning. A family member has to sign for it. I need to confirm you'll be at the house."

"How did you get my number?"

"It's on the order form as the secondary contact."

That's weird. I shrug. "Oh. Well, yeah. Sure, I'm not going anywhere."

"Dispatch is routing a special van since you're so far out. Should arrive around noon."

"I understand. I'll be here."

I hang up. I forgot to ask what was being delivered.

The coffeepot in the kitchen calls to me. I go, pour a mug, and add cream. Sliding onto the pine bench, I hunch down with my manuscript and wrap my fingers around the cup of steamy brew. I need to get focused. After a long moment, I carry the music book to the piano and run the first notes.

Where do you go from here, song? Give me a clue.

I rub my forehead until my hair is standing on end.

Finally, I go and stare out the stormy back window. Dawn's first light rims the steel ocean with metal streaks. As I watch, a thought comes to me.

If Dad and Hunter are working together, there must be a record of it in his office. It's wrong to go behind Dad's back and look. Still, I can't help my curiosity. If I'm going to do it, I have to move fast. Mr. Creedy's due to open the store at any moment. I have twenty minutes at most.

Sammy perks up and lurches to his feet as I dash for the guest bedroom to change out of my pj's. His claws scratch the wood floor as he scrambles after me.

Quickly, I wiggle into jeans and a checked blouse and snatch my oversize blue Juilliard hoodie off the ladder-back antique chair. Then I kiss the top of Sammy's nose.

"Back in a few."

With Dad's store keys in hand, I sprint outside.

THE THORNE COUNTRY SUPPLY SIGN still hangs at an angle from the storm. There's no sight of Mr. Creedy—yet. The gravel lot is empty.

I slide the key into the lock and turn. A bell jangles when I open the store's glass-paned front door. Familiar scents greet me: warm, dry smells of golden hay and pet food; aging wood; leather leashes, collars, and horse tack; and numerous varieties of soap. Earthy smells, too, like peat moss and planting seeds, and fancy organic topsoil.

I hurry past rotating racks of seedling packets to Dad's office, which is tucked into the rear of the store. The door's locked. I work my way through the jumble of shop keys and find the correct one. Inside, three tall file cabinets dominate the right wall. I open the drawer with the letter *P* and riffle through for *Phoenix Research Lab*. Nothing. I move on to *R*, and then *L*. No luck. Nothing under *C* for *Cayman*, either.

Strange.

Neat stacks of paper lie on his desk. I go sit in his swivel-back chair. The macaroni-decorated pencil cup I made for him in elementary school is right there next to the phone. A delighted laugh bursts from me; I can't believe he kept it.

Now I really feel guilty. I hate to imagine his face if he found me going through his private drawers.

He must have *some* file on Hunter.

The bottom drawer is bigger than the rest. Locked. I try the keys.

None fit.

A sound outside makes me freeze. I hold my breath.

Just the wind.

Whatever's important is hidden away. I go through the top drawer one last time. My heart leaps when my fingers touch something hard and square, tucked at the very back. I drag it out onto the desktop. It's an ancient, scuffed photo album.

The cover opens with a papery creak.

Mom looks up at me. My breath catches and my fingers go to her face.

Why would Dad keep this out here, and not in the house? Does he think this holds some key to her death? Is there something inside he's been studying?

I turn a page. It's another picture of Mom; she looks around five years old. She's wearing such a funny, endearingly serious expression that my stomach twists. I'd forgotten about these photos. I remember seeing them when I was little. I never noticed where she was. Now, after all these years, I see the picture for what it is. She's in an airport. There's a baggage carousel behind her. I wonder where she's going. Somewhere very snowy and cold, obviously. She's wearing winter boots and a giant, fur-lined parka, and has one small arm wrapped protectively over a dog carrier crate. The dog inside, a black Labrador, peers up at her through the bars with trusting eyes.

I imagine her alive in that moment and breathe her in.

Unable to fully catch my breath, I bend forward and give her a kiss, trying to hold on to the ghost of Mom.

I flip through the pages.

Tucked into the back is a notebook.

This I've never seen before. The rise and fall of my chest escalates.

There's only one entry. It's in Mom's small, slanted scrawl. What's strange is that the first paragraph starts right in the middle of a sentence. Was there a notebook before this one, and she's simply carrying on here, having run out of space in the first book? What's happened to it? Does it still exist somewhere? I flip through the rest of the book, yet it really is empty apart from this. So why only one page? Is it possible this was . . . her last entry?

It's too real, these pen strokes, this physical evidence of her. My fingers grow damp, and I blink hard against the threat of tears. I can almost hear her voice as I read.

and I can only now conclude that it is the height of human folly to tamper with the human code at such a minute yet critical level. Humans are not made to be divine. And doctors are not meant to play God. It is only by divine intervention, that I stumbled upon the way to correct what's been done.

I have inherited this legacy, and I will never shy away from the blame. It lies heavily upon me. After this, I cannot in good conscience contribute further, and caution all those mad enough to do so. Pray all goes well.

I read the baffling words several times. I knew, even as a small child, that her work consumed her, but what could she possibly have done to feel such guilt? Mom was incredibly caring and conscientious of others. So what made her write that?

And what did she mean, humans were not made to be divine? As in godlike? That doesn't make sense. But could this be a clue? Is this strange legacy the reason why people chased her down and killed her? What happened that made fate tear her away from me? From us?

I stare at the door. Mom had her secrets. Dad used to question me about them. They never married, even though I'm sure they loved each other. I lived with Mom, and she worked at a lab outside Washington, D.C. Dad mostly lived in New York. We only saw him on weekends. It's unlikely I'll ever learn the answer. Who could I ask? Mom is gone. She's been gone since I was five.

The digital clock next to the phone blazes at me. It's getting late. My right leg is curled under me and has gone numb. I stretch it out, and it starts to prickle.

I close the cover and replace the notebook and the album in Dad's desk drawer. Then my eyes fall on a stack of papers next to the phone. The words *Phoenix Research Lab* stare up at me from a printout. I grab the sheet, wide-eyed. It's a purchase order. An order in Hunter's name.

And the delivery date is marked for today.

My heart rate increases. I scan the contents. Dad would want this delivery made. I'll be doing him a favor. I should definitely fill his order and take it up there. Hunter will be expecting his goods to arrive.

Only instead of Dad making the delivery, it will be me.

Besides, I can return Hunter's jacket while I'm at it.

The memory of those piercing amber eyes searching mine is enough to send thrills of energy through me. I need to calm down. So I'm a little charmed. There's nothing wrong with that. It's not like I'm planning to let anything come of it.

Maybe I'll get a chance to clear up some of these mysterious questions. I don't want to find out anything bad, but surely Hunter wouldn't be doing something wrong. Would he?

I ignore the small voice screaming *No way, Dad will be furious if I go*, and take a closer look at the list of items. Nothing out of the ordinary, except there's a lot of it. If I'm going to do this, I need to get moving.

I run for the store's cash register. Maybe the PRL access card key isn't there anymore. Maybe Dad took it.

Praying, I shove my fingers into the secret spot.

I breathe in relief. Got it.

The clock is ticking. Mr. Creedy is due anytime.

I SPRINT FOR THE HOUSE, GRAB Hunter's jacket, and return to the shop. There's a roll-up door for deliveries at the back. Dad's cube truck is parked next to it. Ears trained for sounds of Creedy's car, I start to panic. I don't want to have to explain myself. It takes forever to track down the right bags of straw and oats and lug them outside. What Hunter wants with them is beyond me. I had no idea they were keeping animals.

My heart is slamming.

Wheels on gravel send it into overdrive. Time is up.

"Hi, Mr. Creedy," I call as he gets out of his car and stares at me in surprise. "I'm going to deliver this order." I wave the slip.

His feathered white brows shoot up, and he says, "Well, now, hold on there, Aeris—"

Before he can complete the thought, I climb in the cab, slam the heavy door, and lurch out onto the street.

I'll just have to apologize for taking off when I get back.

The giant square side mirror reflects Mr. Creedy's creased face. His mouth is open, his kind, rheumy eyes are frowning. I can't wave or smile or anything. I'm too busy focusing on driving this thing.

Sure, I've driven it before.

That doesn't mean I'm good at it.

In my hand, the shifter knob shakes, sending vibrations up my arm. I head down the road, away from town. I'm going to hear it later. I must seriously be crazy.

As I drive, I flash to the phone call I received earlier and the package I'm supposed to sign for. I'd better hurry.

The road twists, winding down into a thick stand of trees. On the far side, it snakes up again, opening onto a plateau. Choppy ocean surges beneath the cliffs. Storm clouds mount like grimy giants roaming across the sky. Mottled shadows paint the forested hills emerald green, the cliffs stony gray, the ocean quicksilver.

I spy the long finger of land jutting out into the Atlantic. Another five minutes and I'll be there, using Dad's pass to let myself in. A twinge of nervousness makes my foot ease off the gas. With a choking rattle, the engine threatens to stall. I gun it in panic, not wanting to be stranded out here. Dad's cube truck lunges forward, and I let up on the accelerator.

Relax. It's only a delivery. I chew my lip. I'm sure Hunter will be happy to get his jacket back.

Only a mile left to the promontory entrance.

I have no idea what to expect.

I haven't driven this close since the day Dad and I came out here together, before Hunter's people bought the land to build the Phoenix

Research Lab. That was three years ago.

Some memories stick in your mind with vivid clarity. I can still recall every single thing about that afternoon.

Dad was living in New York. I was at Juilliard. We'd returned to Deep Cove to visit his summerhouse, and to take a vacation ourselves. I hadn't seen it since those long-ago summers with Ella and Gage. Because of the full-time tenant, we'd stayed away. But now his tenant was moving, and Dad needed to assess the place for any problems before finding someone new.

On our second day in Deep Cove, he announced he wanted to show me something.

We climbed into the Range Rover and headed up this way.

I was joking around. Asking what the big mystery was.

"I'll tell you when we get there," he replied.

I knew we were headed toward the big country estate on the promontory. I'd heard about the massive home with its open parklands and narrow road in. People claimed it was haunted. The couple who lived there were recluses. Few guests came and went through their gates.

Dad and I turned the final corner toward the vast residence. We were met with the sight of construction vehicles blocking the entranceway. To my surprise, Dad looked dismayed.

He maneuvered the Range Rover into a grassy ditch. We climbed out, slamming our doors, and approached a red-faced man in a hard hat and orange vest. His nametag said MIKE.

"What's with all the construction?" Dad asked.

Mike shrugged his rounded, sweating shoulders. "Someone bought the place." A tractor began emitting high-pitched beeps. It lurched in reverse. He jabbed out a ruddy hand. "Watch it, you gotta step back."

"Who bought it?" Dad asked.

"Some fancy research operation."

"Researchers?" Dad's voice grew wary. "What kind of researchers?"

"Dunno. Money up the wazoo, though."

"I wish I'd been notified when the place went up for sale. Who made the deal?"

"Private handover."

A tense beat followed.

"Who was the purchaser?"

In answer, Mike pointed his thick, grimy index finger at an engraved plaque, still in its plastic wrapping. "That's all I know."

Dad stepped closer to the sign, and his face blanched.

"What is it?" I said.

"Nothing."

His words didn't match his grim tone.

I quickly studied the thing myself, trying to determine what had him so upset. A frolicking dog formed the central figure, a Labrador with a bandanna around its neck. Tongue hanging out and smiling in the way dogs do, it chased a bird in the sky. Soaring upward, the bird's forked tail and sharp pointed wings reminded me of something. Underneath the raised relief, the words *Phoenix Research Lab* were printed in large letters.

Dad cleared his throat. "Thanks. We'll be off, then."

"But, Dad," I said. "What—"

"We'll get out of your way," he told Mike. "Thanks for the heads-up."

"Not a problem. Have a good one."

"You do the same."

In the car, Dad let out a big breath, and then gave me a smile that was surely forced. "How about lunch?"

"Why were you so upset back there?"

"I wasn't. Surprised, that's all. Now how about we get on with our vacation. Pizza? Because I'm starved."

As it turned out, the visit was more than a vacation. The lab wasn't the only place in transition. Rather than finding a new tenant, Dad decided to move back into the summerhouse. Not only that, he took over his tenant's small tack-and-saddle-supply operation and turned it into Thorne Country Supply.

Today, three years later, it strikes me just how odd it was for Dad to give up his bustling work in the city. He'd claimed a change of pace would be good for him. He'd transferred his whole life here.

What changed his mind?

The Thorne Country Supply delivery truck continues to rattle as I approach the entry to the promontory.

No construction vehicles now.

In fact, the area looks quiet and sterile. Towering stone walls block off the prying eyes of drivers who approach along the road. Poles bristle with high-tech surveillance devices. Camera lenses peer out at various angles.

I'm reminded of a border crossing.

I slow, wary, feeling like I've entered a James Bond film. Am I being watched? Hopefully security is expecting Dad's truck. If I'm lucky, they won't look too closely at the driver.

Both hands turning the giant steering wheel, I maneuver into the driveway. It's paved with smooth blacktop, a contrast from the bumpy road. Pressing the brakes, I halt the truck before the towering metal gate. There, mounted dead center on the massive bars, is the plaque. The one that made Dad blanch.

He never did tell me what he'd wanted to show me here.

I lean forward, face close to the windshield, and study what's visible beyond the gates. All I can see is a road leading inward, bounded on either side by trees.

Hunter's domain is incredibly official. And incredibly mysterious.

It matches him perfectly.

I slide the key card from my pocket, wondering where I'm supposed to swipe it. Where's the intercom box? Scanning left and right reveals no sign of such a thing.

Wind swirls around me when I open my door. I climb onto the cold pavement. To my right, waves crash far below, white and frothy, charging the air with salt. A gust carries the cries of sea birds.

There must be a place to insert this thing.

Because I'm going in. There's no stopping me now. My timid heart is fighting to get me back into the truck, back on the road away from here.

I shut it out. I can't stop. I won't stop.

I've come this far. It's not about the jacket, or the delivery. Something in there is calling me. Questions that need answers. A man I need to speak to, if only once. If only to clear up this mystery, this confusion, this painful longing that's beyond all reasonable proportion. If I can just see Hunter, I know I can fix it. Make it stop. Understand it. That's all I want.

Or at least all I'm willing to believe.

EIGHT

To the right of the PRL gates stands a ten-by-ten-foot concrete bunker that probably once acted as the estate's guard shack. Now it's faced with steel. There's no visible door, but it appears to be my best bet. I approach, key card in hand, scanning for a slot.

Three feet from it, the steel slab slides sideways with a hiss and reveals a dim interior.

Faint lights blink in its depths. I'm not good with cramped places. Especially dark ones. Cold sweat prickles at the base of my skull. I wish I had Sammy with me.

Out loud I say, "Now we're getting somewhere."

Legs wobbly, I step into the concrete shack. Inside, it's the size of a large ATM booth.

Whoosh. The door whips shut.

I stand deadly still, eyes struggling to conform to the darkness. The floor beneath me is a metal grate. That much is clear. Wind gusts up through it, making it rattle. I squint warily down through the waffle slats. All that's visible is empty black air. Wafts of panic begin to rise. Maybe the floor is attached by a hinge that swings down to dispose of unwanted visitors.

My claustrophobia goes into overdrive.

I have to get out of this booth. Now.

There's no knob on the door. No trigger. I slam my right shoulder hard against it, again and again. It doesn't budge. What is this? Am I seriously trapped in here?

"Open up!" I cry, banging on the cold metal surface. "Let me out!"

Nothing.

"Open, you stupid piece of junk!"

My rage has no effect.

The door couldn't care less how freaked out I am. Fumbling in my pocket, I pull out my phone. I'll call the police, that's what I'll do.

Except there's no signal.

Damp, icy wind whistles up from below, sweeping through the grill. It rushes up my legs. I press my body as close to the wall as I can get. My phone has a flashlight. The beam is powerful. I point it downward.

A bottomless hole drops away.

All that's keeping me from falling is this eight-by-eight grill. Closing my eyes, I swallow.

"Please insert your card."

The polite voice rips a small scream from my throat.

On the wall directly to my left, a panel has slid upward. An ATM-style machine blinks in the semidarkness.

"Insert card?" I whisper. "I'll insert the card all right."

Shakily I replace the phone in my pocket and get out the key. On the monitor, the words PLEASE INSERT NOW blink in blue block letters. At least I'm getting somewhere. If only back out the door from where I came. In fact, that's exactly what I want.

To get out, back in the truck, and away from here.

There's a recessed hole beneath the monitor. I bend and see the slot located at the back. Sticking my hand in there is not exactly inviting, but I do it, holding the key straight. Blindly I jab it until it meets the insertion slot and slips inside.

A whirring sound makes me whip my hand back.

Not fast enough. A metal bar clamps over my wrist. My hand, still inside the hole, is manacled in place. Then a red light begins to flash.

Uh-oh.

"State your identity," the robotic female voice says.

"My . . . I'm . . ."

"State your identity."

"I'm here from—"

The band tightens. It presses painfully into my wrist. My fingers are turning numb.

"State your identity."

"Aeris Thorne!" I shout.

"Processing."

I try to wrench free.

"Name not recognized."

"Jack Thorne's daughter!" I cry. "Thorne Country Supply. I'm making a delivery, for god's sake. Just a delivery." I'm almost sobbing. It's pathetic and infuriating and terrifying.

"Processing. Please wait."

Like I have a choice?

Tiny metal gears sound under my hand. I think I'm being released. Instead, a needle jabs my index finger, drawing blood. A spray that smells of disinfectant follows.

"Still processing. Thank you for your patience."

Patience? This is insane! It's checking my blood? For what? Proof I'm related to my dad? That's not possible, is it?

"Identity accepted."

With a pop, the manacle releases my hand. Behind me, the door slides open.

"Please exit the booth. You have sixty seconds to drive your vehicle onto the property."

I stumble backward, rubbing my wrist. Unbelievable. No wonder everyone hates this place. Was that even legal? On the pavement, I put my injured index finger in my mouth. I start walking to the truck, fast.

The giant gate begins rumbling sideways, opening.

I'm angry and frightened.

Inside the truck, the warm leather seat is a welcome comfort. I turn the key, and the engine roars to life. Then I shift into gear. If I'm going to make a break for it, now is the time to leave, to get out of here. Fast.

Instead, I aim the front wheels toward the compound and rumble through. Behind the truck, the gate slides closed.

No turning back now.

The lane winds through pristine stands of pine. On the far side, a white post-and-board fence springs up next to the road. A stunningly beautiful horse gallops into view.

Hunter has horses?

Of course. Why didn't I put that together from the items he ordered?

Black mane and tail streaming, the stallion tosses his head, matching my speed. Under his pounding hooves, a puddle explodes in a glistening spray. I watch him move, imagining I'm riding rather than sitting inside this enclosed cab. Finding the buttons, I roll down both windows. The hoof beats are music to my heart.

Cantering alongside the truck, the stallion seems to share my goal.

I doubt we'll get equal reception, though, from whoever's waiting ahead.

Rolling grassy hills run to the distant cliff. Off to the right, the fence leads to a sprawling, well-tended barn, white with an emerald-green roof. To the left, far away, I spy a grand manor house. It stands on a rise, looking so magnificent my breath catches.

The house must be over a hundred years old. If that's the lab, any signs of modern technology are well hidden behind the warm, earth-colored bricks. I'm reminded of a manor house from some Victorian-era novel or movie. The kind with butlers and a downstairs staff, and dozens of bedrooms for weekend guests. A place with high tea and manicured gardens for strolling among the roses. For whispered confidences, and forbidden alliances.

A pothole in the road gives the truck a jolt. I'm bounced in my seat.

I hadn't realized the barn would be so far from the house. It's a good half mile away. In my imagination, I pictured this all so differently. I saw myself arrive, and by some magical coincidence Hunter would appear. But why on earth would he be down at the barn receiving deliveries? He's a researcher. That's not his job. It all seems ridiculous now. He'll be up at that grand house in some lab, working. I can't go barging around looking for him.

Even worse, I have to go back and explain to Dad why I up and decided to make his delivery for him. And that I took the key out of his secret spot in the register to do it.

I cringe.

If Mr. Creedy hadn't seen me leave in the truck, I'd turn around right now and pretend I'd never come. Unfortunately, I've dug my hole and there's no getting out of it. I breathe deep. I'll deliver the load and find someone to leave the jacket with. When that's done, I'll go. End of story.

The horse veers off, galloping away.

I downshift. I'm almost at the gravel lot that fronts the scrubbed wooden barn. Then I'm rumbling across it, kicking up dust and squealing to a stop.

The area is deserted. I wrench open the heavy door and climb down, jumping the last foot. Gravel crunches under my chocolate-brown oxfords. Muddy puddles here and there still shine from the earlier rain. Feeling exposed and nervous, I zip the Juilliard sweatshirt to my chin and pull the hood over my hair. Quickly, I go around back and unlatch the bolt. Then I hit the button that raises the roll-up door like an electric garage.

My skin prickles and I whip around, expecting to find someone there. It's deserted.

Shaking off my trepidation, I haul out a sack, shoulder it, and approach the barn door. The wood is warm and dry to the touch. It creaks open easily and thumps against the wall, making me wince.

Practically tiptoeing, despite the hefty sack, I enter. Horse stalls run down either side. Dust motes swim in narrow shafts of light that stab through knotholes and gaps in the worn outer walls. I start walking, looking for a place to put the delivery. My feet make scuffling noises on the worn redbrick floor. I glance into the first stall, over the open upper half of its Dutch-style door. The stall's completely clean, as if long unused.

The bag is growing heavy. I drop it for now and keep walking. Five more empty stalls follow.

There's at least one horse that lives in this vast, regal structure.

I saw it outside.

My thoughts roam to Grandpa's ranch in Montana, a place of cooing doves and nickering horses and the comforting smell of straw. If they're keeping horses here, they had to get them from somewhere. Is that the connection between Dad and Hunter? Dad had some of Grandpa's famous thoroughbreds shipped out here? If that's all that's going on, why the big secrecy?

Unless . . . what?

Unbidden, a frightening thought slips into my mind. What would a research lab want with horses? Are they doing something to the animals? Experimenting on them? Has Dad found out? The thought makes me sick. That can't be it, can it?

I consider running away.

I don't, though.

I have to know.

The seventh stall is different and I sense I'm getting somewhere. A lofty bed of fragrant hay fills the rectangular space. It's the sort that invites stolen naps on lazy afternoons.

Quiet words, muffled and deep in the distance, drift to me.

I freeze.

"You got yourself into this," comes the low, rumbling voice.

Hunter.

More words follow that I can't catch.

I back up. I should go. My foot makes contact with something metal. A bucket. It clangs along the floor at an alarming volume. I pause, horrified.

"Victoria?" Hunter calls.

Oh no.

"Curiosity got the best of you, did it?" he shouts.

I turn and sprint.

A thick arm wraps around my neck. I freeze. *Oh god.* A guard must have followed me. It can't be Hunter—he's too far away to sneak up on me that fast.

Terrified, I lurch forward and kick back with my right leg.

There's a small, deep "oof," and the arm tightens.

"Let go," I gasp, struggling wildly.

I should never have come in here. I should never have driven through that towering gate.

"Let me go!" I cry again. "I'm not doing anything wrong!" I wish I knew something, anything, of fighting. Of self-defense. I'm growing winded, too winded to explain what I'm doing here.

Desperately, I try to struggle free. The arm tightens, and hard muscle digs under my chin. My head is forced up and back, so that it's pressing against a solid, powerful chest. Fingers pull my hood away enough to expose my right ear. I feel warm breath on my neck.

The deep voice is quiet. Commanding. "Go ahead, wear yourself out."

He's no security guard. His voice is the one that's consumed my thoughts for three straight days. Impossible though it seems, he's there, behind me, holding me in a tight embrace.

My limbs turn unsteady.

"Um," I whisper through lips that have gone dry.

Sturdy hands spin me around, squeezing my arms hard through my hoodie. I revel in the familiar touch of his fingers, of his broad hands that are holding me upright. Waves of electricity pulse down my arms and into my body. I'm hovering somewhere between fear and awe, hot with a desire that's completely unlike me.

Hunter recognizes me instantly. He releases me as if he'd been caught holding his sister's doll. He looks surprised, pleasantly, perhaps. A smile starts at one corner of his mouth. So contagious that I smile, too. Then his expression shifts and he steps back a foot.

"Wait. How did you get in here?" His brows are low and unnerving, his irises the tawny, luminous color of amber in sunlight.

"Through . . ." I point vaguely toward the road. "Through the gate."

"I see." His gaze moves to my lips, my faltering smile, and back to my eyes. We're still so close I can smell his warm scent. "It's just—a little odd to find you here."

My hood falls back all the way, and I feel suddenly exposed.

"Yes, well, let me explain that."

He raises a hand and steps farther away. Even so, it's like we're magnetized. "I don't mean to cut you off, but I'm right in the middle of something." A loud whinny sounds in the distance.

"What's going on?" I ask.

The whinny comes again, more urgent. I lean past him, trying to spot the horse.

"I don't suppose you know anything about mares?"

"Actually. . ." I flash to Grandpa's ranch. "Yes. I do."

"Then come on."

I'm so surprised when he gives my wrist a tug that I jump.

"Hurry."

What could have happened? Hopefully nothing serious.

Whatever it is, I need to get focused. And not on him.

I can't believe he keeps horses. As usual, he's dressed nothing like I picture a researcher should dress. More like some special ops guy about to head out on a mission. His powerful legs are clad in black army fatigues. His T-shirt is black, too, and sticking to his muscular back in all the right places. He's sort of scary, yet sort of beautiful, too.

Worry begins to blot out my excitement. The closer we come to the whinnying animal, the more I start to wish I hadn't made such fanciful claims. Yes, I know something of horses. To say I could help an injured one would be stretching the truth. Seriously stretching the truth.

NINE

FROM UP AHEAD, I SENSE fear. But maybe it's me who's afraid.

"What's your name?" he shouts as we hurry down the row of stalls. His stride eats up the distance so that I have to run to keep pace.

"Aeris."

There's a supercharged pause.

On a laugh, he says, "I suppose it would be."

"Sorry?"

"Never mind. I'm Hunter, by the way. Glad to actually meet you."

His words give me a fuzzy feeling. "What's going on? Is the horse hurt?"

"Not hurt, but she's definitely feeling some pain."

"I don't understand."

He stops and his big thumb and long fingers circle my elbow. A pulse seems to shoot between us. Then he gestures over a stall's half-open Dutch door. A horse lies on a bed of hay, the golden hues stained. The animal's chestnut coat, beautiful once, is drenched and matted with sweat. Straw sticks to her sides. She's clearly rolled over, probably writhing in discomfort. Her belly is wildly swollen.

Large dark eyes swivel toward us, and the heavy head rises up. She looks exactly like Dakota. My favorite horse. It's almost uncanny.

"Okay, Poppy," Hunter says, his voice a low rumble.

The liquid-brown eyes meet mine. I read something pleading there.

"She's pregnant?" I say. "She's having it now?"

"No stopping her, I think."

The realization hits and I feel a surge of excitement.

"A baby horse. Wow."

"I know. Right?" He releases me and unlatches the stall door. My skin is almost cold in the absence of those strong fingers. He's grinning, and there's a small dimple etched into the angular plane of his right cheek that makes him almost boyish. Gone for now is the dark aura. Instead he's as floored as I'd be if I was about to welcome a foal.

"Who's your vet?" I say. "Why aren't they here?"

"I have an expert. But he's not answering his phone. I was about to start looking up local vets."

Dad. He's talking about Dad. That must be why Dad was in Hunter's car yesterday, why he told Hunter it wasn't time when he came into the shop. But now it is time.

"I don't suppose you know anyone?" he asks, hopeful, searching my face.

"I think it might be too late," I say. "Look."

The foal is emerging. Tiny hooves have appeared.

"You're right. Guess it's down to you and me."

I nod. "We can do this, right? I'm sure she'll be fine."

"Absolutely."

In the stall Poppy tosses her head, the whites of her eyes showing beneath thick lashes. Her round velvet nostrils are damp and flaring. Breath wheezes in and out of her. It's all so fast that mere moments pass, and then the tiny foal lies in the straw. Completely still. Hidden in its protective sac.

"Should we be doing something?" he asks.

"Something's wrong. It's supposed to be getting itself out of there. I don't think it can breathe inside that bag."

Hunter wrenches open the stall door, and the two of us bang into each other in our rush. He's solid as a wall and I almost land on my butt. His hands steady me, fastening firmly around my slender hips even as he's diving to his knees beside the foal.

He's fast, and in an instant its face and limbs are clear. But the foal is still lifeless.

"Here's a blanket," I say. "Try rubbing its chest. I've seen that done before."

"Thanks." He takes it and scrubs the small ribs. "Come on, little one."

"Maybe something's blocking the airway?"

"Good idea. Have a look."

I crawl around Hunter's back, open the foal's mouth, and feel inside with a finger. "Doesn't seem like it."

From behind us, Poppy lets out a gentle chirr. I look at her, and all I see is my Dakota.

"Hey, it's okay." I go to her head and scratch her soft cheek, just the way Dakota liked it. She responds with a low whinny. Her gaze is damp and it's like the color is fading from her eyes. A wave of fear washes over me. The pit drops out of my stomach. She's in trouble.

"Poppy?" I say, putting both hands on her neck and listening to her unsteady inhalations.

"She's moving," Hunter says. "She's breathing. Aeris?"

But my focus is on Poppy, on those eyes that have taken on a silent white haze.

"No," I whisper. "Don't go. Please."

"What's happening?" Hunter asks, his concern plain.

I shake my head.

"Here, watch the foal," he tells me.

I do so, taking hold of the dazed little horse. "Your mother's tired, that's all," I whisper stupidly.

Hunter presses one ear to Poppy's heart.

"No," he growls.

My hand goes to my mouth as I share his agony. He maneuvers her long front leg, one that has known fields and jumps and days galloping across pastures, until he's able to cup his hands over her heart. His back and arms are thick with muscle. Still, strong as he is, I don't see how he could possibly do chest compressions on her. She's too big. Yet clearly he's not ready to let her go.

I watch him rise to his knees and thrust down into her ribs. Her rumpled coat actually depresses. Deeply. It surges up again. He thrusts a second time and then a third. Over and over, keeping the rhythm of her heart. His strength astounds me. It's unnatural. It's inhuman.

My arms clench around the filly; my eyes are glued to Poppy's face.

"You got this," I tell Hunter.

He keeps going, jaw gritting, tirelessly fighting.

I don't know if it's ten minutes or thirty minutes or an hour. I hold my breath until it's painful, as if doing so will help her live.

Finally, he slows.

"What's wrong? Why are you stopping?"

"It's no good." He presses his slick brow to Poppy's broad, matted neck. "I tried, girl," he whispers to her.

"No," I say, my voice fierce. Angry. Furious. "No! Don't stop. There's still a chance."

"It's too late," he says, his voice muffled.

"How can you say that? You're a doctor. What about your research lab? You must have machines. And drugs."

"We can't help her."

"You're just going to give up? What about the filly? She needs her mother!"

He sits back on his haunches, his arms on his knees, his hands hanging. His closed lips press tighter together. His amber eyes flick to me and then the foal.

"There is something you can do, isn't there?"

He hesitates. Or maybe I only imagine the hesitation.

"No." There's a pause and he shakes his head. Weary. Sad. "No, there isn't. I lost her."

My arms sag around the tiny newborn.

"Like you said, I should have had a vet here."

"It's not your fault."

The foal nudges her way toward Poppy, making pathetic, tiny sounds. But her cries go unanswered. They'll continue to go unanswered. Like mine have since the moment I lost Mom. I watch her press her small body to the big, silent one, knowing it's the one moment she'll feel the touch of her mother in this life.

Against my will, a sob escapes from my mouth. I clap my hand over it.

"It's no one's fault," I whisper.

Hunter's arms come around me. He smells of warmth and safety, of clean skin and vibrant life. I cry into his shirt. He pulls me closer, fitting my forehead to the nook beneath his chin. He strokes a hand through my hair, smoothing it away from my cheek. His chin is hot and sanded with stubble. His pulse beats against my temple, pounding in time to my own.

"That's life," he whispers. I'm not sure if he's telling me that or himself.

I nod, my forehead against his hard collarbone.

"Death is the darkest of thieves," he says.

WE'RE BOTH SOMBER AS WE cover Poppy with a tartan blanket. There's not much more we can do in this instant with the newborn in need of immediate attention.

"We should get the filly to a new stall," Hunter says.

"Good idea. I'll help."

"How about you grab some fresh straw while I carry her."

"Okay, great."

I find a wheelbarrow and load up. My throat's still raw and my mind's still there against Hunter's chest, feeling his shirt against my cheek and his legs pressed to mine. What was I thinking, crying? Why couldn't I have held it together? Still, the pain of seeing Poppy die wasn't easy. It's the last thing I could have predicted when I headed over here to see Hunter.

And there's one small joy. The foal is alive.

I hurry to find them both.

"Down here, Aeris," Hunter calls.

The sound of my name on his tongue makes my ears tingle.

"Coming!"

He catches sight of me and my wheelbarrow, and his mouth does this cute half quirk. I must be a complete mess. "There you are. Look." He indicates a high window with his jaw, still holding the filly in his big arms. "The sun's coming out."

I glance up to see rays bleeding between the clouds.

"Nice," I say, and quickly scatter straw across the stone floor so he can put his heavy bundle down.

Feeling eyes on me, I turn to catch him studying me. His gaze flicks down the curve of my cheek, across the shape of my face. There's that curiosity I saw before. He reaches out with his hand, and I'm frozen, breathless, until I realize he's pulling a piece of straw out of my hair. Then he's walking away, his heavy black work boots disappearing in the hay, and crouching next to the foal. He strokes her head and ears.

"You doing okay, little one?"

There's something so familiar in his actions. In his voice. I can't help the odd feeling that I know this man. Have we met before? Not in Deep Cove, yet someplace else? When he'd held me, his touch had actually felt recognizable. And his scent, too. He'd smelled of safety and salvation.

I don't hug a whole lot of people.

And I'd especially remember hugging him.

He glances over his shoulder at me, and I smile quickly.

"She's looking good," he says.

"Much better," I agree.

Her head bucks a few times, ears wicking backward and forward. Then, as if to prove us right, her stilt-like legs unfold, and she wiggles awkwardly.

"Oh my gosh, I think she's trying to stand," I say.

"I think you're right."

Hunter jumps back to give her room, and we retreat to the wall. She makes a funny little bleating noise. Her miniature front hooves come forward, and she plants them beneath her.

"Go, girl," I say, warmed by the sight as well as the feel of Hunter so close at my elbow.

Slowly, haltingly, she rises partway. She pauses, bracing herself. Then, with a start, she topples over, glossy and rust-colored and shimmering in the slanting light. The second time is almost a somersault. The third, she practically does the splits. It's amazing and funny and endearing. This filly is less than thirty minutes old; she's claiming her life moment by moment.

We're both trying not to laugh, but it's hard.

"Almost there. Come on, girl," Hunter urges.

This time, she jams her hind legs firmly in place, hooves spread wide in a stubborn survival stance. Her auburn coat burns as if with licks of fire.

My heart actually leaps into my throat. "Way to go!"

"Yeah!" Hunter says.

As if having made her statement, she careens into the straw.

"She's going to be one little firecracker." Hunter props his back against the stall door. "We need to give her a name. Any ideas?"

"Me?" As it happens, a name had popped into my head. Still, naming her would be a sure way of getting too attached to a horse that isn't mine. So I just shrug.

He uncrosses his arms and his irises flicker. "What was that? You holding back?"

"It might be more of a guy's name."

"Try me."

The light catches his hard cheekbones and smile creases next to his mouth, making my stomach do little flips.

"Uh . . . Blaze?"

"Blaze?"

"I just thought, because of her rusty color, but it's probably not great."

"I don't know about that. I like it. It suits her."

"Really?"

"Yeah." He goes and pats the filly on her side, dragging my gaze with him. "What do you think, Blaze? We need to get you something to eat, huh?"

So Blaze it is. She's certainly doing a quick job of working her way into my heart. But she doesn't belong to me, and I don't belong on the research lab property. Honestly, I need to get a grip. The truth about me sneaking in using Dad's key is going to come out sooner or later. And given his and Dad's tense relationship, it's going to be awkward.

"I saw feeding bottles in the tack room," he says. "I was told to get colostrum in case of emergency. Never actually thought I'd have to use it. It's in the freezer up at the house. You mind staying here with her?"

"Not at all!" I say, too brightly.

I guess sooner or later has arrived. Because once he's outside, he'll see Dad's truck. And then it's going to be explanation time.

TEN

FIFTEEN TENSE MINUTES LATER, I sense someone staring at me. I spin and catch Hunter with his brows knitted. He eases his way into the stall.

"Hello," I say.

"Got it."

"Great."

He says nothing about what he must really be thinking. Instead, he lifts a baby bottle. "I'm not much of a pro when it comes to these things."

"Here, let me." I take the warm bottle. I should just blurt it out. Admit that, yes, I stole Dad's key. "Maybe you should hold her."

"All right." He braces her between his knees. "So tell me again how you got in?"

Under his scrutiny, I grow flustered. I was right. It's awkward. More than awkward. I press the nipple to her mouth. She refuses it at first, struggling away. "Yeah, about that . . ."

"I don't quite recall what you said earlier."

I squeeze a little milk onto her lips. She licks at it.

"Right—well, through the gate."

Blaze's tail starts whisking around as she drinks, whacking Hunter in the back.

"That I figured. I'm still confused. Did Jack help you get in?"

"No . . . look, I . . . I found your delivery order for today, and Dad's out of town, and . . . I thought you'd be needing the supplies. So I came up here, and that's it."

"Dad? You mean Jack Thorne?" He nods. "It's all starting make sense." Instead of the tension easing, though, it grows. "How come I've never seen you in the store?"

"I don't live here. I'm visiting."

Blaze struggles, and I tilt the bottle slightly. It's almost empty. I know it's important not to let her head rise too high or the milk can enter her lungs.

"This puts a different spin on things."

"Does it?"

All the warm, fuzzy feelings are gone.

"So he set you up to this?"

"Up to what?"

Hunter rubs his face with his free hand, and when he looks up, his amber eyes are stony. "You tell me."

I realize what a mistake I've made by coming. How could I have sobbed on this man's chest? I knew there was bad blood between him and Dad. Clearly it's spilling over onto me.

"This has nothing to do with my dad."

"Come on, Aeris."

"He was called away on an emergency. He doesn't even know I'm here."

Blaze pulls away, and we both stand. Hunter's presence is larger than life, powerful and enigmatic and striking in this enclosed space. I feel almost claustrophobic.

"I saw your order and I thought you might need it. And I had to return your jacket. And I saw you and Dad in the store acting weird, and I was curious, okay? And if I'm being honest, I wanted to meet you, talk with you, without being in a nightclub, or Gage barging in. But clearly that was stupid. The only reason I'm happy I came is for Blaze."

Hunter's hands unclench. He wipes them on his fatigues. "Okay."

"Exactly."

"Somehow, I actually believe you. But I still don't see how you used a borrowed card. Security measures should have stopped you."

"Well, they didn't. Look, I'm telling the truth. I made a mistake. Okay? Why didn't you question me earlier, if you were so worried?"

"Guess I was enjoying the help."

"Oh."

"But I should let you get on your way. You leaving town soon?"

I don't see what that has to do with anything. I shrug and run my thumb down the side of the empty bottle. "Just tell me one thing."

"What's that?" he says, cautious.

"Why don't you and my dad like each other?"

A dove coos in the eaves far above. Wings flap to life as it rises and escapes through an open window.

"Never said I didn't like him."

"You didn't have to."

"I respect him. A lot."

"I thought you hated each other."

"Not me. He's a good man," Hunter says. "I know where he's coming from. Especially now."

"And where's that?"

"We're both trying to do the right thing. Even if we disagree on how it should be done."

"What are you trying to do?"

Hunter swipes at a fly and unlatches the stall door.

"Hunter."

He pauses, hand on the latch. "Look, your dad helped me restore this barn and bring in the horses. And I'm really grateful. But now he's been asking all these questions and—well, they're not questions I can answer. Our work is classified, and I have a responsibility to my colleagues. And I guess he's not happy with me."

"Why would he care about your research?"

Hunter's eyes are on me. His thumb traces the shape of the metal latch. "You sure he didn't send you here to question me?"

"That's what you thought?"

"So I'm wrong?"

78

"Yes, you're wrong. And you still haven't told me what he wants to know."

"Maybe you should ask him."

I shuffle my feet in the straw. "All right. I will. I'll tell you this much. He's a good guy. And if anything, he's worried about this community. People aren't happy about having a lab here that's researching contagious diseases."

"Understandable."

"And he'll be upset he let you down today. He would have wanted to be here."

"I know."

"Well, the other thing you need to know is that you can't leave this barn for the next twenty-four hours. No joke. I remember a mare dying in childbirth on my grandpa's ranch and people took shifts watching the foal. About eight hours in, it got some kind of infection. Blaze is nowhere near out of the woods yet."

"Right, I should run an immunoglobulin test on her."

I glance at Blaze, her awkward limbs akimbo as she dozes in the hay. I wonder if she's related to my Dakota. Poppy sure looked like her. Maybe they were sisters. As I watch her breathe, I know what I have to do.

"If you don't mind, I want to stay until my dad can get here."

He appears startled. "You mean until tomorrow?"

"We have to feed her every two hours. All day. All night."

"You're offering to stay here?"

"Yes. My dad wouldn't leave, I'll tell you that much." *And neither would Grandpa.* Since Dad provided the horses, this filly is clearly one of his. Which makes Blaze family. And I'm not going anywhere until I know she's safe.

"The barn's not heated," Hunter says.

"Fine with me."

"It's going to be a long, cold, uncomfortable night."

"That's not a problem."

The truth is, he can argue all he wants. We already lost Poppy. I'm not leaving.

Hunter must see this because he rubs his forehead. "You're stubborn as hell."

"Guess I am." I pick up the feed bottle and gesture at Blaze, who's starting to make impatient, chirring calls.

"And here I thought I was bullheaded."

THE AFTERNOON PASSES QUICKLY, TAKEN up by our focus on Blaze. Yet the uneasiness lingers. A thread of tension underlying everything we say.

After what happened earlier, it's a lonely feeling.

Evening descends. In the hall, I sink onto a hay bale. He comes out and stands next to me, arms crossed, broad back propped against the sturdy wood planking.

"Storm's coming," he says.

I nod. "It's going to be a big one."

Around us, the shadows are growing longer.

"Why don't you take a break," he tells me. "Go outside and stretch your legs before it hits."

"I'm fine."

"You've been cooped up for hours. We've got a long night ahead. Get some fresh air."

I take the hint. He wants to be alone. "You're right."

In the hall, part of me feels almost numb. Another part is so pent up it wants to burst. I thrust my way out into the cool, clear dusk.

My eyes roam along the road and follow it up to the house. The place looks nothing like a research lab. I see no signs of modern technology. Why would Hunter and the others choose to retrofit a rambling estate for their work instead of using some glass-and-steel structure built expressly for their special needs?

And why did Hunter claim Dad's so curious? Maybe he's imagining it.

The truth is, I've been suspicious of Hunter on too many counts—that first night at the club, and here, about why he was keeping horses. Both times, my mistrust was beyond wrong.

Standing in the paddock is the lone stallion that galloped alongside the truck when I arrived. I go to the fence and climb the bottom two rungs. He acknowledges me from a distance with a soft, nickering whinny.

"Hey, boy," I say.

At this, he approaches. Painful experience taught me to be cautious with a strange horse, especially such a big one, yet he shows no sign of skittishness. He dips his head. I reach out slowly and run my hand down his nose.

He makes a deep, rumbling horse noise in his chest. Friendly. Welcoming.

"I think you might be a daddy," I tell him.

He rubs his muscular neck against the fence. I give him a hand, scratching his smooth coat. I have a sudden urge to ride, far and hard with the wind on my face.

I climb over the fence.

"I bet you're a fast runner, aren't you?" I ask, hopping down next to him.

His nose bumps gently against my shoulder.

"How about it?" I ask.

He prances a few steps and tosses his head. It's all the invitation I need. I'm on his back in a flash. He's already moving as I wind my fingers tightly into his mane. Suddenly I'm that girl again on Grandpa's ranch. The one he bellowed at for riding bareback, yelling that it was dangerous to charge around without a proper saddle and tack.

I braved his anger a dozen times. More. He didn't understand how I craved the freedom of those rides. Just me and the horse, moving like the wind, running from everything and everyone, from the past and the future and all in between.

Exactly like I crave it now.

Maybe this stallion does, too, because we're riding hard and fast, bent together like an arrow with no target in sight. His hooves send clods of loamy-scented earth flying. To our right, the fence whips past, a white blur of post and board. I see a red-and-white jump, and we arc toward it, and then we're airborne and the wind is pulling tears that wet my lashes and I'm laughing.

He's incredible.

I squeeze his left side with my leg, and he responds instantly. We wheel around, take a second jump and then a third. Finally, we canter back toward the barn.

Hunter stands outside, hands on hips. His brow is all bunched up in something close to anger.

Uh-oh.

Those fierce eyes stay fastened on our approach.

"Glad to see Ranger didn't kill you," he tells me as we pull up.

"Kill me?" I say. "Why would he do that?"

"He's half wild, that's why."

"Half wild? Seems pretty docile to me." I pat Ranger's neck. "Aren't you, boy?"

"Ranger is a lot of things," he growls. "Docile is not one of them." Despite his irritation, he almost looks impressed.

I move to get down. Hunter reaches for me, his strong hands closing around my waist. My skin practically vibrates in reply. Unwilling to show his effect on me, I keep my face neutral as he lifts me to the ground.

"Fun's over," Hunter tells me. "And I'd appreciate it if you didn't go around jumping on the backs of large, unfamiliar animals. You could have been hurt."

The sizable horse snuffles my hand. "I think I know what I'm doing."

"I think you were lucky."

"Luck had no part in it." I scratch Ranger between his ears. "Did it, big guy?"

Hunter stares at us for a long beat. Finally, he motions me toward the open barn door. "Let's get inside. Ranger needs his oats, and we need to get back to Blaze."

The sound of a car engine comes to life in the distance. A black SUV winds its way down the long, curving lane toward the barn's gravel lot.

"Someone's coming," I say, stating the obvious.

"That'll be Edward. I asked him to bring supplies down from the house."

At this news, I'm overtaken by a timid twinge of unease. It was one thing to argue with Hunter about staying. But is this Edward going to confront me about trespassing?

Hunter's gaze roves over me, reading me like a book. "Since you and Ranger are such good friends, go ahead and take him in. I'm sure someone as resourceful as you will have no trouble finding his stall."

"I'm not sure if that's a compliment or an insult."

"Nor am I," he says with a shadow of a smile.

"Fine," I reply, and lead the horse through the door.

IT DOESN'T TAKE LONG TO get Ranger settled. Then I hurry to check on Blaze. She's sleeping heavily. Hunter appears quietly. We stand together and watch her doze.

His big hands hold a picnic basket, a pile of army blankets, and a pillow. The sight of his tanned, muscular fingers makes me recall how they felt on my waist when he helped me down from Ranger's back. Protective, though god knows why, since he's clearly beyond annoyed with me. And Ranger wouldn't have hurt me. Still, my heart does a tiny flip.

Maybe he isn't quite so standoffish after all.

This whole day has been up and down and past imagining. I wonder what Ella's going to say when I tell her we spent the night together.

That's when it strikes me. We really are about to spend the night together. Alone, the two of us. In a big, dark, empty barn. And despite everything, it's all I can do to squelch down an image of us rolling in the hay.

ELEVEN

"Pillow's for you," Hunter tells me, setting everything down on a bench in the hall.

"I won't be needing it," I say quickly.

He gives me that now-familiar quirk of his mouth, and his eyes are smiling, and I wonder if he's laughing at me. "Suit yourself. Here, give me a hand with this basket. You must be starving. I know I am."

"I am, too," I say, glad of a subject change.

I get busy pulling a workbench over for a table and laying out the food. Hunter pushes a pair of hay bales against the wall and drapes them with a blanket, forming one long, makeshift padded seat.

"After you," he says.

I sit and he settles in beside me, tugging the workbench close. His thigh almost touches my leg. Even with the tension still between us, it's somehow more intimate than any moment I ever shared with Trey. Hunter's arm presses against mine, marble-hard and sculpted and way too sexy, and I quickly pull away.

"It all looks delicious," I say, flustered.

"Thank Edward." Hunter gazes over it all, one brow rising. "He sure went for broke."

There's hot roast chicken and a loaf of crusty bread with cold butter. A hearty salad with tomatoes, cucumber, and feta. A large wedge of cheddar cheese. Half a peach pie. Several bottles of mineral water. A tall thermos of piping-hot cider, and a second one of coffee, along with a quarter pint of cream. Thinking back to Foggy Joe's, I wonder if the coffee is for me.

I pour us both cups of water.

He sets out plates.

Neither of us speaks. Maybe we have nothing to talk about.

"Look," he says. "Since we're stuck here, let's try to leave our differences behind for a while. What do you think?"

I nod. "Okay."

As we start eating, there's a slow loosening of tension. The conversation starts and stops, and starts again.

He's buttering a thick slab of bread when he glances at me. "So tell me something. That night on the road. Did you really enjoy that Mozart piece?"

I stop piling salad onto my plate and look at him. "Yeah, actually. I did."

"I thought no one under thirty—well, hardly anyone—likes classical music."

"You don't exactly seem the type yourself."

He laughs. "Really? I'm not sure how I should take that. What type do I seem like?"

Now it's my turn to laugh. "I don't know. That was uncalled for."

"Maybe not."

"Wait, I'm right?"

"I didn't say that," he says. "Only that you're entitled to your opinion. Truth is, when I was a kid, my dad thought attending performances was prestigious. I associated classical music with tight-fitting, uncomfortable dress-up clothes, being forced to sit still in a dark theater while my father snored next to me in his seat."

I grin at this image of Hunter as a boy. "What about your mother? Did she enjoy it?"

"She did. She used to tell me that if I listened closely I'd hear the world's soul."

Wow. I like this woman.

"So if you don't like classical music, why were you playing Mozart in your car?" I say.

"I guess I changed my mind." He finishes slathering his heel of bread with butter and offers it to me. I shake my head.

"Best piece, the crust."

I pause, my mug halfway to my mouth, and say. "Wait, that's my line."

"Well, at least we have one thing in common." He waves it in front of me again. "Go on, you know you want it."

"Um—" I can't help laughing. "Okay. Thanks."

Our fingers brush and I meet his eyes. There's a lightness there, an opening. If I'm not careful, I could tumble into that bright gaze and never want to leave.

He leans one elbow on the bench, angling toward me and resting his chin in his hand. "So how did you know that was Mozart? Or was it a lucky guess?"

I tear off a bite, and my mouth tips into a little grin. After swallowing, I say, "I'm going to be first violinist in the New York Philharmonic come fall."

"You're kidding." His hand claps down on the bench. "Seriously?"

I nod.

"How? Where did you study? I'm really impressed."

And so I'm answering his questions, telling him about learning the violin, and about my secret dream of composing, and even about my relationship with Trey and how he wanted me to move to the Midwest and turn down the symphony's offer.

"He sounds like a self-centered idiot. I can't believe you gave him the time of day."

"He wasn't *that* bad."

"I, for one, am glad Troy Sheila went back to where he belongs."

"Shields. Trey Shields."

"Whatever. Good riddance."

I'm not sure why this is so funny, but it is. His face glows with devilish amusement. I'm still grinning as we pack up the picnic basket together.

"I like your smile, Aeris Thorne," he tells me. "It sure lights up this big old barn."

I swear I better be careful because I'm in serious danger of falling for this man.

WE GO AND ATTEND TO Blaze, who glances up all wide-eyed, tugging at my heartstrings. It's getting easier to feed her, or so I think, until she shoots out one hoof and catches Hunter in the shin.

He curses loudly. I drop the bottle.

"Are you all right?"

He rubs his leg, wincing. "Yep. My fault. Carry on."

For an instant, I get this ridiculous vision of us as parents muddling our way through our baby's first night home and almost laugh out loud. Hunter's bent, tousled head rises to question my silence. He catches my grin and smiles back, making my heart stutter. In this moment it's like we've been together in this barn, in our solitary world, for a small eternity.

I don't know when the shift happened, yet where there was unease before there's now an electrical current of anticipation under everything we do and say. A breathless beauty to the world, like we're shooting stars racing across the night sky on an impending collision course.

"How did you get into horses?" I ask.

"My mentor. I was studying in Europe. He was a horse fanatic. I caught the bug from him."

"So you rode a lot there?"

"If you want the truth, I was blustering that horses can't be hard to ride so he invited me on an expedition. Two months on horseback in the Mongolian steppes with a bow over one shoulder and arrows on our backs and no idea where our next meals were coming from. I was bruised from one end to the other—and that includes my ego, before I finally got the hang of it."

"Two months!"

"It puts either the love or hate of horses in your blood. In my case, love won out."

"That sounds amazing. I'd give anything to do a trip like that."

"You would?" His rugged face is the picture of amazement.

"Yes, are you kidding? Who gets to do that? Ride away on horseback for two whole months?"

His brows go up a notch. "I'll hold you to it, if I ever do it again."

His words reverberate through me and I can barely breathe. Is he toying with me? Then I swallow and match his dare with a smug grin. "I'll be there."

With a laugh, he shakes his head and strokes Blaze's ears.

"What?"

"Nothing."

"Is it because I'm a woman? You think I couldn't handle?"

"No. Maybe."

"Well, you'll just have to wait and see, won't you?"

"I'm looking forward to it. Very much, actually," he says.

I follow him out of the stall. The air is chilly as we sit together again. He fetches a candle from the basket and lights it, setting it nearby. I pull my knees up, drawn to his warmth.

"What's it like out there, really?"

"Vast. A million stars at night. Sparks rising from the fire. Horses chirring. You're this tiny life-form out in the middle of the plains and the rest of the world disappears."

I can almost see the firelight flickering on his tanned features, the tiny circle of our campground glowing in the darkness. I'm struck by a pang of longing. Of course it's only a dream. Or maybe hopeful thinking. After tonight, who knows what will happen. I have the Philharmonic and he has his work. Yet for now, I savor it as though it could be real.

Spurred on by our easy intimacy, I hear myself say, "I have a confession to make."

"Oh?"

I have his full attention now.

"I don't actually travel much."

"Why not?"

"I have this habit of putting my music first."

"Then you'll have to bring along your violin. Anything else I should know?"

I laugh. "Okay, maybe there's a reason Mongolia appeals to me—I'm weird about crowds."

"As in?"

"Honestly? Normally I wouldn't be caught dead someplace like the Zenith Club. They terrify me."

"I don't like crowds much, either."

"And there's another reason why your trip appeals to me." Before I can stop myself, I blurt, "I love riding, in fact, I've always, desperately, wanted my own horse."

Did I just admit that?

He opens his mouth to speak, but before he can say something he doesn't mean, like that we can share Blaze, or that he'll let me come and ride her, I quickly say, "What about you? Is there anything I should know about you?"

He assesses me long and hard, and I'm sure he's about to say he doesn't want me prying.

"I'm obsessed with my work, too," he admits.

"Really? I like that."

He gives me a half grin. "And you're not the only one who avoids bars. The night we met is the only time I've ever entered a club without being dragged in."

I laugh. There's heat in his eyes, and it radiates down my middle, all the way to my toes. I'm madly aware of the heat of his thigh against mine. He lifts his rough fingers to my cheek. I practically melt forward.

"Crumbs," he says, and brushes them away.

His hand is trembling ever so slightly. My heart is slamming in my throat. His own pulse beats visibly along his jaw, which is dark with stubble. My eyes move to his mouth, and I think he's about to kiss me.

At that moment, Blaze's cries come to us.

We both stand quickly, nearly upsetting the table.

EVENING PASSES INTO NIGHT AND deepens toward dawn. At four thirty I allow myself to lie down for a moment on the hay bales. I wake in inky darkness to find thick blankets draped over me. The barn creaks as it settles in the coolness. There are gentle rustlings in the distance, the sounds of Ranger shifting in his stall.

Out of nowhere, I recall the fact that I was supposed to stay home to accept Dad's package. I groan, softly. I hope Mr. Creedy took it. And thinking of Mr. Creedy, he must be wondering where I am. Did he call Dad? I'm going to have some serious explaining to do.

I peer into the shadows, trying to make out Hunter's form. I sense him sitting just out of reach. His breathing is barely audible. He's clearly awake.

An ache fills my chest. Had he been about to kiss me? Or had I read him wrong? Because he hadn't come close to trying again. If anything, he's been preoccupied and distant.

Maybe he's thinking about Dad again.

Maybe I need to get a grip while it's still possible to stop from tumbling head over heels. I have a goal—no boyfriend until I reach it. That is my rule. It's a good rule. Really. Truly. I'm glad he didn't kiss me.

Well, maybe *glad*'s not exactly the right word.

WE FEED BLAZE, AND THEN I return to my resting spot and curl up alone.

Early light filters through my closed lids. I jolt upright at the sound of hooves. Hunter is leading Ranger down the long row between the stalls. There's a horse blanket slung over the stallion's back.

"Going somewhere?" I ask.

"Good. You're awake. I thought we could take a ride."

"We?"

He pats Ranger's thick shoulders. "This guy needs some exercise, and I want to show you where I'm going to bury Poppy. If you're interested."

"You mean—you and me, ride Ranger . . . together?"

"You're small and he's a big guy. I don't think he'll mind."

I'm not exactly thinking of Ranger's discomfort—although I should be—but more of my own at being so close to Hunter. Apparently that's the last thing on his mind.

"It'll be faster than walking," he tells me, "and I don't like to leave

Blaze too long. It will be time to feed her in another half hour."

As we hurry out the barn door, I run to keep pace with his stride. Yesterday's rainclouds, which had loomed on the horizon, have marched closer. They charge overhead, shadowing the landscape in shades of gray. Across the open fields, misty light slants beneath the rapidly moving cumulus. The strong lines of Hunter's face are silhouetted against the stormy sky.

He eyes the distant treetops that sway in the rising wind. "We don't have much time."

A warning drop spatters on my face.

"Are you up for it?" he asks.

"Of course. Let's go."

Hunter mounts easily and then practically scoops me up with one arm and seats me in front of him.

"Comfortable?" he murmurs in my ear.

I gulp. "Yes, fine!" I squeak.

In one swift movement, Hunter pulls me tight against him, grabs Ranger's mane with his free hand, and urges the horse into action. Ranger doesn't need much prodding. We're off like a shot, thundering across open ground. Hunter's muscular thighs grip my own. They hold me in place with their steady strength and pressure. And even though we're fully clothed, it's primal, carnal almost, to feel my backside rubbing up against him. I dig my hands into Ranger's mane next to his and try not to think too hard about it.

I force myself to concentrate on what a skilled horseman he is. Hunter doesn't jostle. Instead, he matches my rhythm. It's like we were born for this, to canter together at headlong speed.

Soon, we're following the cliff's edge. Wind gusts off the churning ocean.

My eyes drift farther, down to the beach far, far below.

I start in surprise, jerking upright against Hunter's broad chest.

It's Gage's beach. There's the ring of cabins. A dark-haired guy steps out a door. One of Gage's tenant buddies. He's carrying a big black box that's trailing something. Wires, maybe.

My eyes spot Gage's truck, parked next to the bigger building in the center. The lodge. It has a new deck that juts over the shore. Standing on the broad wood planking, staring up at us as we gallop, is a man whose dirty-blond hair shines like a speck in the gray light.

Gage.

Arms planted stiffly at his sides, his gloom seems to radiate all the way up here. I can picture his clear blue eyes, his frank candidness that earned my childhood trust and glued our friendship together. I tug at the collar of my hoodie, which feels somehow too tight. Yet he can't tell who I am, can he? The only reason I know it's him is because that's his place.

As for me, I don't belong on this cliff. I'm little more than a shape against the sky. He'd have to be holding binoculars to identify me.

So why does he keep staring up here?

There's something odd about his stillness. He's frozen, intent. Despite the distance, I get the sense he can read my face, can read my stunned expression as though he were two feet away.

Of course, that's impossible.

Inexplicable guilt floods me. I'm not betraying him or Dad by riding with Hunter. Their reservations are not mine. I'm a free person. It's no one's business what I do or who I spend time with.

Hunter guides Ranger away from the edge, and Gage is lost from view. I'm torn from my reverie as we enter a shaggy copse of trees. Their emerald branches shelter a small clearing. There's a giant boulder on one side, all covered with moss and lichen. Sparrows twitter among the wildflowers growing at its base.

Hunter pulls Ranger to a halt at the edge of the grove.

"This is the spot." Hunter jumps down and lifts me to the ground.

"It's beautiful."

"I come here when I want to get away."

What would he want to get away from? His work? Or does he simply like being on his own? I cross to the boulder and touch its mossy surface. Dewdrops cling to tiny white blooms scattered among the green. I like this secret place. It feels sheltered. Magical, almost.

He joins me. "I figure Poppy would like it here."

"I think you're right."

"She was a good horse. A good listener, if that's not too strange to say."

"Not at all. Horses make some of the best friends."

We ride back a different way, trotting slowly across the grassy fields.

Mist sparkles in Ranger's mane, sliding down our twined fingers. Lush green growth rises from the ground to tickle my ankles. We plow through it, releasing rich earthy smells into the damp, heavy air. They blend with the scent of Hunter—warm and alluring.

I could get used to this life. To being out here with just him and the horses.

Still, the tension between him and Dad lingers like a ghost. I don't know what's got Dad so worried. Hunter's great. Why can't Dad see that?

From here I can make out the estate's house. The old place is still beautiful, yet looks almost Gothic under the stormy sky. Again I wonder why Hunter chose such a place for his work. What contagious diseases are they studying, exactly? What kind of cure are they developing?

For some bizarre reason, the warning from Mom's journal pops into my mind. About toying with the human genetic code and her baffling statement that humans were not meant to be divine. What does that mean, *divine*? Godlike? Superhuman? What?

If there's anyone I can talk to, it's Hunter. He's got to be familiar with gene therapy.

"What is it you do?" I blurt.

"What's that?" he asks, sounding is if I've pulled him from some contemplation.

"What are you researching at your lab?"

There's a pause. "It's . . . tedious. I'm afraid you'd find it less than interesting."

"You know, my mother was a scientist," I offer. "A geneticist."

His muscular left arm, still fastened tight around my waist, tenses.

I try not to focus on the breathless ripple it sends through me. "She died when I was little, so I don't know a whole lot about her work, but I found an old journal of hers."

"You have your mom's journal?"

I carry on. "Yes. This may sound crazy, but . . . if a doctor was working on some kind of genetic medicine and came across a discovery that could give humans certain . . ."

"Certain what?"

"Uh . . . okay, this is going to sound odd. But I guess what I mean is, divine qualities."

He stiffens, and I know I must sound completely crazy, yet I'm in too deep to stop. "Divine?"

"Yeah. I don't know, like, superhuman, maybe?"

"That's an odd question. What made you think of it? Did she write about it?"

"Yes. So would you think it's wrong, or wouldn't you?"

"I would." His tone is oddly flat. "Medicine is one thing. But I don't believe anyone has any business playing God."

"What if someone was really in trouble and this could keep them alive. What if something like that could have saved Poppy?"

"I still wouldn't do it."

"But you're a doctor, aren't you? Don't you want to save lives?"

"I'm a researcher."

"If you were researching genetics, and it was a friend or family member dying? You'd help them if you could, wouldn't you?"

His fingers, knotted in Ranger's mane, have turned almost white at the knuckles. The silence stretches out between us. Have I offended him?

Finally, he says, "You're assuming there'd be no side effects. Would you want to be saved if there was a downside? Because I can guarantee there would be. Probably a horrible one."

I ponder this and stare at the wet earth, yet that's not what I see. In my mind's eye, I'm standing on the precipice of loss. I stare into its cruel depths, thinking of Mom's death, knowing the mother I lost will never return.

Quietly, I say, "I would want them to live. I would choose life."

His chest is pressed so close to my back I'm almost certain I can feel his heart beating against my ribs.

"We'll walk from here," he tells me, dismounting.

I slide from Ranger, suddenly cold.

TWELVE

It's a jolt when I spot a tall, slender figure waiting for us by the barn.

Victoria.

How could I have forgotten her so completely?

Her sleeveless chiffon dress half billows, half clutches at her legs. She's devoid of makeup apart from her lips, which are like two bright crimson petals. Her serious, deep-brown eyes move over me, never leaving, taking in every inch.

I have a desperate urge to smooth down my wind-messed hair. But what's the point? I slept on a hay bale. I'd still look half feral next to her otherworldly glamour.

I glance at Hunter, whose face is a mask of calm.

Wait, they're not an item, are they? No. Oh no. Inwardly, I groan.

What bubble have I been living in? The gray daylight feels too bright.

Victoria's fingers circle her narrow elbows, and I get this ridiculous urge to hide behind Hunter. Instead, I put even more distance between us.

"So this is our visitor," Victoria says. I catch an accent. British, perhaps?

"Aeris, meet Victoria. Victoria, this is Aeris."

"Did you enjoy your evening?" she asks him, ignoring me.

"If you call staying up all night nursing an orphaned filly enjoyable, then yes. Why are you wearing that odd expression?"

"Odd? I thought it was one of my better ones."

He rolls his eyes, yet there's no malice in it. We've reached the fence that abuts the barn. He pauses there with a hand in Ranger's mane. I wrap one arm around a splintered post and lean against it.

"Aren't you wondering how she got in yesterday?" she asks.

"Through the gate, as far as I can tell."

"I should probably go," I say.

Hunter holds up a hand. "Wait a minute. Actually, I am, Victoria. You installed the device. I thought it required more than a key card. A biometric scan. Retinal, or something."

"*Mmm-hmm*, yes." She glances at me. The arched amusement in her doe eyes is worthy of *Vogue*. "Or something."

I flash on the handcuff that held me in place. Of the grate with the empty hole underneath. Of the sting of a needle and smell of disinfectant.

"I'll show it to you sometime," she promises. "It's quite fun."

Hunter lets out a sharp laugh. "If you think it's fun, it must be awful."

Her mouth curves up, and her eyes twinkle in wicked amusement. "Maybe you should ask Aeris?"

A flash of anger strikes. I don't like being spoken about in this way.

"We don't need fun," Hunter says. "We need effective. What if she'd been someone dangerous?"

"How do you know she's not?"

"Seriously?" I say, tired at being stuck between them and angry for falling under the illusion that Hunter liked me. I scowl at him. To my chagrin, he steps closer to my side, bringing Ranger. If I didn't know better, I could almost believe he's being protective.

Scoundrel.

Why does he have to look so damned handsome?

Victoria shoots me a cold glance. For an instant, I feel off balance. Threatened, even. Maybe this isn't about the two of them. Maybe it's about something else, something sinister. What are they shielding in here?

"Anyway," Victoria says. "I let her in. She's Jack Thorne's daughter."

"Vic, I hardly think a woman making a scheduled delivery can be called dangerous."

Her control slips and her eyes spark to life. "I can't believe you're doing this," she hisses. "After everything I just went through!"

"Victoria."

She stops, continuing to glare.

This day is really starting to take its toll, because my imagination is going into overdrive. They're staring at each other, and it's more than a staring contest. It's as if data is flowing back and forth between them. They're communicating somehow. I latch onto an excuse. Maybe it's because they clearly know each other really well?

People don't communicate by glaring at each other.

Intermittent raindrops flick my skin. Watching Hunter and Victoria battle it out, I feel beyond nervous.

Victoria lifts her chin. "I think we should have a closer look at her, don't you?"

He doesn't reply.

In one hand, she's holding a flashlight I hadn't noticed before. She moves with astounding speed. She's in front of me in an instant. I back against the fence, yet there's nowhere to go. Her hand comes up and she aims the beam at my eyes. First the left, then the right.

I wince under the brilliance.

Victoria's lips part in surprise. The look is so brief I nearly miss it. She snaps off the beam, glances at the sky, and says, "It's raining. I don't like rain."

My pulse races as I draw in a breath. That's it? No explanation?

"I'll see you back at the house," she tells Hunter.

He reaches out to commandeer the light and pockets it in his black fatigues. "Satisfied?"

Her shoulders stiffen. She says nothing and strides off.

"What was that about?" I ask.

"Vic's eccentric," he mutters by way of an excuse. "It's been a long night. I'm sure you need to go."

"Yes. But I should stay until Dad—"

"No. Let's get you back to your truck."

"Okay, actually, yeah." After what just went down, I do want to get out of here. If nothing else, Hunter's proved he can handle Blaze, and Dad will be back soon enough. I trudge ahead. "If you don't mind, I want to say good-bye to Blaze."

"All right."

We part at the door. Hunter leads Ranger to his stall.

I find Blaze up and waiting. She trots unsteadily to me.

"Hi, cutie," I say, going down on one knee and wrapping my arms around her neck. I breathe in her horsey scent, smooth down her tufts of baby foal hair. "Grow up big and strong," I whisper. "I won't be here, but you're family. You're doing great. Your mom would be proud. Grandpa, too. I'll be thinking of you, okay?"

Reluctantly, I release her and go to leave. She tries to shove her way out of the stall with me.

I kiss her nose. "Bye, baby," I whisper. "Sorry, but you have to stay here."

My stomach aches as I lock her inside. I hear her nickering all the way down the hall and out the front.

In the lot, the cube truck waits. Hunter strides out after me.

"I need to unload your order," I say.

He crunches across the gravel and opens the cab door. "Climb in. I'll take care of it."

"It's my job."

"It would be better if you got in." Maybe it's the dark sky that's turned his amber eyes almost ink black.

"Fine. It's your stuff." At this point, apart from Blaze, I wish I'd never come.

He hands me up into the leather seat and turns away. I close my fingers around the ghost of his warmth. What had I been thinking? Lulling myself with the idea we could be together? It had seemed that way. Like we'd been wrapped in a dreamy cocoon for two. Talking about our lives. Fantasizing about a trip we'd never take.

The cocoon is gone, and it's time to fly far, far away.

The truck rocks as Hunter proceeds to offload the supplies. Then he's back at my open door. Raindrops glitter in his hair.

"I'm sorry about you and Victoria," I say.

He shakes his head. "Don't worry about that. She's just concerned about the project."

His tone is not what I expected. Maybe I'd read him wrong.

"Are you guys—"

"What?"

"You and Victoria . . . are you—a couple?"

"Me and Vic?" He laughs and some of his lightness returns. "God no. I mean I love her to death, but not in a million years. Besides, I don't think my buddy Ian would take too kindly to that. Which is odd, since they spend half their time at each other's throats."

"Oh."

His eyes drop to my oxfords, which are all muddy against the high cab floor. Absently, he nicks away the grass and dirt with one knuckle. My heart starts thumping all over again.

"Look," he says, "I'm really glad you came. But you can't be here. She's right. Having you on the PRL grounds . . . it could be . . . dangerous."

Dangerous? There was that word again. "You let my father in."

"That's different."

"How? Other people come here, don't they?"

"Trust me. We can't do this." His voice is almost gruff.

What's that supposed to mean?

"So we'll never see each other again?"

He wipes his knuckles on his pants. "I really enjoyed meeting you, Aeris."

My eyes roam across his face as he tilts his head up to look at me.

There's a pull in the air so tense it's like gravity between us. My throat pounds with the thrumming of my heart. I wonder what it would feel like if he climbed into the cab and pressed his lips to mine. I don't dare move for fear of falling into him. Or maybe he's falling into me. Because his hand comes up to the doorframe as if to hold himself away.

"Don't invite me in." His voice is low. "You won't like it."

Heat rushes all over me. He's wrong. I think I would.

Hunter closes my door and raps the cab in good-bye. I watch him turn to leave and then I'm rolling down my window.

"I'm not the one who's afraid," I call. "You are."

He pauses, shoulders tensing, and I wince.

Did I seriously just say that?

Slowly he turns. "You think I'm afraid?" His straight dark brows pin me in place.

I want to sink into the seat and disappear.

His chin goes up. He paces closer. Puts one hand on the sill. "There's a chamber music performance Friday in New York."

His words hit me with such force that my breath catches.

He's not smiling. It's clear he's fighting some internal battle. I realize that a line's being crossed. If we go any further, there will be no stepping back. For either of us. When did it leave me—the belief I could approach this man with safe, slow steps and bolt away when we came too close for comfort? Because if we do this, it's all or nothing.

The air is charged, electrified.

I swallow. "And?" I say.

"And I can imagine twelve reasons why I'm going to hell for this, but would you like to go?"

"Yes."

"I hope you're not afraid of small planes."

"I'm not." Even if I were mortally terrified of them, I wouldn't admit it.

He finds my fingers and I'm breathless as his thumb brushes over the back of my hand. "All right."

"All right," I say back.

His eyes soften and his mouth turns up a little, and those addictive smile lines appear in his tanned, masculine cheeks. "Drive safely, Aeris Thorne."

"I will, Hunter Cayman. Take care of Blaze."

"Yep. I bet she misses you already."

He steps back to let me leave. The key shakes in my icy fingers. I'm on fire with nerves and excitement. I insert it into the ignition and turn. The engine rattles to life. He stands, arms crossed over his broad chest, as I pull onto the paved lane. He's still there, his tanned skin gleaming with rivulets, until a curve in the drive and a grove of trees obscures the view.

What have I done? I want to whoop. But what about my promise to myself to not get involved again?

And what am I going to tell Dad?

Up ahead, the towering fence appears and security cameras swivel toward me. The rain increases in tempo. It begins to drum a fervid beat against the roof of the cab. I spot the looming gates that span the exit. They open wide as I approach.

I guide the truck through and its wheels shudder over the metal strip.

When I'm out, the gates clang swiftly shut.

The rain seems more brutal here on the deserted road. Cold slips through my shirt. I fumble with the heater. Muggy air blasts from the vents, fogging up the windshield.

I swore I wouldn't open my heart again. I swore nothing would disrupt my focus on music. And what do I do? Fall for the only guy who's on my friends' and family's blacklist.

Then I remember his arms around me as we rode bareback across the fields. I lose myself in a daydream that's filled with the sound of his voice in my ear. It's just for the summer. A few good weeks. Before I go back to New York.

A squirrel dashes across the road. I'm torn from my reverie and crane toward the side-view mirror. It's there, scampering away.

I catch sight of my hazel eyes in the mirror. What had Victoria been searching for when she'd pinned me with her flashlight? Her actions had been beyond strange. And why had she left so abruptly? Was it something she saw?

My breath catches.

Or something she didn't see?

Something I witnessed in Hunter's eyes outside the dance club? I recall him lowering his dark glasses when that car came zooming around the corner. The high beams caught his pupils, and for a second they'd appeared to reflect like the pupils of a cat.

Is that how she'd expected mine to behave?

Except they didn't?

No. That's too crazy. The incident outside the dance club had been a trick of the light. Hunter didn't have cat eyes. Not today. Then again, what if I'd shone a beam into them, the way Victoria had into mine?

I wipe the mist from the window and keep driving.

Something strange is taking place at the PRL. But *what*? Is it related to their work? Clearly they haven't accidentally infected themselves with whatever contagious diseases they're studying. If anything they seem super healthy. Glowing with life. Hunter is as strong as any athlete.

So what is it?

The truck careens through a puddle. I grab the wheel, willing it under control. The motion causes a flicker of pain at the tip of my index finger. I'm reminded of the security booth with its handcuff, its "biometric scan," and the metal-grating floor that drops away to nothing.

Does Dad endure that process every time he goes there? I can't believe he'd accept such treatment.

A better question might be—*how am I going to explain to Dad why I made a delivery to the Phoenix Research Lab?*

He must have gotten Hunter's messages about Blaze by now. Maybe he'll be so preoccupied he won't care. I should call him. Easing off the gas, I fumble in the glove box for my phone.

My cell's dead. A quick search tells me there's no charger in the truck. There's probably no signal out here anyway. The clammy interior makes my clothes stick to my arms and chest. Outside, the storm is a gray velvet blur.

I'd been on such a high around Hunter. Now I'm drained. Worried about facing Dad.

The seat jostles my damp thighs. I switch on the radio. Static. Rounding a bend in the twisty road sends music blasting through. It's recognizable yet too fuzzy to bear. I turn it down and keep it on anyway. This coastline feels lonely. Maybe it's the weather, but it's almost scary.

Ahead, out of the gloom, a narrow driveway approaches fast. The entrance is marked with a wooden mailbox nailed to a mossy stump. Gage's place. It's not much relief, even if it is familiar. What if he sees me? What if he really did recognize me on the cliff? What if he's pulling out of the drive and waves for me to stop? What will I say about where I've been?

After that incident in Foggy Joe's, his feelings toward Hunter are pretty obvious.

I hate the thought of having to pick sides. Gage and Ella versus Hunter. No one should have to do that.

Slowing, I glance down his gravel lane. It's all shadowed with heavy wet branches. Deserted. Relief.

I step on the gas.

Five minutes later, the engine knocks and stutters. I check the gas gauge. Empty. *Not now.* Maybe that's why Mr. Creedy was trying to flag me down.

"Come on, you can make it," I urge. There are still several miles to go.

The truck keeps moving, sputtering along, the wipers whacking back and forth. A large, unmarked transport truck jams past. The force sends my own truck rocking. Weird to see one of those out here. Are they allowed on these small roads? What could it be delivering? Top secret supplies to the Phoenix Research Lab?

Thinking of deliveries sends a groan from my lips.

Dad's delivery!

How could I have forgotten? Yesterday I'd promised that guy I'd be there. He said they had to make a special trip. I should have at least called. I completely blew them off. I feel horrible.

The truck chooses this instant to die.

Frantic, I pump the gas pedal. Nothing. Before I'm stranded in the middle of the road, I crank the wheel and ease onto the shoulder opposite the cliff. The truck rolls to a silent stop.

Rain drums on the roof. Although the door is locked, I feel oddly vulnerable. Alone without phone service. I peer through the spattered windshield. Maybe if I wait a while, it will stop.

Except it doesn't.

Time passes achingly slow. No one drives by. Not a soul since the transport truck. I'm freezing. It has to be at least 2:00 p.m. My oxfords are cold and sweaty at the same time. I'll walk. At least I have my hoodie.

I could go back to Gage's. But I don't feel like being grilled as to why I'm out here. There's no way he actually recognized me up on the cliff riding with Hunter. It only seemed like it. And I don't feel like lying. It's easier to walk the extra distance back to Dad's, even if it is raining.

I zip up my hoodie and catch sight of Hunter's jacket. I forgot to return it. I inhale the scent of him before setting it back down.

Climbing out, I lock the door. Turning my feet south, I head off on the cold trudge home.

Wet, rotting leaves mix with the scent of damp earth. The road winds along, descending into a tight curve. High branches temporarily shelter me. On one side, crystal droplets cling to a mossy wall. It's like a picture from a fairy tale. Only the fattest raindrops hit me, exploding on my nose, the top of my head, my hands.

I leave the sheltering trees and follow the ocean bluff. The road veers inland and I'm soon surrounded by exposed, scrubby meadows. Half frozen, I walk faster. I reach a thicket of overhanging trees. I'm drenched and my toes are numb. I pause only momentarily before pressing on.

I reach a familiar abandoned field and know I'm close to Dad's. I decide to cut across the overgrowth. Jaw clenched against the chill, I stumble along. The image of the spa tub at Dad's swells in my mind until I can almost feel my toes dipping into the swirling, steamy hot water.

Long grass whips against my thighs, trails against my fingers. The rain falls in gentle gusts. Ahead, gnarled apple trees crouch in the tall weeds. They're the same trees I can see from the guest room window.

Maybe in the fall I'll come back and pick apples with Dad. I could try my hand at baking apple crisp, with warm cinnamon and brown sugar, served hot, still steaming—

I nearly slam into the back bumper of a shiny black SUV. It's parked in the grass behind the trees. Is it a wreck?

No—definitely not. Too shiny.

I creep toward the driver's side. That's when I see a man in the front seat.

With binoculars. Staring at Dad's house.

THIRTEEN

WHY WOULD SOMEONE STATION THEMSELVES in the field across from Dad's house? Facing his front door? It's like he's hiding. But why? I'd stand and confront him if not for the warning bells in my mind that are clanging out a discordant beware.

Is Dad home?

Gingerly, I crane through the bushes at Dad's driveway. His Range Rover's back. And I see movement through the front window. At least four people inside.

The driver door opens, and the driver steps out.

I crouch and melt as best I can into the thick growth. The branches protest and I'm only partially covered. He's got his back to me. For now.

Salt-and-pepper hair, clean, military cut. Dressed in blacks: black vest festooned with loops and mesh and pockets—bulletproof, maybe. Black pants. Black watch. Black leather boots. And a metallic, high-tech prosthetic hand.

Don't turn. Don't see me!

A phone is pressed to his ear.

"Tell Jack Thorne he has my word. He cooperates, no one gets hurt."

No one gets hurt? My cramped legs start to shake. There's something oddly familiar about his gravelly voice. Recognition dawns. He's the one who called about the package. To make sure I'd be home. He wanted me there, in the house. Yesterday, when Dad was gone.

There was no delivery. It was a trick.

"Then make him cooperate."

Oh god. My fist goes to my mouth. This can't be real. What are they going to do to him? Horror mingles with the raindrops trickling down my icy skin. Clenching my teeth to keep from chattering, I back into the cage of leaves.

"What loyalty can Thorne possibly have to Cayman?" the man says.

As in Hunter Cayman?

Whatever's being said on the other end earns a flurry of curses. The man squeezes the doorframe with his metal hand. Like a horror movie, the frame creaks and warps under the pressure. He's monster strong.

"Tell Perkins and Guzman to kick him harder," he growls. "I don't care what you have to do. Just find out where he hid the damn thing."

They're hurting him. Bile rises in my throat, and outrage surges in my veins. How dare they? I picture them pummeling Dad in his safe, sane living room, and I want to vomit. A branch jabs deep into my lower back. I let it, too scared to move. I have to do something. But what?

"He's bullshitting. He has the PRL key."

At this, goose bumps break out across my skin.

No, he doesn't. I do.

I need to stop this. If it's the key card he's after, I'll give it to him. Anything to get them away from Dad. Through the open car door, the dash is just visible. On it, a gun lies in wait.

The man gives a short, egotistical laugh. "Enough, don't kill him, yet." It's congenial. Like he's out for a couple of beers with his crew. "Plenty of time to satisfy your bloodlust later, Anders."

Are they going to kill him either way? Despite the frigid air, heat washes over me in a slick of terror. *Dad. Oh god, please don't hurt Dad.* My mind flares with images of him beaten to death. I struggle to block them out.

This can't be real. This can't be happening. I can't let them hurt him. I can't let them tear him from me. I won't.

I realize I'm trembling, hard, because the branches pressed into me on all sides have started to shake. If the man turns, he'll see the twigs twitching. He'll come and investigate.

Who are they? Why do they want the key? *Why do they need to get into the PRL?* I don't know what's going on at Hunter's lab, but this is crazy.

I have to get help. Fast. But how? We're over three miles from town.

Maybe if I run—

"You know what?" the man says, wiping the drizzle from his blond buzz cut. "Forget it. Change of plan." He's got his left arm draped casually through the open window, his right foot up on the SUV's running board. "I'm getting pissed. Let me talk to him."

Pause.

"Jack Thorne?"

A moment passes as he listens to Dad's reply. From the way his prosthetic hand tightens around the phone, I don't think he likes the response.

"Yeah, well, I've got your daughter," Iron-fist lies. If only he knew it's not far from the truth. "So you have a choice. Either I shoot her dead, or you drive us out to the research lab in your Range Rover and unlock that bio-scanner for me. Make up your mind. You've got ten minutes."

If only I could tell Dad he's lying.

"You'll see her when I say so." The man looks at his watch. "Now you have nine and a half."

I'm moving before I know what I'm doing. Edging away slowly and painfully on all fours. Thorns jab my palms. Giant wet leaves cover the ground like discarded plastic bags.

I have to get to the shop—to a phone. I only hope they don't see me.

Beyond the gnarled apple trees, I stand and run, skirting wide until I come up on the road. Two lanes of rutted, wet blacktop. Twenty feet of total exposure. Hopefully, I've put enough space between the orchard and me that I won't be spotted. Holding my breath, I sprint into the open.

Bulrushes populate the ditch on the far side. I crash into them, my legs plunging unexpectedly deep so that I topple completely. I land at an angle, cupped by slippery-wet broken stalks. Velvet bulrush heads wave wildly. My whole body clenches against discovery, against the fear of shouts, of pounding footsteps.

No one comes.

I stand. My right ankle sends up a searing blast of pain.

All I need to do is get to the feed store. Customers must be there. It's the middle of the day.

The clock is ticking. I have to move.

I clench my fists against the raging throb of my ankle and lope toward the store. I'm coming at an angle, from the side. What stands out is the empty lot. That's odd. Then I see the CLOSED sign on the door. Weird. With no witnesses to guard me, I can't risk the front entrance. It's too likely they'll see me. I'll try the back way.

It takes an extra few minutes to change direction and work my way through the brambles. When I reach the rear wall, I pause at a darkened window. It's grimy with rotted leaves and pebbles on the sill. I press my nose to the surface. The greasy glass makes it hard to see through.

Half the lights are switched off inside.

I make out the rack of seed packets. A little farther, a lump resolves itself into an overturned chair. I gape, frozen at the mass of ropes and the frail, bony body strapped to it. Mr. Creedy gapes back at me. He doesn't see me, though. He'll never see me again. There's a small red hole in the middle of his forehead.

Dead.

Poor, old Mr. Creedy is dead.

Terror makes my head spin. It's like I'm lifting off the ground, zooming upward in a bubble of fear, amped as though I've drunk fifty cups of coffee. My breath comes out in pants. I avert my head, trying to shut away the image. I turn back and he's still there. Still staring. It's not a bad dream. This is real.

Fingers shaking, I wipe rain from my face.

Blackness creeps over me. *No, god.* I can't let it. I can't pass out.

Oh, Mr. Creedy, how could I have been so terrible to you yesterday morning? Driving away, without listening, without explaining, like you didn't matter? You do matter. I'm sorry. I wish you could hear me say I'm so sorry.

Anger floods me. Who are these monsters? I straighten and am preparing to head for the door when instinct makes me glance one last time through the window.

A shadow falls across Mr. Creedy's prone form. Then a man steps over him and crosses to the register. I duck out of view, heart slamming. What am I going to do if I can't get in there to use the phone? The nearest house is too far, especially with my twisted ankle swelling by the minute. And I don't even know where the nearest police station is. I've never even seen a police car around here. Maybe there isn't one in the county. Maybe a county this small shares one with another county.

I'm wasting time on nothing!

I can't just confront the men in Dad's house. They'll kill us both. Iron-fist made that clear enough. Once we're of no use to him, we're dead.

The shed in the backyard—that's where I need to go. I need to get at Dad's four-wheel ATV and drive for help.

It's our only hope.

Open grass stretches between the store and the house. I get down on my belly and start crawling for the shed. Mud squishes between my fingers. My sweatshirt inches up and sodden grass rubs against my belly. My ankle throbs as I drag it along. I'm completely behind the house now. All windows are in view. I crawl past the barbecue and smoker. They're glossy with rain. I catch sight of fur, unmoving, between them. Then blood. Black, almost, in the grim light.

"Sammy," I sob, unable to hold the name back in my throat.

The fur moves. My heart starts beating faster. Please, let him be all right!

Ears perk up slowly, and then his head. He sees me. Or smells me. His tail flops once, twice, and he lets out a whimper. I put my hand to my mouth. The desperate need to run to him and try to fix him tears holes in my chest. Blurs my ability to think straight. I have to think straight, though. There's no helping him, not like this. If I try now, we're all gone.

He whimpers again, and I motion for him to stay quiet.

"Stay, Sammy, stay," I whisper, knowing he can't understand.

All he understands is that I'm not going to him. That I'm leaving him there to die.

Time is running out. Hating myself, I keep moving.

The shed is now ten feet away. I reach the door. Locked.

Panic rises. I roll into the shadows and fumble in my front pocket for Dad's extra set of keys, the ones I used this morning to get into the shop. The ring holds four brass-colored Yales, the truck and Range Rover keys, and one with a black plastic fob. The Yale marked with yellow tape is for the store. I try another. Too big. The second one slides home. Using both hands, I shove on the accordion door. It opens sideways, making plastic grinding, grunting noises as I pull it wide.

Musty air spills out. A dusty-winged brown moth lies dead on the floor, its lustrous eyes still shining. Shovels and rakes all clotted with earth stand erect along the far wall. If I were a hero in a film, I'd use one as a weapon and free us all. But I'm not a hero. I'm just a person.

In the middle, hunched under a camouflage tarp, lies the daunting form of Dad's mean, four-wheel ATV.

Hyperaware of any sound from outside, I slide the tarp off and scrunch it into one corner. The wicked machine with its four huge tires is something a futuristic droid should drive. Sanded steel bars everywhere, a leather seat high up in the middle. CAN-AM OUTLANDER MAX XT in block letters stenciled down its tail.

Dad told me once he took the limiter off and it goes eighty or ninety miles per hour. I have no clue what a limiter is, but I told him he was crazy to even think of driving it half that fast.

Who's the crazy one now?

From outside comes the medium-pitched hum of an engine. Past the house, a section of road is visible. I catch sight of Iron-fist's SUV driving along it. The engine grows louder. I know it's in the driveway. I hear it slow to an idle.

Time is up.

He's come for Dad.

A helmet dangles from a hook. I grab it and wrench it on. My fingers are trembling so hard I can hardly fasten the strap. It's too big, slipping forward over my eyes. I shove it back and climb onto the ATV, straddling the leather seat. The key with the plastic fob fits the ignition. A thrill of panic shoots through me at the sound of the engine. I aim the front wheels toward the lawn and twist the right accelerator handle. The ATV leaps forward, almost throwing me off. Instantly I let off the gas.

I jolt to a halt. Right there, outside. Right in the middle of the back lawn.

I know I'm in naked view to anyone who glances out the window. The ATV is loud. Seriously loud.

My heart slams and I've barely gone five feet. I shoot a glance at the kitchen door. It's opening. I have to get around the house. Past the SUV in the drive. *Oh god, I can't do it. I can't do this!*

Don't think, Aeris! Just drive!

My legs are shaking as hard as the thrumming monster under me. I give the accelerator a twist. One of Iron-fist's men comes out the back door. Military. Navy SEAL or special ops. Except there's no visible insignia. No marks of office at all. What he does have is a gun.

He plants his feet wide, points his arms straight, and aims.

"STOP YOUR VEHICLE!"

I force my terror down and rocket forward.

The gun explodes. I'm around the side of the house. I'm numb. Am I hit? No, I'd know. I'm sure I'd know, and I'm still driving, still moving. Sliding around to the front. Onto the driveway. *Oh god, there he is.* The man from the SUV. The man in charge. Iron-fist himself. He's snaking around his vehicle's front grill to face me; his powerful prosthetic hand is drawing a weapon.

It's the tourist man from Dad's store. The one with the buckskin gloves and too-crisp flannel shirt. The one who claimed his wife was dying. The one with the creepy, pale-gray android eyes.

"Hello again," he shouts. Then he laughs.

A jolt of recognition from somewhere deep inside floods my consciousness. A childish, primal fear grips me. I've heard that awful snicker before. In my nightmares. In a place that smells of blood and burning steel. I thought it lived only in my imagination. But his laugh is real. A sound that has lingered like a fingerprint in my mind.

His shaved jaw juts out a little, jaunty almost. There's a glint in his eye, a hint of delight at my unexpected attack. It's obvious he sees me as a challenge easily taken down and toyed with. He thinks I'll falter, ease off the gas to avoid hitting him.

Not today, mister.

Not ever.

I wrap my fingers tighter around the knobby, soft rubber grips. My whole body clenches with a need to attack him. Worse. To destroy him.

I twist the accelerator all the way.

The ATV bucks. It lurches up on two wheels, nearly tipping me into the dirt. Then the front end slams down, and it takes off like a bat. Flying. He shouts and dives clear.

I skid out of the driveway and onto the slick road. The front door to the house opens. Three guys built like tanks spill onto the walk.

Some insane, reckless part of me, one I had no idea existed, slows the beast enough to dig out the Phoenix Research Lab key card. I wave it high.

"Come and get it!" I shout.

Then I bust across the road.

Iron-fist barks, "GET IN THE CAR, GET IN THE CAR, GET IN THE CAR!"

Like some military sergeant on training day.

They want to go to the PRL? I'll take them there. Just let them try to get through. I'd like to see it. But no one said I had to make the trip easy on them.

I turn into the abandoned field, praying to God they've left Dad alone. I fly past the orchard, sending rotten apples falling. I fishtail through a puddle and mud sloshes up my legs. I keep moving, keep going, willing Dad and Sammy to be okay. Oh please, let them be okay.

I weld my gaze to the bumpy ground, my fingers to the handlebars. Towering stalks rear up out of the gloomy rain. A boulder. I swerve. I'm moving way too fast to be safe. Stupid tears blur my vision and I scream.

Why is this happening? I'm supposed to be here on vacation, visiting Dad, trying out his smoked fish, playing music, and composing.

This has to be a joke. This isn't me. My life is predictable and safe.

Stop it, I tell myself.

I'm nearly across the field. Less than fifty feet of pine and scrub separate me from the winding road. Too late, I spot the tree root.

I clamp the brakes and nearly tumble over the handlebars. The Outlander slams into the root and goes airborne. Then, with a grinding crunch, it touches down and snakes sideways. Branches tear at me. Frantic, I try to touch my foot to the ground. Big mistake—my shoe is ripped away.

Brakes locked, engine whining, I skid between the towering pines that border the field.

I'm still sliding. Across the narrow road.

I hear the roar of a tractor-trailer. Then the driver blares his air horn in alarm. Halfway across the far lane, I skate to a stop, the ATV stalling. The eighteen-wheeler careens past, spraying me with grit while I stare wild-eyed, imagining the soft, sickening crunch of my skull.

My breath is ragged as I frantically restart the Outlander. I can't seem to get enough air. I'm shaking so hard I think I might pass out. Rain gusts around me. My sweatshirt is sticking high on my back. I feel exposed but don't bother to yank it down.

My grand plan to drive to the research lab and toss the keycard over the gates seems suddenly ludicrous. Stupid beyond all reason. I should have gone the other way. To a police station. Even though I've never seen one. Who do they call when there's trouble? It's a pointless question. I have to keep going.

Driving is easier on the road. The wet forest whips past.

At least two miles to go.

No one will be there. Hunter won't be waiting. No one's going to come out to defend me with guns blazing. They have no idea what's headed their way. There are cameras, though. Iron-fist and his men won't shoot me in plain sight, not in front of all those security devices. Would they?

The stalled store truck is exactly where I left it. I blow past. Spot Gage's mailbox, closing in fast.

Please be there! Please come driving out, Gage!

Deserted.

What could he do, even if he had miraculously appeared? I keep going. Fully committed now. Unbidden, thoughts of how the whole town is suspicious of Hunter bubble wild and fast into my mind. Winding left, the trees open up. What if there's a basis to their fears? What if there is something horrible going on up at the lab? What if the men chasing me are the good guys, and I've got it wrong?

No. If they were the good guys, they wouldn't hurt Dad. Or Mr. Creedy. Or Sammy.

Another sob threatens to choke me.

I slide through a turn, almost losing control. Hunter said it was dangerous for me to be at the PRL. Why did Dad warn me off Hunter like he was trying to protect me? Crushed pine needles send tingling air into my lungs. The odometer reads 55 MPH. Rain pricks my cheeks, and I'm terrified and alive all at once.

Beyond the ragged cliff edge, sheer walls drop to the churning ocean far below. Gusts fling up salt-tinged billows. Sensing something behind me, I glance back.

Big, high headlights. A wide, glossy front grill. Iron-fist and his men. They've caught up.

I crank the engine until the odometer reads 60 MPH. 65. Then 72. The curve comes up too fast. Wheels thumping, I careen off the road. Hover along the edge. Sliding. I wrench hard and somehow the wheels grip, yanking me back to safety. Pulling me along a short straightaway.

My pursuer's high beams light up the misting rain. Grow brighter. Closer. From a hundred feet back comes a loud pop. The next instant, my earlobe flares. I've been shot.

I duck and open the throttle all the way.

"Almost there, almost there," I gasp, seeing the final bend, and then the gates coming up. My eyes are so wide, the whites are burning.

"Hunter," I scream at the cameras, even though there's no way he can hear me. *"Hunter!"*

From behind, a bullet makes contact with my leg.

*Thwack-thwack*s ring out as more gunshots strike the Outlander. The stench of exploding rubber floods my nostrils. Shredded tire parts hail past. Still holding on to the handlebars, I'm toppling, spinning, careening through the air. The ATV is head-over-heels. I'm grappling with an eight-hundred-pound monster, kicking myself free, aware of it flipping around me and the sharp moving parts underneath, of the searing exhaust, and thinking of the skin on my face—*please don't let it touch my face*—and then I see the forged steel gates. *Oh god, not the gates. Not like that.*

Hands grind dirt. Body still airborne. From somewhere behind me, the engine screams.

I slam into the barrier first. Shoulder blades, ribs, ankles.

The brick-shaped ATV sails at me in slow motion.

Mom.

You protected me once, but nothing could stop this.

Not today.

Maybe it's been coming for me ever since.

Bringing me back to you.

The crack of my bones is deafening.

FOURTEEN

SOMEONE IS TOUCHING MY FACE.

Gently.

Large, rough fingers. They trace my cheekbone with such yearning tenderness that my soul aches to respond. The touch ends, launching me into blackness.

I feel nothing but the fragmentary trail of sparks left behind by that strong hand.

My body is featureless. A cloud, fuzzy and floating.

No arms, no legs, no fingers, no toes. Just that cheek. I drift away from the sparks, unable to hold on, desperate to hold on, slowly falling, grasping at the sensation, knowing that was my anchor and I've come loose.

I see it then, emerging in the fog. Snapping and winging out of reach. A man with arms that could lift a vehicle full of men and guns. A man who ripped the doors off a monstrous SUV. A man with flashing catlike eyes, reflected in a pair of headlights bent on destruction, who tore my pursuers in two. A man who gathered me into him and bore me away.

Terror. I'm terrified of his strength even as I claw to stay in the warmth of his grasp.

I tumble down from the vision, a feather in the current.

Submerged until I'm all gone.

THE PRESENCE IS THERE AGAIN. Pulling me back, calling me back, around me like a force field. Male and powerful, warm and steady.

It's no use, though.

I'm slipping.

There's not enough of me to hold on.

"Aeris!"

The voice explodes in colors. White and purple and red.

Human heat surges close by, swirling inward. A cheek touches mine. Rough skin. Stubble. That's what it is, stubble.

"Aeris." His voice is a hoarse whisper.

So sweet. Oh, so sweet to hear him call me. I ache with the pleasure of his voice. Liquid warmth rolling through me, swelling my heart.

"I'm not letting you go," he says. "Hear me? Not letting you go."

I want to reply. Where's my mouth? How do I reach my mouth?

"You were right about Poppy," he whispers.

He's gone then and I spin around his words, puzzling over their message. Poppy. There was a mare. Dakota? No, not Dakota. Soft brown eyes. Pleading for my help. Something happened to her, though. A joyous moment gone wrong. There was a shoulder, too. His shoulder, and I pressed my face into it.

A lurching sensation rolls through my being. A sob, maybe. I watch it like waves on a stormy ocean, rolling and smashing, wet and dangerous.

Voices, low and urgent.

Two men, one woman.

Instruments, clicking metal objects. Beeping machines. A heartbeat echoes, sounding strange. Arrhythmic and staccato. Not good music at all. Don't they know the tune? That beat will kill you.

"Jack wants in," comes the woman.

"Jack can stay in his seat and keep giving blood," the man who touched my cheek replies.

Hunter. That's his name. Hunter.

The beeping heartbeat slows; the pings grow random. Have they stopped?

Ping.

That's good. Pings are good.

A clock ticks against the wall. Click, click, click, click, click, click—

Ping.

"We're losing her. One milligram atropine. Now!"

"Blood pressure dropping."

Rushing sounds, people moving. Images, hazy at first, grow clearer. A big, bright room. So bright. A table in the middle, directly below me. I'm on the ceiling, staring at an operating theater. A body lies on the table, mangled arms and legs, bleeding everywhere. Shreds of checked fabric cover part of the body's torso. I have a shirt made out of that fabric. I put that shirt on in Dad's guest bedroom.

"Atropine, point five milligrams."

I stare at the man below me, working to revive the body. I recognize the broad shoulders, the big hands, the way he stands protectively over the inert remains of a woman. Like a knight on the battlefield. Like an armed warrior trying to fight off death.

"*Come back to me,*" he whispers.

I want to. Oh, how I want to.

"*Come back, little bird,*" he begs.

A memory flits by, bittersweet and wistful and too ancient to grasp. I watch his powerful hands cover my chest, trying desperately to hold my life in. His words come to me then, words he spoke into my hair as I sobbed against his chest when we lost the mare. *Death is the darkest of thieves.*

Beeeeeeep.

The ominous sound pierces the room. Pierces me high above, and I fear now I'm never going back.

Hunter sags against the table. "This can't be happening." He slams the beeping machine, and it goes silent.

"We're out of options," says the man with red hair peeking from his cap.

"You're wrong, Ian. It's my job to save her, and I damn well intend to."

Voices grow urgent. Garbled.

Dad's in the room, shouting, trying to get near me. He's alive, safe!

"Get out, Jack," Hunter rages. "Do you want her to live? Then get out and let me do what I have to do."

I'm fading.

It's not painful. Just a sensation of dying light. Like a fire fading to embers and finally, softly, darkly, going cold.

Hunter.

If you're coming for me, come soon. Oh god, please, come soon. . . .

FIFTEEN

A PLUNGING FORCE STABS THE CENTER of what's left of me. It explodes in a sunburst of tendrils, rays shooting outward in all directions. Millions of arms and hands, grabbing, seizing, clutching.

My consciousness slows its outward drift, stops, frozen.

Then it all comes rushing inward. Pieces of my mind smash against one another, slam into place. Whirring and clicking, smelling of blood and electricity and disinfectant. The engine in my chest roars into action. Hammers in earnest, in joy, in celebration. My mouth opens, and air charges over my tongue, runs deep into me, forces my chest to rise as it conquers the farthest reaches of my lungs. Warm liquid sensations swirl into my shoulders, surge down my arms into my fingertips that curl with delicious pleasure.

It's beautiful. Sensations and smells of this world. This wonderful world. Where Dad still exists, and Sammy, and music, exquisite music, and the dark-haired man I long to see.

My eyes fly wide.

He's there. Right there.

"Hunter!" I gasp.

He nods and there's a wobble to that normally strong mouth. It's as though he doesn't trust himself to speak.

From farther off, I hear a female voice say, "Shit."

Victoria.

The operating table and its bright lights and beeping machines are a modern island in the beautiful old room. Oak-paneled walls are straight out of a study you'd see in a royal palace. A painting stretches across the ceiling overhead. Pale blue sky with fluffy clouds and butterflies. Thousands of butterflies in fiery shades of orange and yellow. Painted branches bloom in profusion along the ceiling's borders. On the painted tree limbs are cocoons, some bursting open as winged creatures emerge, others being built by fuzzy caterpillars.

My head drops and my eyes drift from the dizzy ceiling to Hunter's face. His surgical mask is pulled down under his well-shaped jaw. Dried blood stains his neck. From when he carried me.

Hunter sinks down until our heads are level. "You scared the hell out of me. You know that?" He gives me a half smile.

"Dad," I croak. "You have to help Dad."

"He's here. He's perfectly safe."

Of course, he was in the operating room. I heard him. Relief gives way to fresh shock at a fragment of recall.

"Our dog—"

"Sammy's all right, too."

Hunter smooths away my hair, and my skin tingles faintly in response. My sluggish brain takes a moment to process it all. Sammy looked so hurt. And Dad—they were kicking him and beating him. I breathe out. Dad's all right. Sammy made it. *Thank you, God.*

The chase comes back to me, vivid images fast and rough.

Me approaching the gates. Screaming at the cameras. And then Hunter was there.

"I saw you . . ." I break off, staring at him, trying to make sense of it. How had he gotten there so fast? He lifted the ATV off me and threw it. *He threw it!* An eight-hundred-pound vehicle. At the windshield of the men who were chasing me. I saw it smash. No, it wasn't possible. A vivid dream. Was I even conscious?

"What do you think you saw him do?" Victoria demands.

Emotions surge over me. It's weird, though, because they're not my feelings. They're hers. I sense them almost as clearly as if they were my own. Wariness and anger flow from her, resounding on a different pitch than if they'd come from me. Hers is a faster, more refined vibration. She's suffering an overlying emotion that colors it all.

Fear.

Victoria is afraid. It's the kind of fear that makes my stomach churn. I don't know how I'm feeling it, just that I am. Is it because I hit my head? It's coming on so strong I need to make it stop.

Hunter's stormy amber gaze snaps from my face to hers. "Out."

Her mouth opens in surprise.

"Go," he says, pointing to a mahogany door set in the far wood paneling. It has a brass knob that looks to be from another century.

"Yes," she says. The door creaks as she opens it and marches out of the room.

Hunter may as well have flipped a switch. The crippling fear disappears, leaving me drained. How did he know I was upset by her emotional turmoil? Was it the look on my face? Can he read me that well?

From beneath my heavy lids, I notice the red-haired man leaning against a steel counter.

His face is grim. "So you're the lucky girl who's captured Hunter's interest."

The way he says it sends a chill over my prone form. I say nothing as he straightens and crosses under the blazing lights.

"Back in a few," he tells Hunter, who has moved to a flashing monitor.

Hunter grunts in reply.

The door opens again. This time, I catch a brief glimpse of a warmly lit room with overstuffed chairs and rich carpets before it clicks shut.

"You're going to be just fine," Hunter says with a calm strength that cushions me. He wets a cloth at the sink and rubs it softly over my face. "You doing all right? You've had a bad shock."

It was more than shock. But his attention distracts me. I close my eyes as he continues to stroke the hot fabric over the bridge of my nose and forehead. Clearing away the blood. Still, he can't completely wipe away the remnants of Victoria's fear that cling like a knot in my disembodied center.

Did he notice what I sensed from her? Did she? Or is he right? I'm in shock. I need to stop freaking myself out. I need to calm down. Splintered recollections barrage my mind. I can still hear Hunter begging me to come back to him. And then—

"You injected me with something," I whisper.

"I injected you with a lot of things."

My pulse throbs in my temples. "I thought I was going to die."

"You think I would have let you do that?" He puts down the cloth and touches my cheek with his thumb. I turn and press my face to his palm.

A bout of nausea takes hold. I wrench my face away. The ceiling wobbles and begins to spin, butterflies flying in a circle above me.

"What's going on?" Hunter says.

"I'm going to faint."

"Deep breaths, there you go. I got you." He checks my blood pressure as he talks.

I breathe in, gulping air until I can speak. "I would've been dead if you hadn't come."

"Yeah. Well." He looks away. "It's my own damn fault you had that key."

"You couldn't know that. So thank you."

"Don't thank me for trouble I got you into," he growls.

"Try and stop me," I whisper.

He grows unnaturally quiet and then says. "I'll never forgive myself."

I'm fading fast and trying to keep my eyes open. I know I'm badly hurt. Mangled, even. I should be afraid. His presence soothes me, though.

"Guess we won't make that concert," I say.

He lets out a low laugh. "Exactly my thoughts when I saw you leading that chase like some batgirl out of hell."

"Seriously?"

"No."

"I didn't know what else to do. The only way I could think to get rid of them was to throw the key through the gates so it would be gone."

His mouth opens, his brows draw upward, and then he shakes his head. To my surprise, he lets out a bark of laughter.

"What's funny?"

"You."

I'm struggling to speak. "What are you talking about?"

"You just take the bull by its horns. You don't even know how to stop. You jump on and go for it."

"What choice did I have?" I swallow and a dizzy wave hits me.

"That actually wasn't a bad plan. Most people would have hidden in the bushes until the bad guys left."

"How did you get there so quick?"

"I was nearby," he says vaguely.

I close my eyes. I can't fight the creeping blackness much longer. "I just wanted to save my dad and Sammy."

"You did, Aeris." His voice is soft. "You did good. I'm proud of you."

I glance down to see his strong hand against my arm, but something's wrong. It's like my arm is dead. An amputated limb.

I can't feel it!

Adrenaline spikes me out of my stupor. I attempt to wiggle my fingers. Nothing. Then the real fear strikes. "Am I paralyzed?" I cry.

"No. I think it's only temporary."

I stare at him as a phantom feeling of cold floods into limbs I can't actually sense.

"You think?" I say.

"Let's take it one step at a time."

My music. My work. My soul. My root. *Will I ever be able to play again?*

I clamp down on the question. I'm not ready for that future. I can't get enough air. Blackness narrows in, pressing at the edges of my vision. Blood drains from my head.

"Stay with me, Aeris," he says, concerned. "Come on."

The sheet rustles at my side, and he takes my disembodied hand.

Numb or not, I sense the connection immediately. A wall. No—almost a force field around him—seems to rip loose. His emotions stream into me like water from a scorching river. A jarring rush. Masculine and completely unlike my own. Urgency. Guilt. A savage protectiveness. For me. So fierce it makes my breath hopscotch.

I stare at him, mouth open, and let it rush in.

My own emotions surge back like the outgoing tide and seem to slam into him. It's intense and beautiful and astonishing, and I don't want it to stop. This wild, inexplicable exchange. My heart starts to pound. If I told him what I was experiencing, he'd think I was crazy.

The heart monitor pings faster, ringing in my ears. It doesn't matter that I'm numb. I'm shaken. I hear it. Thanks to the machine, Hunter can, too.

That's great. That's all I need. A broadcasting device.

He steps away, quickly. A wall comes down and I no longer feel him. If I felt him at all. Maybe the drugs they gave me are messing with my ability to think straight.

He adjusts an IV bag. "Don't worry. I'll have you back the way you were, I promise." His voice is ragged. "Good as new."

My eyes grow damp and I blink, hard. *Please, let it be true.*

He smiles to reassure me, yet it's strained. "There's going to be pain. I need to warn you. But you're up for the fight. I know it."

I nod.

"I'm going to get your dad."

I'm left with the orange-red sea of butterflies overhead.

I hear Dad's familiar stride. Panic flares in me out of nowhere. Inwardly, I flinch away with an awful, unreasonable terror. A wild, animalistic instinct winds up inside for a fight. I'm injured; I need to protect myself! But that's ridiculous. Dad wouldn't hurt me.

Blinding terror rises higher and higher and flies from my mouth in a groan.

"Aeris." His gruff voice barely covers his shock.

"That's close enough," comes Hunter's voice.

It's Dad, it's just Dad, it's just Dad. . . .

Reason fights with dread. I have to destroy him, get away, have to find safety, to find a dark hole to heal my wounds.

Dad calls, "Peanut, if you can hear me, I love you." His voice breaks. "You're safe. You're going to be fine. I promise, everything's going to be fine."

Pain flares to life in my right leg. White hot. I gasp as it moves to my left leg, and into my hips. What was numb before is now on fire. Dripping hot fire, like flesh melting over a bonfire of violent flames. I open my mouth to scream.

Nothing comes out.

I'm dropping away from consciousness. Howling pain is coming along for the ride. It's flaying me alive, and there's nothing I can do to stop it. No way to cry out for help.

I realize now what hell must be like.

I'm drowning in molten lava, bones melting. I have to get out. Voices penetrate suddenly, from a long way off. I strain, agonized, toward them.

"Let's get her into a recovery chamber." Hunter's voice. A recovery chamber? I puzzle over the odd choice of words. "We can save the chitchat for later."

"Make that you," Ian says. "I want no part of this."

"It's our duty, on about a dozen levels of which you are fully aware, to keep the patient in this room, in this very house, alive."

"Don't tell me my duty. And if you think I'm going to talk technicalities with her dad, you're wrong."

My body throbs as I try to cling to the conversation.

"Out of everyone, you're coming down on me?" Hunter says. "When you're always raging about restrictions?"

"Not about this."

"You know who she is. You saw her blood sample. You would have let her die?" Hunter pauses. "Don't walk away from me."

My blood sample . . . my pounding brain struggles to grasp what he's saying. I recall a prick in some security booth—here, outside the gates. It took my blood.

Footsteps grow farther away.

"What's done is done," Hunter calls.

The footsteps stop.

"She has multiple fractures in both arms and legs," Ian says sharply. "Broken ribs, extensive organ damage. She was crushed against a gate by an eight-hundred-pound moving vehicle. Look at her." The sound of a fist slamming metal is followed by a curse. "Thorne saw her—he knows she should be dead. It was all over his face. You shouldn't have let him in."

"Well, I did," Hunter says.

"*Damn the present*, remember? Remember that? The agreement that keeps the feds and every Jack, Dick, and Harriet with a budget out?" He's nearly shouting. "You think we want them in here? Me, or Vic, or any of us?" His rage sends me riding on a wave of terror. I sense he fears for his life. Worse, for his sanity. "She was dead."

Dead? I was dead? That can't be true.

I feel a phantom prickle across my scalp as I share his panic, unable to block the pummeling current of dread.

Did Hunter use some experimental drug to restart my heart? Did he break some rule? Even so, it doesn't justify Ian's wild fear seeping through my bones.

Another presence enters the room. Waves of soft, female energy pour over me, wise and comforting, soothing the raging fire.

"That's enough," the woman's voice says. "Let our young friend rest. The last thing she needs is to hear you boys bickering."

"Bickering?" Ian snorts. "Don't you get it?"

"There's no turning back. I think we should make her feel welcome."

"Yeah? For how long, Lucy?"

"As long as it takes," Lucy says.

"You were in trouble once, Ian, remember?" Hunter asks.

"How can I forget when you keep reminding me?" His bitter feelings flood me. "I'm going to find a drink."

Hunter says, "Good luck with that."

"Yeah." Ian lets out a harsh laugh.

I breathe out, spent.

"The police are here," comes Victoria's voice. "They're demanding to see her."

"Damn it," Hunter growls.

"They can't hurt us now," Lucy says. "Let them in."

A second later, hard, squeaky shoes make tracks across the floor. A man coughs. Two more mutter words I don't catch.

Fiery pain grabs me and yanks me into a volcanic abyss.

The brightly lit room and its people are lost to me.

There's no way back.

SIXTEEN

I HAVE NO IDEA HOW MUCH time has passed.

Occasionally, I hear voices. Hunter, Victoria, Ian. Commenting on my status.

More than the voices, however, it's the emotions of the people in the room that I latch onto for distraction. It's the only thing that brings me some measure of relief. How I feel them, I don't know; yet they comfort me. Is it a side effect from the accident? Forced solitude that's making my senses stronger? Complete imagination, perhaps? Insanity?

Whatever the cause, it occurs to me in this moment that people wear emotional signatures. I feel Victoria in the room with me now. She's a fierce blend of satire and sharp edges, with an odd vulnerability underneath that I can't quite put my finger on.

There's a clank of metal instruments dropping on a tray. Small wheels rolling across the floor. Buttons clicking on a keyboard. The sound is mildly muffled, as though my bed has tall, solid sides.

I'm getting that same fear from her again. It's deep and blended with churning confusion. Anger warring with fierce caring. For what, I can't tell. Her emotions are just that—emotions with no further information attached. Like hearing jarring movie music with a blanket covering the TV screen.

Ian enters. A wave washes between them and I follow its movement, letting it obscure my own agony. It's love, for her.

"Don't worry, it's under control," he says.

"Is it? We don't know that." She's not accusatory. She's looking for reassurance.

"The levels are experiencing significant die-off. Look here, at the numbers."

Are they talking about me? No, must be some research thing.

"They *were* dying off," she says in a stiff tone. "Now they're holding steady."

"A brief plateau. It's going to be fine."

"If not?"

Alarming waves hit me. Dark and loud. Pummeling me from their end of the room. Their frightened feelings mix with my pain. It's like they can sense me in the same way I sense them. As if my pain is affecting them internally. Injuring them.

"Ian," Victoria demands, "and if she's not under control?"

"Then we'll deal with her."

His tone fills me with terror.

"How?" she demands.

There's a long pause.

"I've got to get out of here," Ian growls. "It's too much. It's giving me a headache."

I desperately try to pull back from him. Why do they want to get me under control? What's happened to me?

Things grow jumbled then. My legs are shattering. Every one of my bones is exploding. I'm like the giant oak in front of Dad's house, aflame. Tree limbs cracking and sputtering in the blaze. Over it all comes the sound of my unfinished composition.

I can't go on. I just can't make it.

Mom's here.

Oh god, thank you, Mom. I miss you. Need you.

Her cool hand touches my brow and drapes icy wet cloths over my flaming eyes. I want to tell her what I'm going through. I don't need to, though; it's clear she understands. The fierce sympathy that flows from her soothes me.

When she speaks, it's with Victoria's voice. "I wouldn't wish this on anyone. Not even you."

I fade for a while, into a place of blissful silence.

How many hours have passed?

Hunter's in the room. His emotional signature is instantly recognizable. It's a barrage of contradictions I'm coming to know. Guarded yet expansive. Cheerful yet sober. Stubborn and dark, but with a bright streak leaking through. Solid yet wary—of what, I can't see.

It's a surprise when I hear Dad speak. I didn't feel him there. I strain to use my newly honed senses, imagined or not, to detect how he's holding up.

He's blank.

"How did you find out?" Dad says. Grim.

"From her blood sample at the security booth. Victoria ran a trace. That was when it all started making sense. You, for one."

I'm trying to focus, yet the more I do, the more the earlier fear I felt toward Dad starts creeping up. Enraged that I could fall prey to such a hallucination, I clamp my terror down by sheer force of will. The effort leaves me spent.

"Look. She's alive," Hunter says. "And she's going to be fine. Exactly as she was. No long-term effects. You could at least be happy about that."

"I am. By god, yes, I am." Dad sounds older. Tired. Beaten down. I want to hug him and tell him not to worry.

"The worst of it is over."

"I wish you'd told me all this before."

"I'm sure you can appreciate why I didn't," Hunter replies.

"Can she hear us?" Dad asks.

There's a beat of silence.

"No." Despite Hunter's calm voice, angry self-condemnation bubbles beneath the surface. "She'll be out for another few days."

I hear Dad's comforting footsteps draw closer. There's his familiar, homey scent. The sheet rustles under my chin as he pulls it higher. I want to call out to him, yet my mouth won't move.

"I don't want her knowing about this," Dad says. "What you've done. She's suffered enough. She has her whole life ahead. Promise me. One man to another."

"You don't need my promise. I have no intention of standing in her way. We want the same thing."

They're leaving now. I don't want to be abandoned. I'm in agony. Stop.

It was easy to be brave out on the road, driving for my life. Yet all my pluck has disappeared. My endurance is nearing its breaking point. I can't go on. I just can't make it.

From across the room, Dad is speaking. I grit my teeth and listen hard.

"I still want answers. I don't care how long it takes. I'll find them with or without your help."

Is he talking about the attackers?

"I want them as much as you do. She deserves that much," Hunter says, gruff. "I'm sorry." Sadness leaks out, real and true. "We all cared about her, no matter what you think."

Wait, what? Who are they talking about? For an instant, I think it's Mom. Of course, that's not possible. Hunter's too young to have known her.

Dad grunts.

Hunter clears his throat. "I only hope we've made you gain a little trust in us. In me."

"I'll think about it," Dad replies.

I've heard that tone before, though. It's going to take a lot more than apologies to heal the conflict between them.

I slip away, the flames crackling around me, tugging at this strange mystery as I go.

I'M PACKED IN AN ICE bath.

I awake, wild. Hunter is stronger. He's speaking to me, low and fast, trying to keep me there. Gasps tear from my mouth. I fight harder. The noise of my bandaged limbs slamming into porcelain echoes in my ears. Am I in a cast? Am I naked?

Hunter keeps piling more ice over me. My teeth chatter.

Strangely, the room smells of flowers. Peonies.

The touch of his fingers on my forehead is soft, gentle. Sweetness mingles with the pain, sweeping the horrors away and lifting me above them.

Yet something's wrong. My pain is no longer just my own. It's in him, too. The fire is starting to rage, to tear him down. It's like I've infected him with my alarming affliction.

I'm imagining it.

I must be imagining it.

No! There it is again, broadcasting loud and clear, pouring out from his center, the flares hot and wild. His fingers spasm in agony against my cheek. He rips his hand away.

"No," he growls to himself.

Am I causing this? Am I hurting him? Desperately, I struggle to untangle my senses from his.

Go, my mind shouts at him. *Go! You have to go.*

Then he starts to hum. Low and rough, the sound of someone not used to music. It's a lullaby. I'm not sure if it's me he's trying to comfort or both of us. His voice resonates in his chest. Off-key or not, I know that tune. Even without the words.

It's Mom's lullaby.

Land of the white wolf
Home of the reindeer
Where still the mighty bear
Wanders at will

White sea and frozen shore
I will return once more
Boom diddy-ah da, boom diddy-ah da, boom diddy-ah da,
*   boo-oo-oom*

There, where my true heart lies

I'll set my igloo
Close to the twilight edge
Silent and still

White sea where you were born,
You will come home that morn,
Boom diddy-ah da, boom diddy-ah da, boom diddy-ah da,
*   boo-oo-oom*

Land of the Amarok
Home of Anguta
Here comes my true lost friend
Wandering still

Sleep sweet most precious young
That's how this song is sung
Boom diddy boom boom, boom diddy boom boom, boom
*   diddy boom boom boo-oo-oom*

We float together to the time of the beat, and our pain begins to fade. Can he sense my emotional body the way I sense his? I listen like we're two musicians, straining to hear his retort. To my surprise, a faint stirring comes to me. And then he's there, pressing against my own emotions, holding them, caressing them in a way that's foreign and strange, yet somehow natural.

He offers hope, and I link into it, trailing notes of fear. He soothes those away, buoying my heart with caring and brightness. Our shared pain is shoved deeper, a gritty undercurrent beneath a shower of shooting stars. It's wonderful. Incredible. The way humans should always be. I'm breathless and he catches my breathlessness. Laughter bubbles up in me like starry champagne; it swirls into him until it breaks from his mouth in a chuckle. It's staggering, this merging of souls.

No, not any soul. His.

How is this possible?

Still he hums on, off-key yet perfect beyond words.

Victoria's presence flares in my periphery. The hurting roars back.

"I used to sing that to her," she says, her English accent coming out stronger than usual.

"I know," Hunter says, voice tense as he clamps down on his pain. "With the way you had it stuck in our heads, it's not likely I'll ever forget it."

"You've really done it to us, you know that?" Her voice is tight. Tired. Worried.

He doesn't reply.

"You have to stop this," she tells him. "What about the others? They're coming soon."

"Don't tell me what I already know," he says. "I've reached the same conclusion."

"It's for the best."

"Is it?"

"Come on, Hunter. We've all been through it!" Victoria's emotions always have a sharp edge. Sympathetic or not, they rattle.

"Not me."

"Yes, well. That's what's got me most concerned."

"For my tender heart?" he scoffs. "Or that I'll do something insane?"

"Both."

"Relax. Maybe I don't deserve to feel safe, but you do. I won't put any of you at more risk."

Together, they lift me from the ice and place me amid crisp sheets that smell of freshly washed cotton. An inkling of worry tugs at me. I reach out to Hunter to gauge his inner state and meet a solid wall of calm.

Victoria said he had to stop this. Stop what?

I drop off into a troubled, restless sleep.

Hunter comes to me in my dreams. He speaks gently to me, words of comfort. Stroking my forehead. Kissing my cheek. The feel of his lips against my burning skin obscures all else. I've dreamed of his kiss since that night in the barn, wondering how it would feel. I yearn to throw off my chains, force my unmoving arms to break free and wrap around him.

In my dream, his heart responds to mine, thumping hard and loud. He runs his rough fingers along my jaw, barely touching. Sparks shoot wild through my skin, mingling with his, swirling down into my belly.

"Stop feeling this way." His voice is ragged. "It's killing me."

The dream slips out of reach. Try though I do, I can't bring it back.

SEVENTEEN

A SOFT BREEZE WAFTS OVER ME, perfumed with rain-washed grass cuttings. Warmth radiates across the bridge of my nose and my parted lips. I sigh, stretching slightly, a good ache running the length of my limbs and down my arching back. I can't quite fully move, though. My arms and legs are caught by something.

My lids flutter wide.

And then I remember: I'm paralyzed.

Shock catapults around my skull until I realize my left hand is clenched. Wait, I can feel my left hand. Oh my god. I really can.

I try to move under the clinging, fluffy duvet that's been pulled up to my neck. Finally, after much awkward thrashing, I manage to send the duvet slipping over the side. Air creeps across me, and the flesh on my belly prickles under its touch. I wrench my head up, afraid I might be naked.

No, thank god. I'm dressed in a light, sleeveless gown. Wires run from my chest to a softly beeping heart monitor. I stare at the casts. Four of them—one on each leg from toe to hip, one on each arm. My right hand is completely encased. But my left hand is free. And I'm still clenching it hard. I relax my fingers and breathe out.

So I'm not paralyzed. He was right. Yet only time will tell if I'll still have the ability to play music like before. A queasy burning fills my stomach. I focus on the room.

It's so pretty I spend a moment taking it all in. A large vase of pink blooms stands on an antique wood dresser. The walls are painted in rosy hues that blend with the floral design on the cream curtains. Antique moldings edge the ceiling. A chaise longue with a quilt thrown over it begs to be curled up on with a book. An alcove in the far corner holds a deep window seat piled with cushions. A fireplace is partially hidden by a screen painted with two swans, their necks curving to form a heart. For a ridiculous moment, I expect a butler to appear.

Footsteps creak nearby. I'm suddenly nervous.

"Hunter?" I call.

"It's good to see you awake," a reedy voice says.

Not Hunter.

Turning, I struggle to catch sight of the man coming into view.

He's older with mostly white strands in his carefully combed back hair, wearing a black tailored suit. A throwback from another century. He holds a long-necked silver watering can and a cloth. His movements are quiet and efficient as he fills the vase. Okay, wait. There really is a butler? Have I entered some comic book dimension?

Unnerved, I try to reach out to him with my senses. Nothing.

Instantly, I feel silly.

"I'm afraid I have you at a disadvantage." His face is nice when he smiles. Open yet polite, the kind of face that turns amused rather than annoyed by life's trials. He folds the cover and sets it on a trunk at the foot of the bed. "I know your name, but you don't know mine. I'm Edward."

I feel ridiculous, lying here. There's a queasy burning in my stomach. Still, I manage, "Nice to meet you."

"The honor is mine."

"Where am I? Am I in the research lab?"

"Yes. In the west wing of the original house. We felt you'd be comfortable here."

"It's like something from a storybook."

"The man who built it had a daughter. This was her bedroom."

Having watered the plants, he sets down the can and retrieves the duvet from the floor.

"Are those flowers peonies?" I ask.

"They are. A fellow horticulturist?"

"No—I've always liked them. They were my mother's favorite flower."

"Yes." Pause. "They grow in the gardens."

"They're enormous."

"They're the original plantings. It's quite a sight when the buds appear. The whole garden comes to life with blooms and butterflies."

"Isn't it a shame to cut them?"

"Lucy suspected they might bring some comfort. Besides, it's our duty to enjoy such beauty. Even," he adds, "when one is stuck indoors."

"Lucy?" I ask, recalling the woman's name from the operating room and the day the police came. "Is she a doctor here?"

The click of feminine heels sound in the doorway. Without even turning, I know it's Victoria. I cringe.

"Lucy is Edward's wife," she says. "And a surrogate mother to the rest of us misfits," she adds in a wry, humorous tone. Yet I almost believe there's truth in it. She's dressed in high tan boots, a leather micro-skirt and camel cashmere sweater. Her eyes are lined with copper pencil and a similar shade gleams on her lips. How a person can make copper lipstick attractive is beyond me, but she does.

"I'm off. I'll be back with lunch," Edward says.

He's leaving me here with her? Alone? "Oh, I'm really not hungry," I say.

Victoria crosses her arms, reading my face. "Do I alarm you?"

I glance at Edward for help.

"Victoria, be nice."

"This is me being nice."

The older gentleman actually looks amused. "Yes, I suppose it is."

He nods at me and departs. I'm left, horrified, wanting to call him back. A bee drones through the half-open window. It starts bumping against the glass.

"Where's Hunter?" I say.

Victoria ratchets me into a seated position. "Not here."

"When's he getting back?"

"I couldn't say."

"But he'll be back later today, right?"

"Oh no. I don't think he'll be back in the foreseeable future."

I gape at her and my stomach bottoms out. *He's gone?* "Doesn't he have research to do?"

"I hardly think that's any of your business."

The buzzing bee grows more urgent. She swivels and tries to shoo the trapped creature out the window. It zigzags upward and is hidden among the drapes.

So he just left? Without even saying good-bye? The stupid heart machine starts pinging faster, and I can hardly breathe. "I don't understand, I thought . . ." *What, that he'd be waiting at my bedside like a prince from a fairy tale, looking into my eyes as they fluttered open? Gently kissing my forehead?* "I didn't realize he was planning to go."

"You thought he'd share his plans with you?"

Is that anger in her voice? I try desperately to reach out to her with my senses. I'm almost sure a faint deflection shoots from her. Then nothing. Try as I do, she's blank. That's when I realize the truth. It was all in my imagination, thinking I could sense their emotions. All of it.

Just like I imagined Hunter had deep feelings for me.

"Hunter's a busy man. He has numerous duties," she says.

Is that what I was to him? A duty? I close my eyes, aching and unable to ward off the depth of the blow.

"What about Blaze? He just abandoned the filly?"

"Your father's taking care of her."

I stare at the swans, tracing the shapes of their twined necks. "I don't suppose he left a note or anything?"

"No." She holds out a small plastic cup and picks up a glass of water from the nightstand. "Here. Take this."

I frown into the cup, struggling to hide my emotions. There's a marble-sized metal ball inside. "What is it?"

"A pill."

It's unlike any pill I've ever seen. I peer at the thing. It reflects my pale face. "It's huge."

"Yes, well, bottoms up."

I roll it back and forth. "Is this really necessary?"

"If you want to live, yes." She taps her foot. "Just swallow the little beast."

"Easy for you to say. You're not the one doing it. I can hardly choke down a baby aspirin."

Her face lights with a flash of anger. "You have no idea how lucky you are. So stop staring into that cup and take the damn thing. And be happy about it. Because you're alive and you're getting better and you're going to walk out of here and that will be it. You'll be normal, Aeris."

Her outburst shocks me. She looks pained, and it becomes clear she's actually concerned about me, despite her harsh attitude.

The truth is, I could be stuck in a shared hospital ward right now surrounded by sick patients. Instead, I'm in what amounts to a luxury, private care facility. They have all the latest machines and medicines, and they've taken exceptional care of me. Perhaps beyond that—doing things I don't even want to question.

She's right. I need to get back to my music. I have to practice before September. I have to be in complete working order. There's no way I'm losing my hard-won position in the Philharmonic. More than that, I need to disappear from Hunter's world. From any reminders of him. If this pill can get me there, I don't care how big it is.

I tip it into my mouth. It weighs heavily on my tongue, and I feel a mild sense of panic.

Victoria hands me the water. "Quick, a big gulp."

I nod and do so. An odd, acrid smell fills my nostrils. I fight to stop gagging. Once the pill starts moving, it's like a bowling ball, tumbling back and down, down, down.

After she leaves, I call Dad from the landline beside my bed. I hadn't realized how shaken up I am until I hear his comforting voice.

"I'll finish up here as fast as I can. See you shortly," he tells me.

Alone, I stare at the ceiling. This beautiful house is far from what I expected. I would have thought they'd have cleared out a room like this and filled it with beakers and Bunsen burners.

But then what do I know?

I thought Hunter would be waiting for me to awake, like a prince.

I curl my good arm around myself, squeezing and unsqueezing my fist and praying that I'll still have my old abilities. Closing my eyes, I recall Hunter's warm, low voice humming a lullaby with the two of us wrapped together in its melody. How had I read him so wrong? Were his feelings for me like my feelings for Gage? I cringe, knowing what Gage must feel and the bitter sting of rejection.

Hunter knew he'd done his duty by me, and so he left. He didn't care the way I do.

But it's over. He's gone. And he's not coming back.

Dad sits on a chair next to my bed. We talk quietly about Sammy and Blaze.

"The foal's doing really well. I told Grandpa about you staying up all night with her. He said you're a chip off the old ranch."

I laugh and picture her small, velveteen face. What a time that had been. Both tragic and joyful. For a while, Hunter, Blaze, and I had existed in our tiny bubble. We'd muddled our way through, side by side. For Hunter and me, it had been a night of confessions, of shared dreams, of sitting so close our legs touched. And in the morning, on Ranger's back, he'd held me to him like we were lovers.

"Oh, before I forget, I brought you some things." Dad hands me my iPod. I cling to it like a lifeline. Next he shocks me by pulling my composition manuscript from his leather bag.

"What made you think I'd need this?" I ask.

"I notice stuff."

"You're awesome." I keep it on my lap, unwilling to voice my fear that my muscles won't be quite the same.

"Mr. Creedy's funeral was a few weeks ago. Most of the town showed up."

"I'm going to miss him."

"Yep. Me too."

"Have they found the people who did this?"

"There's an investigation under way. That's all I know."

"But they must have come to question you. Why did those men want to get in here? And how did they know you had the key?"

"I guess they were watching me."

"What if they come back? I'm worried about you."

Dad eyes the heart monitor and strokes the damp hair from my forehead. "I'm fine. I gave up my PRL access card. I'm no use to them. The only way I can get in is if Ian or Edward meets me at the gate. It will all be sorted out."

"Were those men military? What did they say to you in the house?"

"Not a lot. Nothing worth repeating. I wish I could tell you more."

"What's so important in here that they'd want to break in?"

He shakes his head. "I couldn't say."

"Maybe they want to steal an infectious agent?"

"Maybe. I should let you rest." He stands. "Ella and Gage have been asking about you."

"Tell them hello."

When I'm alone, the silence in my room is oppressive. It crushes in.

Never have I felt so trapped.

Did I matter so little to Hunter that he felt a good-bye wasn't necessary? What happened between us?

I won't feel sorry for myself. I won't.

There's no point to it.

Angry, I stick out my tongue and lick the salty tear that betrays me. Through blurred eyes, I find the fireplace screen with the pair of painted swans. They're centered on its curved, rectangular surface, two heads bowed in an eternal embrace.

Hunter doesn't want these feelings of mine.

The realization squeezes my chest so I can hardly breathe.

I never wanted them, either. This sort of pain is exactly what I was trying to avoid. So how have I found myself here alone?

EIGHTEEN

A FEW DAYS PASS. I SPEND the time trying to work out new bars to my composition. Unfortunately, they won't come.

Victoria and I do basic exercises to bring mobility back into my hips and shoulders. My left hand is now fully functional, which gives me hope. The wires and monitors are gone. She supplies my medication—two red pills in the morning, the strange silver one at noon, two blue pills at night—checks my blood, listens to my heart, sits with me while I eat.

The fear that I won't be better by September is rarely far from my mind.

Yesterday, we argued.

"I want to know about that security booth," I'd said. "I'm pretty sure taking someone's blood is illegal."

"It's private property. No one asked you to stick your hand in there. If you don't like it, too bad. You shouldn't have stolen that pass. Personally, I think it's quite clever to have a DNA record of people trying to break in. Move your arms up and down. That's it, ten more reps."

Even with the casts, the mobility in my shoulders was coming back quickly. "Wait, that's right, I heard you talking about my blood sample in the operating room."

"I very much doubt that."

"No—I did. Someone said they recognized me and I think . . . you were afraid or . . ."

"Afraid?" she demanded. "And how would you know that?"

I examined her face, and for one crazy moment, I wondered if she was testing me.

She waited, arms crossed. I tried to recall the words I'd overheard. They were gone.

"You know," she said, "in my experience, it's people like you, the innocent-seeming ones, that end up causing the most trouble."

"Well, that's a blanket statement."

"You're here, aren't you?"

Today, in comparison, Victoria is subdued. She combs my hair as I watch in a hand mirror. Thanks to Dad's helmet, even though the visor had been up, I'd suffered little damage to my face. It's healed now.

Her gentleness surprises me. She's almost mothering. I'm embarrassed at being cared for by her in this way.

"I was tired of looking at your stringy bedhead," she tells me.

Strangely, I find her pointy attitude better than pity. I laugh.

In fact, I think I'm coming to like her for all her harshness. I don't think she's actually malicious. Maybe the opposite.

Maybe her jagged manner is a wall because she cares too much.

THE SOUND OF INCOMING MAIL pings on my iPod. It's a message from Professor Darcy.

Dear Aeris,

I hope this finds you well.

A new music firm that creates sound tracks for movies and TV recently contacted me. Your exceptional skills continue to draw interest. They're looking for new talent and asked me to get in touch to see if you're available to apply. I know you have your hands full with the Philharmonic. The reason I forward this is because of your deep passion for composing.

If you decide to apply, good luck. You deserve it.

Take care,

—Andrea Darcy

Goose bumps race along my arms. All morning I've been listening to my favorite sound track: Ólafur Arnalds's haunting music for the TV drama *Broadchurch*. His work and life are an inspiration.

To think I could follow in his footsteps, write scores to gripping stories—it just seems impossible. Like a dream that fell out of the sky. It's everything I want—to get paid to compose. I could juggle it with the Philharmonic. I know I could.

And if not?

I can't think that far ahead. I click on the link. They want samples of my compositions. I attach two. It's surreal. What if they don't like them? Maybe I shouldn't do this. I'm baring my soul, and, after Hunter, I'm not sure I could weather another rejection.

My finger hovers over my iPod.

Then I hit send.

THE FOLLOWING MORNING, EDWARD—FORMAL EDWARD who is amazingly strong, given his elderly, tall, slender frame—lifts me into a wheelchair and conveys me out for a stroll.

"It's too much trouble," I try to tell him.

"For me or for you?"

"For you, dragging me out here."

"I assure you I'm quite up to the task."

"That's not what I meant." I try to twist around to see his face, without luck.

"Besides, technically I'm not dragging you. That would no doubt cause quite a bit of discomfort on both our parts."

"You're teasing me."

"It would appear so. Here we are."

We turn alongside the house and out into a vast, English-style garden.

"It's beautiful."

"I would have felt personally responsible had I not taken you here during your visit. Especially since, as you say, peonies were your mother's favorite flower."

I inhale deeply and look around. More and more I question the oddity of this place. A horse barn, gardens, beautifully furnished rooms. Hunter's choice of clothes.

The sun sends long shadows slanting among the giant peony plants. The blooms are huge. Blush-pink ones that exude a rich, heady perfume. Lazy bumblebees flounder around them, sinking and rising as they move from bud to bud.

The sound of a man humming makes me turn quickly. For a heart-beat, I think it's Hunter, and my pulse races out of control.

A flash of red hair appears beyond a hedge.

Ian.

My spirits sink. He scares me, although I'm not sure why. I shrink back in my wheelchair, longing to escape. As if seeing my trepidation, Edward comes to stand behind me, putting the weight of his steady hands on the push handles. I wish he would bear me swiftly away.

Ian wears a lab coat over his waffle henley and cargo pants. It's the first sign I've seen to suggest that research really is being done here. Even if, like Hunter, he doesn't match my clichéd image of how a scientist should look. Yes, his pockets are sagging with pens. But his shoulders are huge and his waist is lean, and I doubt there's a millimeter of fat on his six-foot frame. They must have a killer gym in this place.

A liquor bottle dangles from one hand, two thirds of its amber liquid gone. The other holds a cut glass tumbler that sparkles in the sunlight. Catching sight of me, he scowls.

My left hand clenches and starts to sweat.

"Hello," I call in a voice suddenly hoarse.

Ian raises his glass to me and takes a slug.

"Healing well, are we?" His tone is clipped.

"Yes, thank you." He makes me nervous. "I'm sorry to have caused so much trouble."

He stares into the amber liquid. "Yeah, well. Promise me one thing."

"What's that?"

"Take your meds."

I'm stunned. That's his request?

"Religiously, exactly as directed." His face is stiff.

"Of course."

His fingers tighten around the crystal glass. I'm afraid he might crush it. "This isn't a joke. I need your promise, Aeris."

"Yes, I promise."

Ian's eyes go to Edward's face. "You damn well better keep it."

I watch him go, my stomach roiling.

If I'd wondered before, now I'm certain. The treatment is suspicious, something they're working on here. I call after him. He ignores me and keeps walking.

I'd wanted to ask Edward to take me to the barn to see Blaze. Now, however, I want to go back to my room. Nerves are turning my legs to jelly in my casts.

Before we leave the garden, Edward cuts a bouquet of peonies and I hold them in my lap. As I finger the soft blooms, my mind spins with questions. Something's not right about this lab. Or about the people who work here. Hunter's beyond strong. Or had I imagined the speed and strength with which he'd saved me? And I still can't get past that flash I'm sure I saw in his eyes. And then there's Iron-fist. What is it that he's desperate to get his hands on? The pills I'm taking? I can almost taste the strange, acrid silver ball. What's in it? Will there be side effects? I feel fine now, but do they even know?

Back in my room, I watch Edward arrange the blooms in a vase.

"I'd like to stay in the chair for a while."

"You sure you're comfortable?"

"Perfectly."

"Very good. Will you be needing anything else?"

"No thanks, Edward."

"I'll check on you in an hour."

I wait until Edward's footsteps have died away. Then I test out my ability to wheel my way out the door. For the first time, I'm moving through the house alone.

Nineteen

I'M SURPRISED AT THE STRENGTH in my left hand and arm. I wheel down the hall and peer through each door in turn. Despite the casts, I feel good. I'm not sure what I'm looking for. I guess I'll know when I find it.

There's a sitting room with floral-print chairs and a clean fireplace. Next come two unfurnished rooms. Farther on, I find a game room with a billiard table, a dartboard, and a liquor cabinet. A decanter rests on a side table next to a half-full glass. I picture Ian tucked in the depths of some leather armchair, so I hurry past, turning one corner and then another, not stopping until I feel safe.

I reach a hall hung with paintings. Landscapes, mostly. A shiny brass door handle catches my interest, and I decide to have a look. It's unlocked. It swings open, and I find myself staring into a man's study.

Hunter's leather jacket lies folded on a chair.

My heart stutters.

How is it he still has such a maddening magnetic pull on me?

I enter and shut the door. This room is definitely his. His presence is everywhere, from the faint woodsy scent to the heavy oak furnishings to the packed bookshelves full of medical tomes, field guides on flora and fauna, bioengineering textbooks with titles I can't even begin to understand. It practically crackles with his aura.

I'm intruding. I shouldn't be here. But neither can I go.

Slowly, I approach his sprawling desk. The teak floor creaks under the wheels. I continue until my knees are pressed against the side.

The broad surface holds oddities from medical instruments to calculators. Next to a half-empty glass of water lies an open notepad. I back up and maneuver around to it. From the way he threw the pen down and left his drink here, it's like he's about to return. Then a horrible thought hits. He can't actually be here, avoiding me, could he? I push aside the idea as ridiculous and study his notes.

The tiny drawings and calculations are so dense the pages are nearly black. I pore over them and can make no sense beyond references to blood types.

I glance up and see a framed photo. It's clearly old given the clothing worn by the couple in the picture. The man looks like Hunter, although sterner somehow. The woman's smile is kind, and she has his eyes. It must be his grandparents.

I avert my gaze, feeling bad for snooping. I'm reminded of how I searched Dad's office all those weeks ago. I hadn't learned anything about the PRL, or about Hunter. But I'd found Mom's cryptic journal entry with her warning about human genetic modification.

Hunter and I had talked about it the day he and I went riding. I'd asked him if he thought it wrong for a doctor to seriously modify a person's genetics if it could save the patient's life. He'd gone all stiff and I had to press him to reply. What had he said?

"I don't believe anyone has any business playing God."

But if Ian was telling the truth about me, that I was dead, isn't that exactly what he'd done? Played God?

I turn my attention to a thick folder. It contains investment information about a company called Vogel Instrumentation. Nothing that promises answers.

"Where are you, Hunter?" I whisper into the silence.

The faint tick of a clock is the only reply. I should go back before someone finds me here.

On my way out, I pass the chair with Hunter's jacket. Unable to help myself, I pause and pull the heavy object into my lap. Then I hug it to me and breathe in his scent. I let myself dream we're back in the barn. None of this ever happened. We're safe. We're going to that concert.

Chest aching, I press my face to his coat.

The instant I do, I double over in pain.

My teeth clench as heat roars up my arms and spreads along my neck and into my mind. Lurching forward, I nearly tumble out of the chair. My breath comes fast and sharp. For a second, the pain falters, breaking off, and then comes again. Like a radio broadcast, tuning in and out. Raging and then dull, static and then coming through loud and clear.

As sweat pours down my sides, it dawns on me that this is not my pain. It's coming from outside me. Coming from a distance, radiating in and out.

Then I sense a rush of emotions. Masculine and angry. And protective, fiercely protective. I recognize that emotional signature. I know whose pain this is.

Hunter's.

Did I infect him, then? Is that what this is? Is that what happened?

Or am I going crazy? Am I imagining all this?

Desperately, I try to reach out to him, to feel for a response. The flames grow so intense tears leak from the corners of my closed eyes.

Hunter, what is this? Where are you? Tell me. Show me. I want to help!

In response, I feel myself being thrust backward. It's so powerful I'm thrown back in the chair and the jacket slips from my arms. A wall slams down between us. I realize my ears had been roaring, because now the room is dead still.

I'm sweating beneath my casts. My left hand is drenched. I reach down and pick up Hunter's coat. *Don't shut me out*, I think, even as I begin to question my own sanity. Cautiously, I press my face to the leather again. This time nothing happens. I try and try.

There's no point. I'm going mad. That's the only explanation.

Abandoning it on the chair, I turn and wheel myself out into the hall.

Footsteps sound from around a corner. They're drawing closer. I want to be gone. Frantic, I start to push myself along.

Then I hear Victoria's voice. "Hunter said he left it on his desk."

"I hope so," comes Ian's reply.

Any second, they'll see me. I try the nearest door. Locked. The second one whispers open under my urgent push. Swiftly, I enter. The room is dark. A moment passes before my eyes adjust. Closed curtains block off the far wall. I make out lumps of what must be furniture draped in sheets. Then I catch sight of the piano, and I forget everything and everyone.

A Steinway.

I cross the room in an instant. I can't help myself. It takes some effort to shove the bench clear. Then I'm sitting at the keys, and I begin, very softly, to play. One-handed. My fingers are stiff. They don't respond like they used to. Fear wells up, yet I shove it down. I'm playing, and that's enough. Here there is music. Distorted or not, I'm playing.

"How did you get in here?" Ian demands.

I swivel in my seat. I realize my face is damp with tears. I scrub them quickly away.

He's wearing his lab coat. Now, however, across his left side is a dinner plate–sized crimson stain. Is that . . . blood? My eyes snap to his. I sense worry flowing from him. It blends and swirls with my own uneasy fear. What caused that ugly blotch?

Should I bluff? And say what?

"I was tired of sitting in my room."

"Who told you you could go snooping around?" Ian demands.

"No one."

Victoria pushes in behind him. "There's no point getting uptight, Ian. I would have done the same thing."

"This area of the facility is off limits!"

"It doesn't look much like a facility," I counter. "I don't see any high-tech labs or anything. It just looks like a house to me. And if this room's so top secret, why is the door unlocked?"

"This room isn't—that's not the point," he growls, fuming.

"I've never been in here before." Victoria strolls past him, glancing at the shrouded furniture. At the piano, she runs a finger along the dusty top.

"You play pretty well one-handed."

"Thanks," I say.

"I didn't know this was here. I would've brought you. It's a lot better exercise than what we've been doing." She moves around the room, lifting covers and peering underneath. "We don't use this part of the house much. But you know what our facility's called, right? You know what we do?"

"Exactly my point," Ian interjects. "You can't just go sticking your nose wherever you feel like. It's called Phoenix Research Lab *for Highly Contagious Diseases* for a reason. I don't give a damn if you're bored or whatever the hell drove you out here. What if something happened to you? Isn't it enough that we saved you once already?"

"I'm not trying to cause trouble."

His glare shifts to Victoria. "It was a mistake putting her in this chair. Who authorized it? You? Edward?"

"Calm down. There's no harm done," she says.

He flaps his arms. "Oh great. Really?"

"I want to go home," I say. "Now. I've been enough of a burden. Call my Dad, and he can come get me."

"You can't." Ian's voice is flat.

"What do you mean?" I demand.

"It's not safe," Victoria says. "There's no way you're ready. You're not recovered enough. You still need rehabilitation. And your drugs need monitoring."

"What kind of drugs are they, anyway? I mean, why do I need drugs for broken bones?"

Ian starts to say something, but Victoria raises a slim hand. "It wasn't just your bones. You were injured internally. You experienced near organ failure. You might feel fine, but you're not. Not yet."

I consider her words. Then I raise my eyes to Ian. "You said I was dead. I heard you say it."

His mouth opens. Beneath his flaming red hair, his forehead puckers. "I said what?" He starts to laugh. "I said you were dead?"

"I heard you!"

"Look, I'm right in the middle of an experiment, and I don't have time for this." He's laughing now.

"I know what I heard," I say.

He scratches his head. "If you were dead, Aeris, we wouldn't be having this conversation. I'm good at what I do, but I'm not that good. If I were, I sure as hell wouldn't be slogging away in some lab. I'd be waving my magic wand over terminal cancer patients and getting rich."

His outrage is so thick I can't help wondering if he's telling the truth. Emotions are not like words. They don't carry the same information. Am I wrong? Did I dream what he said? I was unconscious for a long time. Three weeks.

Uncertain, I stare at the piano keys.

"Okay, are we done here?" Victoria asks.

"I know I am," Ian says.

"I can make my own way back to my room."

"I'll take you," Victoria says.

I sense Ian's relief. "Make it quick. We need to get back to work."

"Right-o, slave driver."

He rolls his eyes.

We part ways in the hall.

"Ian gets his back up, but he's not that bad when you get to know him. He's just a little overprotective and he worries," Victoria tells me.

I mull this over, not sure I agree with her assessment. "He looked pretty upset."

"It's good to shake him up. Keeps him on his toes."

This is just the sort of comment I've come to expect from her.

I can't help grinning. "He's always so serious. Is he ever nice?"

"I'm not sure. No, I don't think he is. Oh wait, there was that one time—on second thought, that may have been a mistake."

"Are you serious?"

"Kidding. Stick around long enough and you'll see he can be quite funny sometimes."

I know in that moment I won't get the chance. As kind as Victoria and

Edward have been to me, and Lucy, too, with her short, friendly visits, I have to leave.

I recall what happened to me in Hunter's study. I'm going mad cooped up in this place. Forget the questions—forget all of it. I want to get back to my life. I need to put this behind me. I'm getting out.

TWENTY

As soon as I'm alone, I call Dad.

"Please," I beg him. "You've got to take me home."

"I don't know, Peanut."

"I'm fine. If anything happens, you could just take me to the hospital, couldn't you?"

There's a heavy pause.

"All right. Tomorrow night after I take care of Blaze, I'll come for you."

"You can't let them know."

"Don't worry. We'll do it quiet-like."

"I love you, Dad."

It takes a long time for me to fall asleep. When I do, I slip into a nightmare. I'm in the apple orchard, crouched behind Iron-fist's black SUV. I know he sees me. Horrified, I play dead. His feet crunch through the grass toward me. He kneels and puts his face up to mine to see if I'm breathing.

I can't hold my breath. I need air. I suck in a mouthful.

He seizes me and shakes me hard.

"*I knew you were alive,*" he shouts.

I wake in a sweat. My eyes fly open and I see I'm not alone. Victoria's lean silhouette is parked near the window. She opens the heavy drapes. Dawn light filters onto my face. I squint against the brightness.

"You look like hell," Victoria informs me.

"Thanks."

She shrugs one narrow shoulder. "Just saying."

I groan. "I had the worst dream."

"Let me guess. Ian turned into a dragon and burned up the piano."

I laugh. "No."

"Too bad. He'd be kind of cute with a snout." She goes to a stainless-steel cart just inside the door and selects a syringe, several blood-collection tubes, and some packets of alcohol swabs. Needles still make me woozy. Better to stare out the window and watch the dawn's bruised clouds scud by.

"Did you know the whole town is scared of this place?" I ask.

"Are they?" She peels off the syringe wrapper. "No one's ever told me that."

"You probably don't talk to them."

"That's not fair. I go dancing at the Zenith Club. As I recall, you saw me there."

"Should people be worried?" I ask. "Is it possible someone could get infected by what you're studying?"

She wipes her right hand on one leather-clad thigh. "Anything is possible. Not in the way you're thinking, though."

"What is it you're researching?"

"It's not something I'm at liberty to talk about."

My frustration makes me bolder. "Why have I never seen anyone besides you, Ian, Edward, Lucy, and Hunter? How can this be a research lab with no staff here?"

"There are others."

"How many?"

Her stony eyes level me with a long, piercing gaze. There's a wall between us, between me and everyone here.

"Thirteen." She says it casually.

There's nothing casual about it, though. The air is thick with tension, and it's as though a brick has tumbled clear. I press on, urgent to tear out another.

"Thirteen people? They must be really quiet."

Victoria smirks. "Yes, well, they're not here at the moment."

"Where are they?"

She raises one brow and inserts the needle. "As it happens, we have a sister facility. Overseas."

I wince away from the thrusting syringe that's lodged deep in my vein. "Overseas? Whereabouts?"

She switches the full vial of blood for an empty one. "Switzerland, actually."

Switzerland? I feel suddenly dizzy. Switzerland is where my mother died. I stare at Victoria, whose gaze is trained on my arm.

"Have you been there?" she asks. Her voice is nonchalant as she extracts the needle. Still, there's a curious quality to her doe eyes when they meet mine.

My heart is pounding. "Once," I manage through dry lips.

"When?"

"I was little."

She goes to the stainless-steel cart. "Never again?"

"No." My tongue is parched. "Never again."

Does she know what happened to us in Switzerland? She couldn't. I was only five. Victoria could have been at most eight or nine years old. And it was barely in the news. The authorities said we'd suffered an unfortunate accident on the winding roads. They insisted my mother's driving was at fault, even though I knew better.

A man clears his throat.

I catch sight of Ian in the doorway. Fear makes my stomach lurch.

"Giving away classified information?" he drawls. "Aren't we chummy."

"Don't be a bore, Ian. It doesn't suit you." Victoria's impenetrable expression has snapped firmly back into place. "Neither does oozing around as though I can't hear you."

He crosses his arms over his broad chest.

"Toddle off and leave us to it, darling."

"You're infuriating, you know that?"

"It's why you adore me." It's the lighthearted armor she uses to fend off the world.

Ian snorts and leaves.

My heart is still pounding at the mention of Switzerland. I look up to see that everything about Victoria is now clammed up tight. Her shoulders, her tense fingers. Her clipped movements as she clears away my blood work and wheels the metal cart toward the door.

There, she pauses.

When she turns, her eyes are different. There's caring. Real, honest caring.

"Are you all right?" she asks.

"I'm fine," I reply quickly.

Her eyes go to her hands, which are clutched around the cart handle. I sense she's about to tell me something. Her mouth opens. Words seem to hang there. Finally, all that comes out is, "Okay. Good."

Her heels echo into the distance and disappear.

Maybe it was the concern in her tightly drawn brows. Maybe it was her unexpected kindness. Whatever the cause, I can't hold the childhood memory at bay a second longer.

It slides over me, tasting of tears and blood.

Mountains and pine trees. The car, with Mom behind the wheel. Me riding in the front like a big girl. Our happy singsong dying on her lips. The paleness of her cheeks when she looks in the rearview mirror.

"Mommy? What's the matter?" I hear my five-year-old voice ask.

"Make sure your seat belt's fastened, okay, honey?"

I press on the metal buckle, doing as she asks. Pine trees whip by my window. So fast they start to blur. The high alpine road is narrow and twisty with hairpin turns. There are no guardrails. Far below, a river cascades over jagged rocks.

"Mommy, you're going too fast!"

I see a car move up behind us in the side mirror. It's almost attached to our bumper.

I'm frightened.

Mommy's eyes go to the rearview mirror. Her usually comforting voice makes a tiny, "Oh!"

And then our car does the unthinkable. It tumbles sideways, right over the edge, and I'm screaming and the river is coming closer, and we're flipping in slow motion, and somehow Mommy rips off her seat belt with the strength only a mother could have and throws her body over mine, and we slam and roll, slam and roll.

The sound. The awful sound.

Explosions of shattering glass.

Squeals of grinding metal.

The blaring of a horn. Our horn.

The jarring halt.

The warm wetness of Mommy against me.

Long stunned moments pass.

I start to cry.

"My baby," she whispers, her voice so weak I'm frightened. "I got you. You're okay. You're okay. I love you so much."

I put my small hands on her cheeks. "Mommy, are you hurt?" I'm scared for her.

She doesn't answer.

My heart starts beating fast like a bunny rabbit's. Pitter-pattering out of control.

Something clinks and pings off the side of the car. Then come several pairs of footsteps crunching and sliding down the sheer embankment toward us.

"Shh," Mommy tells me, her voice thick with pain and fear. "Quiet as a mouse."

I nod.

She shifts over me so I'm hidden completely. There's a volley of kicking and angry voices as the crushed trunk of our car is wrestled open. I hear our suitcases being dragged out. Men wedge open the back door. From my position, I can just peer between the driver and passenger seats. Mommy's purse is lying on the backseat. A muscular hand comes into view and picks it up. The image is burned into my mind. Those thick pale fingers. The tattooed initials on his forearm that read WB.

He bends over us and I hear the glove box open. His cologne makes me want to gag.

"I wish you'd behaved more professionally, Julia," he says.

He knows Mommy. He called her by name. Why isn't he helping us?

"Move out," he tells the others.

They're leaving us trapped in the ravine, in the wreckage. Mommy keeps silent until their scrabbling footsteps have died away.

I smell smoke.

"Honey, I need you to be brave. Can you be brave for me?"

I nod. Anything, anything. "Yes," I say, clinging more tightly to her.

Mommy coughs. "You need to get out of the car, okay? You need to crawl out the back."

"No!"

"I'm coming right after. I'll be right with you." With great effort, she rolls sideways. Blood runs from her scalp, down her soft cheeks.

"Please, hurry," she whispers.

"You're hurt, Mommy," I sob. Her arms and legs bleed from awful red gashes. She's turning pale.

Smoke billows over us, making us cough.

"Hurry!" She lifts me, and we both slip over into the backseat. She's strong; she's going to be all right. "I love you," she tells me, kissing my forehead. "I'll always be with you, Aeris. Never forget that." She thrusts me out the back door, hard.

At the same time, the car explodes. A ball of fire roars skyward. I'm thrown across the hillside. I hit rocks.

The world goes black.

A man is holding me in his arms and walking fast. I cry out and struggle against his flannel-clad chest.

He soothes me with gentle words. "It's safe, you're safe."

"Mommy! Help my mommy!"

He holds me closer. "She's with angels now."

"No!" I scream, sobbing and fighting hard.

He lets me punch and kick him until I'm exhausted, never letting me go. His neck is bristly, and finally I burrow into it, crying until his warm skin is drenched with my tears. We walk for hours like that, his big arms cradling me tight. It's pitch black and he never stumbles once, not once down the rocky, steep mountain.

I must have fallen asleep. When I wake, I'm in a bustling police station. A uniformed man with a big mustache tells me I'm safe.

"You're lucky that hiker found you," he tells me. "He carried you more than thirty miles."

Lucky? How can I be lucky when Mommy's gone?

Still, I wish I could have thanked him.

Now, in this old house, in this room, I cry like I did then. I cry for the man who saved me, who comforted me, who left before I got to see his face. I cry for the little girl who lost her mommy. But most of all, I cry for my mother.

I sob knowing I couldn't get her out of the car. I sob until I'm choking. I drown in the unbearable truth that she died for me. *Mom, I didn't want you to go.*

My throat is swollen tight and my chest aches, and still I cry some more.

TWENTY-ONE

I WAKE TO THE SOUND OF someone in my room.

My eyelids are swollen as I glance up and start in surprise. "Dad."

He raises a finger to his lips and bends to lift me. One arm under my legs, the other under my shoulder blades, he moves me swiftly to the wheelchair. Moonlight streaks the windowsill.

"Hold tight."

I do, gripping the chair as he whisks me down the long, brilliantly lit corridors. I feel terrible, escaping with no good-bye. Or thanks. They saved my life. I'm grateful. Yet I have to go. We hurry past half-open doors as nervousness ping-pongs in my chest.

"Almost there," Dad says.

Just let us get out undetected. I can see the front door. My fingers turn clammy.

Then we're on the broad gravel drive. Damp, misty air creeps under my fiberglass casts. The breeze snatches at the hem of my nightgown as we hurry to Dad's Range Rover, which is parked under a clump of pine trees. He helps me into the front passenger seat.

Then I remember something.

"My meds," I blurt out. "I forgot."

"Where are they?"

"In my room, on the side table. Three bottles."

"I'll be back."

The moon emerges from beneath a cloud, casting eerie yellow light over the dashboard. *Hurry, please hurry.* I hear footsteps and wrench around.

"Got them." He hops in the driver's seat.

"Good work, Dad."

He puts the car in drive, and the big house shrinks behind us. Guilt twists through me. I'm sure Ian will be glad to hear I've left, though. And now Hunter can come back because I won't be here to bother him.

"I missed you, Peanut," Dad says.

"Thanks for coming to get me. I really missed you, too, Dad."

We're nearing the barn, which gleams silver in the darkness. Its doors are fastened shut. Blaze's presence pulls at me. She'll be bigger now. I want to wrap my arms around her neck and kiss the white star on her forehead and apologize because I have abandoned her these past weeks.

Would she even know me?

I'm silent as we pass the gravel lot. Here and there, tires have dug permanent tracks in its surface. Are any of them mine, remnants from the day I snuck into the barn? The day Hunter caught me from behind, engulfed me in his arms, and pulled me close to ask who the hell was trespassing on his property.

He'd meant it to be threatening. It sure hadn't felt that way. Not even with his warm breath against my ear and his fingers tight under my jaw.

I'm such a fool. I need to stop thinking of him. But I can't stop. It's not like switching off a light. Feelings don't work that way. They linger in the chasms of the heart, welling up without warning, reminding us of the one who was lost.

Dad glances over as he downshifts to take the corner. "How are you doing?"

"Glad to be coming home."

"That makes two of us. Sammy will be excited."

I smile.

Fog swirls in from the left field, heavy as cream in water. The mist catches the front grille and billows around us, locking us in a veil of obscuring white. Dad switches on his high beams. The bright lights create blinding patterns and only manage to tunnel a few feet. Out of nowhere, the gate appears.

Dad brakes and stops ten feet short.

I stare at the place where I was crushed.

The steel bars glide open and we pass through. There's no sign of damage, no remnants of awful gore. It's like nothing happened here. I press my face to the window as they close, watch them gleaming in the Range Rover's taillights.

Then I see it.

The PHOENIX RESEARCH LAB plaque in the middle, the one with the dog—the black Labrador retriever—chasing the pointed-winged bird. It's been cracked in two.

THE FOG TURNS TO MISTING rain. Dad switches on the wipers and follows the twisty road.

"Has there been any news about the investigation?" I ask.

"Not enough."

"Did they catch the bad guys?"

"Not that I've heard. They fled the scene way before the police showed up."

"So there weren't even—like, dead guys?"

"Dead guys? No."

I try to recall that stormy night. I still don't get how Hunter reached me so fast. A vision flashes into my mind—of Hunter lifting the ATV into the air and throwing it at my attackers. But that's ridiculous. No one can lift an eight-hundred-pound vehicle. I can almost smell my blood and hear the shouts around me. Had there been a fight? Had Ian been there, too? And Victoria? I remember a woman's shrill scream before the world went black. Maybe it had been mine. The harder I try to focus on the vision, the faster it slips away.

"They won't come after us again, will they?" I ask.

"I don't see why they would. We have nothing they want."

"No. You're right. We don't."

Vague fear winds around my ribs and cinches tight.

"I've installed a security system in the house. Not that we need it. I just don't want you coming home to any more surprises."

I nod as unease sizzles through me. Iron-fist is out there, and who knows what he wants. The damp chill claims my feet. We fall silent awhile, Dad focusing on the twisty, fog-obscured road.

"Dad, can I ask you something?"

"Sure."

"I heard you and Hunter talking about a woman. Who was she?"

"A woman? No." He keeps his eyes carefully on the road.

"I heard you. You told him you wanted answers about her. That's what you said."

He's silent so long maybe he hopes I'll drop the subject. He'd said a woman. Not Mom, though, because Hunter's too young to have known her. So then, who? The mist blurs the windshield and the wipers slam it away. Over and over. Mist, slam, mist, slam.

"Dad?"

"I'm sorry, Peanut. Whatever you think you heard, you heard wrong."

I stare at him, confused.

He wouldn't lie, would he? Is it possible he's telling the truth? As if to reassure me, he reaches out and squeezes my left hand. I can feel how much he loves me, how much he was worried about me. It's good to have his big hand around mine. Maybe he's right. I've been confused a lot, lately. Maybe this is just one more thing.

WHEN DAD CARRIES ME THROUGH the door, Sammy is all dancing legs and earnest yips. He scrambles after us through Dad-land, past softly gleaming leather and wood scented with lemon polish, and the piano, which I'll get to play whenever I want.

In the guest bedroom Dad sets me down and Sammy bumps into me in all his furry earnestness.

"Oof." I wrap my arms awkwardly around his quivering neck. His fervent affection, despite my abandoning his broken body on the back lawn, makes tears prick at my eyes. "I'm so glad you made it, buddy."

Dad helps me under the covers. My eyes close, and my head drops back. The last thing to cross my mind before dozing off is Victoria and Edward's reaction when they find me gone.

I should've left a note. A thank you, at least.

Turns out I'm no better than Hunter.

A COMMOTION AT THE FRONT DOOR wakes me. Dad's words are drowned out by a woman's high, commanding voice.

"Where is she?"

My eyes fly open. Wan morning light bleeds through the half-shuttered window. Victoria appears in my doorway, surreal and striking in this house. She's wearing a bloodred leather ensemble: a fitted jacket, skintight skirt, and tall boots. Her luminous face is as scary-beautiful as ever.

"Hi," I manage.

Her eyes sear into me. There's an awkward beat.

Finally, I say, "You could wear a Red Cross hat with that."

"A Red Cross hat."

"Yes. A leather one."

"Do you have any idea of the scare you gave us?"

"I figured it was better this way."

"You're coming back with me. Now."

I pluck at the covers. "No, Victoria, I'm not."

She stalks to my bedside and sorts through my medication. "Did you take the red pills?"

"Not yet."

She shakes two out and thrusts a half-empty glass of water into my hand. I swallow them with the tepid liquid.

"You can't stay here. It's too dangerous."

"I'm perfectly safe, and there's no way you're dragging me back."

She rubs her face and I know she's worried. I sense it, faintly, stirring through me.

"I'm sorry. I should have left a note. I've been a huge burden on you guys, and you've done enough. I'm really all right now. And I'm hugely grateful. If I haven't told you that, I am. I mean it."

Arms crossed, Victoria studies the bookshelf. It's vacant apart from my violin case. She touches the clasp. Emotions jangle beneath her hard surface. It's clear my words have touched her, but not enough to ease the jarring pings of worry. So the linked effect has returned. Not that I'm about to tell her.

She paces to the dresser and picks up what appears to be a letter in a heavy envelope.

"I'm surprised you're getting mail here. This isn't your actual residence, is it?"

"Let me see that."

She hands it over, and then it all comes rushing back to me. My application to the music company. All else is forgotten as I tear it open.

Dear Ms. Aeris Thorne,
APPLAUSE has reviewed your application. We'd like to see you in person. We have an interview slot at 3:00 p.m. on July 22. Please call or e-mail to confirm your availability. Our offices are located in Hartford, CT, at the address listed above.
Sincerely,
Nathan Biggs, CEO

"I can't believe this! They want me to come for an interview."

"Who?"

"A movie sound track company." I glance at the address again. "In Hartford."

Victoria's smooth brow creases. "How did they find you?"

"I was recommended. I applied."

"When do they want you there?"

I'm so dizzy with excitement that for a moment I'd forgotten my injuries. "Two weeks."

"That's not going to work."

She's right. Still, I say, "Are you out of your mind? No way am I turning this down."

"Tell them you'll come later. In a few months."

"It doesn't work that way. They won't wait. It's everything I've ever dreamed of. I have to go." And I realize now it's the truth. I'm going, casts and all.

"Let me see that." She snatches the letter with her willowy fingers and studies it. I wait for her reply, but she sets it down as if the subject never came up.

"You need to come back to the PRL. I can't keep you safe here."

"I'm not coming back, Victoria. I'm sorry."

She walks nervously to the window, twitches the blinds, and peers out.

"I'm right down the road. I'll call you if I get sick, promise."

"I don't know how to convince you. You're not my prisoner. Please, stay inside, take your meds, focus on getting better. I'm trusting you."

"Tell Edward and Lucy good-bye?"

She gives me a curt nod. As I hear her give Dad the wheelchair we abandoned in the PRL's front hall, it dawns on me that although she came, she knew I wouldn't be going back.

WHEN SHE'S GONE, I MAKE Dad sit next to me on the four-poster bed.

"I want to know about Mom."

"What can I tell you?" His black beard has grown back out, half hiding his face.

Dad and I never talk about her, so it's a struggle. It comes out in a rush. "I was thinking about the accident in Switzerland. Victoria told me the PRL has a branch there. I know this is a long shot, but is there any chance Mom was connected to the research lab?"

He stiffens.

"Have you looked into it?"

"She kept her work from me, Peanut. You know we weren't living together."

Before I can stop myself, I say, "Was I a mistake? Didn't you love each other?"

"Of course we loved each other." He's gruff. "But she had a lot going on, and we agreed it would be better to live separately. Until she was ready."

I feel hurt and anger rising. I've kept it down too long. "What was more important than us being a family?"

"There are times when life isn't that simple."

My anger turns white hot. Everyone has been putting me off and putting me off, and I won't stand for it.

"What aren't you telling me, Dad? I'm not going to sit here and listen to you claim you're in the dark. Because you're not. You're hiding things from me. You have no right. She was *my* mom. She would have wanted me to know, and I resent you trying to protect me! I won't be shoved away any longer. What happened to her belongs just as much to me as it does to you. More! I was the one who lived with her. I was the one she kept by her side. I was in the car, not you. I was with her when she died."

Dad stands abruptly. It's clear I've wounded him. How could I suggest Mom loved me more when I know how heartbroken he was over her death? He's never loved another woman since. But I'm furious. Beyond furious.

"Your mother loved you more than anything. And if I ever learn the truth of what happened to you two that day, I promise you'll be the first to know."

I hear his brutal honesty. Am I being paranoid, believing he has answers that don't exist?

"Wait, Dad?" He's already angry, so what's one more thing? "I went through your desk. I found—"

"You went through my desk? Really, Aeris? Why?"

"I found Mom's photo album." My voice breaks. "Did you ever think I might want to see those pictures, too?"

He rubs his head and blows out a sigh. "I shouldn't have kept it in there. You're right. You should have it. I'll bring it to you."

DAD'S AT THE SHOP. I sit near the piano in the wheelchair and open the photo album. My forehead scrunches as I study the one of Mom and her dog. An odd sensation tugs at me, as though a message is staring up at me, yet I can't quite puzzle it out.

Then my breath catches. I examine the black Labrador in the crate, looking cute in his red bandanna. It's a lot like the dog on the PRL plaque. The one on the front gate. The logo. The dog chasing a phoenix. A Labrador dog, with a bandanna around its neck.

No. It's a coincidence. It has to be.

The journal is still there. I open it and ponder her cryptic words. *Doctors are not meant to play God.* Was it also a coincidence that Hunter had said nearly the same thing?

Was there a link here?

I touch her pen strokes.

Is it possible the PRL and Hunter's research are part of Mom's legacy? Could I be alive because of her work?

Images come in flashes. Symbols of regeneration. The painted butterflies on the domed ceiling in the operating room. The caterpillars and cocoons bursting with life. The fiery bird that the lab is named after. The phoenix that dies and comes back to life.

Just like I heard Ian claim I did.

Was I dead on that operating table until Hunter intervened?

If Mom had somehow been involved in uncovering a key to human regeneration, and her legacy is still under way at the PRL, it explains why Iron-fist is so desperate to break into the facility. Yet it's not perfect. Far from it.

I haven't allowed myself to think of my frightening episode in Hunter's study, yet now it rushes into me in all its pain and horror. What if what I felt from him was real? What if somehow, by some inexplicable force, I did sense him? What if whatever he did to heal me is contagious and I infected him and that's why he left? Because he's sick? A cold bubble of worry breaks over my skin.

The ringing phone yanks me from my reverie.

I roll into the kitchen and read the caller ID.
Gage.
After a moment's hesitation, I pick up.
"Hello?"
"I heard you were back. Want a visitor?"

TWENTY-TWO

IT'S GOOD TO HEAR GAGE's friendly voice on the line.

"Word gets around quick," I say.

"Small town, you're the big excitement. Well, at least for me and Ella." I can hear his grin. "So what do you say?"

"I look pretty funky."

"I can manage funky."

"Don't say I didn't warn you. Okay, yes. Come over. That would be nice."

"I'm ten minutes away. Need anything?"

"Nope. Just knock."

I wait at the piano, playing one-handed and fretting over the call I made earlier to Applause before I could get cold feet. I spoke to a woman. She confirmed my interview. I'm going. I promised I'd be there.

The knock comes, two long, three short, and I burst out laughing. I can't remember the last time I heard that.

"Coming!" I shout, and trundle to the door. With my good hand, I fumble with the lock and then wheel myself back a few feet. "It's open."

His blond head peeks around the corner. He's wearing a big grin and carrying a grocery bag.

"Thanks for dressing up," he says.

I'm wearing what fits over my casts: flannel boxers and an oversize T-shirt that reads I'LL BE BACH. "Yeah, no problem. Took me hours," I joke. "What's in the bag?"

"Stuff."

"Sounds good. Want to sit in the kitchen?"

"Lead the way."

The bag contains a pack of playing cards, two supersized Mars bars, a box of powdered doughnuts, and a six-pack of ginger ale. Summer fort food. "Nice," I tell him. "Except for one thing. I still don't play poker."

"Good enough. War or Crazy Eights? You remember those, right?"

I laugh.

We're halfway through a fierce game when he says, "I sure am glad you made it."

"Really? 'Cause I'm about to beat you," I tease.

"I'm serious. I just wish you would've gone to a hospital, instead of letting those freaks take care of you."

"Freaks?" I freeze. "That's pretty harsh, Gage. They saved my life."

He rips a fresh can from the six-pack, pops the tab, and stares at it as froth bubbles up through the hole.

"I was unconscious. It's not like I had a choice. But even if I did, there wasn't time. I would've bled to death waiting for an ambulance."

"You could have been airlifted," he says.

"There's no way."

"They sure have you convinced."

"I was there!"

"How do you know they weren't exaggerating? Maybe they didn't want you going to a hospital. Ever think of that?"

I gape at him. "That's ridiculous! Look at me. It's not like I needed a few stitches. I was hurt. Badly."

He twists and untwists a used candy wrapper, worrying it into a knot. When I can take it no longer, I snare it from him and stuff it in the empty grocery bag.

"Did it ever occur to you," he asks, "that your accident could have given them the perfect chance to do a little human research?"

"No," I lie.

"You were there for four weeks. Why didn't they send you to a hospital after the initial emergency was over?"

Blood thumps in my temples. "Let's just play, all right?"

He sips his drink and draws a card. His words have hit home, though. The game ends in a tie. I watch him shuffle the cards in silence.

"Gage?"

He glances up, his cornflower-blue eyes brooding beneath his scruffy blond hair.

"What exactly happened to you in the military?"

His mouth opens. I guess it's the last thing he's expecting.

"Maybe it's none of my business," I say. "I just—"

"No—I'll tell you. I want you to know." Gage shoves his thick hand through his hair. He glances out at the sea, cracking his knuckles. "A group of us got in trouble doing something stupid. We were goofing off—it's not important what we did. But we got sentenced to six months' confinement. There was this medical trial no one wanted to enter, so they gave us the choice: Be guinea pigs for three weeks or serve time. We took the three weeks."

"Is that normal?"

"Definitely not. It came up in the hearing later—but at this point we were a bunch of idiots who saw an easy way out."

"So the military does medical trials?"

"It was run by a private contractor. You might've heard of them. Blackbird?"

"I suppose, in the news, I guess. What do they do, exactly?"

"They're basically an army for hire. They're real bastards. The government calls them in to do its dirty work. They have a huge training facility four hours away. And this weapons factory that you wouldn't believe."

"What do they make?"

Gage's bulging shoulders are hunched, and the muscles are working in his jaw. He puts his head in his hands and mutters, "You name it. Custom tanks, dirty weapons, surveillance, robotics. That's not the worst of it, though." He meets my eyes. "The CEO has a special interest in humans."

"What do you mean, humans? How do you develop humans?" As soon as the words slip from my mouth, a creepy sensation rushes over my body.

"Resistance to biological weapons and diseases? That's one way. It gets a lot nastier, though. These freaks are trying to build human supersoldiers."

"You mean, like, making people artificially stronger or something?"

"Yeah. That plus a whole lot of other transhuman mutant shit. Subdermal armor. Robotic implants. Body mods so people punch harder. Run faster. Jump higher. Mods to make them drink less, eat less so they can survive where other people can't. Brain links so they can control soldiers like it's a video game. With retinal cameras embedded in their eyeballs. That way generals can move them around without endangering their own precious hides."

"That's insane. Are you serious?"

"Deadly."

Gage hasn't told me about his own trial, though. Were they exposed to a biological agent? Is that what killed his brother? Or had Gage been . . . modified? Without meaning to, my eyes roam over his shoulders, down his arms to his hands. He looks normal. Strong, yes, but . . .

"You know what," Gage says, forcing my gaze up to his. "On second thought, I don't really want to discuss this."

"Sorry. I shouldn't have asked." But I'm dying to know.

"It's fine. I guess I'm just not ready to talk about it."

"Can you tell me this? Is what happened connected to Hunter Cayman? Was he involved?"

"He was there. I saw him there, Aeris."

"Where? Are you saying you saw Dr. Cayman at Blackbird during the experiment?"

Gage nods.

My heart crawls into my throat.

"And then, a couple of months ago, I saw Blackbird's CEO up at the PRL. He flew there in his helicopter. I was standing on my dock. I saw him land. I watched him get out."

"How did you see that far? Did you have binoculars?" I say.

Or was it just like you seemed to see me that day Hunter and I rode along the cliff top?

He ignores my question. "You want to know why I don't trust Cayman? Because he's in cahoots with Blackbird's CEO. Brewster King. The criminal who killed my little brother."

The *beep-beep-beep* of my noon dosage alarm jolts us both. I fumble for it and quickly switch it off.

"Something important?" Gage asks.

"No! Not at all," I say, too bright. "It's nothing."

Although Victoria cautioned me numerous times on the importance of taking my medication exactly at noon, I keep playing cards. Ian's words ring in my mind. *Promise me one thing. Take your meds. Religiously, exactly as directed.*

I have to get Gage out of here. But maybe, after all he's said, I don't want to take them.

And if I don't?

"Victory!" Gage says, and I realize he's won.

"Well played," I tell him. "I'm kind of tired. I should—"

He leaps up. "Right, sorry, I should have asked. Let me help you to your room."

"You don't have to do that."

"You sure? Let me take you there."

"No, really, Gage. I'm good."

"Okay." His face registers disappointment. At the door, he bends, gingerly places his arms around my neck, and kisses my cheek. It's sweet and I can't help wishing he created sparks in me the way Hunter did. He's a good guy. Safe. Reliable as a brother.

When he's gone, I hurry to the guest room and grab the large bottle with the heavy silver pills. The clock reads 12:25. Are these things truly safe?

I picture Victoria. And kind Edward and Lucy. No way would they hurt me. I'm alive because of Hunter. He might have left, but he saved my life. On the operating table, he'd pressed his warm forehead to mine and begged me to return to him. And I did.

The pills plink against one another as I shake one out. Round and weighty, it presses into my palm. I meet my frightened hazel eyes in its brilliant surface. A nervous flutter thrums in my stomach.

I don't know what Hunter's connection to Blackbird is. I can't help thinking Gage read it all wrong. It's true that when Hunter left, he hurt me deeply, and there's no excusing it. Gage believes he's evil. I just can't, though. He wouldn't have done terrible experiments on me.

One thing I know for certain: In the barn with Blaze, I felt goodness in Hunter's soul. He hadn't been acting. It had been real.

I place the pill on my tongue, tilt my head back, and let it tumble down my throat.

Oh, Hunter, what's going on?

I close my eyes and batter myself with the memory of his rough cheek against mine, of the gentle words he whispered in my ear, of the protective hands that fought to save my life. Then I hold my ache close, because it's all I have left of him.

As the afternoon wears on, I haul myself carefully into bed. I'm exhausted. Ocean-scented air creeps through the open window. An occasional breeze flutters the curtain and caresses my face. An emerald butterfly wends its way in and flits about the room. It comes to rest on the bookshelf.

Pain flares in my right arm. Letting out an involuntary cry, I clench it with my good hand. Searing heat rips through every limb, and I double over. It's happening again, the scorching horror of the hospital. I'm burning. A throbbing, raw hell that nothing can stop except death. I rip at my casts, desperate to be free of them, certain my skin is dissolving underneath. My back twists in an arch, and my head thrashes against the pillow.

"Stop," I beg. "Stop it."

Sweat drenches my hair. I curl onto my side, shuddering in fear. My belly is clenched so hard it feels as though I've done a thousand sit-ups. Is something wrong with the drugs? Or is it because I was late taking the silver pill?

"Someone, help me," I whisper.

From out of the void, there comes a response. A rapid, distant stirring. Arms, tendrils of arms, reaching toward my heart.

The pain lessens, but only briefly. It erupts again, pulling me under. Terrified, I ride out wave after wave. After what feels like hours, the attacks grow farther apart and finally cease.

Spent, I lie panting and stare at the white ceiling.

I have to call Victoria.

I fumble for the phone and stop. She'll take me back to the lab.

I can't do it.

Sammy's erratic trot makes a beeline my way. He lumbers up to me and presses his damp nose against my hand. His velvet ears move like radar dishes, alive with worry as if verifying I'm safe. To my embarrassment, I blink back a pathetic tear.

"How did you know I needed you?" I whisper.

He puts his chin on the bed, and I lean my head next to his.

"You're a good boy," I tell him.

Could the timing of the pill really be that critical? Or am I experiencing some buildup of the meds, and the timing was simply coincidental? I wipe my good hand on the sheets. I don't ever want to go through that horror again. It will turn me insane. No one emerges from hell without eventually paying the price. They'll have to commit me. Will I have to fear this always? Will I have to take the meds forever?

If I was hurt badly a second time, I'm not sure I could go through with it. People who are burned at the stake die within hours. Maybe minutes. I don't know. But the bonfire tore at my body for weeks.

I love life. More than anything.

Yet given the choice, I couldn't brave the horror I went through at the PRL again.

I would choose death instead.

I STRUGGLE INTO THE WHEELCHAIR AND head straight for the piano. I need to wipe the fear from my mind. It's close to four when Ella shows up. I'm so glad to see her I practically suffocate her with my heavy casts as I give her a hug.

Her cheeks dimple in a broad grin. "Good to see you, too. You don't look nearly as bad as I thought you would."

I laugh. "I'm calling it plaster chic."

"Ha!" She laughs. "I never noticed you had such good skin. You're all kinds of glowy."

"Am I?" I put my fingers to my cheek. Come to think of it, my skin does feel different. Smoother.

"You sure Cayman didn't comp you a little cosmetic treatment while you were out? Laser peel?"

"Not that I know of."

"Can you imagine? That would be funny."

We head into the living room. I hadn't given my skin much thought, but she's right. Could it be a side effect of the drugs? A good one, yes, but is it the only one? Sweat prickles under my arms. No, of course not. There are the flames. The pain. What if it comes again? What if I have those attacks for the rest of my life?

"So I told my mom I'd get her the same one. Can't you just see her with it?"

"I'm sorry, I just drifted off there for a second. What are you getting your mom?"

Ella laughs. "Never mind. It's boring."

"It's not! Sorry. I'm out of it today."

She slides her hands under her jeans-clad legs and leans forward, eyes shining. "So give me the dirt. What happened with you and Dr. Cayman?"

"Uh . . ."

A brisk, salty breeze rattles the half-open sliding-glass door. Her heart-shaped face is expectant.

"What's he like?"

"I didn't really see much of him."

"Seriously? That's too bad." She sits back. "It's funny. Even though I said you weren't his type, I got this weird feeling that day we drove past him in my car. I got this vibe like something was going on between you two. You were so tense and he was—it's not like he stared at you; it's more like he was trying not to."

Outside, the damp greenery has grown so lush from all the rain that plants are crushing one another. I'm tempted to spill all of it and cry on Ella's shoulder. Maybe it would feel good to talk.

"You read him wrong," I say.

"Bummer. He's cute. Correction, not cute. Hot. Seriously hot."

"Yeah, he is. . . . too bad he's not my type."

"That whole type business is ridiculous. It's not about that. You never know who you might like. Sometimes a guy asks you out, and you go. Maybe you have an okay time, so you decide to go on another date. After a while, you're a couple."

"I don't think I ever want to date a guy until I get used to him."

"That's not what I'm saying."

"It's what happened with me and Trey. Which is why we didn't work out. I want a guy who makes my heart pound from the first moment I see him. I want his voice, when he speaks my name for the first time, to make my knees tremble. I want him to see me the way I'm seeing him, like a revelation, like our whole lives have led up to this moment."

"Who wouldn't?" Ella says. "Unfortunately, that only happens in romance novels and fairy tales."

THE NEXT FEW DAYS ARE spent between the piano and my laptop, punctuated by daily visits from Ella and Gage. There's a large Wikipedia entry on Blackbird detailing its rise to power and its link to various military scandals. The company's like a cockroach—it just shakes off trouble and moves on. Reports of Gage's medical trials are small and vague.

I search for Brewster King, the CEO Gage mentioned. The guy has done an amazing job of staying under the radar—I can't even find a photograph. Another search that leads nowhere is for a link between Blackbird and Hunter Cayman.

Mom's journal and the questions about Switzerland has sparked fresh interest in me, as well. I wonder if it's worth tracking down people she went to school with. I could get a class roster from her college days. And what about the company she worked at? I know Dad tracked down her old coworkers years ago but didn't learn anything that led to answers. Is it worth revisiting them? What if she was doing freelance work on the side? Had those people been contacted? Who were her mentors, if any? I know the man who attacked us knew her.

But how?

His words have echoed over and over in me, down through the years.

I wish you'd behaved more professionally, Julia.

What had he meant?

I pick up the journal and read it for what feels like the hundredth time. A tiny memory comes to me. It could be nothing. Then again . . . it was about butterflies. She'd told me about them in detail, their life stages. How they regenerated. She'd been obsessed with them. She even kept a small collection of them in her lab. Wait—she'd kept live ones. I jerk upright as I recall them flying around in a glassed-in room. Was that real or my four-year-old imagination at work?

Whatever the case, there's no online record of her and such a lab existing.

I'm hunched over my laptop when I get the distinct feeling I'm being watched. I bolt upright and wrench around. My door is open. The hairs stand up on my arms. I wheel quickly toward the hall. Empty. My skin vibrates with the certainty that I'm not alone. I tour the whole house, yanking open closets, peering behind curtains and under tables. Not a soul.

In the guest room, I go to the blinds and twitch them aside the way Victoria had the day she visited. Feeling trapped and defenseless in my wheelchair, I squint at the apple orchard where Iron-fist hid his SUV.

It must be the light, because I can see every single leaf in clear detail. Green and vibrant and laced with veins. Was my vision always this good? Maybe it's the strong sunlight after weeks of gloomy storm clouds that's making the world so clear. Or maybe . . . it's like my skin.

I rub my forehead. Regardless, I don't see anyone hiding out there. No metallic reflections behind the trees. So then why do I feel like eyeballs are drilling into my neck?

The sensation of being watched looms all day. The next day, too. Maybe I'm being paranoid. Dad had said Iron-fist was monitoring him before their attack. Did that include surveillance inside the house? Could they have taken fresh interest now that I'm here with the meds?

I search my room for hidden cameras. I search the whole house. I've heard they can be tiny and undetectable. No matter where I look, I can't find the source of my suspicions.

TWENTY-THREE

It's shortly after eleven in the morning when Ella and Gage show up.

"A double visit? Awesome," I say.

"We're taking you on a mini getaway," Ella announces.

"Really?" I rub my dirty hair. I've run out of oversize T-shirts and boxers and am wearing a white knee-length nightshirt decorated with black music notes over underpants. Oh, for the days when I can pull on a pair of jeans again. "Forget it. It's one thing to have you guys here, but I don't want to scare the rest of the world."

"You look great," Gage insists. "You're injured; so what? It happens."

"Anyway," Ella says, "We're taking you out in the boat. You won't see anyone. It'll be good for you to get some air. Liven you up."

"Sounds tempting." I recall Victoria's warning to stay inside and get better. To be honest, I'm not sure what staying inside has to do with it. Edward took me out to the gardens at the PRL and I haven't enjoyed the outdoors since. That can't be healthy. Besides, I'd love to escape this sensation of being watched.

"What do you say? Come on," Ella urges.

I cave. "Let me just call my dad and tell him."

The phone in the shop goes to voice mail. He must be busy with customers.

"I'll leave him a note."

Thirty minutes later, we're on the dock. Ella and I laugh as Gage carries me onto his boat, joking about pirates and lasses in plaster casts and billowing nightshirts.

From my position on the cushioned bench seat, I watch them toss off ropes and push away from shore. They're right. It's good to get out in the open. My eyes find the cliff that belongs to the PRL. The small section where Hunter and I rode along the top appears deserted. The longing I thought I'd overcome rises hot and painful.

I turn and focus on the surging green ocean.

The engine roars to life. I need this escape.

Ella whoops and grins at me as the twenty-foot cruiser powers away from shore. Under the open sky, the breeze rushes through my hair. The boat flies seaward, cresting and falling over the whitecaps. In the distance, the dock shrinks rapidly until it disappears into the rocky shoreline.

Gage shoots me a smile, and my lips curve up of their own accord.

The sea begins to rip away the past weeks. Even my casts feel lighter until I'm barely aware of them. A pod of dolphins springs out of the ocean. We shout, and Gage steers closer. They're all glossy and spinning and chattering away. They disappear into their secret underworld and we race farther on, chased by cormorants and flashes of silver herring. Stretching farther and farther from Deep Cove until its choking chains snap and fall away.

A town appears in the distance, perched along the shoreline. From here, the buildings look like toy models. Gage's cheeks are ruddy as he motions at it with his head.

"There's a great fish-and-chip place over there. We can pull up with the boat and get food to go. Want to?"

"Sure. Sounds great."

Gage aims the boat shoreward.

Three feet from the starboard rail, an ash-white seabird coasts alongside the boat. It turns to probe me with its shiny black eyes. From the pilot's chair, an alarm starts to beep.

Worry jerks me upright. It reminds me of my own alarm. The one that tells me to take my pills.

"What's that beeping?" Ella asks.

I glance up at the bright afternoon sun. I don't have to look at the time to know it's well past noon. Probably closer to one thirty or two. The alarm continues to beep. A sickening sensation slithers into my belly.

"We're passing over a reef," Gage says. He flicks a switch, and the alarm goes silent.

I lick my lips, which have gone bone-dry. How could I have forgotten to bring my silver pill after what happened? "We should head back."

He eases off the throttle. "What about lunch? Are you getting seasick?"

"No! No, I'm fine. I just—I changed my mind."

"Come on, Aeris," Ella says. "Lunch won't take that long. And we can get it to go if you're so worried about people seeing you."

"Wait, let her be," Gage says. "What's going on Aeris? Is something wrong?"

"I forgot my medicine. How long will it take to get back?"

"An hour if I gun it. Do you want me to?"

My hands are icy slick. An hour? At this point, it's already way too late.

Maybe what happened last time I was late taking my silver pill was a coincidence. In fact, it's been more than two hours and I'm perfectly fine. No flames. No heat. If anything, I'm a little chilly. Yes, it was definitely a coincidence. The attack happened only minutes after I took my dosage. In fact, it could have been the dosage itself that caused it.

I'd be sick by now, wouldn't I?

I feel free out here. I don't want to go back yet. I chew on my lower lip. On the other hand, what if it was because I'd been late taking it? Ian and Victoria had been so insistent that I follow the dosage rules. I rub my face.

"I hate to be a downer, but I need to go home."

The white bird cries out and banks over the waves. It spears a fish, and the fish wiggles desperately to get free. I watch the bird wheel off. It heads for land, for some hidden nest where it can devour its prey in privacy.

THE TREMOR BEGINS IN MY right hand. Shaking overtakes my fingers. Ella is talking. I smile at her and clench them to make them stop.

White heat explodes behind my eyelashes. Convulsions rip through me. My arms and legs hammer wildly, sending me tumbling out of my seat, scattering cushions until my flailing casts are hammering against the fiberglass deck. Frantic, I open my mouth in agony. Hellfire licks at my brain. My scream is so hot it turns the air into billows of scorching mist.

Ella is screaming, too. "Oh my god! Call 911! What's happening to her? Call 911!"

The world becomes a blur of whining engine noise, a wild slamming place as the boat crashes over crest after crest. Wailing sirens and blinding flashes of red light rip through my distorted consciousness.

An ambulance.

The shore.

People.

Gage's huge hands restrain me, carrying me to land.

"Careful with her," he barks at the four medics it takes to strap me to the gurney.

Sweat pours from every inch of my body. Crowds press in and I can't breathe.

"Get away," I beg.

The ambulance walls close around me. The door slams shut and we're off, wailing and careening in a van of beeping equipment. *Medicine.* The word flares. *Medicine!* I force my heavy eyes wide and struggle to focus on the faces around me. Something creepy is going on. The people are not normal. They look alien and strange. I curl away in revulsion.

There he is—Gage—the one who can help. He's beside me. Why are his features all wrong? Ugly and horrifying. A wild impulse to attack sends my arms lurching for his throat. The restraints check my assault. I sob in frustration.

What am I doing? It's Gage! My friend.

"Hang on." He squeezes my arm. "We're almost at the hospital."

"I need my medicine." Sweat pours from my scalp. "My medicine!"

"They'll know what to do."

"No! It's in my room. Dad knows. Please!" I gasp. "I need my medicine!"

It's like a mantra. Over and over I repeat the words, crying, wailing, whispering, pleading. Down the streets. Across the emergency unloading area. Through the antiseptic hallways filled with monster-faced patients and brutish alien workers with hungry eyes. What has happened to the world? Why has everyone turned to demons? Or have they all been this way and I never noticed?

The gurney flies through a pair of double doors. I thrash hard, my body on fire, my mind clenched with the need to attack.

A woman, white-masked, bends over me. I bare my teeth at her, growling.

"This should calm you down."

The needle pierces my belly. I sink away from her into a dim, raging hole of fire.

A COOL, FAMILIAR HAND TOUCHES MY forehead. I sigh into it, filled with impressions of comfort and home. My eyes flutter open and Dad's mountain-man face peers into mine.

"Feeling better?"

I dry swallow. "Much." Then I bolt upright. "My medicine."

"I gave it to you an hour ago."

"The silver one? How did you know?"

His tone is vague. "The instructions on the label."

How much does he know about my cure? Because more than ever, I'm certain it's not normal. "What did the doctor say about me?" I ask, studying his reaction.

"You had a high fever and a blood test came back showing low glucose levels. She said either of those could have caused your seizures. She put you on a glucose drip and is thinking about antibiotics, but your fever's down. She thinks it was probably the shock of being out in the boat, combined with too little to eat. Right now, she's keeping you under observation."

He gives no sign of suspecting anything beyond that.

Then again, he did give me the silver pill. "What do you think, Dad?"

"I think I'm worried as hell. I wish you hadn't gone out on that boat."

My head flops back. "I'm sorry, Dad. I'm sorry if I scared you."

He squeezes my hand.

"I'm freaked out," I whisper. "I'm scared about the drugs I'm taking."

"I am, too, Peanut. As soon as you're out of here, we're making a visit to the PRL."

So he does know Hunter's methods were unorthodox. I can see it in his face.

"Maybe we should talk to the doctor," I whisper.

The color drains from his cheeks. "No. Hunter warned against you seeing a doctor. He said they might take you off your meds, and that could cause serious problems." His voice is low, urgent. "I'm sorry, I almost lost you a few weeks ago. Hunter has medicines that aren't exactly in the public domain. You wouldn't be here without him. I want us to go there tomorrow before we decide anything further."

All this time we've been hiding our knowledge from each other.

Movement catches my eye, and I glance out the door of the sterile hospital room to see Gage and Ella in the hall. Their faces no longer resemble scary monster masks. They simply look concerned. Whatever happened to me clearly twisted my vision into insanity.

Tentatively, Gage steps inside. "You okay, Aeris?"

"Yeah. Turns out I just needed a shot of sugar."

"Jesus, Aeris," Ella says. "You scared me shitless."

"I scared myself," I reply.

The hospital bustle resounds through the half-open door: loudspeaker announcements, carts wheeling past, the squeaky shoes of nurses.

"Can we go home?" I ask Dad.

His face is grim. "They want to keep you overnight for observation."

Dread creeps over me, shortening my breath. "Dad," I whisper, "I need to get out of here."

"I know. It's easier this way. It's only until tomorrow."

"I'll stay with you," Gage volunteers.

"No," Dad says. "I'll do that myself. Better get your boat back. It'll be getting dark."

At six, after a horrible meal of powdered mashed potatoes and dry chicken, I banish Dad to the cafeteria.

"You should probably get something to eat, too," I tell him.

He nods. "I won't be long."

I'm left with the pinging of strange machines and sheets that smell of vinegar and bleach.

With him gone, my mind flashes back to my monstrous hallucinations. Gage and Ella had looked inhuman. Grotesque. Like hideous bogeymen. I'd wanted to attack them, kill them. What had come over me? What if it happens again? I could hurt someone I care about. Like Dad or Sammy.

With nervous hands, I crumple and uncrumple the covers until they're damp with sweat.

From the hallway, heavy boots blend in with the patter of orthopedic footwear. I quail under a sudden fear that Iron-fist has come after me. What if he's tracked me here, to this bed? Waited for Dad to leave the room so he could get me alone?

The footsteps carry on past my door.

My muscles unclench, and clammy sweat drips down my ribs. I'm exhausted, bone deep. I stay awake long enough for Dad to return and then nod off into a numb, dreamless sleep.

The sound of low, urgent voices tugs me awake. I blink in the dim light of dawn and see Gage and Dad in the light of the doorway. I fumble for my red pills, gulp them down, and hide the bag back under my hoodie.

"What's happening?" I ask, rubbing the sleep from my eyes.

"The store's on fire," Dad says. "Firefighters are working to put it out."

I recoil at the grisly news. "On fire?"

Gage says, "I came right away so your Dad could go back."

"Dad, hurry—what are you waiting for?"

His hands are in fists. "I'm not comfortable leaving you."

"Gage can take me home. The police need you there. Go."

He mauls his neck, haggard with shock.

"I'm serious, Dad, go. What about Sammy? What if something's happened to him?"

192

He nods once. "All right. You'll only be here for another hour or two. They said they'd release you when the doctor comes in around seven. I told them Gage is a relative. He'll be able to stay in the room."

He kisses my forehead, and then he's gone.

"Don't look at me like I'm some wretched casualty," I tell Gage.

"I wasn't."

"You were and it's unnerving. I'm just injured, temporarily. I'm still me. Still the same person." *I hope.*

"Duh, of course you are. Even if your hair *is* a little greasier than usual."

I roll my eyes. "Great, thanks, that makes me feel so much better."

"Here," he says. "Move over."

"What are you doing?" I say on a laugh.

"Joining the team."

"Ow, hey!" I say as he shifts me over a few inches and lies down on his back next to me.

"Boy, they don't exactly make these beds comfortable, do they?"

"That's because you don't fit."

"And what are these sheets made of? Small-grit sandpaper?"

"Stop it," I say. "Someone's going to come!"

"You're right." He puts a finger to my lips.

I snort and let my head flop back onto the pillow. We stare at the ceiling in silence.

"You really freaked me out yesterday." His voice is uneven.

"Hey, I thought you were joining my team."

"I'm trying to, Aeris." He shifts so he's looking down at me. Then his stubble is grazing my lips and his mouth is pressed against mine.

For a moment, I'm so caught off guard I'm motionless.

His familiar, callused hands weave into my hair, and his chest presses down against mine. I can feel his pulse slamming. This is Gage, my best friend. And this is all wrong. I struggle away, afraid—not of him but of the hurt I'll see in his cornflower-blue eyes.

It's why I've desperately tried to keep this moment from ever occurring.

"Gage, stop. Gage!" The words are crushed against his lips, and my indignation is rising. Hurt be damned, I don't want this. With my casts, it's hard to get my arms in position to push. I do, finally, and shove at his chest. It's rock hard, like flesh over steel armor.

"Stop it. Quit it!"

He jerks back. I don't say a word, because he's reading it all in my eyes. His face flushes. He slumps away from me, head falling onto the pillow, one muscular arm thrown over his face.

"Sorry."

"Look, you're one of my best friends. You know how much you mean to me. It would kill me to lose you. I just—I don't want that."

The arm stays in place. Is he mad?

"I don't want to lose you, either," he murmurs.

His voice is thick. He can't possibly be . . . crying, can he? I want to comfort him. Instead, I pluck at the dirty edges of my fiberglass cast where it's gone all jagged.

From the doorway comes the sound of a woman clearing her throat. An unfamiliar doctor stands there dressed in a green shower-cap-style hat and shoe coverings. Her arms are crossed and her lips compressed.

Gage slides out of the bed, shoves his hands in his pockets, but remains next to me.

"Hi, Doctor," I say, acting like she didn't just see us kissing. "I'm ready to get signed out."

She gestures at someone in the hall. Wheels creak outside the doorway, and then two aides step inside, pushing a gurney. That's odd. Maybe the wheelchairs are all in use? It'll be kind of strange to get pushed out to Gage's truck on that thing.

"I just need a minute to change out of my hospital gown."

"That won't be necessary," the doctor says, coming to fuss over me with her stethoscope.

"What do you mean?" I ask, laughing. "I'm not wearing this thing home."

She fails to smile. "We need to perform a few more tests."

"What are you talking about? I'm supposed to leave."

"I've been ordered to perform a series of labs."

"By who?"

"I received a call from the authorities, and I have to follow up."

"What authorities?" I demand, my voice harsh to hide my concern.

"I'm not at liberty to discuss that."

I glance at Gage. His cheeks are pink. Is it a hangover from our kiss or something more? A few days ago, he'd practically ordered me to visit a regular doctor to make sure I was all right. I'd refused. I recall his awful stint in the military. Could he be suspicious enough of Hunter to have contacted one of the investigators on their case?

I stare at him. *Can't he just be happy I'm alive?*

"Who did you call?" I say.

There's a beat.

I'm suddenly furious. "Gage?"

"No one. But I'm glad someone did. They *should* check you out."

"I don't want to be checked out. I thought you were on my team. You told my dad you'd take me home!"

"And I will. God, Aeris, I'm on your side."

I turn to the doctor. "How did these authorities hear about me? Did they just call you out of the blue?"

"We file reports on all patients in a central database. Your name was flagged as a person of interest. You're the woman who crashed outside the Phoenix Research Lab for Highly Contagious Diseases, correct?" She emphasizes the words *contagious diseases.* "Apparently the PRL falls within some governmental jurisdiction. The government has the right to do some checking up."

"I'm not giving you permission for this. You have no legal right."

The two aides strong-arm me onto the gurney. With an ominous clank, bars rise into place so that I can't roll off.

"I was told I could go home. I'm a free person, a citizen. You need my permission before you do any extra tests."

"Not when the order comes from a higher authority. You're being investigated as a public health risk."

"A public health risk? That's absurd. Who's this authority?"

She sighs. "If you don't want me to perform the tests, you're free to talk to my contact. However, I guarantee he'll simply repeat what I've told you. Is there some reason you don't want to cooperate?"

"I need to call my dad. Right now."

His phone rings and rings. I try three times. A fourth. Still no answer.

"Aeris." Gage puts his hand on mine. "His store is on fire."

My hair is sticking to my forehead. I swipe it away and dry swallow.

"It's your call. What do you want me to do, Miss Thorne?" the doctor says. "I think you're overreacting. These tests are for your own good."

Maybe she's right. Maybe they are. Despite what Dad said earlier, it's not my job to keep things secret.

If only I'd taken the silver pill on time. If only I'd never come to this hospital. If only I knew what Hunter did to me. He should have told me.

I guess now I'll find out.

A janitor pushes a mop past the doorway, leaving a trail of pine-laced antiseptic fumes. They assault my nose and make my head ache. Perhaps this is for the best.

"All right," I say, committed now. "Let's get this over with."

LIGHTS BLARE DOWN FROM THE lab ceiling. Bleach and sanitizing hand-wash scent the air. There's a thermometer clenched between my teeth. A needle protrudes from the back of my hand. Crimson blood flows into a tube. Cold instruments prod my skin. I cringe and struggle to remain calm.

I can't. I'm scared stiff. Of what, I'm not even sure.

Two aides lift me onto an X-ray table. Impersonal, gloved hands shift me into position and drape me with a heavy, rubberized shield. The clammy weight presses against my thin hospital gown. Machines whir and click. The process is repeated until I've been twisted and laid out in every possible position.

I watch the face of the X-ray tech, behind his window. His face shows nothing. When he steps out into the hall, it's another story. He's babbling, shocked.

I cower on the table.

"What did you find?" I demand when the X-ray tech returns, jutting out my jaw.

"It's not my place to say."

"I want to call my dad."

"Discuss that with your doctor."

I'm furious now, desperate to get out and away from these people. I'm wheeled into another room. When the doctor enters, I practically shout my request.

She nods. "We'll be releasing you shortly."

I'm so surprised my tongue merely stutters out a relieved "Oh."

She goes to a metal rack and removes an instrument. It looks like a power saw. The device whirs to life, and she takes my wrist, pressing the blade against the plaster.

I try to pull back. "What are you doing?"

"Cutting it off."

"My hand?"

"Your cast, Miss Thorne."

"Why?"

"Because your bones are not broken."

TWENTY-FOUR

I DON'T BELIEVE HER.

"You're insane. Of course my bones are broken."

She holds the X-rays up to the light. "They aren't now, and they never were. Not a single fracture, not a single scar in the bone."

"But I'm telling you, they were."

"And I'm telling you you're wrong. Whoever did this is either deranged or has a sick sense of humor."

Rapidly, brutally, she severs the fiberglass. The saw whines. The cast screeches in protest. Then, carefully, she peels the hard cocoons from my arms and legs.

Limb by limb, she frees me from a prison of lies.

I perch naked apart from my gown. I'm too terrified to move lest my arms and legs come unhinged—flop at inhuman angles. A few feet away, the doctor disposes the remains of my fiberglass incarceration. It hits the bottom of the metal trash can with a resounding clang.

"I'm telling you, you mixed up my X-rays."

"We did not mix up your X-rays." She takes my right arm and moves her hands up and down its length, squeezing here and there.

"Any pain here? No? How about here?"

"Maybe we should do the X-rays one more time."

Head bent, she gives me this look that says *Drop it already.* From her frizzy hair to the blue smudges beneath her eyes, it's obvious she's overworked and annoyed. Clearly she has other patients to get to. More important ones. Patients without fake injuries or orders from investigative agencies. She slips me into a pair of disposable green booties.

"Stand for me, please. Careful."

Suddenly I want to laugh. I want to scream. I don't know what I want, really. Answers, I guess. Yes, that's what I need. I won't get them from her, though.

The recovery table paper crinkles under me as I slip gingerly forward. My toes touch the ground. It's icy through the thin coverings. She takes my hands and helps me wobble to my feet. Nothing happens. Nothing snaps. I stand there feeling like an idiot.

"You'll be a little stiff. That's expected."

I nod.

"The front desk can arrange some rehab sessions. An aide will take you back to your room."

She opens the door to the bustle outside. I'm helped into a wheelchair. Eyes seem to fasten on me from every direction. The nurses' station. The other hospital workers. I guess gossip moves quick. I'm the patient some agency is investigating. The one with four broken limbs that aren't really broken. I scan the sea of pitying eyes.

Look at her. She's not even hurt. Poor thing. So obviously naive.

I've known audiences like this before. Sure, most people wish you the best, yet what about those who long to see you squirm? If I were feeling daring, I'd shout, *It's a miracle, I can walk!* Like someone on a religious TV show. Instead, I raise my chin and focus my attention on the elevator doors, willing them to hurry up and open.

Upstairs, Gage's jaw drops, and he stares at my limbs in amazement.

"Don't even ask. You were right," I tell him.

He doesn't say *I told you so*. He doesn't need to. It's in the curl of his lip when he closes his mouth. In the shine of his eyes.

"Let me get dressed. Then we can go."

To his credit, all he says is, "I'll be outside. Shout when you're ready."

Alone, I sink onto the bed.

Hunter lied.

Gage was right.

He lied to me.

My heart constricts as my faith in Hunter's goodness topples. He left me trapped with no explanation. I trusted him. And Victoria, Edward, Lucy, too. Acting like they cared about me. All along it was a lie.

Why?

There's a phone beside the bed. I pick it up and ask the hospital operator to connect me with the Phoenix Research Lab. It takes a few minutes, and then Victoria comes on the line.

"I'm at St. Mary's General Hospital," I say, foregoing any greeting. She knows my voice. "We need to talk. Come to my dad's house. One hour. Show up or I'm calling the police."

Before she can answer, I slam down the receiver.

I recall what Ella said about my smooth skin. I yank up the hem of the hospital gown and stare at my newly exposed thighs. Then my arms. They're flawless. I can't find a single scar. Not even the faded gash from the ice skating accident. Every tiny blemish is gone as though airbrushed away. So my bones were fine, yet they fixed my skin?

My mind spins, seeking purchase, seeking steady ground. Were they fine or not?

The digital clock on the bedside table clicks from 11:59 to 12:00. Shaking, I pull the leather satchel from its hiding place and heft it into my lap. Dizzy flutters twirl in my stomach. *What do I do?* What the hell am I supposed to do? Take the silver pill? If I don't, it's clear what will happen.

If I do?

Hunter, what did you do to me? How do I reconcile this with the caring man who held me in his arms and sang to me? The man with the cocky, warm smile and the rumbling laugh. The one with eyes that I could drown in. Yet he's a scoundrel of the worst sort. Once again I'm in his grip, yet this time it's not the kind of grip a girl dreams of.

Fingers shaking, I pry the lid from the bottle.

A lukewarm glass of water sits on the table. With a swift gulp, I swallow it down. Then I pull on the long white nightshirt with the music notes from yesterday, haul the satchel over my shoulder, and climb into the waiting wheelchair.

Banging on the door. Gage calls, "Aeris? Come on, we need to go."

"Ready!" I call, sounding more confident than I feel.

Gage is strangely nervous as he wheels me out to his truck. He must still be embarrassed about our kiss. I tune him out, lost in my own bubble of fear. No one can help me. No one can pull me out of this mess. My bones are well, but I'm not.

I need to get up and move.

"I want to walk," I tell him.

"You're too weak. Let's just get out of here."

"Gage, I want to stand, stop pushing."

"Okay, okay."

Before I can move he comes around and props me on my two legs, holding me as if I were a newborn foal in danger of tumbling over. "There. Good?"

"Yes, if you let go."

He raises both hands, palms up.

My nightshirt flaps loosely against my bare legs, making me feel exposed and naked. I expect my knees to shake and wobble. Oddly, they don't. I take a deep breath and a wondrous strength surges through my freed limbs. My muscles ache with the need to run. Away. Hard and far from my fear.

"Put this on. You must be freezing." Gage hands me his heavy GORE-TEX jacket. This time, unlike outside the Zenith Club, I do.

"Now can we leave?" he asks, impatient.

I nod and climb in.

He hands me my bag and I clutch at the horrible thing. What happens when the meds run out? Will I have to take them for the rest of my life? I stare into my lap as he abandons the chair and climbs in. Another thought strikes. Something even worse.

What happens if I can't get more?

Gage speaks first. "What the hell was Cayman doing?" He wrenches the car into gear and roars out of the lot. "Sticking you in those casts? I thought he was a freak, but the guy's a sadistic psycho."

I hate it. Hearing *Hunter* and *psycho* in the same sentence. I hate it more than anything. How could I have fallen for him? At the same time, dread prickles all over me. Never have I felt so alone. So isolated in this horrible reality. My mouth is nearly numb with terror.

What's in those pills? And why did he put me in those useless casts? What did he do to my body?

I dig my fists deep into Gage's pockets, pulling his coat tight around me. My knuckles bump up against several small, tubular shapes. I fish them out and stare at a wrapped syringe and an unused blood-collection tube.

"What are these?" I ask, holding them away as Gage swipes at me.

"They're nothing."

"You stole these from the hospital? Or do you just carry needles around with you?" I stare at him as color floods his cheeks. "Wait, were you going to take my blood?"

"No! No, of course not."

"You're a horrible liar, Gage. You were when we were kids, and you still are."

"Fine. It's because I care about you, okay? I wanted to make sure you were really all right."

"So, what? You were just going to take my blood without even asking me? Don't you think I've had enough of that from Hunter? And what about the hospital? You think you're going to find stuff they didn't? You're no doctor. What the hell?"

"No—I was going to ask you first. Of course. And yeah, I'm not a doctor, but I have a scientist friend who knows stuff, and I thought he might be able to run tests the hospital couldn't. That's all. That's it. Like I said, there must be some reason Cayman put you in those casts. Don't you want to find out?"

I stare down at my bare feet. Wiggle my toes. They're blue with cold.

"Obviously he wanted to keep you trapped," Gage says.

"Trapped? If he wanted me trapped, he would have kept me at the research lab." *Although Victoria did try to make me come back.* "Anyway, Hunter left. He couldn't care less about me."

Gage keeps checking the rearview mirror. I twist in my seat. The traffic is light.

"What's wrong, is someone following us?"

"No, we're fine." His fingers wring the steering wheel. "And even if he left and you went home, you were still trapped. Why?"

"I don't know."

He scoffs. "So if it wasn't about keeping you under control, then what? He lied and said your arms and legs were broken for fun? That's almost worse."

"My bones *were* broken." And as I said the words, I knew it.

"I'm sure it seemed that way to you."

It didn't just seem that way. In the operating room at the PRL—when the police came—the researchers were afraid. Ian claimed they'd suspect I should be dead. That I was too damaged.

"I was crushed," I insist.

"A lot was happening; you were being chased. Obviously it was confusing."

"I was thrown against a huge iron gate and the ATV hit me. Square on. I watched it. I heard my bones break. Don't tell me what did or didn't happen. You weren't there." I pull my knees up to my chest and wrap my arms around them. They feel bare and thin without their thick fiberglass shell.

"Okay," he concedes. "You were hurt. And probably needed stitches. Which you got."

"My bones were broken!"

"Not according to the X-rays."

I put my forehead to the glass and stare out at a cluster of dilapidated houses. On one tiny front yard, weeds sprout through the remains of a rusted-out bed frame.

I lick my dry lips. "I don't know what's real anymore."

"What's real is that someone triggered that alert. Why else would the authorities order those tests?"

"But what authorities? You sure you didn't call anyone?"

"No." He slams his fist on the dash. "But like I said, I'm glad someone did. I thought Cayman performed the same operation on you as they performed on my unit."

"Maybe they did."

"Nope."

"How can you tell?"

"The X-rays would show it." His voice is grim.

"Wait, what operation did they perform on your unit?" They'd been operated on? I thought they'd been exposed to some deadly infectious agent. I dry swallow. "What would your X-rays show?"

He's silent, his dark pupils fastened to the road.

"Gage? What would they show?"

The run-down houses have given way to open pasture. Birds huddle on the wires, watching us pass.

"We don't talk about it."

"Who's we? You and the other soldiers they experimented on?"

His shoulders are hunched forward. He nods.

"You and the guys living down at your compound?"

"Yep."

I'm stunned by his weighty tone, by the meaning in that tiny word. The blacktop snakes out in front of us, snakes up the wild coast, snakes toward home. Toward a place that seems on the surface so peaceful. It's not. Gage's jaw is tense. I know suddenly that hidden along the ocean bluffs, a war is gathering.

"Please tell me what's going on. Please tell me what happened during that experiment."

I can see the decision battling in his mind. He wrenches the steering wheel, slamming the brakes at the same time. We skid onto the shoulder, fishtailing and kicking up dust. When the truck comes to a stop, he thrusts open his door. Salt air rushes in, along with the sound of distant waves.

"What are you doing?"

"Showing you."

I open my door. The blacktop sends blinding rays of hot sunshine blasting upward, radiating warmth along my legs. Gage lopes along the gravel edge, heading toward a signpost that warns of dangerous curves ahead. He shoots me a backward glance. Then, casually, like a runner grabbing a baton in a relay race, he lifts the sign from the ground, taking the poured concrete base as he goes. He keeps jogging; it's effortless.

I watch in disbelief as he stops and tosses the thing into the air. It whirls skyward, flipping end over end, flying at least thirty feet high. Bits of dirt rain down from the weighty lump of concrete stuck to the bottom. Reaching its full arc, it slows, stops, and comes plummeting down.

"Watch out," I gasp, even though I know he can't hear me.

With one hand, he catches the pole and proceeds to wrap the metal into easy knots. He could be tying his shoe for all the effort on his face. There's none. Literally none.

My jaw is hanging open.

Witnessing Hunter fight those men in my half-conscious, shocked state was one thing. This is real. This is happening. Gage is bending a giant metal signpost into a pretzel. His face flashes red as I gape at him. There's pride, though, too. For all his anger, he's almost smug.

He saunters toward the truck. "Probably shouldn't destroy public property like this, huh."

"No. Probably not."

Unwinding the knots takes a little more work. "Guess I tied them a little tight."

Finally, he replants it in the dirt. I'm so shaken when he climbs back into the driver's seat I can't find my voice. When I do, I squeak, *How?*"

After starting the car and guiding it onto the road, he holds out his forearm. "Feel it."

"I'm not sure I want to."

"Just feel it, Aeris."

I do. "Seems pretty normal."

"Squeeze it. Harder."

Suddenly I know something's off. It's like earlier, when I pressed against his chest to push him off me. His chest had felt like skin wrapped over armor.

"Is it—is there metal under there?"

"Metal and Kevlar and a whole lot of stuff I don't understand."

"And you thought they did that to me? That's what the doctors were looking for in the X-rays? Why, because I was Dr. Cayman's patient?"

"That and the convulsions, your high temperature, a lot of things. It happened to us. The body doesn't take kindly to having that much metal shoved inside. Ask my brother. Oh right. You can't. He's dead."

"And they did that to you without your consent?"

"Oh, we gave our consent. We just had no idea what we were consenting to when we signed ourselves over to Blackbird, to Brewster King and his Franken-doctors. They called it an unfortunate program gone wrong. The doctors were arrested, of course. And the military was pressured to release us with decent pensions. Basically, they bought our silence. Works for me. I don't want people knowing I'm a freak."

"And this guy, Brewster King, why wasn't he arrested?"

"The worm wriggled clear. People like King know how to get out of things."

"So that's it? He's just carrying on?"

"For now. Believe me. Justice will be served."

I press my forehead to the side window and stare out at the blue sky. All I'm seeing, though, is Hunter lifting the ATV off me and flinging it through the air.

Pieces start falling together. Flying together. Slamming into place.

I recall Gage and Hunter facing off in the Foggy Joe—seeing Gage's stiff, brutish frame matched against Hunter's own powerful, fluid body. A bionic man against a mortal beast.

Hunter didn't make me into a metal soldier.

Oh, he did something to me. Of that I'm sure. Hunter's not normal; I see that now. Yet he isn't like Gage, either. Whatever he did, he made me more like him. And Victoria. And Ian. Lucy and Edward.

I picture the ceiling in their operating room. The caterpillars, the cocoons, the butterflies. I see my broken body on the table. Hunter bending over me, begging me to come back to him. I feel the needle stab my heart, the strange electric pulse, the flames rushing through my limbs, the burning fire melting my muscles. Melting my bones.

He saved me. He saved my broken body on a molecular level.

I know why Gage saw Blackbird's CEO visiting the PRL. King's company designs military weapons—be those guns or futuristic soldiers like Gage. Blackbird took the brute-force approach. But Brewster King knows there's a better way, a technique to rebuild a human from the inside, with his or her own blood, muscles, and bones. A way to make them healthier, stronger. Strong enough to throw an eight-hundred-pound ATV through the windshield of a truck.

I grab the door handle and squeeze. Nothing happens. It doesn't crush between my fingers. Feeling self-conscious, I glance at Gage. He has no idea what I'm thinking. At least the awkwardness of our kiss is gone. We're friends again. Closer than friends. We're both hiding horrible secrets. Although he's still not privy to mine.

"Shit," Gage says, eyes narrowed on the rearview mirror. "Shit!"

I twist in my seat.

Five big black SUVs are coming up on our tail fast. Through the nearest tinted windshield, four broad-shouldered men in dark clothing are visible.

Terror ricochets down my spine.

"Maybe they're just in a hurry," I hear myself say.

"Yeah," he growls. "I don't think so. Hold on." He presses the accelerator to the floor and we bolt forward.

The SUVs increase their speed. A police siren whoops, and lights whirl to life on all three vehicles.

"It's the police," I say. "It's just the police! Stop."

"They're not the police." His eyes are on the mirror.

I wrench around and stare, hoping against hope he's wrong. A hand reaches out the passenger window. It's holding a rifle.

"Gun!" I shout.

"We've got bigger problems."

A shot pings off the truck bed. I hunch down, facing front, and my eyes peel open in dismay. Two more SUVs are coming at us from the opposite direction. They fill both lanes on the narrow road, driving parallel. Spikes jab forward from their armored grills. They're going to hit us. They're going to plow right into us.

"Gage!" I scream, bracing my arms and legs against the dash.

The distance is closing.

Four hundred feet.

Three hundred feet.

Two hundred feet.

A rock wall to the left. To the right a coastal cliff. Gage slams the brakes and we skid, whirling in an arc so tight the truck tips up onto two wheels. Still, the SUVs come at us, driving hard.

"They're crazy," I gasp, holding the door and bracing.

"Come on, come on!" Gage growls.

Whining, the engine grinds as he aims for the narrow gap between them. I see a driver's face, and then we hit hard, still tilted, somehow forcing our way through in a scream of grinding metal and broken glass.

We made it. We made it out the other side. Glass fragments spill into the lap of my nightgown. The wheels slam down, and Gage looks triumphant. Except the axle must be broken because we're spinning again, spinning around and around, burning out rubber, and then the truck flips like a bug onto its back, and still it spins some more so we're hanging from our seat belts, papers raining down from the sun visor, glove box crashing open and spewing its contents, dizzy and upside down until we stop, facing the open road ahead and no way to get out of here.

"You okay?" Gage asks, unclipping and dropping down to land on all fours on the ceiling.

"Yes," I say, breathless and terrified as I fumble with my seat belt.

He catches me as I fall.

From outside, a loudspeaker squeals. A voice comes on. "Come out with your hands up."

We freeze, staring at each other.

"Leave your weapons in the car, and come out with your hands up."

"They think we're armed," Gage says.

"Are we?" I ask, hopeful.

"Nope."

My heart thunders in my chest. I'm breathing fast. My throat's sore with the floating stench of burned rubber. The megaphone squeals again, grating and loud. A person coughs.

"Gage." The man's raspy voice makes us both jolt. "You recognize me, don't you? Your old buddy, Brewster King?"

Gage isn't the only one to recognize him. I know him, too. Iron-fist. The man with the creepy, cold gray eyes. The one I found spying on Dad's house. The villain who chased me down and almost killed me.

All along it's been King. I should have known. Should have put it together. It's been in front of me this whole time.

Did Brewster King and his company, Blackbird, have enough authority to order my tests at the hospital? Had he instigated the patient watch list after my crash outside the PRL? Or did the unfamiliar doctor who showed up this morning work for him? Had it all been a bluff?

How did he know we were on this road?

Gage's lips peel back from his teeth, and the tendons—or whatever's in there—bulge in his forearms.

"Not very impressive driving, but I guess that skill wasn't part of your program," King calls.

"I'll kill him," Gage growls.

"It's the girl I'm interested in. Send her out."

"Like hell I will," Gage shouts.

"As you recall, I know exactly what you're made of. You're not strong enough to take us all on. Send her out, and I'll play nice."

Crouching in the upside-down truck, I study our pursuers through the cracked rear window. The vehicles are lined up for attack. Why don't they just come for us? Are they afraid? Afraid we're armed? *Afraid of Gage?*

Shattered safety glass grinds into my palms and knees. Daylight streams through the windows. It catches the shards and makes them flash like diamonds. I blink against the brightness. That's when I see my reflection in the broken rearview mirror that lies in front of my hands. In the shards' starry light, my irises reflect up at me like a cat. The way Hunter's had on that fateful night outside the Zenith Club. Reflecting in a way that's completely inhuman.

The whole world seems to go silent.

It's like someone pushed pause.

It's like there's no breathing, no movement, nothing. Just this eternal vacuum of shock.

I'm no longer who I was. I'm different. I'm a freak.

Then the world comes roaring back.

"You can't win, Gage," King calls. "Send her out or we'll simply shoot until you're both incapacitated, and I'll come get her myself. Messier than I'd like. I could live with it."

Gage puts his face to the broken driver window. "This is bullshit! She's normal! Cayman didn't modify her. Let us go."

Over the megaphone, King says, "I'll decide that. Send her out. Or do I need to come get her?"

Gage reaches for the door handle. "Stay in the car."

"No way. I can't let you do that," I tell him.

"I've been waiting for this for years. I'm going to kill the bastard."

"No. There's too many of them." I fumble in his jacket pocket for the syringe and vial. "Wait. I have an idea. We can give them my blood. That's what they want, isn't it?"

"No way in hell am I giving him your blood. If this bastard tracked you down, Cayman did something to you. And obviously I was wrong about them working together, because he'd have no reason to stage this takedown."

"I don't care. Let him have it." I shrug out of his jacket. "Quick. Help me make a tourniquet."

"No, Aeris. Don't you get it? I'm not giving this asshole your blood.

I don't want him to have it. He's dangerous enough without him owning Cayman's secrets, too."

I freeze. He's right.

"What about your blood, then? We can call his bluff, say it's mine."

"He won't go for it." Even still, he's wrapping his arm tight and then his crimson life force is flowing into the tube.

"Time's up, Gage," King calls.

"We're coming out," Gage shouts back. "Tell your men to back off." He caps the blood container and pulls his sleeve down.

Quickly, I snatch it from him, before he realizes what I'm doing. Then I turn and kick open the passenger door. I'm so worked up that the power in my legs sends it screaming under my assault, and it nearly breaks from its hinges.

I don't want to die. No one wants to die. Letting Gage die for me, however, is not an option. This isn't his fight. I brought this on myself. I never should have stolen the PRL key.

My speed surprises even me.

One second I'm in the truck.

The next I'm through the gaping hole and standing, barefoot, on the blazing tarmac.

TWENTY-FIVE

"Aeris!" Gage howls.

I'm running, holding the tube of blood, yet his cry is so heartrending it makes me pause. I turn back to look at the sound of tearing metal. Gage is ripping the driver door free. It's in his hand like a shield as he comes at me, his eyes bloodshot with rage.

"Back in the truck," he barks. "Get back in the truck!"

King calls, "She wants to come, Gage."

I'm rooted to the spot now. Halfway between the overturned truck and the mass of armed men in black fatigues. I open my mouth to speak. It's parched and my words come out as a strange croak. "Here's my blood!" I raise the tube high in my clenched fist. "It's what you want, isn't it? You can have it. Just let us go."

"Bring it to me," King calls.

"Promise you'll let us go."

"You're in no position to bargain. But bring it over and I'll think about it."

"Stay where you are," Gage growls.

King's next to his vehicle now. His pale eyes are trained on mine. Sun reflects off his prosthetic arm as he motions me forward. I obey his command. I start walking.

A rage-filled roar rips from Gage's throat. He charges past me, thrusting me backward, and flings himself toward the men. I stumble and fall as five men in combat gear lope forward to meet him. The tube rolls away, yet I only have eyes for Gage.

Gage's dark blond head rises half a foot above the rest. A man lunges. Gage spins, fast, slamming the door's edge hard into the attacker and knocking him to the ground. The fight becomes a blur. Arms and legs, kicking and punching. The door moves at lightning speed, slamming men down. The others are quick, too, though, and I see Gage lose his shield and double over.

I scramble to my feet.

"Stop!" I scream, and sprint toward him. A man slams his boot into Gage's head once, twice, three times. "Stop it!"

Gage rolls away and sways to his feet. Blood flows from his mouth. He reaches me before I reach him, running to close the distance. His big hands grab me—his left hand takes me by one arm, his right hand closes around my thigh. And then, as if I weighed no more than a doll, he lifts me high and flings me hard. I fly over the low wall, toppling end over end until the world spins out of control. My body whumps into a thicket of grassy overgrowth. For a moment, I lie dazed, the wind completely knocked out of me.

I roll onto all fours and strain to suck in a breath. It won't come.

Then it does in a rush.

I leap to my feet and see Gage holding them back. But for how long? They're a small army. He's just one man.

A fresh fighter exits the SUV King arrived in. He's larger than the rest. Hair the color of rust and cut like a jarhead's. As if sensing his presence, Gage glances up and the man grins. Jarhead paces forward with a swagger to his step. The others, meanwhile, drop back.

I hear Gage shout something. A name, perhaps? Do they know each other?

And now the fight is on. But this time it's real. Before I thought I felt fear. Now I'm sick with it. These two are equally matched. Yet Gage is already winded. Jarhead commandeers Gage's arm and he's twisting it hard, and Gage shrieks as it bends out of the socket.

I'm over the wall and I'm screaming. The pavement is rough and gritty under my bare feet.

"Brewster King!" In that instant, my words are drowned out by the appearance of a black airplane.

It swoops over the treetops less than a quarter mile away. Pontoons, the kind used for landing on water, jut like giant talons from its belly. They have a plane, too?

On the road, the fighters freeze, and every head turns skyward to stare at its approach. All sound is drowned out by its deafening roar. Lower it comes until its pontoons loom so close I see rivets shining on the struts. It buzzes over us, just missing the tops of the black SUVs.

On the road, gunfire rings out. They're not aiming at Gage, though. They're firing on the plane.

Bullets spray upward, aimed directly at the aircraft's midnight-colored underbelly.

Despite Gage's bad arm, he's managed to take up his door shield. He slams it into Jarhead's face. Blood spurts in a high arc. From behind Gage, a fallen man lurches to his feet. A knife glitters in his hand.

"Look out!" I scream.

Gage whirls. The blade rips through his good bicep, and there's a sick metal-on-metal sound. Blood spurts from the wound and my stomach lurches. Armor or not, he's still mortal. Somehow he keeps moving, bringing his door-shield down on the knife-wielder's neck and chest. The man crumples just as Jarhead fastens his hands around Gage's throat.

"Stop!" I shout, "Leave him alone."

I sprint forward. Bullets rain down on the pavement from the plane overhead, stopping me in my tracks. The acrid taste of panic burns my mouth. Whose side is the pilot on?

A gunman climbs onto an SUV roof and points his weapon skyward. The plane keeps coming. Straight for him. Low and lining up with the roadway. If the plane keeps going, it'll hit the gunman. What is this, a suicide mission?

Gusting air sends my nightgown beating against my bare thighs.

Then I see him.

The pilot.

A dark-haired man with intense amber eyes, whose jaw is set in rage. A powerful figure, poised and capable and ready to attack. The man I can't stop dreaming of. The man who deserted me. The one who tore my heart in two.

Hunter.

We're so close now that his eyes meet mine.

Determination floods through me. His determination. Foreign yet familiar. Powerful and possessive, furious and appalled, charging me with fresh hope, and I don't know if I'm imagining it, wanting to imagine it's real, but I feel it. I don't know why he left me. I don't know why he lied. This one thing, however, I know is true. Gage and I are no longer alone.

He's here for us.

He came back.

The gunman on the SUV opens fire. *Rat-tat-tat-tat* explodes upward. Bullets shred the plane's right pontoon.

Still Hunter keeps coming at him. The man scrambles from the roof. Not fast enough. The pontoon spears his chest, sending him airborne.

Triumph, however, is fleeting, for the plane rises up, only briefly. A moment later, it limps toward the cliff's edge and falls out of view. My heart lurches in my chest. They must have hit the engine. It splutters and grows silent, replaced by the faint, distant crash of waves.

I stare in horror at the empty space. *Hunter, no!*

Shouts sound behind me.

"Run!" It's Gage. "Run, dammit!"

In the next instant, his attacker overwhelms him, taking him down and pounding his fists and heels into him. Three others are sprinting toward me, their black boots hammering the pavement. Ruthlessness is plain in their eyes. To them I'm no human. I'm a specimen. An anomaly to be dissected and preserved in a glass jar. My courage drains away. I stumble backward, clutching at the front of my nightgown, unable to force my legs to run. The hard blacktop ends. My bare feet skitter on the gravel shoulder and my heel catches. I trip and go down hard. My hands find a rock. I pick it up and throw it as hard as I can.

It flies straight as a missile, so fast it whirrs, straight toward the closest man. He goes to duck. Too late. Bull's-eye. I stare in horrified fascination as the man staggers backward, clutches his bleeding face, slumps to his knees, and falls over.

I'm up again. I find another stone and hurl it. Miss. Another and another. I'm fast and strong as hell, but my aim is for shit. The two men are fencing me in. Backing me toward the cliff. Far, far below, the frothy ocean is edged with hungry rocks. Rough grass jabs the soles of my feet. I'm throwing sticks now. Garbage. Anything I can get my hands on. I'm almost at the edge. There's nowhere to go.

I turn and look.

There, where the cliff meets the sky, fingers appear.

Big, strong fingers.

They latch onto the dry dirt and grass. Then Hunter lunges into view, flying up and over and landing in a crouch. Dirt stains his thick forearms. His jaw is knotted in rage. His black hair is drenched and dripping down his forehead. Our gazes meet, and here at the edge of the world, I'm falling for him all over again.

"Aeris." His fingers close around my wrist as if to confirm I'm real. He pulls me to him and I feel his lips in my hair as he mutters, "Thank god."

His eyes flick past me to my pursuers. He's all bulging shoulders and lean torso, and there's a dangerous look to him that sends a chill trembling across my skin. Even if we don't survive this, I know this now: He does care. And so do I.

He releases me, and his powerful leg muscles propel him forward. He flies past so quick he's a blur of movement. The pair of thugs close in, smiling. One lunges. Hunter moves like an animal, fluid and fast. The other attacks Hunter from behind. I drive my elbow into his kidneys. Hunter spins and breaks the man's arms. He falls to the ground, screaming.

"Your meds," Hunter demands. "Where are they?"

"In the truck."

More men are running at us now. I count twelve or thirteen. People are shooting.

"Get them," Hunter says, half pulling me as I sprint to the upside-down vehicle. Bullets fly past, barely missing us.

"We need to help Gage!"

He shoves me through the passenger door. As soon as I'm in, he's dragging the truck to the cliff's edge, holding it in front to shield us from the gunfire. We're moving fast, incredibly fast, and I'm clinging to the hanging seat belt, jerking up and down so hard I nearly tumble from the gaping door hole.

He stops and I lurch to a halt. The medicine satchel flies through the open door. The bottles scatter.

"Pick them up," Hunter shouts.

Men are closing in, I see them through the rear window. I crawl out. A glass tube glistens in the weeds. Gage's blood sample. I'm sobbing suddenly, wondering how everything went so wrong, and I snatch it up and shove it, along with the meds, into the bag, zipping it shut.

Gage is on the ground near King's SUV, trying to get up. He can't, though. He's hurt.

Then our assailants are here.

The grinding of tearing metal sounds at the front of the vehicle. Hunter is wrenching the bumper free. He swings it like a giant ax. Two men go down.

"Aeris," Hunter shouts. "Come on!"

We're at the edge of the cliff. He's pulled us back here. His hands grab my waist and lift me to face him. His chest is firm against mine; his arms hold me as though I weigh no more than a feather. His face is inches from mine.

"Wrap your arms around my neck."

I look to Gage, who has somehow gotten to his feet. He's fighting hard, fighting to keep back the men. Jarhead, the enhanced one, is circling for a fresh attack. Dark blotches stain Gage's golden hair. Blood.

"We have to help him!"

"I have to get you out of here."

"I'm not leaving him."

Gage turns, his eyes bloodshot, his nose streaming red. Still he sees us, sees me sobbing and staring at him in desperation.

"Go!" he yells at Hunter. *"Get her the hell out of here!"*

Hunter's grip around me is almost painful.

"Let go," I cry, fighting to get down.

He holds me tighter, yet I sense his indecision.

On the road, Gage swipes at his oversize opponent. It's clear his injuries are making him weaker. Others are coming at us now. There are too many against too few.

"I'm sorry," Hunter says. "He's right. It's the only way."

I hammer his rock hard chest with my fists. "Let me down. Let. Me. Go!"

"He's fighting for you, Aeris."

"I don't want him to!"

"I won't let it be for nothing." Locking me in one arm, he carries me over the edge. "I won't let you die."

One look down and my eyes peel wide. The rock wall drops straight under us; a sheer face ending in an unforgiving, distant shoreline. He's cradling me to his chest with one arm, the other grips a barely-there crevice. His toes, too, have found purchase in impossibly small gaps. Wind whips over us, lifting my hair and swirling it around my cheeks.

"Hold tight," he says. "I need both hands to climb. With your legs, too. Wrap them around my waist."

I hesitate.

"Do it! Fast!"

I obey. Clinging to his neck with all my strength I wrap my legs around him. My skirt cinches up and I'm acutely aware of his hips, of his rough shirt fabric rubbing against my chest, of his pulse racing against my skin. I feel it in my cheek, racing as fast as my own.

He moves quickly with certain confidence. I have no right to feel safe here, not with Gage up there fighting. I'm shocked and sickened that there's no going back. No getting back to yesterday to take my meds and stop this horror from ever happening. The thought of losing someone else, losing someone I care about while I survive, sends my brain into panic.

First Mom, now Gage?

My mind threatens to spin out of control, to break. I feel darkness closing in.

A thought wells up in me, a feeling that resolves itself into words. *Brewster King will pay for what he's done.* I choke back a sob.

Inches from my face, Hunter's neck is corded with strain.

"You're okay, almost there. Hang on," he says, mistaking my sorrow for alarm.

His shirt grazes my cheek as he moves fast, lowering us down the cliff face. Out of nowhere, I'm reminded of a time long ago when a tall, dark-haired stranger bore my five-year-old self screaming and sobbing away from a different devastating accident. His skin smells of sweat, masculine, fierce, angry, and alive.

Suddenly I'm there again, fighting to get back to Mom, back in the Swiss Alps, back to where a stranger gathered me in his arms and carried me through the night. I'm being pulled away again when I should stay.

Gage, I'm sorry! I don't want to leave you there!

I have to live. If only to see King suffer.

Rat-tat-tat explodes over our heads. Bullets whiz down in a hail of deadly, metal fire. They hiss and spit past my ears.

Hunter swings left, so fast and sudden I lose my grip around his neck.

I scream. Oh god, I'm sliding down his body! His legs are moving, toes seeking gaps in the wall. I hear scratching, his fingers scraping down the rock face, trying to grab on. I'm still sliding. My hands rake his chest, rake the belt that's covered by his T-shirt. I can't grab it! The cloth is in the way! My hands are on his thighs now, and my legs are dangling.

"Aeris," he gasps.

I'm screaming, screaming.

Tiny waves crash and froth on the miniature boulders, dizzy and distant and waiting.

His fingers swipe at my neck. They clutch my bag strap and for a wonderful moment my descent slows.

"I've got you," he cries.

"Don't let me go."

"I won't."

"I don't want to fall! I don't want to fall!"

Then the strap snaps. My fingers flail upward as it's torn away and he's holding it and reaching for me and I get one last touch of the leather satchel, grasping at its curved, smooth bottom, desperate to hold it somehow but not able.

"No!" His voice rips me with its agony.

Air.

It whips around me, buffeting my skin, my hair. My stomach lurches up into my throat. *Hunter*, I try to scream. Nothing comes out.

I'm alone.

Alone in a vast expanse of air that's compressing as the earth flies at me with deadly speed. Boulders rush to meet me, jagged toothed tombstones, waiting, thirsting to receive me.

Silence. All I hear is the rush of wind. I don't fight. There's no point. Nothing to be done, no decisions to make. Nothing but the knowledge of my last breath.

Dad, I wish I could tell you how much I love you.

A body hurtles past, startling me so that I jolt and twist in midair. It's Hunter. He's dropping so fast he's a blur. He must have been hit. I watch him plunge, my mind oddly detached. We're so close to the ocean that details in the rocks are visible. Seaweed surges in sparkling pools. Jagged crevices hold scuttling crabs, their sharp pincers working.

A wave crashes, sending up a violent plume that mists my skin.

Hunter hits first.

I close my eyes. Squeeze them shut. *Please, God.*

Let it be quick.

TWENTY-SIX

FOOTSTEPS POUND THE ROCKS. I hear him. Over rocks, splashing through water. Running. My back slams into the curve of his arms. I fall against the slickness of Hunter's wet chest. And then we're tumbling in water, rolling and thrashing in the surf, and I'm gasping as his hands push me to the surface. I cough, eyes streaming in the salt-charged foam that churns relentlessly and threatens to pull me down again.

For a moment, he holds me to him, burying his face in my hair.

"Swim," he whispers, urgent.

"How did you—"

"Doesn't matter. Swim. Now!"

The water plane is there, anchored offshore. One pontoon, the damaged pontoon, wallows half beneath the surface. I straggle at Hunter's side, thrashing in the frigid water. I'm a good swimmer, but the water's ice cold. Teeth chattering, I kick harder and crawl forward, fighting off the growing chill.

His hands seize me, and he pulls me to a stop, holding me against him and cursing.

I follow his gaze up to the cliff. A man stands there holding a giant metal tube. I know what that tube is—I've seen one before. In an action movie on TV. My trembling grows more violent.

"Is that a rocket launcher?"

A flash lights the end of the tube. Then a missile explodes outward. It flies toward us, winging downward with terrifying speed. No, not toward us—toward the plane. They're trying to cut off our escape.

The missile hits, exploding water sky-high. The blast sends my head snapping back. Frantic, I thrust hair from my eyes. The plane's still there.

"Missed," Hunter notes. "Come on, before someone who can shoot gets hold of it."

Panic makes me abnormally strong. I swim toward the plane with strokes more powerful than any I'd consider myself capable of. Even the deadening cold is no match against my growing swiftness. Still, it's not fast enough for Hunter. His left arm wraps around me and hooks under my armpit. He hauls me at inhuman speed across the surface.

The nearest pontoon bobs a foot away. He leaps onto it and helps me out of the water as he thrusts the lightweight door open. We climb in and he tosses my bag into the foot well and pulls my door closed, fastening it shut.

Through the misty window, I stare up at the cliff. The gunman is loading a fresh round.

Hunter starts the engine, impatient, his big hands working levers and knobs and switches, his amber eyes focused and in control.

I'm not, though.

"Hurry!" I cry, staring up at that gaping barrel.

The engine thrums to life, strong and throaty. It rises to a steady, throbbing whir.

"They won't shoot, not with you in here."

I watch the gunman on the cliff, cringing, waiting for the flash. Hunter's right. It doesn't come. The plane limps across the water, picking up speed. The shooter lowers the rocket launcher and watches us go.

A gust takes us, and we lift off. Winds batter the wings. The plane climbs higher, and soon the cliff top is visible. The cars are there, small as black toys. The road snakes in either direction. Gage's truck lies upside down, forgotten. A knot of men stand around a prone form on the pavement. From this distance, the glint of his blond hair is barely visible.

I press both hands to the glass. My face turns hot with tears. "Oh, Gage, what have they done to you?"

The plane banks left, and all I see are clouds.

Gray and heavy, they consume us both.

How can this be happening? How can I be flying away from my best friend? This is my fault. And he's paying for it. My heart squeezes so hard I almost throw up.

We have to get him back. Please don't let King kill him. Please.

We fly in silence, the plane roaring south.

I stare at the sky. Gage told me his friends are planning to destroy King. When we land, I'm going straight to his cove. We'll take down that monster together. Obliterate him. Limb by limb. His twisted company, brick by brick. All of it, until he's no more than a name on the wind. An item in a Wikipedia entry. Dust.

That's my only sliver of light—I will avenge him. And for now I have to focus on that. I grit my jaw and swallow my tears, my whole body clenched until I'm exhausted. Spent.

I'll never forget what you did for me. Ever. I will owe you always until I can make this right.

My agony narrows into a little stone in my belly. It lies like a sharp weight. Right beside the stone that belongs to Mom. The pain fills me with new fire.

I'll avenge you both.

The sky is black and icy as my soul. Hunter's hands are busy entering coordinates into some digital device on the dash. His blunt-tipped fingers make deft, knowing movements. Water leaks from his T-shirt, dripping down the tanned skin of his solid arms.

For a moment I allow myself to imagine he's what he appears. Good and honest and true.

He's not all those things, though. I'm sure part of him cares for me. Yet he lied. He did things to me. And he left me alone without a word of explanation. He's playing the hero today. For how long, and to what end?

"I want answers," I say, weeks of pent-up frustration blending with my fear for Gage. "I want them now. What the hell did you do to my body?"

"You're cold," he says. "There's a blanket in the back."

"I'm fine." I look down at my wet nightshirt and realize I'm completely exposed. Scowling, I grab the blanket and pull it over myself.

"There's no point in keeping secrets any longer, is there?" he says quietly. "I've made mistakes. Big ones. This never should have happened. I'm sorry, Aeris."

Clouds blow past, trailing water droplets along the windows.

"Just tell me what you did. Right now."

"That night we spent in the barn was . . ." There's a thread of pain in his voice. He stops and turns to study me. Power and worldliness radiates from his face while tiny lines of disenchantment are etched around his eyes. "Do you really need me to answer that?"

"Yes."

"When you were on my operating table, I kept thinking of us riding Ranger together. I remembered everything you said about losing the people you care about, and I made a choice. An irresponsible one. I went against every principle I stand for. You didn't know what you were in for. How could you? It's what I wanted. Simple as that."

"Bringing me to life?"

"Yes."

Finally, the unvarnished truth—I was dead. And yet I'm not. I'm here in this plane above the earth. And he did what he'd been so vehemently against so that I could live.

"Why did you leave?"

"I needed you to get better without me there."

"Why?"

His eyes go to the windshield. There's that shuttered look again, like he's worried. Like he's hiding something. I try to reach out and sense his emotions. I can't feel a thing. It's just me. Me going crazy.

"Did I make you sick? Is that it?"

"You? No. Definitely not."

"So you wanted me to get better without you there, but when you left, I already was, wasn't I? When you sang to me. I woke up the next morning."

He shoots me a glance, his startling amber eyes curious. "You were aware of me?"

"Yes. Look, I'm done with all these secrets. I want to know what's actually happening to me."

"You're healing."

"Obviously. How?"

"It's a process."

"A process? If you won't explain it, then I will. Because I'm pretty sure I have it figured out. So stop me if I'm wrong, but your drug sent me into some wild, hyperfast healing mode. A doctor told me my bones were never broken. She had no clue. They were, and they fixed themselves in record time. You know how I know? Because it felt like hell. Like my whole body was tearing itself down. I was on fire. It felt like I was melting inside. Maybe I kind of was until my bones started reforming."

In the darkening sky, the cabin has turned murky. The colored dashboard lights catch the angles of Hunter's face.

"I'm right. Aren't I?"

"Pretty damn close."

My feet are cold against the metal floor. I stare at my toes, the nails somehow impossibly perfect as a child's. "My mom was obsessed with caterpillars. She told me once that when they enter a chrysalis, their cells go back to their original state. They become cellular building blocks, the kind that can turn into anything. The caterpillar melts inside its protective shell. And gradually their cells become new things. A new body, new eyes. New arms and legs. And something extra the caterpillar didn't have before. Something special."

"Wings," Hunter grinds out.

"Exactly. And when it's ready, when its change is complete, it crawls out and emerges like a phoenix. Reborn into something new."

"That it does."

"That's what happened. Isn't it? The drug doesn't just fix bones. It changed my muscles. My skin. Even my eyesight. I'm not normal anymore." My voice wobbles and I struggle to keep it steady. "I don't know what I'm becoming."

"You will be normal. I promise you that."

He reaches for me, tentative, and then his fingers close around mine, and, for a moment, I allow myself to get lost in the caress of his big hand. Then I pull away and cross my arms. I'm not ready to trust him. Not even to voice my suspicions that Mom might have been involved in the PRL twenty years ago. Anyway, that was long before his time.

"I know you don't trust me," Hunter says. "It kills me I wasn't there for you. I am now and I swear—I won't let anything bad happen to you."

Despite his claim, I sense his worry wrapping around my heart, threatening to choke out all hope. Once again I'm capturing his feelings in the same way that a stereo captures radio waves. Would he think I'm mad if I told him?

The tops of the towering clouds create a majestic path on either side of the tiny plane. They're so solid one could almost imagine stepping out and climbing among them. Air currents bump the plane, and I wonder if those bullets did any damage to the engine.

"How long will I have to take the pills?" I ask.

"I don't know."

I stare.

"We've never done this before."

My mouth drops open. "What? I thought you and Victoria and the others—"

"What I mean is that we've never knocked down the modification."

"Knocked down?"

"Reset a person's DNA back to normal, return it to how they were before."

I struggle to digest what he's telling me. "You mean turn the butterfly backward into the caterpillar? Back into the worm? Is that what you're saying?"

"Humans were never meant to be butterflies. But you were never a caterpillar—not in my book."

Against my will, my heart skips a beat and starts to race. I won't let him do this to me. I'm not falling under his spell again. I raise my chin. "What about you? Why haven't you reversed the effect on yourselves?"

He reaches over and tucks the blanket around me. "It's a long story. You need to rest. It's been a heavy day."

"I'm fine." I edge away from him, closer to my door.

He's right, though. The stress of it all crashes over me like a black icy wave. There are too many things to think about. Gage. Dad, I have to call Dad as soon as I get to a phone and tell him I'm all right.

I think of King and his vicious attempts to harvest my blood. What about the researchers? Why hasn't King gone after them? I'll ask Hunter tomorrow. When I'm not so tired. This much I know: Until I'm normal, until the modification has been knocked down, King and his men will chase me. Hound me until they run me into the earth.

I pull my bare toes onto the seat. It's cold up here in the sky. From beneath my lashes, I watch him. I watch his aristocratic, mysterious face, those steady, capable eyes trained on the darkness ahead. A fighter. A researcher. A liar who bound me in casts and yet still makes my heart pound uncomfortably hard in my chest.

Part of me trusts him completely. Part of me longs to lean into him and let his arms protect me from my fears. Another part isn't so sure.

The argument Gage and I had that day we played cards and ate candy comes back to me—

Maybe they didn't want you going to a hospital. Ever think of that? . . . Did it ever occur to you that your accident could have given them the perfect chance to do a little human research? . . . You were there for four weeks.

A lot can happen in four weeks. Especially three of which I have little memory of.

Hunter still hasn't explained why he put me in casts. I had a right to know how he'd changed me. From the start. And I still do. No matter his motives, no matter that he's trying to protect me. I am an experiment. His experiment. I'm taking his experimental drugs. For how long, even he doesn't know and he's the doctor.

I'm nearly too numb to be frightened. Or maybe I'm growing used to the small fissure of fear that hums in my belly, constant and unsettling.

Gage had said Hunter and King were friends. I'm certain now they couldn't be.

Still, like the last time Hunter came to my rescue, he's once again in control. Before, I was in his secret lab. Now I'm in this unmarked plane. I'm his passenger yet also his captive. With no phone, no money, no proper clothes, I have little chance of getting home on my own.

If nothing else, I'm going to get answers. I have so many questions. I'll get to the bottom of this. No matter what.

For now, I have to trust him. Because anything else is too awful to contemplate.

I'm so drowsy. The wild, frantic stress drains from me and turns into a glowering worry that drags me down, drags me under into a deep, dreamless sleep.

I wake to the sensation of the plane descending. A sliver moon glows weakly in the dark, twinkling night. We drop below the cloud cover. Stars wink out, replaced by a blur of gray. I squint to see the ground. There's no sign of an airport, just pitch-black countryside.

Trees, fields. A building in the distance with a glowing yellow light.

Hunter touches my shoulder, pulling me fully awake.

"Where are we? Why are we flying so low?" I say.

"Landing."

"I don't see a runway."

"Runways are overrated. Fasten your seat belt."

"Overrated? Great." I sit up quickly and push aside the blanket to snap on the safety belt. It's one of those things that crosses over both shoulders and locks over my breastbone.

Not a minute too soon.

A grassy field comes up at us fast. I grab onto the door with one hand, my seat with the other, bracing myself.

"The pontoon! What about the broken pontoon?" I cry.

"Hold on and pray."

TWENTY-SEVEN

I DO AS HUNTER SUGGESTS. I pray hard and quick and stare at the approaching ground. It zooms up to meet us, impossibly fast.

The wheels bounce violently.

Then they settle into a brisk, lopsided roll. We limp across the field at a hasty clip.

"Nice work." Hunter slaps the dash as though slapping the shoulder of a good buddy. He toggles switches and dials and the throttle. I look out at the grass whipping past. Flaps on the wings engage, rapidly slowing our progress. Before we reach the tree line, he wheels the plane in a U-turn. The lumpy ground jostles me gently as we taxi.

"Where are we?" I ask.

"Every guy needs a secret hideout. This is mine."

"Secret hideout, huh?"

He shoots me that grin of his, the one I remember from the barn. There's that angular dimple etched into his right cheek. "Yep. You're officially visitor number one."

"I feel kind of honored."

"Reserve that thought. You haven't seen the place yet."

For a moment, our banter brings back the easy familiarity we shared all those weeks ago. Then I'm back on my guard. What is this place? And when can I call Dad? How can I get news of Gage?

A large metal building appears out of the blackness. It's long with an arched roof and flat front secured with huge double doors. A Quonset hut. Hunter parks the plane a hundred yards from the tall entrance. He hops out, leaving the engine running, strides to the doors, and hauls them open. Then he gets back in the plane and drives us inside.

I unbuckle my seat belt. By the time I've shrugged out of it, he's at my door, reaching a hand to help me to the ground.

"I can manage," I say

He backs up and watches me.

Half a dozen faint white bulbs glow overhead. There's an SUV parked in the semidarkness. A Porsche Cayenne. It's black and shiny like his other wild ride, and although it's too big to be a sports car, it looks fast and powerful. Everything about Hunter is fast and powerful.

"Pretty impressive hideout," I venture.

"Really? You like it?"

"Seeing as it's the only hideout I've ever visited, I don't have much to compare it to. But yeah, it's not bad."

At this he rolls his eyes with such exaggeration that my teeth tug at my lower lip to hold back a smile.

To be honest, I can't believe he owns an airplane hangar with an unmarked water plane and a shiny, luxury getaway car. What reality does he live in?

"Come on. This way." Hunter looks almost sheepish as he leads me to a regular door in the back of the hangar. It's secured with a key code panel. He types in a bunch of numbers and the lock clicks open. "Ta-da."

I see an apartment that can only be described as over-the-top masculine.

"Interesting," I say.

Low, discreet lights glimmer everywhere. A spotless concrete floor enhances the industrial-style furnishings. Lots of open space. To the right stands a brushed stainless-steel table with two chairs made of the same metal. The kitchen cupboards and freestanding counter are matte black. There's a matching half fridge.

Far to the left is a bed made up with white sheets and pillows and a gray wool blanket. A bedside table holds a digital clock, a light, and a stack of books. From here they appear to be medical texts. Nothing remotely resembling light reading.

There's no sign of a TV. Instead, a long bookshelf takes up most of the central area. It's stuffed with more books. Hardcovers with long, technical-sounding titles. The kind of books that used to fill the house Mom and I shared. At five I'd flip through them and marvel at how smart she must be. Like a goddess, all-knowing, because how else could she interpret such dense paragraphs, complicated diagrams, and bizarre mathematical equations?

There's only one truly inviting chair. It's positioned next to the shelves. His hideaway is like an extension of his study back at the PRL.

"It's very you," I say.

"Is it?"

"Definitely."

"We're safe here, anyway, and it should warm up soon. Hopefully you won't find it too uncomfortable."

I glance at the bed. Of course there's only one. Why would there be more? "No. It's . . . great."

"I'll sleep on the floor," he says, clearly reading my thoughts.

"I will," I say, awkward.

His face says that will never happen.

"I'm serious. If you have an extra blanket, that's all I need," I insist.

"Come on, the bathroom's back here. If you want, you can take a hot shower to defrost. I'll find you some clothes. They'll be big, but I guarantee they'll be warmer than those damp clothes."

I pause. "I need to contact my dad. And I want to find out if there's any news on Gage."

He shakes his head. "Too dangerous. King's got ears everywhere. He'd trace us the minute the call went through. Victoria will have contacted your dad. She knew I was headed to get you."

"What if they try to go after him?"

"It's you they're after."

"And what about Gage? Do you think they—"

"There's no point speculating until we can get more information."

"Maybe they let him go."

"Maybe. Gage has a few tricks up his sleeve. He won't go down easily."

I'm glad he doesn't claim everything's going to be fine. Nothing's fine, and I don't know when it will be ever again. His fingers work the back of his neck, even as I sense his need to comfort me. There's a pull between us, as though he's about to stretch out his arms and wrap me close. Even if I wanted him to, I don't deserve anyone's comfort.

I clear my throat. "I better get in the shower."

"Right. I'll find those clothes."

Alone, I undress and turn on the faucet. Was it just this morning the doctor cut me free? It seems like decades ago. Shards of gravel are embedded in my skin. I step beneath the hot stream and scrub my hands and knees and feet. Hunter's shower gel pummels me with the bright, crisp scent of lemons, a too-bright smell that wars with my dark thoughts. I scrub hard until the skin is red and all the grit is gone. Then I let the water scorch me, trying to burn away my worry and fear, my chaos and bottomless guilt.

As I'm drying myself, there comes a knock at the door.

I open it a crack and Hunter hands a shirt and pants into the steamy room. Our fingers touch. To my chagrin, a pulse, electric, shoots down my arm and all the way into my body.

"Thanks," I say.

"Hold on. Stay there." His hand pulls back and reappears holding a short coil of rope. "I had to wing it with the belt."

"That'll work," I say.

His T-shirt smells good. Like him. I pull the enormous thing over my head. It falls to my knees. I slide into the pair of soft fatigues and knot the rope at my waist. The cuffs require six roll-ups until my feet are showing. Instead of shoes, he's supplied me with two pairs of thick wool socks. I layer them on and check myself out in the mirror.

Lovely.

I try tucking his shirt in, which looks dumb, so I pull it out again.

Then I shuffle through the door.

Hunter is in the kitchen, opening a jar of spaghetti sauce. He turns as I step out of the bathroom. His gaze shifts from my face to my socks and back up again, taking me in so completely that I stiffen and my arms involuntarily cross over my chest.

"I look ridiculous. I know."

"I wouldn't say that." He leans back against the counter.

Whatever. Finding myself at a loss for words, I step past him to the two-burner hot plate. "What are you making?" Like it's not obvious. God. Could I think of anything more intelligent to say?

"Pasta. It's the only thing I can cook."

"Sounds good. Want help?"

"Sure."

I find a pot and fill it with water. "So what's it like to know how to fly an airplane? To be able to go anywhere you want?"

"I won't lie. It's great."

"Have you ever been afraid you were going to crash?"

"Not yet," he says.

"When did you learn?"

"Oh, a while ago," he says, his tone vague.

"Do you have any brothers or sisters?" I ask as he dumps the sauce into a pan.

"A sister. She's gone now."

"I'm sorry. Were you close?"

"Growing up, yeah. She would've liked you. You would've liked her, too, I think."

"So you're the only one left. That must be hard."

"It's not so bad." Still, an emotive sensation curls into me. Sorrow. It's as old and as heavy as the stones of a lost city. My mouth opens in surprise under the weight of it. He turns away and adjusts the flame. Or can he tell that I sense him?

"My sister got sick a while back," he says by way of explanation. "Enough about me. I want to hear about you."

"What do you want to know?"

"I want to know you."

At this, I actually laugh a little and I feel the tension easing. We serve up two plates and sit. The conversation comes slowly. It's like we're getting reacquainted. All the time I'm sensing his emotions, faint as ghostlike tendrils between us. It's hard to stay focused. Finally I let go and let the emotions do their thing. It starts to feel like music, like a soundtrack under our words. I should be frightened. I'm not somehow. It's actually enjoyable. My own emotions expand and contract with his, so that it's like we're dancing, the words and feelings lacing us together.

And then I remember where we are and the things he hid from me, and I push away my half-eaten plate. My stomach aches, and I don't even know how I ever took a single bite.

"I want to know about the casts," I say.

He sets his fork down carefully. "I wondered when that would come up. Then again, I thought you might have puzzled it out."

"And how on earth would I have done that?"

One of his brows arcs upward.

"Okay. Let me guess. If you're the good guy—and I'm still not completely sure about that—"

"I am the good guy."

"You'd probably say you did it as a cover-up."

"Tell me—how would it look if some brutally injured woman walked out of our facility four weeks after an accident without a single scratch? I knew you'd refuse to stay put. I knew King would be watching. And the police had seen you firsthand. This way, the world would see what they expected to see. It was a ruse, that's all. And it didn't work."

"You could've told me. I would've been careful—I would've played along."

"I needed you to get better, not worry about your treatment. I didn't want you burdened with our secret. I was trying to protect you. That's all."

"Because you and the others—what you've done to yourselves—it's a secret?"

"Yes. And it would hurt all of us if it got out. We'd lose our freedom."

I recall King's men, who'd chased me down like I was a specimen. A thing to be put under glass, dissected and studied piece by piece.

Rain begins to patter against the curved metal roof, slow and steady. I believe him. That was the fear I felt from Ian and Victoria. And although I don't agree with him keeping things from me, I begin to understand a little why he might have.

"I don't want any more people getting hurt. It's my secret now, and I won't share it with anyone."

THE RAIN IS COMING DOWN as I inspect Hunter's bookshelves. I notice an old record turntable in a cabinet and crouch down.

"Does this work?" I ask.

"It does, but there's no needle right now."

He crouches by me on the concrete floor. Our bodies are not touching, but I'm aware of his warmth and size and solidness. If I move even an inch, our legs would press together. They feel almost magnetized. I pull out an armful of vinyl albums.

"Chopin's nocturnes? Arthur Rubinstein's version? He played it brilliantly."

"Really? Those were my mother's. I'm not sure I know it."

"Opus nine, number two in E-flat major? You'd recognize it for sure. It's been in movies, TV shows, some video games, even, I think. And there's this great British rock band called Muse that did a version that's like Queen meets Chopin."

"Queen meets Chopin, huh?" His eyes flicker at me, crinkling at the corners. "How does it go?"

I put my head down for a second, searching for the lyrics. "I think it starts out something like . . . *You and me are the same. . . .*"

"Sing it."

I roll my eyes. "All right. You asked for it."

I sing until I forget the words, and I trail off into the nocturne. His expression warms in recognition of the notes. They're beautiful and almost

SUE WYSHYNSKI

painfully nostalgic. His carefully crafted walls, if that's what they are, seem to be slipping. I close my eyes and glide over the threshold as his world opens up to me. It's a place of heavy, swirling dark emotions. Yet there are pinpricks of lightness. I don't know how or even what I'm doing, but I continue to feel my way forward and brush against a barely concealed field of desire. I can almost sense him pulling me closer, and I let him for a moment before my consciousness spins away. I hum and fly deeper, entering the dark, tortured shadowlands of some indefinable wound. It's caustic, boiling, ancient, and almost boundless. It startles me in its intensity, and I focus all my attention on it, trying to see, trying to understand, trying to know—

"That's enough," Hunter says sharply.

"Oh!" I say, my eyes flying open. The sensation snaps off.

"We have a long day tomorrow." He stands abruptly. "You should get some sleep."

I rise, horribly awkward, desperately eager to escape. Was that real? Or had he been reacting to some weird expression on my face? Had I looked like a crazy person? Because right now I feel crazy. Almost hungover, like I'm having a sick reaction to what just happened.

"If you have that extra blanket—" I begin.

"You're sleeping in the bed." His stony face brooks no argument.

I glower at him. I don't appreciate being barked at. Maybe he's the good guy. But it doesn't mean he's a nice guy. Whatever. I'm done. I just want this day to be over.

Stiff-backed, I say, "Fine." Fully dressed, I tug up the sheets and crawl in.

He takes a brief shower and switches off the lights. I hear him settle into the leather chair. I turn to face the wall and do my best to shut him out.

As I start to fall asleep, my thoughts go to Gage and Dad and Sammy. All evening, anxiety has made it impossible for me to fully relax. Now that I'm alone, my worry roars into the fore.

Please, dear God, let them be all right.

TWENTY-EIGHT

I WAKE THE NEXT MORNING TO an empty room. For one panicked moment, I have no idea where I am. Sounds come from the airplane hangar. Then it rushes back.

It's Hunter. He's humming.

I carefully make the bed so it looks like it did before—with crisp military corners.

After how last night ended, I badly want to keep my guard up. There's a fresh shirt and pants laid out. They're soft and smell of his laundry soap. It would be a lot easier if he wasn't so thoughtful. Yesterday he told me he wanted to know all about me. Despite everything, the more time we spend together, the more I care about him. He has some dark secret, though—that's clear. I'm afraid of the troubled shadow that torments him.

Part of me longs to be able to free him from whatever it is. Another part knows it's too big for that. Weeks ago, outside the barn, he warned me away. Is that why he was so abrupt last night? Because I'm getting too close for comfort?

In the bathroom, I take the red pills and dress quickly. My worry for Dad, Sammy, and Gage, fear about my modification, and confusion about Hunter show in the blue shadows beneath my eyes.

Hunter continues to bang away in the airplane hangar.

There's no point delaying this. Bracing myself, I pad out the door into the big, arched space. The plane looks large and impressive, enclosed in this personal room. The Porsche Cayenne SUV is there, too, shiny and new and mobile.

Hunter appears, sauntering around the tail of the plane. He's got a bucket in one hand, a large soapy sponge in the other. He's wearing a pair of low-slung, faded jeans, rolled up to just below his knees. And that's it. His feet are bare. A dusting of hair runs the length of his arms, looking like it would be soft to run your fingers over. His chest spans at least five, maybe six of my hands, tapering downward into a well-sculpted six-pack. The masculine curve of his hip bones draws my eyes even farther downward, toward that low waistband and . . .

This is ridiculous! I'm ogling him. How does he do this to me? I'm staring at him and feeling the most outrageous erotic sensations rippling down my belly.

Pull it together! After last night, you need to be distancing yourself!

I tear my gaze upward. His devilish eyes are fastened on mine, and his mouth turns up into a half grin.

"Good morning," he says.

"Yes, hi."

"There's not much for breakfast, I'm afraid. Half a loaf of bread in the freezer, peanut butter and jam if you want toast."

"I'm fine. How's the plane?"

"Sturdier than she looks." He motions with his sponge at the bucket. "Just washing off the salt water. I made a few repairs. Have to get parts in at some point."

Silence follows. We've run out of things to say. I shuffle my feet, tongue-tied.

"Guess I'll go empty this," Hunter says.

He disappears and I see one of the giant doors crack open a few feet. Wan sunlight pours inside. There's a splash of water being tossed and then he returns.

"I'll just rinse off and we can go," he tells me.

"Go? Where?"

"Victoria told me you have a work interview in Hartford."

"I forgot about that," I say, stunned at how far away Dad's house and that world seems. "But it's not for another two weeks. You think I need to hide out for that long?"

"I'm not sure. But we need to stay somewhere. I have a relative in New Haven. It's forty minutes from Hartford. We can hole up there while we're waiting."

"I guess you don't want to stay here." Obvious. Maybe I don't, either.

"Can't. That was my last packet of spaghetti."

"Won't the interview be too dangerous?"

"Can't imagine it'll take more than an hour."

I knot my fingers. "I'm going to be able to stop running, right? Because otherwise, what's the point?"

He sets down the bucket. "Yes. As soon as you're clear, I'll make sure King knows. Even if that means meeting face-to-face."

"Maybe I'm already better?"

"Maybe. But I don't think so. I have a blood kit. Let me get cleaned up and we'll see."

I follow him back inside. "Why am I so important? Why doesn't King go after you?"

"He's tried. You're an easier mark. If he comes after us, he knows he'll lose. Like always."

Maybe. Or maybe someday Hunter and the others will mess up.

"I just want you better, Aeris. I hate that you're feeling threatened. I hate that I put you on the run."

"You know what? I don't care. It's a lot better than being dead."

He emerges from the bathroom in jeans and a fitted heather-gray T-shirt. His brushed steel watchband makes his already thick wrist look even more muscular. He opens a cupboard and takes down a small, hard plastic suitcase. Inside are various needles, alcohol swab packets, some glass petri dishes, and a few bottles of liquid.

"Here, rest your arm on the table."

I do as he says, aware of his intoxicating nearness. The brush of his fingers electrifies my forearm. His face is unreadable, yet the faint color in his cheeks tells me he feels something, too.

He's competent, and I barely feel the prick of the needle.

"Hold that." He nods at the cotton ball pressed into the crook of my arm.

I press on it as he withdraws the syringe.

"Now we'll see." From the case, he takes a petri dish and squirts my blood onto it. Next he adds drops of various fluids. My blood changes color, turning darker until it's a deep shade of blue. Blue as a starry sky. Blue as ink, and now rapidly turning black. He grimaces and carefully washes the contents down the kitchen drain.

A pulse, dark and stormy, seems to shoot from his back, straight into my heart. It's brief, disappearing almost as quickly as it began. Whatever the results are, I know they're bad.

"How is it?" I ask.

"Better."

"But not good enough."

"Not as good as I'd hoped."

He's obviously disappointed, and I wonder how long we're going to be trapped together, running from King. He must be wondering the same thing. My stomach aches.

He joins me at the table. "There's something I need to say. Last night I was rude. I apologize. No—" He holds up one hand to keep me from replying. "Don't say anything yet. Just listen. The drugs aren't working as quickly as I'd hoped. And I can't in good conscience keep hiding this."

I wait, staring, wondering what it could be.

"After last night, you deserve the truth."

"What truth?" I say, although somehow I already sense the answer before he tells me.

He doesn't speak. Instead, it comes across from him like a release. Like a dam slowly inching open until a few drops trickle into me. It's a feeling, an emotion, a sensation. Totally masculine. Totally his. And if there were words attached to the emotion, they'd be saying something like, *You al-*

ready know. You know without me telling you. Aeris, you know.

My eyes snap up to his, and he nods.

So it's true. I'm not crazy. I feel a lump in my throat. Half relief, half disbelief. I'm not crazy. I can sense him. And he knows it. One hundred percent knows it. And now I'm angry.

Because he can sense me, too.

He didn't tell me. I thought I was going mad, and he didn't tell me?

My mouth opens to speak, yet all I can do is stare into his eyes. Sensations come flooding in. A whole river. An ocean. Bursting into my mind.

All of it, everything. The knowledge of how he's feeling as I look at him, or as he looks at me. Both, reflections yet different. Mine. His. Confusing and hard to pull apart, like mirrors facing each other and replicating unto infinity. Other sensations, ones I can't put names to because I don't know what thoughts are behind them. Concern, perhaps. Caution. Watchfulness. I never realized how much free-floating emotion exists in a person's body, a person's mind, until mine starts blending with his.

It's too much.

The flow is too strong. Way too strong. I frown, twisting and struggling under the weight of so much information. My synapses are firing out of control. The room fades out of my vision. Desperately, I try to focus on my surroundings. On the table. On my hands that are gripping the chair so hard I fear my fingers might break. I throw them up and clap them to my ears.

"Stop! Make it stop!"

It does. He does.

I go limp, sagging onto the tabletop, burying my face in my arms.

"So it wasn't just me," I whisper. "How could you not tell me? You knew what I was feeling."

Hunter rubs his face.

"You had to know everything I was going through," I say through gritted teeth.

"I thought if you experienced some minor emotional link, you'd believe it was nothing. A fluke."

"Minor? It wasn't minor. That's pretty damn obvious. How could you not tell me?"

"It's more than you and me that's at stake here. I broke our number one rule by saving your life. A consensus was reached. I voted to tell you, but the others wanted you kept in the dark. In their opinion, it was the only way to protect you and themselves at the same time. Humans want what they can't have, and empathic abilities would fascinate a lot of people. The human psyche is not ready for them, I can tell you that much. It never will be. They're a curse. I had to stick by their decision. But do you see on some level why we'd want the truth hidden?"

I stand, overwhelmed. It's all too alien to seem real.

I need to do something. I want to feel normal, safe. I go to the kitchen. There's a box of tea. I'll make tea. That's normal. I grab the kettle, fill it with water, and plug it in.

How could he keep this from me? I had every right to know!

The water begins to boil, and so does my indignation.

I glance over my shoulder and his eyes snap to mine. I realize then that although he's locking himself in, part of him can sense my swelling emotions. Does the connection always go both directions, or can he sense me even though I can't sense him? If so, it's just one more way he has control over me. From the hospital to this forsaken place, even into my mind.

I have no secrets from him. No private feelings. No silent dignity.

The kettle whistle blows high and loud. I yank the cord from the wall and dump the scalding water into a cup. It splashes onto the counter.

"All that time you knew I was sensing people, you said nothing. I could have lost my mind!"

"You didn't. And if we had sensed that, we would have told you the truth."

"We? So Ian, Victoria, all of them can read me?" I glare at him. "And so that's why you're telling me now? You think I'm losing it?"

He's a powerful, solitary figure, alone at the kitchen table. His rugged face seems so steadfast and honorable and true. I want to trust him. I so badly want to trust him. What is he really, though?

He grunts. "I'm telling you because from when I picked you up on that road, it's been a losing battle keeping you out. Obviously last night I couldn't. That's why I was angry. Not with you, with myself."

The tea leaches dark orange ribbons into the hot water. Both my hands are braced against the counter. They're shaking. This isn't how human beings are supposed to work. Tampering with the mind to open up connections between people is disturbing, impossible. Unthinkable. "I don't get it. This is what you've been researching? Linking yourselves up this way? Why?"

"It's not like that."

"Then what is it?"

Hunter remains silent for a long moment. I can still feel the threads faintly between us.

"It's a side effect. A horrible side effect of the genetic modification."

"I didn't feel it between me and my dad. Or my friends, Ella and Gage."

"Because they're not like us."

Us. Me and him. Because I'm no longer normal. No longer a safe, sound human being. I'm something different.

"Who is 'us'?"

"You and me," he says. "Victoria, Ian, Edward."

"And Lucy, too?"

He pushes back his chair. "There are others. Thirteen of us."

I let go of the counter and straighten up. He's right. On some level, I can sense them all. It's like low-level chatter. Perhaps because Hunter's physically closest, he's the loudest. There are others in the near distance like the wind in treetops. If I focus really hard, I realize I can sense Victoria's emotional signature. *She's worried.* From farther away comes the faintest murmur like the burble of a tiny stream—the people across the ocean in Switzerland, perhaps.

"And they're all struggling to shut me out?"

"Yes."

I think of Ian, who wanted this the least. No wonder he was so cold.

So angry.

"Is that why you left, then?" I ask.

"Partly." He's holding back. "I wanted to stay, Aeris. It's different for me. Harder."

"Why?" I ask, more deeply hurt than I could ever imagine. "Why is it different for you? You act like you care for me, and you're the one who turned me into what you are! I heard them try to stop you from doing it, from saving me. And then you leave them to take care of me while you disappear? You made me one of you. You could have at least told me the truth. I never asked for this. I never told you to inject me on that operating table. Yes, I wanted to live. But I never told you to use some experimental drug to restart my heart."

"Stop." His palms are facedown on the table, muscles twitching in his wrists.

I'm breathing hard, my chest rising and falling under the oversize shirt.

"It's different for me because I injected you with my own blood."

Hunter's words hover ghostlike between us.

His blood.

"I thought you gave me a drug."

"There is no drug. Not anymore. It's gone. It's been gone for a long time. I didn't even know if infusing you with my blood would save you. I certainly didn't realize it would work almost instantly. We were shocked. There you were, eyes open and speaking." He shakes his head. "We've been keeping up walls between us for so long that when you came into your awareness on that table, we were caught off guard. I had to send Victoria out, to pull herself together."

I remember that. I remember him ordering her from the room.

He rakes a hand through his hair. "I had no idea that injecting you with my blood would create a more direct link between us. It's not like with the others. It's stronger."

As we face each other, understanding passes between us. We're in this together. More deeply than either of us could have imagined. We were drawn to each other before the accident. Yet now there are threads knotted around both of our hearts, tied tightly and pulling us inextricably near. In some ways, we're closer than two people could ever hope to become. And in others, we're miles apart.

"You were ill," I blurt out as the realization comes to me. "After you left. I felt you. I made you sick because of this."

"No. That was different."

"And you came to me once at Dad's, when I was afraid."

"What was that about? I only knew you were frightened. I couldn't tell why."

"I was late taking the silver pill."

His face pales. "So that's twice? We can't let that happen again."

"No. And last night when I was singing it felt like I was crossing over into you or something—is that how it works? Is that what you do to me?"

"Honestly, I spend most of my life trying to avoid it."

"But it could be so interesting."

"I'm not so sure."

"You'll have to teach me to put a up a wall, then. It's only fair."

"You're right. But I can't lie. With you, it is appealing. I'm not blind to the temptation of what it might be like to explore it further. But earlier, when I showed you what we were capable of, for a minute I thought I wasn't going to be able to regain control. It's never happened to me before. It was like being pulled into an ocean current. One minute everything was fine, and the next I thought we were both going to get swept under."

I try to laugh. "What are you saying—that we almost got locked in each other's minds?"

"Yeah. I am." He shrugs. "It felt good at first. Damn good. But I almost couldn't stop it. I almost didn't want to."

TWENTY-NINE

The door to the airplane hangar stands open, and the grassy runway is just visible.

"I have to go outside," I say.

He sends his chair scraping back. "I could use a walk. If you don't mind the company."

I shrug, but am somehow glad when he reads that as a yes. The world is awash in morning glow. We stroll along the plane's landing path, stepping over crushed daisies and dandelions. The sweet, tannic scent of rosebushes permeates the air. I spot them blooming in great tangled masses like rolls of barbed wire blossoming into life.

When I reach them, I pluck a half-opened bud.

"Aeris?" Hunter says abruptly. "I don't think we should wait."

I turn, surprised.

"You need to be able to protect yourself. I know it's too late to say sorry for what I put you through, but I am. And I hope you'll see that someday."

It feels good to hear his acknowledgement, even if I am still mad at being kept in the dark. Judging by his furrowed brow and pleading eyes, it's clear he means it.

"Okay. . . " I say. "Apology accepted."

He blows out a sigh and the worried lines on his face ease. "I'll make it up to you. I promise. Starting right now. Let's do this."

I won't lie. I feel my excitement rise at the thought of being able to control my empathic ability. Although what happened in the hangar scared the living daylights out of me, there's an addictive pull that has begun to take hold. I want this. I want to know everything about it.

"Copy me. Cross your arms over your chest, tightly," he says. "It helps, in the beginning, to have a protective stance."

I do what he says.

"Good. Now glare up at me like you don't trust me. Use your eyes. Like you're pushing me away with your expression. Like you're building a distance between us."

I give him my hardest, mistrusting stare.

"Okay, ouch. I guess I deserve that, but it's a little intense coming from you."

"Just doing what you tell me."

"Yeah." His mouth curves with the hint of a grin. "I just didn't think it would come so easy. Then again, I have been a bit of a bastard. . ."

"Hunter. Can we get on with it?" I say, struggling to stay serious.

"Okay, right. So keep that look. And start to imagine a barrier of ice around your heart."

"Stop grinning," I tell him. "And it might be a little easier."

"Right. Good point. Wouldn't want to break your concentration."

I groan. "You're not exactly good at this. Hurry up, or I'm going to start laughing."

The feeling comes to me then. An energy—a presence, his presence, pressing into me. He's crossing the breach. Slipping into my arms; or maybe I'm slipping into his. I frown harder and tense my whole body, trying to shut him out. Still he keeps coming, wrapping around me.

And then, of all the terrible things to do, he tickles my soul. I swear it's the only way to describe it. He's giving me this ferocious, unbearable urge to laugh. I feel his humor inside me and it's so contagious that it's all I can do to keep glaring. I squint and wrap my arms around my ribs. I won't laugh. I refuse to. Freeze, Aeris. Freeze him out!

I imagine myself as the Ice Queen. With blue lips because I'm so cold.

At this, the first giggle emerges. I clamp my lips together. He doesn't let up, he keeps prodding me, goading me, relentless, going after me until my belly aches with the desperate need to laugh. And then we do, both of us, until I'm wiping tears from my eyes.

"Stop," I plead, holding up both hands. "Stop! I give!"

It takes a few minutes before we're both able to get serious again. One after the other, he tries different ways to attack me. With my arms crossed, I lower my lids and push him away. It's impossible.

"I can't do it."

"You can. Concentrate."

Then it comes to me. Fear: a fear so apocalyptic that my insides seem to turn to liquid. The ground loses its solidity. Terror roars in my ears. What's fueling this? A memory of Hunter's? What could make him suffer such horror? He keeps going at me.

I'm frightened. What if I can't escape? What if he can't stop it?

My teeth begin to chatter.

"Don't let me in," he growls. "Shut me out, Aeris. I'm just your audience. Do you understand? Shut me out!"

My audience? How is he my audience? And then I get it. I know what he's trying to make me do. Pretend I'm on stage. That's the one place I know how to shut people out. I imagine I'm playing. I focus my whole being on the tune. The heat of my blood drains.

The fear slips away.

I look at him.

"Can you feel me?" he asks.

I shake my head. "No."

"Nothing?" he says.

"Not a thing." I've done it. For now, when I concentrate, I can control it.

We remain standing mere inches away from each other. The floral-scented air is thick with breathless anticipation. We're rooted to the center of our world. His brow quirks and I'm almost tempted to let him in just to see what he's feeling. But I'm pretty sure I don't need supersenses to know he wants me as much as I want him.

"I warned you once before," he says softly. "You need to protect yourself from me. And I'm not just talking empathically." Yet his face doesn't match his words. There's a softness in the lines of his dark brows that makes me want to touch them.

"Why?" I breathe.

"My life is a mess. I don't want to drag you into it."

"I'm already there."

"You're not. This is only temporary. You and me, being here. Together."

I'm still holding the rose I picked earlier. The thorny stem bites into my palm.

"What are you saying?"

"I have to protect you. I want to. But that's all."

Birds twitter, singing around us. I don't believe him. Not when I see the rise and fall of his chest and the tightness of his hands at his sides.

"You'll be free soon," he says. "Back to who you were. Our link will fade and . . . then it will be gone."

Gone.

The word pulls me from my reverie. Our link will be gone. Of course it will be gone. The knowledge of its coming loss stabs me with surprising force.

I'm just beginning to grasp the power of our connection. I don't want to lose it already.

"You're going to be back to your regular life soon, the Philharmonic, your music." He pushes one hand through his hair. "Look, this will all just seem like some bad dream. Which is how it should be. We don't belong together."

I step away from him and pull his shirt tight around me. I refuse to let him see my hurt. How he can play stoic so easily? Well, I can play it cool, too. "I never said we belonged together."

I think I see a flash of pain, but then it's gone.

"So how long, exactly, will it be until I can get back to my real life?"

"I'm not sure," he says. "I hope soon."

Soon. Of course he wants it to be soon. "If you think reverting back to normal is so important, then why don't you do it yourself?"

"I can't."

"Can't? Why not? Why don't you take the pills?"

He takes the thorny rose from me. "You cut yourself."

"I'm fine. Answer the question."

"We tried. The pills don't work on us. They only work if you start taking them right away. We had high hopes, the others, and me, but we learned that we're too hardwired. We don't know how to fix ourselves. Doesn't stop us from trying, though."

"So that's what you're doing at the lab? You're not researching infectious diseases?"

"I'm afraid so."

"But then why claim—"

"Because it keeps people away."

I'm struck by a pang of sympathy. "But . . . how did you know the drugs would work on me?"

"Poppy."

Outrage floods me and I jerk back. "You're experimenting on the horses?"

"You really think badly of me, don't you?" He ruffles his damp hair and an unruly strand topples over his creased forehead. "No. There was a jumping accident and Poppy almost died. Except she didn't, because I saved her."

"You injected her with genetically modified blood? The way you did with me? And it changed her?"

"In her case, I had more time. I didn't inject her with blood. I made a serum. The principle's the same, though. We've isolated the genetic mutation from our DNA. That mutation was inserted into her DNA and forced her broken bones into a healing phase. Afterward, the meds knocked down the genetic mutation—but unlike with you, it only took seven days. She reverted back to normal."

"So you could have saved her again!"

"No. I knew you'd say that. It was too late." Hunter touches my shoulder. "It was her time."

Still, I feel his loss. Pets and horses are friends we never forget. Instinctively I reach up for his hand. We're so close he nearly blots out the stormy gray sky.

"Is it so impossible for us to be together?" I whisper.

Instantly, I wish I could put my words back. I'm out on a limb and I want to hide. He towers over me in this field of flowers and waving grasses. The slanting morning light makes him look almost timeless, like a sepia photograph. He's been hardened by whatever trials life has put him through—that much is clear. He has his own agenda, and I'm not on it.

So I'm shocked when he reaches for me and pulls me close. He's solid, strong. My heart is doing odd little thumps and when he tentatively brushes the hair from my neck, my pulse starts to race. I can see a war being waged in his eyes.

"Maybe just for now," he says.

"Yes. Just for now."

Then he bends closer. I notice that his eyes aren't just amber; they're flecked with a kaleidoscope of tawny browns and greens. I'm hypnotized by the shape of his mouth, and my gaze lingers there, feeling its pull. Am I still breathing? I don't know. Our lips touch and a rush of warmth shoots straight to my toes. He's kissing me, and, oh, is he ever good at it. I'm lost in the softness of his lips and the faint peppermint taste of his mouth and the strength of his body pressed to mine.

When we release each other we stand staring, our chests rising and falling.

Thunder rumbles overhead. Mist flecks my face.

"Rain," I say, the words oddly distant.

"Yes, rain," he echoes.

The sky opens up. Then we're laughing and running across the wildly overgrown landscape as the drops slant sideways.

"Race you," he says at my elbow.

"You're on."

He's off like a shot. But I'm quick, too. A lightning-speed me. I'm laughing, amazed at my power. I can't believe he kissed me. An amazing kiss. I had no idea it could ever feel like that.

BACK IN THE HANGAR, HE wraps his arms around me, and I swim in the scent of him, a cool, rain-washed fragrance that makes me feel so alive it almost hurts.

Through the wide entrance, the world sparkles with misty wetness. It feels safe here. Distant. I could walk out in the field, wander to the trees, stare up at the sky, spend time sorting things out. The city promises oppression. Strange people, crowds. I wish we didn't have to go.

Here, it's like time has come to a stop.

Here, it's just me and Hunter.

And our link that I'm only now learning to control. Who knows how much longer it will last? Who knows how amazing it could be? What if we were kissing and we let our emotions merge and—

"I'll start loading up," Hunter says.

I glance up. "Uh . . . right."

There's that smile of his again. He opens the rear hatch of the black vehicle. I watch him, all six-foot-something of perfect muscle and warm skin. He turns and catches me, his eyes all but daring me to come closer. My stomach starts doing triple somersaults.

"You make it awfully difficult to leave," he murmurs.

"Really?"

"Yes, and you know it," he says.

My teeth tug at my lower lip. "Do we really have to?"

He nods. "Yes. We do. I don't want anything to happen to you. You seem stable, but I don't have any medical supplies here. If there was an emergency, we couldn't risk flying to the PRL, not until the plane's fixed. Besides, we should stay away from there for now. We have to get to New Haven."

OUTSIDE, THE RAIN HAS STOPPED. Sunbeams blaze down through the clouds, lighting up the earth. Before we depart, I shuffle outside in a pair of his combat boots, the toes stuffed with socks. Standing there, I let the green surround me. A carpet of wildflowers, fragrant blossoms in white, pink, yellow and blue, languish under guard of the surrounding trees. Old oaks circle the perimeter, their boughs twining and coming together like the clasping of hands. Swallows flutter, calling out and singing among themselves.

All this time, a low-level hum of worry for my family and Gage has never left my mind. Now it boils up, and the horror strikes me all over again. My stomach clenches and my hands go damp. I just have to know if he made it, if he's all right. When we get to New Haven, I'll find a way to check in. Until then, I have no right at all to feel happy or safe.

Far off, a reddish-brown, four-legged creature with a bushy tail stands dead still in the shadow of a tree. A fox. I cup my hand over my eyes to block the sun for a better view. As I do, it melts into the undergrowth and disappears, leaving a trail of waving grasses.

Behind me, an engine roars to life. Hunter drives the Cayenne onto the dirt track. He hops out, locks the Quonset hut's large double doors, and comes to stand by me.

"See something interesting?"

"A fox."

"I know the one. Healthy-looking guy. He's been hanging around lately."

We stand together, watching to see if he'll reappear.

"Don't beat yourself up," Hunter says. "You gave it your all yesterday. Gage knows that."

I tamp down a piece of earth. Then I face him. "Gage told me he saw you at King's facility. And that King visited you."

"It's true. We've had a long-standing agreement."

"Which is what?"

"He leaves us alone, and we leave him alone. On occasion, he seems to require a face-to-face meeting to confirm our convictions."

"I still don't understand why he hasn't stolen your blood."

"He's one of the few who knows about us, but there are others in a position to keep things in check."

"In the government?"

"Yes. They realize the world has no room for people like us. So they leave us alone as long as we leave the human race alone. We don't modify anyone, they keep out of our business. Those are the rules. It's that simple."

A knot forms at the base of my skull. "Great. And how do they make sure you don't modify people?"

"At this point, we have a certain autonomy. They know we have no interest in spreading it. But they do keep tabs. That's why red flags went up when you stepped into that hospital. They ordered tests, and King was in the loop. As far as he's concerned, all bets are off. You're unauthorized. I broke the rules."

"Will the authorities take action, too?"

"Yes. I don't know what just yet. If I can get you better before we have to face the music, we might escape trouble-free."

"If not?"

"Then I've really opened up a can of worms. For all of us."

"Could they force you to allow them to experiment on you?"

He says nothing. Simply grimaces.

"Victoria, and Lucy and . . ."

Hunter nods and slips his hand into mine. After a time, as if by some mutually unspoken agreement, we abandon our vigil, turn, and head for the car.

The Porsche is all-black leather and plush carpets and hand stitching. It looks brand-new, like it's rarely been driven. I suspect it's only for emergencies. The track confirms my suspicions. Five feet out, the lane turns wild, completely overgrown in places. We bounce along until we come to a stream that's flowing across our path.

"That's new," Hunter says.

He hops out. I watch him kick off his boots on the bank and wade in without bothering to roll up his pant legs. At its deepest, the water reaches his knees. Sunlight gleams on his dark hair, flashes on his watchband. He's such a mix of contrasts—frightening and powerful when he's in the midst of a brutal fight, gentle and protective with the people he cares about.

Bending, he latches onto an object underwater and comes up with a boulder at least three feet across. Mud streams from it as, with little effort, he tosses it clear.

His eyes sweep up to mine and catch me through the windshield.

Maybe it's because we're alone, just the two of us in this lost wilderness, yet for an instant I feel like I'm the only girl in the world. And with sudden certainty, I know that if it were just Hunter and me here, stuck in exile forever, I could be happy.

Maybe he knows what I'm thinking. I know he can sense me through the wall. His smile is deepening, and I can sense him, too, and I'm pretty sure he's thinking the same thing.

Even though I'm growing stronger at blocking him, I don't try. I let him in on my innermost private feelings. It feels daring and crazy and superintense. Maybe I'm reckless for opening myself up when I know all this has to end.

His smile works its way into a grin. He wades up the bank toward my open window, stopping to pick a purple wildflower from the waving grass. At my door, he reaches in and tucks the bloom behind my ear. His fingers trail through my hair, leaving sparks in their wake. There's no need to say anything. To do anything. Because, yes, he can feel my emotions. Yet I can feel his, too. They're so heady and all-consuming that my heart nearly stops beating.

I'm unaware that I'm gripping the doorsill until he takes my hand in his and turns my palm up. Hunter strokes it, and a flash of heat shoots along my arm. His head bends to cover it, and his lips brush my skin like the wings of butterfly. As he does so, his extraordinary eyes come up to mine, mischievous and dancing.

When he releases me, I curl my fingers up and watch him stride around to his door. Seriously, I think I'm in love.

He puts the car in gear. "We're good to cross."

"Okay," I say, still a little breathless. "Great."

Sure enough, the car splashes into the stream and comes safely out the other side.

Leafy-scented air flows through the open window. It catches my bloom from behind my ear, taking it spinning away before I can grab it. I watch it fly, glad to be moving, glad to be doing something. Despite my earlier misgivings about leaving the hangar, it's wonderful to be on the trail.

We cross the roots of a giant tree. Hundreds of last year's dried leaves kick up, flocking around us like birds.

Being out here feels like a release. Like the calm after the storm. Even though the horrors of yesterday hang heavy in my heart.

A small voice inside warns me this is no release, however. This is no calm. It's the eye of the storm. The real hell is yet to come. I don't want to listen. I won't. I shut it out and open my window wider, reach my arm out and let my fingers fly on the wind.

THIRTY

As the morning wears on, the track becomes a dirt lane, and the lane turns into a rolling, two-way paved road with a dotted line down the middle. Every now and then a car appears over the approaching hill. We pass it and crest down the other side, traveling unmolested on our way.

Still, I'm aware that King has numerous eyes around the country. From what I can tell, his organization is huge and well equipped. And not just King. There are the others Hunter mentioned. We're going to have to start being careful at some point.

I remember hearing that governments can track down wanted criminals through city traffic cameras using face-recognition software. Unless we keep our heads down, running will be for nothing.

A tattered billboard in a farmer's field reads, LILA MAY'S AUTHENTIC SOUTHERN COOKING, 1 MILE AHEAD. Which is funny, because we couldn't be farther from the south.

"What do you think?" asks Hunter. "Shall we verify her claim?"

The dilapidated restaurant is the first we've seen since we left the hangar. There are two rusty pickups in the lot and a third that looks brand-new. Hunter leaves a gap of six spaces, parking under a tree. "I'll get it to go. Safer that way."

"All right."

He snags a baseball cap from the backseat. "Any special requests?"

"I'll have what you're having."

His eyes twinkle. "I doubt you can eat that much, but you're welcome to give it a shot."

When he's gone, I'm suddenly nervous. A brown sedan pulls into the lot, completely dark with tint. Before the door opens, a second vehicle whips into the space beside me, a black SUV that grinds to a halt a few feet away. My heart starts to pound. I should have closed the windows. What was I thinking?

I sink down low, my eyes darting up as the SUV door is thrown open.

It's just a woman in a dress. She gives my worried face an odd look as I let out a huge breath. Then she retrieves two kids out of the back.

I don't care if I'm being silly, if it's ridiculous to think King could find us so fast. I've never been so relieved to see Hunter's wide, muscular frame as he saunters across the lot with two giant takeout bags in his arms.

"What did I miss?" he asks, worried as he scans my pale face.

"Rush hour."

"Take a whiff of Lila May's fried chicken and you'll be surprised the whole state isn't trying to get through that door."

We pull down the road a little ways to eat.

"Why are you so strong?" I ask him.

He shrugs and keeps eating.

"I want to know why. You must have an idea. And what about this whole empathic thing? What causes it? I've heard of side effects—headaches, stomach upset, okay, those I understand. But an emotional link? That just happened? By accident? Without trying to create it? How?"

"That's a lot of questions."

"I have a lot of questions."

"Why don't we leave it for now." He reaches for a biscuit.

"I don't see why we should. I need to know these things."

"Actually, you really don't."

"What?" I'm mildly floored. "A little while back, you were telling me everything, teaching me to help myself, and now it's on a need-to-know basis?"

"Those things you *did* need to know. About how to protect yourself, and what my relationship is with King. The rest is different."

Carefully, I wipe my fingers one by one and then ball the napkin in my fist. "It's no different, Hunter."

Before, he was angled toward my seat. Now he turns so that one hand's on the steering wheel and his foot is pressed hard up against his door.

"What are you afraid of?" I ask.

"A day's going to come when you've moved on, and people might track you down, searching for information. And the less you know, the better off you'll be."

"For who? You or me?"

"Both of us. If it were only me—I'd tell you everything. It's not, though. I'm responsible for a dozen other people. They're relying on me. I can't just break a decades-long rule of silence—"

"I'm relying on you, Hunter. Right now. What if I don't get better? Did you ever think of that?"

And just like that, we're at loggerheads again. The smell of leftover chicken turns my stomach. I wish I hadn't eaten so much. But I'm not backing down. Now that I've asked the questions, I can't unask them. I won't.

Hunter's jaw is tight. Finally, he rubs his face. "I know, dammit. I know. All right. Ask. I'll tell you what I can."

And so I'm peppering him with questions.

"I want to know about the pain. And how does it all work? Why does it work? Who came up with it?"

"A scientist many years ago asked himself this question: If a living creature like the butterfly can tear down to its basic components and completely regenerate, could it be possible to stimulate human organs and limbs to do the same thing? In a controlled, localized effect?"

"Okay."

"First he studied the scarlet jellyfish. What's interesting is that when it gets old, it doesn't die. It latches onto a piece of seaweed, morphs back to its original birth state, and grows into full adulthood again."

"Are you serious? What do you mean? They live forever?"

"They can."

"So you're telling me this scientist crossed jellyfish genes with human genes?"

"Not exactly. First, he and his partner identified the code that forces the jellyfish to regenerate. Second, they copied it. Then they tested their theory out on butterflies. Butterflies seemed like a good fit because they go through a chrysalis phase. They inserted the relevant code from the jellyfish into the butterfly's DNA. And a new type of butterfly was born. From there, they started working with human tissue."

"Wait. But why are you so strong? Neither of those things are."

"Actually, you're wrong. Butterflies are extremely strong. Their muscles are highly developed so they can flap those large wings—up to twelve times a second. And unlike human skin, after death a butterfly's wings can remain perfectly intact in a museum or behind glass. We also think it has to do with the number of times we've gone through—what I mean is, the way we heal after each stress or injury. Our bones and muscles are honed and ultimately we grow sturdier. Tougher. Faster."

"And what about the empathic thing?"

He nods. "Okay. Butterflies and jellyfish have flocking habits. They travel in units, moving and communicating. But, of course, they don't speak. They converse in other ways. For butterflies, use of ultraviolet light is the most talked about in scientific circles. We have a slightly different perspective. We think they also employ emotive transference. At least, if what's happened to us is any indication."

"Emotional transference?"

"Like fear. It can drive the whole colony at once. Make them flee. By uniting their emotional state, we think they can induce a shared 'motor mind.'"

"What, like the Borg?" I laugh.

"Exactly. Of course, when their genetic material was introduced into humans . . . well, let's just say we're a lot more complex than a butterfly. We don't want to flock. The end result—"

"Is that you sense what's going on with each other, except instead of being helpful, it's overshare?"

"You got it."

"Wow." I shake my head. "That's madness." Genetically modified people? And here I've been worried about genetically modified foods.

I flash on Mom's journal. What would she think if she could see me now? I lean back and try to digest it all. Hunter starts up the Cayenne and merges onto the road. Switching on the radio, I'm surprised to find reception. Some old Memphis blues jug band. I turn it down low.

"This might sound odd," I tell him, "but I have a strange feeling my mom could've been involved with the PRL twenty years ago."

"What makes you say that?"

"Partly because of what I told you she wrote."

"I'd like to see that journal."

"It isn't much. Only a few paragraphs. There's another reason, though." I slide my fingers along the armrest. "When I was five, my mom and I went to Switzerland. I think she was trying to bring some people her research. We were chased down." I glance at him.

His eyes are on the road.

"She was killed."

"I'm sorry." His hand takes mine and closes completely around it. He feels for me; I sense it loud and clear.

"The people searched her car and took all her files. We never found out who they were. Americans, that much I know. They must have followed her there. Your company is originally from Switzerland, isn't it? Victoria told me. When this is over, I want you to help me look into it. Maybe it's a long shot, but I just can't shake the feeling it's connected."

"Instincts are pretty powerful."

For a moment, I get an overwhelming urge to ask him if he met her. That wouldn't make sense, though. How could he have? He would've been a child.

The road grows busier and wider, and eventually we turn onto a broad freeway. Rushing cars pack every lane. An interstate sign reads, NEW HAVEN, 27 MILES. We're almost there.

"I hope Dad's not too worried," I say out loud, the words escaping before I realize how large they've been looming in my mind.

"He knows this is the best way to keep you safe."

"But what about him and Sammy? Are they safe?"

"He knows how to protect himself."

"I hope so."

As we drive, I think of both Dad and Gage. I dragged them into this. Guilt presses down, so heavy it colors the world black. The shadows of the approaching city are like the shadows in my heart—ominous and dark.

Shifting in my seat, I pull my knees up and turn to study Hunter.

"Gage thinks you're like King, that you're trying to make supersoldiers."

"Gage said that?" He laughs. "No wonder the guy hates me."

"Why did you ever get involved in this research?"

"It's a long story." There's that tense, closed-down look again.

"I'm not going anywhere," I say.

At this, he lets out a short laugh. "All right." He forcibly relaxes his grip on the steering wheel. "The condensed version. Ian and I were soldiers stationed in a remote location. Victoria, Edward, Lucy, and the rest of our people were there, too, some working as civilians, others as part of the research team. There was an accident. We shouldn't have survived. We did, but had no idea what we were getting ourselves into. And ever since, we've been trying to get ourselves out of it. Looking for a way to undo the effects. That's why we do what we do."

It's the last thing I expect him to say. I'm stunned.

"An accident?" I ask when I find my voice.

"The lab was attacked. We escaped, and this was our only way to survive. We were in a snowbound location; we were injured; we had no food, no radios; we were going to have to walk out. It was live or die. The drugs had been salvaged. We took them. And here we are."

"How long has King been after you?"

"Years." Hunter shakes his head. "Last time he tried, I blew up a billion-dollar research facility of his, and he laid off for a while. Now you come along. You're newly changed. You're not strong like we are. You're an easy mark. And you're outside the rules."

"And if he gets me? Then what?"

He pauses, and suddenly his feelings flow to me unchecked. They're so awful I nearly retch. "It would be a nightmare. If he gives his men an infusion of your blood the way I did to you with mine, you'd be linked to his men. Linked to them just the way you and I are. Just as strong. Just as close. Living with their violence. Sensing it. And you'd have no skills to keep them out."

My heart starts slamming.

"As for Victoria, Ian, Edward, all of us, we'll experience it, too. You'll be like the funnel that channels them through. Everything will pour into us as well. They won't have the skills to put up blocks. There would be no way any of us could withstand the force. All of our carefully constructed walls would crumble in the face of such an assault."

Ian's words in the garden outside the lab come to me then. I remember the fierce way he begged me to take my medications. Now I understand. I finally understand. That's the fear I felt from Victoria, from all of them.

When they look at me, they see their downfall.

If the force didn't kill them, it would drive them insane. Then there are the soldiers—being so many, it would tear them apart. Who knows what terrible acts such a group of ruthless, violent men would commit?

Victoria, Edward, and Lucy treated me with compassion. Even Ian in his own way. It's amazing they were ever kind to me.

It's hopeless to want to stay linked to Hunter. Even though our power shimmers with the promise of a shared, uncharted territory.

I have to get better.

If King gets my blood, not only will he invade me, but he'll invade us all.

THIRTY-ONE

THE DIM HANDS OF DUSK press down upon the earth while flares of man-made light struggle to keep darkness at bay. Cars rush through the twilight gloom. Fast-food signs promise temporary solace. Most people appear homeward-bound, to the safety of locked doors and blaring televisions. Driving alongside them, I feel as if I've been cast out and may never find my way home.

An approaching sign reads WELCOME TO NEW HAVEN. More signs point to Yale University and various landmarks. Parallel to the highway, a freight train approaches, whizzing and clacking.

"This is our turnoff," Hunter says, taking an exit that curves over the tracks.

The railway cars continue on below us, a giant, segmented, high-speed snake, so long I can't see its tail.

Then we're winding through a residential neighborhood. Houses grow larger and grander the deeper we go. Lawns spread themselves wider, homes farther apart.

"What's your relative's name?" I ask, realizing he hasn't said if it's a man or a woman.

"Charlie. Charlie Quinn."

"What does he do?" I ask, surveying the lavish mansions.

"Art dealer. And collector. A successful one."

"Looks like it," I say as we pull into a wide driveway.

"Does he know about you? Me?"

"Yes."

The central focus of the front lawn is a fountain lit with twinkly lights. In the middle stands a sculpture of Venus from Botticelli's *The Birth of Venus*, one hand covering her naked breasts, the other barely covering her thighs with her long, flowing hair. Hunter cuts the engine, and the sound of dancing water fills the humid night.

"He should be expecting us," Hunter says.

At that moment, the front door opens and a man steps out. In the porch light, I catch sight of his face and a shock of washed-out reddish hair, and guess him to be in his late-sixties. He has an upturned nose and a wide mouth, and as he approaches, his lean face wrinkles into a broad smile. With his rangy arms and legs, I'm reminded of a life-size marionette I once saw in a theater.

"Hunter!" he cries. "And who's this beauty you've brought me?"

"Charlie," Hunter warns.

"What's this? Do I hear a note of jealousy? Don't tell me you've found love at last."

"What I've found is your driveway, and I was hoping you'd let us in."

Charlie looks amused. "No, you can't come in. You still haven't introduced me."

"I'm Aeris," I say, stepping forward.

"There you go, very civilized." He offers me his hand. It's warm and bony. His eyes crinkle, and he says, "I'm Charlie. You'll have to excuse my cousin's churlish manners."

"You're cousins?"

"Yes," they say in unison.

I'm slightly surprised, given their age difference.

"As you can see," Charlie adds, "I'm the more attractive one. No bags? Well, come inside. No point donating blood to a bunch of thirsty mosquitoes." He heads back toward his front door.

"I just have one thing." I go to the car for my satchel and lift it from the foot well. It's grown a lot lighter now that the pill supplies are dwindling.

"I'll get that." Hunter drapes it over one shoulder. "Charlie can be a bit much, but he really is a good friend."

"He seems nice. I like him."

"Good," Hunter replies, sounding relieved.

"What are you two whispering about?" Charlie calls. "Better be about me."

"It is," Hunter tells him, and laughs. Then he opens the back door and grabs a black duffel. "Clothes for you and me. Speaking of which, we'll have to get you something else for your interview."

"You don't think these will do?" I say, and make a little twirl on the lawn, holding out his shirt.

"Oh, they do just fine for me."

THE FRONT HALL IS SURPRISINGLY narrow given the expansiveness outside. A suit of armor stands guard in a niche at the foot of a steep set of stairs. Oil paintings ascend upward, disappearing out of view. A small table near the door holds a brass bowl with a ring of keys. Next to it is a statuette of a water nymph.

Charlie is already halfway down the hall. "Come to the kitchen. I'll pour you a drink; you must be thirsty."

"Don't suppose you've got anything edible?" Hunter asks.

"You're in luck. There's beef bourguignon bubbling on the stove and a couple of frozen baguettes waiting to be thrown into the oven."

"I was wondering what smelled so delicious," I say.

Charlie glances at Hunter. "I see you haven't exactly been forthcoming with my accomplishments."

Hunter's mouth tips up in a grin. "No need to swell your head. You do a much better job of it than me."

"Well put, well put. What he's trying to say is that I dabble in gourmet cooking, and I'm damn good at it."

The corridor gives way to a spacious, well-equipped kitchen. Gleaming pots hang from a rack on the ceiling. The gas stove is huge with six burners, and the stainless-steel fridge is enormous. I don't know how he stays so thin with a fridge so large. He practically scampers to the stove, his bony arms working as he lifts the lid from a pot and gives it a stir.

I pad across the rustic tile floor to the counter. Even in here there's art. Pottery urns that appear to be Greek or Roman line the tops of the cabinets.

Charlie gestures at my baggy outfit. "Tell me about this. Is it all the rage? I'll never understand modern fashion."

I let out a laugh. "No! These are Hunter's. I didn't have anything else."

"Oh my. Were you naked and shoeless when he found you?"

Hunter clears his throat. "About those baguettes?"

"All right, all right, I've got them." Charlie digs in the freezer and pulls out two long loaves.

"I can unwrap those for you," I say.

"Excellent. Drinks, that's what I was going to get."

The clink of ice into three tumblers is followed by the fizz of sparkling San Pellegrino.

"I'm sure I've got a few limes in here somewhere."

As he digs around, I feel Hunter's eyes on me, and when I turn to look at him, he smiles. His smile sends a warm glow all the way to my toes. In this enclosed space, Hunter looks huge and muscular, his windblown black hair tumbling over his forehead.

Charlie says, "We'll eat at the kitchen table if you don't mind. The dining room is temporarily housing a collection of Etruscan artifacts."

It's amazing how easily we chat away. Hunter and Charlie are clearly the oldest of friends, and without the least bit of effort, they make me fit right in. I notice, however, that Charlie is careful to avoid the topic of what we're doing here and Hunter avoids mentioning it.

Despite our troubles, Hunter almost seems content.

For a while, the two of them talk while I listen. As they do, I think back to Charlie's earlier teasing—*Don't tell me you've found love at last.* It was just a silly jest, of course.

Charlie's looking at me expectantly, and I realize he's said something I didn't hear.

"What's that?" I ask.

"I thought you might be interested in seeing my antique piano. I understand you play."

He has a piano? Trepidation trickles down my spine, my arms, all the way to my fingers. To sit at the keys would be wonderful. But this isn't like when I had my casts on. Then I could push aside my worries. Now my hands are free and this is the real test. Can I still play? Will the accident have changed me? My hands? Or is it my old fear?

"I'd like to see it," I say, tamping down my emotions.

Charlie brews up some espresso, and I load plates into the dishwasher. We carry our espresso into the living room. There it is. An upright piano carved all over with sinuous leaves and vines, flowering ribbons, and birds darting here and there among them. It's not from this century, maybe not even from the last. It's known players' hands for longer than I've existed. Had it come from a private home or a grand theater? Maybe it livened up some western saloon with girls in satin dresses and crowds of brawling drunk men.

I touch a carved swallow. "It's beautiful."

"1862, rosewood with ivory keys."

"Is it tuned?"

"It is."

"You play, then?"

"Oh no. Not at all. Have a go. Let's get a professional opinion on whether this thing is worth all the fuss made over it."

I slide onto the seat and run my fingers across the keys. I pick out a few notes, and the instrument whispers to life. It speaks to me, telling me I haven't lost it. I shut my eyes in relief, running one scale and then another. It responds under my hands as if it's been waiting for a person to find it and revive it.

"More!" Charlie cries from the settee. "A song!"

I'd forgotten my audience. I glance at him, and my nerves flutter back.

"'Sweet Chariot,'" Charlie says.

"I'll play it. But only if you two sing with me."

"Me?" Hunter barks out a laugh. "Not on your life."

Charlie shoots him a beetling challenge. "Don't tell me you're scared."

Hunter pulls a face and grins.

"'Sweet Chariot,'" Charlie says. "Play on, maestro."

"All right. Everyone knows the words to that," I say pointedly at Hunter.

"Fine," he says with a laugh, and sits down beside me.

His warmth reassures me as my hands find the notes and strike their way across the keys. I don't know what Hunter was worried about. His deep voice is wonderful, and soon the three of us are roaring out the song together.

Swing low, sweet chariot,
Coming for to carry me home,
Swing low, sweet chariot,
Coming for to carry me home!

I looked over Jordan, and what did I see
Coming for to carry me home?
A band of angels coming after me,
Coming for to carry me home.

Once the two of them get going, there's no stopping them. We play and sing until our throats are hoarse and Charlie is digging into a box of vintage music scores for more songs.

There's a bond between these two, so strong that my heart swells. Unconditional—that's what family love is. It holds us safe through the ups and downs of life. It's there for us when all else has fallen away. It's there, no matter what.

Like Dad. And Mom. I realize that's my fear: Music is the magic line that anchors me to Mom. She loved to sing. She was good at it. Really good. We always sang together. Sometimes we even made up silly songs. She actually wrote them down as sheet music—*because you'll want them when you grow up, Ari.*

She couldn't have been more right. I still have them, my envelope of faded, dog-eared treasures. Is that why I chose to make music my life? Because when I play, she's there in every note? Her comforting voice, her fierce devotion, her passion for life. It comes alive, and I feel her hold me close.

It's late when we finally run out of steam and head for bed.

"I'll let you manage your own arrangements," Charlie says. "I have some work to do down here."

"Good night. Thank you for a delicious dinner."

"Thank you, my dear, for making it the most lovely evening I can ever recall."

I beam at him, and as he bends to kiss my cheek, I see a sudden sadness in his eyes.

"Good night," he says as we head off.

His unexpected melancholy sends my thoughts toward Dad and Sammy and Gage. As I head away from the warm candlelight, my stress and fear roll back over me. At the stairs, Hunter puts a hand on my arm, steadying me as I ascend the steep, narrow steps.

Even though I can't feel his emotions, even though he's kept a wall carefully between us all through dinner, I can sense his heat at my back. He's so close, his body almost presses against mine. My pulse begins to thrum in my throat.

Then we're at the top of the stairs. We make our way along another narrow corridor. Hunter stops at a doorway, turns the filigreed knob, and pushes the door inward.

"Will you be all right in here?"

The four-poster bed appears to have been torn straight from a Transylvanian castle. With the shutters drawn outside the windows, I can't help a shiver of trepidation.

"I'm not sure whether to feel safe or terrified."

Hunter grins. "It does look rather medieval, doesn't it?"

"You're sure this isn't Dracula's New Haven abode?"

"Quite. I'll be down the hall. Scream if you need me."

But he makes no move to leave. He smells faintly of the lemon soap from his shower back at the hangar. A frisson of energy passes between us.

"Aeris."

"Yes?"

He puts a hand on my shoulder and brushes his thumb along my collarbone. His emotional guard slips, and I feel him through the veil. It's fierce, passionate, overarching, and all-encompassing. "If something happened to you because of me, it would kill me."

"It won't. I'm fine," I say.

His eyes are two veiled storms. He stares toward the shuttered window as if seeing something far off. I stand on tiptoes and lean into him, feeling the roughness of his jaw against mine. It's so good here when I press my cheek to this tiny space.

His lips brush softly across my skin, and then his firm mouth presses into mine. Even after this morning, it's still a shock to be this close. Heat surges from my toes to the top of my head. Our blurred selves roll into each other in waves. As we kiss, we press against each other so tight it's as if our contact could fuse us into a single being. Just by the mere touch of our lips and our arms that are wrapped tight around one another, we're mirroring and merging until our edges meet and disappear. I don't know where I end and he begins. It's all mixed up and painfully good, and yet I stop myself before we can go any further.

What am I thinking? How can I allow myself enjoyment when other people are in danger?

I'm out of breath as I pull away.

Hunter steps backward, dark and huge in the shadowed, narrow hall.

"I should let you get some sleep," he says.

I nod.

I see then that I'm not the only one with worries on my mind. His brow is clouded. I watch him go, my hands clutching the doorframe.

What demon hangs over his head? What horror is he keeping bottled inside? Is it just King that he's worried about? Or is there something else? I sensed a vast, dark shadow inside him back at the hangar. A painful, roiling wound that lingers in the depths of his being. What horrible dread is he keeping bottled inside?

THIRTY-TWO

MORNING LIGHT FLOODS CHARLIE'S LONG, gently sloping backyard. I admire it through the polished kitchen windows, enjoying the warmth on my bare skin. I'm dressed in one of Hunter's shirts, the cuffs pushed above my elbows.

Every time Hunter and I pass each other, energy trembles between us. The air is supercharged. I try to empty the dishwasher, to get my mind in order, except I don't know where anything goes.

"Leave it," Charlie says. He's fussing over his Cuisinart, blasting up a batch of Hollandaise sauce for the simmering poached eggs.

Unlike last night, he looks oddly disheveled; his faded red hair is flattened on one side. There are fresh creases in his lined cheeks, and shadows are smudged beneath his pale gray eyes. I can't help wondering what project kept him up last night to have him looking so drained. As he removes the Cuisinart lid, it slips from his hand. Pale yellow Hollandaise drops splatter as it skitters across the floor.

"Got it," Hunter says, scooping it up and rinsing it in the sink. "Long night, old friend?"

At this, Charlie turns sharply and gives him a fierce look. I'm shocked at the intensity of his affront to such a seemingly banal question.

"Old friend?" he growls.

A tense silence follows.

Hunter says quietly. "We've known each other for a long time, that's all I meant."

"Indeed we have." Charlie continues to glare. "That's what it is to be old. Take a good look. One late night and the whole world wants to know your business."

"Point taken," Hunter says.

"You're not that old," I say, trying to break the tension. "We all grow older."

Hunter clears his throat. "So. What can I do to help out here?"

Charlie says, "Yes. Moving on. Slice some bread for toast. There's orange juice in the fridge door."

At his command, I go out and arrange a Provençal tablecloth with a bright blue-and-yellow pattern over a round table in the backyard. We cart everything outside and set to eating among the flowers and the birds and the bees.

"It's beautiful back here," I say.

"I enjoy it," Charlie replies. "I'm not one of those fastidious trimmers you see in magazines. Nature should be allowed to grow over a little. Wouldn't you agree?"

I nod. Things have grown over more than a little. Forsythia, hyacinth, and other flowering bushes I can't name sprawl across the lawn, surrounded by skirts of colorful fallen petals. The grass slopes downward, forming a lush green path between the blooms. In the distance, a low wood fence marks the bottom of the garden.

"Is that a park on the other side?"

"It is," Charlie tells me. "Quiet on most days unless there's a baseball game under way."

Hunter butters a piece of toast. "I'll walk you down after breakfast."

Charlie wipes his mouth with his napkin. "Yes, do." There's a peculiar look in his eyes. "I'm sure she'd like to see what's there."

"Why's that?" I ask.

"Charlie's teasing you. It's nothing earth-shattering, unless he's added something I'm not aware of?"

"No, no, it's the same old haunt."

"After that, I'm going to have to abandon you two for a few hours," Hunter says.

"Where are you going?"

"Thought I'd head into town and find a mall. Grab you some proper clothes."

"Wait, what?"

"Me. Buy clothes. For you."

"Okay, caveman," I say with a grin. "But I can't make you do that. I should come."

"You don't trust me? Ah, ye of little faith."

"No! I mean, well, you don't know my size."

His eyes rake over me. "Oh, I think I have a pretty good idea."

I smirk. "I'd rather go myself."

"Yes, well, in a perfect world, you would. It's just not worth the risk."

Charlie stands. "I'll clear up. You two enjoy your walk."

"Absolutely not. We're helping," I say.

Hunter loads at least two-thirds of the table's contents into his capacious arms. "That was the best eggs Benedict you've made yet."

Charlie turns away. "Been working on the recipe. Knew you were a fan."

CLOUDS HAVE ROLLED IN FROM the west when Hunter and I step back outside. I'm surprised at how rapidly they've appeared. When we were eating, I'd seen no sign of a coming storm. In the distance, thunder rumbles, electric and tense.

We walk together in silence, down among the broad bushes. I glance up at his face, so masculine and strong, and wonder what he's thinking.

At the bottom of the garden, we pass a shed so shrouded in clambering rose vines to be almost invisible. A door handle gleams in a shaft of sunlight that shoots from beneath a cloud. We keep walking until we reach the fence. It's chest high and sturdy, if somewhat in disrepair. Hunter stops and leans, half sitting, against it with one foot on the lowest rung. His face is at my height now, and a shadow of stubble is just beginning to show. His hair is tousled and his amber eyes are warm. He couldn't possibly be any more breathtaking if he were a god.

"It's pretty here," I say, and then gulp at the wolfish look he gives me.

His gaze strays to my mouth and back to my eyes again. "That's for sure."

My skin tingles. I'm finding it hard to breathe.

He brushes a hand along my arm and draws me closer. I melt against his chest. The veil between us slips a little.

"Can you know how I feel?" I ask.

In reply, his energy sweeps around me, and we plunge into the ocean of each other.

"I could drown in you, Aeris Thorne," he murmurs.

It seems like eons, the two of us surrounded by fluttering dragonflies and cool gusts that promise coming rain. His lips are on mine and the mind-blowing sensations of outer and inner are exquisite beyond words. I wish I could stay with him like this forever.

CHARLIE'S PUTTERING AROUND HIS DINING room table, examining items in his Etruscan collection with the aid of a magnifying glass. He glances up as we enter. I swear I'm probably glowing as bright as the northern lights.

"Off, then, are you?" he asks Hunter.

"Just have to grab my keys."

"Will we see you for lunch?"

"Can't make any promises. Shopping isn't exactly my forte. Any last-minute advice?"

"No frills," I say.

"What? And here I'd planned to find you a Victorian gown with a lace skirt."

"I suppose just one gown would be all right. For special occasions, of course."

"Of course." He captures my hand and plants a kiss on my palm. "Until then, my lady. Oh, by the way, don't worry if you hate what I get. They're temporary. Victoria's picking up clothes from your dad's and bringing them down next week."

"Speaking of my dad, I need to make sure he's okay. And I have to find out if there's any news about Gage."

Hunter glances at Charlie. "We know your dad's safe. As for Gage, I promise, we'll tackle looking into that when I get back."

I blow out a sigh. At least I know Dad and Sammy are fine. Hopefully, before long, I'll know exactly where things stand with Gage.

CHARLIE IS WONDERFULLY OBSESSED WHEN it comes to his artifacts.

"I could spend several lifetimes cataloging the pieces in this house and tracking their history and never grow tired of it," he tells me.

I pick up a slender glass object that reminds me of a candlestick holder. "What's this?"

"That's to hold perfume, a tear bottle."

"A tear bottle, what an odd name."

He tells me about it and some of the other things. His enthusiasm draws me in, sweeps me up in Etruscan fever.

"Oh dear," he exclaims, glancing at his watch. "I've just remembered an order I put in for two pounds of smoked trout. I hope you don't mind if I leave you to nip out and get it?"

"Not at all!"

He brushes off his hands. "I won't be long. Feel free to explore the house. You never know what treasures you might find."

I laugh. "I'll do that. Take your time."

After he leaves, I poke around, but his amazing collection is unable to distract me. All I want to do is go back outside and stand by the fence and think about Hunter.

Despite the heavy clouds, the back porch is dry and the air is still warm. I walk barefoot through the grass, the soft blades tickling my toes. I return to the bottom of the garden. It's so beautiful. Like a fairy-tale garden, straight from a picture book.

The old fence is soft and smooth with age. I climb up and sit on Hunter's and my spot—or so I've already come to think of it.

To my horror, the whole section groans and sinks to the ground. I leap clear and cringe as I survey the damage. I've ruined Charlie's fence. Maybe I can lever it back up. I climb to the far side, crouch under the main post and put my back against it. One, two, three—I shove and the fence flies up as if it were paper. I spin to see it's now flopped the other way.

That's odd.

I pull on the fencepost. It wrenches up easily, too easily. Right out of the dirt. As I shove it back in place, I'm reminded of Gage's display of strength on the road when he twisted the signpost into a pretzel. I've gotten stronger. A lot stronger. It's baffling. Disturbing. The genetic modification is supposed to be growing weaker. So what's happening to me?

Maybe I'm overreacting. Maybe the fence is constructed of superlight wood?

There's only one way to find out. Among the tall grass lies the stained bowl of an old birdbath. I flex my fingers and then grab the disk on one side and brace my foot against the other. I pull up hard. Nothing. It doesn't split or splinter or anything.

I put my weight into it. And I'm almost laughing with relief. Of course I'm not that strong.

With a snap, the concrete bowl splits in two.

Shards explode left and right. I stand there, gripping one broken half.

Seriously?

I drop it and step away, trembling.

Something flashes on the shed in my periphery. Rosebush tendrils wave in the light breeze, lifting to reveal a square of metal in the center of the door. It's gleaming in the faltering light. Some sort of plaque.

Charlie's words from this morning come to me. *I'm sure she'd like to see what's there.*

Carefully, I climb over the fence and make my way toward it.

Four feet away, I freeze. Then my fingers touch my parted lips as I stare at the plaque's familiar motif: a black Labrador retriever chasing a pointed-winged bird. The last time I saw something identical was on the huge gated entry into the Phoenix Research Lab.

I reach out and try the handle. Locked.

Apprehension whispers around me. It's in the wind. In the rosebushes that prick at my bare forearms and leave delicate scratches that well with crimson beads. I wipe at them and they heal as I watch. No—they weren't deep. That's all.

There's a keypad under the door handle, with alphanumeric symbols. I run my fingertips over the tiny raised keys.

What could the code be? I try out various words. *Hunter.* Too obvious. *Cayman.* Nope, also too obvious. *Charlie. Phoenix. Victoria. Switzerland. Thirteen. Phoenix 13. PRL 13.* It could be anything.

Out of the blue, a thought comes to me. Wouldn't it be sick if it were Mom's name?

I bend close and touch the letter *J*. The silvery key clicks down. Next comes *U*. Then *L, I, A*. Then her last name, *P, E, R, D* . . . This obviously can't be it. My index finger presses the final letter, *U*.

The lock releases with a click.

I'm so stunned I nearly black out.

THIRTY-THREE

My HANDS RUSH TO COVER my mouth. I stand, rigid, as my insides turn to ice.

They've been keeping this from me. Both of them. Dad and Hunter. Mom was involved with the PRL. But what on earth are they keeping inside this place?

What am I going to find out about Mom?

I turn the knob. It rotates. The door swings inward and a light switches on.

Shooting a furtive glance over my shoulder, I wonder how long Charlie will be away. Then again, do I even care? I'm frightened and furious all at once.

My legs are jerky as I step over the threshold. I shut the door behind me. My palms have turned slick. I clench and unclench them, and stare at the tiny landing that gives way to a set of descending stairs. *What's down there?*

My bare feet shuffle across the bloodred paving tiles. When I reach the steps, I place a steadying hand against the pale stucco walls that descend in an arch. Painted butterflies dance along, appearing to fly up and out the door. Their flame-orange wings are identical to those painted on the operating room ceiling where Hunter healed me.

I feel an urge to flee. Instead, I wrap my arms around myself and descend the curving stairs. I count forty-four, and then I'm at the bottom. A winding corridor bends away. The air smells of dry plaster and stone.

I creep along the hall, my hand sliding over the warm surface, following it as it wends right.

Overhead, the painted butterflies are thicker, a flock of escaping brilliance.

Soon I come upon an arched wooden door. There's no lock. I push it partway open and peer into the chamber. It's oblong, oval with a ceiling that curves gently up and over. I'm reminded of a bear cave—or perhaps a cocoon. Yes, that's it. A cocoon.

But it's not the shape of the chamber that makes me take a step inward. It's the box.

A long glass box. A human-sized glass box. The sort of box you expect to find holding a sleeping Snow White, trapped in suspended animation.

Except it's empty.

Light shines down on it, streaming from a recessed halogen in the ceiling's highest point. Rays glint over the polished object, catching a set of jet-black carbon-fiber hinges. I back away from it and stumble against the door. Clutching at it for balance, I hurry out.

I'm baffled and more than a little scared.

Thoughts of Charlie returning make me walk quicker.

Down the hall are three similar rooms. All the same shape, all with a long glass box in the center. The fourth is slightly different: The box is slimmer. A faint, barely there perfume wafts toward me, clinging to the chamber's walls. I've smelled that perfume before. On Victoria.

I can't help myself. I step inside to search for proof she's been here. The door swings shut behind me. Panicked, I grab the handle, twist, and wrench so hard I pull the door partway from its hinges. Fear is getting the better of me—the door wasn't locked.

And there's another thing. The door is now hanging slanted. I'm scary strong.

I grimace at the damage. There's no way to fix it. Not without tools and fresh screws. They'll know someone was down here.

I try to prop the door at a less incriminating angle and notice something odd. There's a clothing hook mounted in the center. It's the kind of hook you have in your bathroom for hanging a robe while you take a shower.

What is the point of that?

Beyond confused, I edge out into the hall, determined to find answers. All I see, however, are more cells. Two-thirds of the way down, I find a cell that's larger. And inside is a box for two. I run my fingers across the glass. Edward and Lucy. This is yours, isn't it?

But, Mom, what does it all have to do with you?

The underground facility comes to a dead end, with one last cell to the right. Its box is wider in the shoulders than most of the others.

It's his. Hunter's. I know it.

Twelve cells in all. A space for each of them?

I swallow the lump in my throat and stare ruefully at the long container.

What is this place, Hunter? What are you, really? What do you do down here in these silent glass boxes?

My feet are like ice as I approach the case and press my hands to it, looking at the empty spot where his head must lie.

"You said you'd tell me everything. But you didn't. Did you? What is this? And why is my mother's name the code to the front door?"

I'm tired of being kept in the dark. I'm tired of letting Hunter call the shots. I'm unable to even call my own dad. To find out if Gage is all right. I asked him straight up about Mom yesterday. Nothing. Not a word of acknowledgment. And then this? I'm a rat in his cage. Fed just enough information to keep me under control. I spin away and punch my fist into the wall. I scream and punch again. Plaster breaks away in blood-flecked shards, and still I keep punching. Kicking. Screaming.

Worry flares in the distance, blending with my frenzy. Worry and fear. Not mine. Hunter's.

He's trying to probe me, desperate to know what's causing this distortion in the fabric of my emotions. But they're not his to know. Not anymore.

"Get out!" I cry, pressing my fingers to my temples. "Get out!"

With all my energy, I raise imaginary hands and push him as hard and far from me as I can. Hunter. Them. All of them.

The world suddenly goes silent.

My head and heart are empty, inhabited only by me. And then I realize just how strongly I've been feeling them all this whole time. Sensing their low-level emotional chatter. I've shut them out. I've slammed up a wall so solid that no one can get through. I hold it around me like a steel aura. And while it should be a struggle to keep it there, it's not.

I'm impenetrable.

I think of Hunter out at some store buying clothes for me. I see him picking shirts and pants off racks, trying to imagine if I'd like them. I see his handsome face debating some purchase, his knotted shoulders huge among the racks of feminine clothes. I see it so clearly that a sob catches in my throat.

Everything has gone completely wrong.

I won't let myself cry. I gulp down my despair and brush the plaster dust off my clothes. No—his clothes. His soft shirt and tightly tied pants. My knuckles should be throbbing. They're not. I pull the sleeves down to cover them and walk determinedly toward the door. I'll go outside and talk to Charlie like nothing's happened.

When Hunter returns, I'll find out the truth.

Then I'll demand he take me back to Dad's.

THUNDER RUMBLES AS I EMERGE, yet the air is bone-dry. I wrap my arms around myself and hurry toward the back porch. Halfway there, I glance up and spot Charlie standing in the shadow of the awning. I quicken my pace.

His faded gray eyes pin me on the bottom step. "Out for a wander?"

"Oh, yes." I'm shocked at my ability to act nonchalant. "It's beautiful out. Did you get your trout?"

"Hunter's never let me down there, you know."

My feet go still. "Down there? To the bottom of the garden?"

"I saw you come out of the shed." His tone is unnerving.

"Did you?"

"In all the years he and I've known each other—and believe me there have been plenty—he's never allowed me to see the high-tech lab or secret facility he's hiding in my garden. But you've seen it. And I'd like to know what's down there. Please enlighten me."

"I—I didn't really get a good look around," I lie, unsure why I can't bring myself to tell him about the glass boxes.

"Ah." He scrutinizes my face, clearly not believing a word. "I see." Something about his eyes alarms me.

I try to hide my unease. "Actually, Hunter doesn't know I went down, either."

"Really."

"I snuck in."

"How did you know the combination?"

"Lucky guess. Please don't tell him, Charlie. I want to ask him about it myself."

He drums his fingers on the deck railing. "Very well."

From overhead comes the noise of a helicopter. I glance up but see only heavy clouds. Charlie turns sharply and goes inside. I have a sudden, obscure urge to run. Instead, with trepidation, I follow.

In the kitchen, Charlie removes the smoked trout from the butcher paper. I watch, awkward, twisting my fingers together.

"You're angry," I say. "I'm sorry."

He slams down a mesh bag full of lemons. They roll free, spilling to the floor. He doesn't bother to pick them up, and I'm afraid he'll yell at me if I do, so I stand frozen and watch his face bunch into a fist of bitter rage.

"How long have you known him? A month?" he asks.

I shuffle my feet, wanting to be anywhere but here.

"Of course I'm angry!"

"Why? What did I do?"

"He's known you a month, and he's given you immortality?"

"Immortality?" I reel at his accusation. Has he gone mad?

"You think I'm crazy? Is that it? Well, how's this? Hunter and I are the same age."

I take a step back. It's like the room's closing in. My head starts to shake slowly in disbelief.

"That's right. Born the same year, two months apart. You're just some girl he met, but I'm his cousin, for god's sake. Look at me! A crumbling old man, while he's a youth in his prime."

"That's impossible," I say.

He ignores me. "I've been the gatekeeper, and for what? My time's running out, while he's got all the time in the world. I could do so many things on this good earth. Look at my work," he says, thrusting out an arm. "You see what I do. You see what I love. I don't sleep. I don't dare— time is slipping away from me, hour by hour, minute by minute, second by second. He has the tools to help me, yet he does nothing."

Maybe Charlie's a raving madman. Yes. That has to be it. It can't be the truth, can it? But what had Hunter said about the jellyfish—they can be immortal?

He's so agitated his face has gone bloodred. The way a person looks when they're going to have a heart attack. I try to calm him with my voice.

"Have you told Hunter all this?"

"Oh, we've spoken about it. Frequently. But his mind's made up. At least it was. Until you came along."

"Well, maybe you should talk to him again?"

"That won't be necessary."

"Why not?"

"Because you're going to help me."

"I can't. I know nothing about his work. I was injured. I was going to die and Hunter saved me. That's all I know. And whatever process he used on me, he's given me drugs to reverse it. We never talked about *immortality*."

At this he looks almost sad. "Then he's a bastard. Really and truly a bastard. I gave him more credit than that. I've never seen him so smitten. I thought he cared about you. Actually, I thought he loved you."

"Maybe he does," I say, surprising myself.

"Not if he's trying to reverse what he did to you."

"I don't believe you," I say. "Immortality doesn't exist. This is real life. What is it you really want from me?"

He cuts me off with a sharp wave of his hand. He marches to the antique glass-front cupboard that holds his dishes and yanks out the lowest drawer. Placing it on the tiles, he removes the folded dishtowels and then toggles a hidden compartment on the bottom. It opens to reveal a small storage space. Inside is a photograph. He offers it to me.

"Have a look."

I'm afraid. Still, I take it. The thing is old—there's no question. All faded and tattered around the edges. I stare at the two young men in the photograph. They're wearing football jerseys. On the left is a younger Hunter, more handsome than ever. On the right stands Charlie, his hair thicker, one arm wrapped around a football, the other around Hunter's shoulders. He's grinning like they just won their game.

"It happens quicker than you think," Charlie says quietly. "You start to wrinkle, your hair grows coarser and the color fades to gray, your eyes grow weaker, and your limbs turn feeble. Meanwhile, he'll be handsome and strong forever."

He takes the photo and stares wistfully at himself. "Time flies. Believe me."

It's truly starting to sink in.

Does this mean I have a choice? Am I teetering on the brink of immortality?

Dizziness swirls up from my stomach, and blackness pricks at the edges of my vision. My hand reaches for the counter and I hold on. I'm afraid I might faint. Are the pills the only thing keeping me from eternal life on this planet? If I stop taking them, will I live forever? It can't be—I almost died when I missed my dose. But what if—what if I just had to wait it out? Suffer through the process? Would I dare? Should I try?

It's so out there, so science fiction.

I see my life stretching out before me—the world carrying on and changing through the decades, on down the centuries. People I love, living and dying. Technologies modernizing and growing. The earth shifting through hundreds of seasons, thousands of seasons, and me living on through it all. It's frightening and wondrous, and I'm filled with a powerful desire to live it, experience it, all of it.

"Don't worry," Charlie tells me. "You and I aren't quite out of time yet. Hunter might have forsaken us, but there's still a way. You're not completely healed. There's still some of the change left in you. Enough for us both to get what we deserve. He owes it to me. I'm sorry, but if he won't grant it, then I'll do what I have to."

"What are you saying?"

His eyes flick to the sliding-glass door, and I turn sharply, my nerves firing on all cylinders.

Two helicopters, a small one and a huge black military personnel carrier, are touching down in the park behind Charlie's old fence. The big one hasn't even hit the ground and men in black fatigues are pouring from the doors.

"What have you done?" I gasp.

"They're going to help us. You and me."

THIRTY-FOUR

I THRUST MY WAY CLEAR OF the kitchen and sprint down the narrow hall to the front door. The pounding of my bare feet against his wooden floor is all too real, too terrifying. This can't be happening. Please, God, let this be some crazy nightmare.

It's not, though. King is coming for me. He's going to steal my blood and use it to inject others. It's going to cause a link between me and them. Dozens of them. Perhaps hundreds, his soldiers, his hired killers.

It's too sickening to contemplate.

I have to get out. I have to hide. At a neighbor's house. In an unlocked car. Anywhere!

I dive for the front door.

The knob turns before I reach it, and it swings open.

Brewster King fills the doorframe. Beyond, I see black cars in the street. He may not be tall, but he's wide, his shoulders straining against his seams. His creepy eyes as they fasten onto mine are the cold pale gray of storm clouds. They tighten into a smile.

"Hello, Aeris."

I cringe away from him, my footsteps faltering as I slam into the suit of armor. I clutch at its metal hands, almost falling in my fright.

"Where's the brave girl who tried to mow me down with her ATV? You were a regular old human back then. You haven't grown faint-hearted, have you?"

I push the hair from my eyes with a trembling hand. "Where's Gage?"

"He's managing."

"What does that mean?"

"You're so anxious. I thought you'd be tough stuff after your first re-casting."

I have to stall, to figure a way out. "Recasting?" I rub my arms and say, "Yeah. It's true, I was in casts. I had—numerous sprains. But I'm better now."

"Don't play games. Recasting, as in what made you better. I hear it's extremely painful." His eyes dart over me. "But obviously quite effective."

"You're crazy." My gaze flicks to his powerful prosthetic arm and back to his face. "My sprains healed. That's all." I need a weapon! If only the suit of armor was holding a sword or a spear. Anything. But it's not. "I don't know what you're talking about."

"Really? You forgot your first recasting? That's impressive. Though I hear it gets a lot more painful with each cycle."

What is he saying? My confusion must be apparent for, as his steely eyes roam over my face, his expression changes.

"He hasn't told you, has he? That's sick. Ha! Not what I expected from the noble Hunter Cayman. Save the news until cycle number two hits?"

"What are you talking about?"

"The recasting process that fixed your bones, made you stronger, heal faster. You'd have to be blind not to notice how abnormal Hunter and his people are. They're strong as hell. Genetically perfect. You think they got like that by going through it once? It's a cycle and every time they go through it, they turn more perfect. Their bones are like Kevlar, unbreak-able. Their hearts are like newborns."

I think of the glass boxes in the hidden rooms beneath the garden and a dark shadow passes over me. That's where they go when they're sick—when they're suffering through a "recasting" nightmare. That's the awful sense of doom I felt in Hunter's silent chamber, a vestigial agony that still lingers in that secret place. It's one of the reasons he wants me to get better. That's the dark secret he couldn't bring himself to tell me. If I stay like one of them, it's what I'll have to look forward to. Always. Wondering when it's going to hit. At Dad's I swore I could never go through it again. Yet Hunter and Victoria, Lucy, Edward, Ian, all of them spend their days under its shadow, knowing the nightmare is coming.

Wait—that's why Hunter left the PRL. He wasn't sick. He was recasting. I sensed his agony when I was in his study.

King is telling the truth.

And yet why am I so much stronger? Is it because I've been through two more small cycles, after missing my noon dose? This narrow hallway seems suddenly smaller; the crawling-vine wallpaper seems to choke the air so that I can't get enough. Trembling, I shift my eyes to the rusted umbrella stand in the corner. Empty. The wallpaper is peeling behind it.

So will my meds keep me from undergoing it again?

I lick my dry lips. "How often—" My voice is hoarse. "How often does this . . . 'recasting' happen?"

"Good, yes. Excellent question. Several times a year, from what I hear. Although apparently everyone responds differently. A severe injury can bring it on, obviously. It's possible other stressors might trigger it. When it starts to take hold, you become quite dangerous. Irrational. Wild. Out of control. Like a rabid animal."

I flash back to my recent hospital emergency, to the monstrous way people looked when I lay strapped to the gurney. I remember how I screamed and struggled, trying to get my hands around Gage's throat.

If I change back to normal, would Hunter attack me when he was starting to recast? The way I tried to attack Gage and Dad in the hospital? Everything Hunter's been trying to warn me about grows clear.

King steps closer, allowing the door to close. "Clearly it's a defense mechanism—a primitive need to ensure your own safety before it's lights out. Once you're in chrysalis mode, you have absolutely no way to defend yourself. It makes sense that you'd want to destroy anyone who's not your kind." He smiles at me. "You're a killer, Aeris; you just don't know it yet."

"That's a lie." As I whisper the words, I know what he's saying is true. I tried to strangle Gage when they had me on that stretcher and the whole world had turned to monsters.

"I'm here to help."

"You really think you can help me?"

Hunter, where are you? Please come back! Please hurry! How do I drop my emotional wall and call you?

"Yes. I do. Come on. Who recasts a person without explaining the implications? You have a life, don't you? The Philharmonic? I understand you're an exceptional talent."

I keep my face frozen to hide my shock.

"Shame that you could also be a rabid killer. What if you start recasting during a performance? That won't go over well in a concert hall. I can make you safe. Stable. Innocent people have been killed by your kind. Take Victoria—"

"Stop!" I don't want to hear it.

"All right. Maybe you want to hear this then. The recasting gets worse. So painful that a number of your kind have killed themselves."

Blood drains from my face and I feel dizzy. *Suicide?*

"What you experienced, my girl, was a walk in the park. There used to be seventeen of you. Now there are thirteen. Correction, fourteen, including you. Before you know it, you'll be coming up on your second meltdown."

My hands tighten around the suit of armor's forearms. "I won't. I'm not like them."

"Is it really like being burned at the stake? Burned and melted for seven days without a second of relief?"

I wrench the suit of armor up and over my head, ducking low at the same time. My strength astounds me. His arms come up but too slowly. I've caught him off guard. It smashes, helmet first, into his face. I push away from the alcove and run. I don't know what I plan to do. Get to the kitchen. Find a knife. Hold him off until Hunter comes back. He's fast, though; he catches hold of my wrist in his metallic grip.

Blood drips from his smashed nose and forehead. He wipes his sleeve across those disturbing, marble-like eyes.

"My car is out front," he says.

"Let go of me!"

"I don't appreciate being struck in the head, Aeris. Let's do this the nice way. Be friends, allies. We'll be seeing quite a bit of each other from now on."

"I told you I'm not like them! I was hurt, that's all!"

"This isn't a game. This is my legacy. Not that you'd listen. But know this—Hunter's a megalomaniac. He wants everything for himself. He's not the only one who wants to keep someone dear alive."

I forgot—he came to Dad's store and posed as a customer. He said there was a woman who wanted a horse. A dying woman. A relative? Mother, sister? Wife? She's real?

For once, I read emotion in those cold eyes. It almost takes my breath away. But he still can't be trusted. He hurt Gage. And then I'm wrenching backward, and my hand is fastening around the porcelain nymph. I fling it at him.

He smashes it away and squeezes my wrist, hard. "I'd rather not damage you."

I struggle to wrench free of his iron-fisted prosthetic. "You're lying about the recasting."

"I'm not."

"How could you possibly know about it?"

"Because after Hunter destroyed half a billion dollars of my research, I agreed to a truce if they'd let me talk with the Winterborn survivors. I wanted to understand their concerns."

Winterborn survivors? Is that what they're called?

"I flew to their facility, and we had an informative discussion. That's how I learned about the problems with the genetic sequencing."

"Hunter said you have a truce. So let me go!"

"Hunter broke it by saving you. What's that saying? No good deed goes unpunished?"

I sink down as if fainting, which I nearly am. My thoughts are confused. Whirling. He loosens his grip and I launch clear and skid away.

Rounding the corner to the kitchen, my bare feet fight for control on the smooth tile.

Uh-oh.

I flail my arms, grasping at the doorjamb. Then I'm ripping the door off its hinges and slicing it at King. His hand punches through the wood as I spin away. The floor is slippery and I go down hard, my butt slamming into the ground. I'm up in an instant, running for the knife block.

Except the kitchen is full of men.

A Viking giant with blond hair and broad shoulders steps through the back door. My heart swells. Gage. He's alive. He found me. By some miracle, he's here.

"Gage!" I cry.

I sprint toward him.

"Get out," I scream. "Run!"

THIRTY-FIVE

GAGE'S EYES ARE ON ME. They're ice blue. Cold as a winter pond.

"Gage, we have to run!"

Something's wrong. He doesn't answer.

I sprint past the blur of people and grab his arm. "Come on!"

I'm pulling him now. Hard. He doesn't budge. Those frigid pools are starting to terrify and break my heart.

"Oh, I'm sorry," comes King's voice. "Did you think he was your friend?"

King stands in the doorway with his arms crossed over his wide chest.

"Let go. Get your hands off me, dammit!" comes Charlie's voice from across the kitchen.

My gaze finds him in the crowd, seated in a chair. Jarhead's behind him. The overpowered giant has his meaty fingers clamped to Charlie's thin, struggling shoulders.

A beaming King clears a path as he strides toward him. "And you must be Charlie."

"What in the bloody hell is this?" Charlie growls. "I told you we'd cooperate. Take her blood and get out."

"Don't worry. We're on our way." King turns to Gage. "Take the girl to the helicopter."

"That's not the deal," Charlie says. "The deal's a blood sample. Take it and get out!"

Gage, meanwhile, walks toward me with such menace I begin to shake all over.

"Don't touch me!" I put the counter between us. "Gage, please! We're friends, aren't we? Please! We're friends, you and me and Ella!"

At this, Gage's footsteps falter.

"That's right, they've brainwashed you. You can see that, can't you?"

From the corner of my eye, I see Charlie try to rise. A thug elbows his head so hard the crack makes my stomach turn. Gage stares at me over the butcher block, over the packet of forgotten smoked trout and a partially sliced baguette.

"I told you," Charlie rasps through rapidly swelling lips, "She's not part of the deal. Take her blood and get the hell out of my house."

King comes face-to-face with him. "The deal was that I'd make sure you'd never grow a day older."

"Yes," Charlie manages, grinding his words. "But—"

"And I'm a man of my word. You, my friend, will never grow a day older. I guarantee it." He pulls a gun from a pocket of his fatigues.

"No!" I lunge past the counter to grab King's arm.

The explosion is stunning in this contained space. The stench of gunfire assaults my nose, and I panic. He couldn't have. He wouldn't!

Jarhead steps away from the chair. Around King's cobra-like back, I see Charlie slump sideways, see him tumble to the floor, see his wide, shocked eyes as he hits the ground. His hand reaches in slow disbelief to the hole in his chest. He draws it away and stares at the slick red wetness.

"Charlie," I sob. "No!" I throw myself past King, past all of them, and fall to my knees over him. In despair, I press my hands to the bleeding wound, try to stop his life from flowing out. "Oh, Charlie, no."

He swallows convulsively and grabs my slippery hand in his. "I'm sorry," he whispers, his voice hoarse. "I'm so sorry, Aeris!"

I squeeze his palm as if I could hold him here in this life, in his house, in his beloved kitchen.

"I've been such a terrible old fool." His faded eyes struggle to stay on mine.

I can't stop the escaping tears.

"Hunter will never forgive me," he says.

"Hunter loves you," I say.

He coughs. "You are a good girl. Meant for him." His eyes roam my face and then his kitchen as if to take it in one last time.

"Stay with me!" I cry.

"Hunter will stop these bastards from hurting you."

I nod, even though I know it's too late.

Charlie slumps, growing weaker, losing his fight. "Don't tell him," he whispers. "He's so alone. He relied on me. He needs his roots. He needs to believe that I—"

Through tears, I say, "He'll never know. I promise."

"You are . . ." A look of gratitude spreads over his pained features. Then he grows still.

I shake him hard. "No, no, come back! Don't die! No!"

His eyes stare sightlessly at the cupboard, at the drawer he pulled out to show me the picture of Hunter and him standing together like brothers. I think of him last night, singing at the top of his lungs, belting out "Sweet Chariot," and squeeze my eyes shut.

"Get up," King says. "It's time to go."

"The hell it is," comes a livid, familiar voice.

Hunter stands in the kitchen doorway. Slowly, he takes in the devastating scene.

His inner presence comes across in a whisper of agonized rage. I focus on him hard, and my wall crumbles. Outside, he's disturbingly calm. His arms rest at his sides in a devil-may-care pose. But under the surface, his energy is supercharged. He's coiled like a beast.

He heard my calls for help. Yet there's no helping this. He's strong. I'm strong. Yet we're hopelessly outnumbered.

"You're trespassing," Hunter tells King. "Leave. Now."

King laughs. "Or what?"

"I think you know the answer to that."

"The girl's out of your domain, Hunter. Plain and simple."

"We both know you're wrong."

Then it's like Hunter's everywhere at once. Slamming men to the ground. Hunter dodges a blade that was aimed for his chest. It slashes his right forearm. He clamps down on the knife wielder's wrist, and there come the sounds of breaking bones and screaming. Catching him by the throat and his belted pants, Hunter launches him hard. The thug hits the range hood and tears it down with him as he falls.

King stands in the center of the room as Jarhead steps forward, arms flexing, fists drawn. He circles Hunter as though circling a wild dog, searching for his weakness. Blood trickles from the cut on Hunter's forearm, but already it seems to be healing.

King grows impatient. His hand rises, and with it, the gun.

"Look out!" I scream, running and kicking King's arm. Too late.

The muzzle flashes.

Hunter flicks sideways, impossibly fast. The bullet catches a man circling behind him between the eyes. A fountain of blood gushes outward—a devilish crimson halo expanding from the back of his head. I shut my eyes, reeling, trying to block out the image now stained on my closed lids, wishing I could unsee it, swallowing against the bile rising in my throat.

Hunter's foot moves in a blur, kicking the gun high in the air and then catching it in his fist. Then he crushes it. Crushes the thing to black-and-silver dust.

"I told you to leave this house. Now, do it," he grinds out.

King picks up a slice of baguette and eats it. Slowly. Casually. Like he hasn't just lost nearly all the men in the room. Only Hunter and King, Gage and Jarhead remain, facing off. Although King only has to call out for reinforcements.

Hunter's eyes flick to Charlie on the floor. They show nothing, yet I feel the blow of his grief slamming into my own. Blackness. Despair. A helpless feeling of floating away from the shore with no way back home. I watch his fists tighten at his sides.

His head comes up and he crosses toward me, looking past my shoulder. "You've joined the party, have you, Gage?"

Behind me, Gage grunts in acknowledgment.

"Nice act back at the cliff. Here I thought you cared about Aeris."

King moves in a blur, pulling a cast-iron pan from the pot rack. Hunter turns a fraction too late. The blow meets his skull and sends his head snapping forward with a crack so loud I'm sure he's dead. But then Hunter spins and the two of them go down, brawling, the pan flying wide and thudding into the cabinet, chairs scattering, the table legs breaking as they and it slam together against the far wall.

Hunter is strong beyond all imagining. *He crushed a gun in his bare hand!* Yet King is strong, too. They're on the floor, King on Hunter's broad back. His iron hand makes mechanical tightening noises as it grinds around Hunter's bicep, which is twisted up at an angle. He drives the weight of his knee into Hunter's throat.

"You didn't think I'd actually be weak, did you?" King gasps, panting. "I might not have your genetic advantage. Well—" He laughs. "Not yet. But I'm doing all right, as you can see. My mechanics can be quite effective. In fact, I'm rather surprised at the outcome. Aren't you?"

I throw myself on King, grab his jaw with both hands, and wrench his head back hard.

Hunter kicks himself free.

Jarhead is right there with a thin piece of metal flashing in his monstrous hands. A wire. Lightning fast, he loops it around Hunter's throat. Hunter butts his head back, smashing Jarhead's face, yet Jarhead continues to hold on. They fall back together, Hunter wrestling with the cord until they're pressed against the oven. The man's ugly lips curl as he tugs hard, causing the veins to stand out in Hunter's throat.

I scream and throw myself at them, trying to tear them apart.

Jarhead's foot comes up and smashes into my solar plexus. I'm airborne and flying across the kitchen. My body smashes up against the doorjamb, and then I'm lying on the hall floor. Gasping.

"Get her to the helicopter," King barks.

I'd almost forgotten Gage. I dart around to see him leaping over the butcher block. His movements are almost doglike, the way his hands meet the surface of the counter and then his feet. I turn to run. He lands hard, jolting the floor with his weight, and grabs me from behind. One hand wraps in my hair, the other snakes around my chest and holds me intimately tight.

"Please, Gage," I gasp. "Please no. You told me you hated King!"

His hand tightens over my chest, and he pulls me closer to him, lifting me in his arms.

Hunter's fury blasts into my consciousness, protective and jealous and seething with disgust. "Bastard," he croaks. "I'll kill you."

"Think of Ella, and Max! Your little brother!"

Gage falters, seemingly confused. I struggle hard, pulling him around so we're facing the kitchen.

Inside, Hunter lurches forward, taking Jarhead with him. They smash against the stove. That's when Hunter gets his hands up under the wire and rips it clear. In the next instant it's manacled around Jarhead's wrists, which are being twisted high and out of their sockets. Hunter switches on the gas burners and presses Jarhead's scalp just inches from the flame.

"Let her go, King," Hunter says.

"You think I'd do that for one man?" He laughs.

"He's your prize boy, isn't he?" Hunter twists Jarhead's arms higher, and there's a sick cracking sound. He shoves his head closer to the flame. The man's teeth are pulled back in agony. "Your number one subject? Gotta be worth a small fortune, this one. Won't be much use if I burn his brains out."

"Ease up, ease up," King says.

"Then let Aeris go."

"It's no use, Hunter. You're outnumbered."

"You want blood? You can have mine. She walks, I go with you. Deal?"

"No way, Hunter," I say.

"An interesting proposition," King says. "Do I have your word?"

"Of course you have my word."

"Release my man."

"Not until Gage takes his hands off her."

King nods at Gage.

His big arms, arms that once belonged to my best friend, release me. Still, he blocks me from getting back into the kitchen.

"Go outside and get in my car, Aeris," Hunter says.

"I'm not going anywhere without you."

We glare at each other.

King swears. His hand is in his vest and out in a flash. He has a second gun. Hunter's still holding Jarhead down when the shot catches him dead center in his chest. Acrid smoke fills the air. I put both hands over my mouth and scream. And scream. Kicking Gage. Punching him.

He holds me back.

A high-pitched wail rips from my throat as Hunter slumps to his knees. Those beautiful warm eyes are on me, and I scream again, driving my knuckles and elbows into Gage's ribs. "No," I shriek. Sobbing. "No!"

Hunter falls forward. He hits the ground face-first and goes still.

"Hunter!"

Jarhead straightens, wrenching his own arms back into their sockets. Then he's dragging Hunter outside, out onto the back lawn and the waiting helicopter.

"No!" I scream, and try to shove Gage clear.

"Bring her," King says.

THIRTY-SIX

I whip around and flee.

"*Hunter*," I gasp, crying and running.

Down the hallway. Over the fallen armor. Through the shards of the broken nymph. Past the dining room with Charlie's Etruscan artifacts all tumbled and smashed on the ground.

Footsteps crashing behind me.

The front door opening. Men.

Not that way. Sobbing. *Hunter!*

The stairs.

My hands wrapping around the bannister. My body flies up them. My legs pumping fast. You can't be dead. I won't let you be, Hunter. Where to go. Where do I go? A window. Bedroom window. My bedroom. Through the door. Slam it shut. Fast! Gage is here. Sticking his hand through the gap.

I'm smashing his fingers. Racked with sobs.

"Back off, dammit! Back off!" I scream.

I'm so overpowered that the handle pushes straight through the wood and out the other side. My arm goes with it through the hole. I'm yanking it back.

Caught. I'm caught.

Gage wraps an arm around my neck and hauls me to the bed. Pins me against the Gothic headboard. My scalp smashes backward and my teeth snap down on my tongue. Blood. Engines outside, the slow whirr of a helicopter coming to life.

"There you are," Kings says. He's got a syringe. "Just in case, you and I aren't leaving without a sample of your blood."

Gage has me in a chokehold. I can't breathe. I'm kicking. Blacking out. The needle plunges in, but the choking hands don't let up. I claw at them. Then I'm gone.

SIRENS WAIL IN THE FAR distance, breaking into my consciousness. The blackness fades to the edges and I gasp, grabbing at my throat. King and Gage are at the window.

King is speaking into his phone. Barking orders.

Hunter. My chin wobbles and I clench it shut.

The blood-collection tube is on the bedside table. And there's my drug satchel. And through the fog I remember another attack—we took Gage's blood. It's in there. I fumble for it. I have to switch them. Fingers shaking. Digging. Clamping around it. I have it. This tube is shorter. He won't notice. My hand is halfway to the table when Gage turns.

"Shhh," I say.

"My blood," Gage mutters.

He remembers? I shake my head, frantic, yet it's too late.

"Dammit." King snatches up both tubes. He looks from one to the other, uncertain, throws them to the carpet and crushes them under his heel.

"Bring her. Quickly." He marches from the room.

"Come," Gage says, wrestling me up from the bed.

My hand launches at his face. His eyes zone in on the needle in my fingers and then I'm plunging it into his eye.

"I'm sorry! Oh god, I'm so sorry," I cry. "Just let me go."

He roars. An animal. Enraged. Wild. I'm off the bed, but his hands grab my shoulders from behind, and like that fencepost he tied into a pretzel, I know he's going to break me.

A metallic whack sounds at my back. Twice. Three times.

Suddenly I'm tumbling to the floor, and Gage's huge form, all two hundred or more pounds, smashes on top of me and I can't breathe. In the next instant, the weight is gone. I see a rag doll Gage thrown, airborne. He slams into the dressing table, sending wood exploding.

Ian stands over me, red hair flaming, holding a shovel. He looks as annoyed as he did the day he urged me to take my medicine.

"Let's go," he says.

I stagger to my feet. "They shot Hunter."

"Out the window. Now." He yanks it up and kicks out the screen.

I get a last glance at Gage, who's lying broken and still on the floor. Blood trickles through my old friend's blond hair. The needle juts from his eye. I let out an involuntary sob.

"Move!" Ian barks.

Over the sill, it's all clear. Yet it's two stories down.

"Jump," he says.

So I do.

I'm falling, arms going round and round, and then my feet hit, hands second, the breath grunting out of me. Ian lands like a cat. We're on the strip of lawn dividing Charlie's house from his next-door neighbors. A sharp look both ways is followed by a wave of his hand.

We check the back first. It's swarming. The smaller helicopter is twenty feet up and I catch sight of King, with Jarhead at the controls.

"He's got Hunter," I say.

"I heard you the first time," Ian snaps, fury pouring from him.

We watch it rise higher, helpless. Then we edge around the front and huddle long enough to see the cars and men filling the driveway.

"Now, while they're distracted," Ian tells me.

"They'll see us!"

"No shit. Don't look, just run."

We break from cover.

For a second, no one notices us. Not for long. Shouts ring out in the storm-charged air. The grass is still dry and soft under my bare feet. I run for my life. We sprint past the first house. Veer around the side. Ian's just ahead of me, his red hair flaming like autumn leaves in the gray light.

I skid down a short hill. Spot the hedge. It's thick and waist high.

Ian clears it easily; my right leg gets caught in the brambles clawing at my feet. I call out and he wheels back, cursing, and rips me clear. The shouts are drawing closer.

"Mirror me," he says.

"Mirror you?" What's is he's talking about? I am mirroring him. Not that I even care anymore. All I see is the bullet striking Hunter's chest and the bullet hole and his wondrous eyes on me. No, dammit. How can this be happening?

"Wake up," Ian barks. "Are you trying to get us both killed? Follow my lead."

"I am," I grind back, running at his heels.

We weave through a block of smaller houses.

"With your senses, idiot," he snarls.

"My senses? *How?*" But then, like light pricking through a window shade, I feel his consciousness probing my legs and arms. I nearly falter at the sensation, and gasp, "What are you doing?"

A bullet zings past, driving into a brick wall.

"Damn it!" he growls. "Are you stupid?"

"No, I'm not stupid."

We've come to a dead end—a long row of attached houses. Ian is on the roof, disappearing over its peak. I scramble up after him.

"Chimney," Ian shouts, and we dive behind it as another shot rings out.

Then we're climbing across the steeply sloping rooftop, the scratchy tiles ripping at my soles, and I'm terrible with balance. My legs start to tremble uncontrollably. There's an antenna. I fall toward it and grab on.

"I'm slipping, shit, I'm slipping."

"You're useless," Ian hisses. "Mirror me or I'm done with this."

"I don't know what you mean." I'm slipping farther.

His probing grows stronger, more urgent. It's not my emotions, though. It's like he's trying to catch hold of me physically. There's a strange sense that my mind is splitting into two pieces—my rational mind that's searching for a handhold on this forsaken rooftop, and a second piece I've never thought about before.

My motor mind.

The mind that allows me to walk without planning each step. To breathe without thinking, to speak without focusing on each articulation. A giant part of how I move through life exists, and I've never given it a single thought.

Now, however, it's drifting farther apart until it forms its own continent in my brain.

My right hand releases the antenna and anchors into the roof tiles. My torso moves upright. My legs stop flailing and my feet catch against the bumpy surface. I'm doing it. I'm doing something. I glance at Ian.

He nods. And I realize our motor skills are beginning to lock together into a single unit.

Is this how flocks of starlings move in those giant, mesmerizing patterns? Not by observing one another and trying to guess the next move, but by communicating via a shared pathway? Why not? Just because humans don't doesn't mean animals can't. Humans think they know everything about this world. We assume other species are like us yet stupider. We have no idea what goes on in a bird's mind, or a wolf, or a butterfly.

I spot hands at the edge of the roof. They're here. King's men have caught up.

"Come on," he urges. "We don't have time for this."

He's right. I force my frantic mind to try to reach out an ethereal hand to him. To my astonishment, a part of him takes hold of it.

"Finally," he grunts, annoyed.

I release the antenna. I stand, arms up at my sides, balancing precariously. I can feel it. I'm harnessing his power. He turns and runs, and suddenly I'm running, too. Keeping pace. We're connected. Completely connected. We're doing it. I'm doing it. My feet hit the sandpaper tiles with certainty, with total confidence. My arms pump at my sides and accelerate me toward the edge. It's his skills I'm using, his training coded into his motor mind. He's sharing it with me, and I'm able to harness it as if it were my own.

We're at the far side. Up three floors. Ian's jumping. I'm so jarred by the sensation, the realization of what I'm doing, that panic sends me snatching at control, trying to stop, trying to take my limbs back.

We're tied too tight, though. My legs keep going, clearing the rain gutter, landing on a garage, and then leaping to the ground. There's a row of attached houses ahead. I spot several SUVs weaving down the street toward us. Thugs are running across the tiny connected yards, catching up.

We clamber up a trellis, my hands and feet acting in complete coordination, moving me in ways I've never moved before, like a trained Marine, like a soldier, like a hero from an action movie. Like Ian. We reach the roof as one.

We sprint across the top, past deck chairs and watering cans and potted plants. Ian's ahead of me, and then he's gone, leaping out of view. I follow, running blindly, leaping and landing beside him on a busy road.

We're standing in oncoming traffic.

A station wagon is closing fast.

My eyes widen, seeing it all in slow motion. The driver, a woman with blond hair. The child in the backseat. The woman's hands clutching the wheel. Her mouth opening to scream.

I don't act. I can't act.

Instead, I close my eyes. This is it, and I don't want to see it.

Ian grabs my wrist. My legs leap into the air. My bare feet slam down onto a hot, smooth surface and keep going. Metal, metal, angled glass— the windshield—then flat metal. I open my eyes and we're dashing across the station wagon roof, a moving automobile, and flying clear of the back.

"Don't fail me now," Ian snarls, still holding my wrist as we leap to the next car and then a third, the drivers' shocked eyes widening as we go.

That's when I see Gage. He sprints out from between two houses.

Dried blood stains his blond hair and face.

"Woke up, did you?" Ian yells as we hit the pavement.

We sprint to the far sidewalk. The sound of a train clacks and whirs beyond the last row of houses. It's the ravine with the train tracks and the bridge Hunter and I crossed over on our way to Charlie's.

We're about to be trapped by the moving train.

"We can't get over the tracks this way," I cry.

Ian keeps running.

Frantic, I try to sense Hunter. It's all a mass of churning energy; is he alive? Am I sensing him or the agony in my own heart?

We burst out past a cluster of dilapidated row houses and onto a wide gravel area. It stretches like a vast wasteland, a barrier between the homes of the living and the roaring commuter corridor that houses the train tracks ahead. In the approaching ravine, the cars whiz at high speed, a deadly, moving wall with no beginning or end in sight.

The gravel rips into my toes, making me gasp as Ian and I hurtle toward the speeding metal snake.

I glance back and see Gage, eye bleeding, his long legs eating up the distance between us. Behind him are the SUVs, bearing down fast. It's only moments before they reach us. I might be able to follow Ian's movements, but I'm slowing Ian down.

There's almost no distance between Gage and us at all.

Ten feet.

Five feet.

From above, a *whump-whump-whump* of helicopter blades slashes the air.

King peers out one chopper window. Jarhead is at the controls. Hunter's not visible, yet he's in there. The metal bird swoops lower. They're fifteen feet overhead. King leans out the back door with a gun. He aims at Ian.

And I leap.

Impossibly high into the air. Flinging myself toward the helicopter. Nearly there. Not close enough. Jarhead angles the chopper toward me as if welcoming me, and my palm fastens around the landing skid. King breaks out into a smile so genuine it's startling. He takes my left hand and hauls me up until I'm standing outside on the narrow metal slat. He's still holding my fingers, crushing them almost, grinning in disbelief and pleasure.

"Hello," I say.

With my free hand, I reach into my waistband. I find the thing I grabbed from the garden rooftop. The shaft of wood is long and smooth. It's weighted heavily on top with metal. A hammer.

I swing it up.

With a crack, the steel head makes contact under his jaw. His head snaps straight back. Whiplashing skull to vertebrae, chin to chest.

Wind pummels through the open door. The air smells of blood and dust and engine fuel. King slumps in his chair with a clatter of his prosthetic limb. I climb over his body. Behind him, Hunter is shackled to the floor with wire ties. His chest is a mass of wet blood.

His head rises up. Half grimacing, he smiles at me. He actually smiles.

"Nice one," he grunts.

I choke back a sob in reply. I'm already working to free his hands with the hammer and my fingers, one eye on Jarhead at the controls. His lips are peeled back in obvious indecision: fly or attack me. I'm ripping with such frenzy that blood is oozing and it's unclear if it's mine or Hunter's. So close. Almost there.

Jarhead jerks the chopper sideways, superhard. It sends me sliding toward the open door, flailing to latch on until I'm hanging half inside, half outside the gaping hole. My legs brace hard. On the ground below, Ian and Gage are a tumble of fists and kicks.

Crawling clear, I loop my arm through Hunter's and work from underneath. King groans. He's coming to. Then Hunter's hands are free and Jarhead is out of his seat, one heavy boot slashing toward my head. I grab his ankle and try to wrench him off balance. He's not falling, though. He's reaching for my throat. His bone-crusher hands are fastening tight. I'm choking.

Hunter's ankles are still tied down, yet he's on King and reaching into his vest. He comes up with the gun and fires, and Jarhead falls sideways. The cockpit rumbles as he smacks down.

Hunter squeezes off a shot between his ankles and he's free. The commotion rouses King to his senses, and he dives for the gun and they're fighting. The chopper is out of control. Clouds and sky spin outside the windows. I leap into the pilot's seat. I have no idea how to fly this thing. The ground is coming up fast.

"Jump!" Hunter screams.

I wrench a lever and we angle hard, still going down.

"Jump!" Hunter yells again.

I glance back.

"Go, I'm right behind you. Go, dammit!"

Flinging open the pilot door, I jump. The abandoned dirt lot rises up with sickening speed. Sixty feet. Fifty-five. I can't survive this, can I? The metal bird descends with me, whipping up a small tornado from below. A sudden spinning motion takes hold of the aircraft. Long blades hammer the air. *Hunter, get out!* The engine lets out a sickening whine, and the helicopter turns faster and faster, gyrating and rolling almost upside down.

Hunter's dark head appears through the door.

It's keeling farther, the angle precarious.

King's got him in a headlock. Hunter's hands latch onto the doorframe, and he extends one leg out. They're standing now, both struggling on the landing skid. The helicopter continues to whirl and they disappear and reappear at dizzying speed. Dust and gravel fly up around them, a wild cloud of grit. We're ten feet from the ground. They'll be pulverized.

"Jump!" I scream.

Hunter leaps, pushing off the skid hard, kicking the helicopter away. The kick sends it only a few feet. Then Hunter's caught against it as a gust rolls it end over end.

My body punches into the earth, and the world turns red.

THIRTY-SEVEN

I'M ALIVE IN A WORLD that's blurred crimson. Dirt clogs my mouth.

I raise my head to see the helicopter crash down with a deafening bang, the blades still turning and flipping the aircraft. One blade stabs swordlike into the earth, pinning it in place. There's a sucking sound like air being drawn in.

I throw my arms over my head and press myself into the dirt.

The whole thing explodes in a ball of fire so hot that it scorches my skin.

Hunter.

Horror surges through me as I stagger painfully to my feet. Beyond the wreckage, across the broad stretch of dirt, the train is clacking and swaying along the tracks. Brown shipping containers, headed for their destination, the busy world carrying on like nothing's changed. Yet it has changed. Because there's no sign of him.

And then arms catch me from behind.

"Got you," comes Gage's voice.

Desperate, I snap my head back into his jaw with a power that shocks me.

He lets go. I sprint into the smoldering ruins.

King lies on the periphery, motionless. I claw through the wreckage. Beyond the flaming hulk of metal, Hunter's dark hair is just visible under a piece of fuselage. I run to him and seize the scorching steel, wrenching upward. It's stuck. *Come on! Move!*

Suddenly I'm five and it's my mother in the flames. A howl, inhuman, issues from my lips and I wrench again. The sound of fire roars in my ears, the awful, familiar scent of burning fuel and metal and plastic singe my nose. The smell that turns my legs frozen in my nightmares. I'm here now. This is real. I'm alive and this is happening. I won't give up. I'll never give up.

The metal groans.

Then I'm lifting it and screaming Hunter's name, and his eyes, those beloved eyes, open and meet mine. I cry out as emotion ricochets between us. Kneeling, I wedge him loose inch by painful inch. He groans, gripping his chest and stumbles upright.

Gage is ten feet away, watching, his form shimmering in the mirage-like heat waves.

Hunter lets out a roar of fury and charges.

Something's wrong, though. Gage stands dumbly, staring from the lifeless King to me to Hunter's raging attack. He's uncertain, surprised, even. He shakes his head like an injured dog.

"Aeris?" he calls out.

Hunter reaches him then. Their clash sends them tumbling.

A siren screams in the distance. The police are coming. Dozens of cars from the sound of it. At the far side of the lot, King's men climb into their SUVs, hauling their injured with them. Ian detaches from their midst, bloodied and angry as he strides toward us.

Gage is losing the fight. He's losing fast. Blood streams from his nose and mouth. His eyes are wild.

"Kill the bastard and let's get out of here," Ian shouts.

"Stop," I shout. Louder, "Stop. Let Gage go!"

They roll through the dust, sending up clouds of brown and red. Hunter's two big hands latch onto Gage's jaw. Suddenly I know what's going to happen. He's going to twist hard and bones will snap, and Gage, my dear friend, will be no more.

"I'll never forgive you! That's not Gage!"

As I say it, I know it's true. King captured him and changed him. Took control of his mind and body. I'm sure of it. King turned him into the pawn, the supersoldier, the tool Gage feared men could become.

This is my fault. I did this to you. I abandoned you on the road.

"Stop it," I shout.

I throw myself forward and wedge between them. Hunter's head snaps up to face me. His hand loosens a little.

That brief moment is all Gage needs to wrestle clear. His eyes meet mine, one bleeding, the other ice blue and baleful. My heart catches in my throat. My Gage is gone.

He turns and lopes, sprinting, toward the fallen King.

The train with its long load still clacks and rattles in the distance. I can see the tail end of the snake, though. The last car, a dirt-brown rectangle, whips along on its frenzied transit toward some unknown destination.

Gage scoops King up in his arms, and his running picks up speed.

Eyes on the train, it dawns on me what he plans to do. "No!" I scream.

"Shit!" Ian shouts, sprinting. Trying to catch him.

It's too late, though.

Gripping King in his massive arms, Gage leaps. He catches hold of the last train car, his blood-crusted gold hair gleaming and blowing in the wind.

He flies away, disappearing into the gloom, just as the first drops of rain begin to fall.

THIRTY-EIGHT

HUNTER'S ARMS ARE AROUND ME.

For a moment, Gage had been lucid. I failed him. I failed my dear friend.

"Thank god," Hunter murmurs, his hand stroking my hair. "Thank god."

I clutch Hunter, sick with guilt and, at the same time, crawling into the comfort of his embrace. He's alive. I never want him to let me go.

"I thought I lost you," I whisper, my hands moving over his bloodied chest. He hunches forward. The wound has stopped leaking, yet it's clear he's in pain.

Coughing, he says, "I'm tougher than you think."

"No kidding," I murmur.

"I guess we're even now," he tells me.

"How's that?"

"King almost got his wish to carve me up into pieces and store me in jars. And I'm strong, but that fire would've killed me if you hadn't got me out. So you saved me back. Twice."

Our supercharged emotions meet, my agony-twisted ones tangling with his. I press my face into him, unsure if the wetness is from the rain or my tears. He feels good. He feels like home.

Ian says, "Enough with the mushy stuff. Let's move."

Hunter takes my hand. "We're heading back to the house."

For once, I'm glad to let him call the shots. I'm too spent, too numb to care. Charlie's dead. Gage is gone once again. Lost. So lost. Is he still in that body somewhere, trying to get out?

"You want to go back there? Are you insane?" Ian says, glancing in the direction of the approaching sirens.

"I'm not leaving Charlie."

"Charlie's dead."

"I'm aware of that."

Ian swears.

"Then run. But after all these years, Charlie deserves a hell of a lot more than that."

We're walking fast now. Rain drenches our skin.

"Listen, he's gone. It doesn't matter."

"It does to me. He'll be buried with honor. He's family. I'm not going to hide and cower and leave him to the state."

The three of us make it back to the house before the flashing cars catch up. There are more police there, though. King's vehicles are gone. Official cars fill the driveway. Officers are surrounding the house with yellow police tape. An ambulance has its doors open.

"Leave the talking to me," Hunter says.

"Gladly," Ian replies.

Hunter detours past the Cayenne, which is parked halfway down the road. He throws on his jacket, zipping it over his destroyed shirt. His face is pale, but he keeps walking.

At the house, he approaches the nearest man and speaks quietly to him. Then we're ushered inside. There's no trace of King's people, only the damage to Charlie's house and his precious artifacts. In the kitchen, given what happened, the destruction seems pathetically small. A broken cabinet. A smashed chair. An overturned table.

A police photographer is taking shots of the room.

Charlie is being placed on a stretcher. He appears to be sleeping, although I know he's not. It's an illusion. It's my mind struggling to believe the soul has left the body when he's so clearly right in front of me. He made a mistake contacting King and paid the ultimate price. I should hate him for betraying Hunter, yet I can't. I just wish he'd come back.

Hunter goes to him, and, despite the medic's protest, he bends over his cousin. I feel his pain as his hands go around Charlie's shoulders. He squeezes him hard.

"Good-bye," he whispers.

Then he's pulling the sheet up over his face.

The medic nods at him, and the three of us—Hunter, Ian, and I—stand together as he's wheeled from the room. I'm awash in Hunter's emotions. Less strong come those of Ian's. Maybe he's too worn down to put up a barrier. Maybe he no longer cares. And so I feel him, too. Remorse. Regret. Sadness. The feelings flood into me, mixing with my own. From farther away, like fires lighting on hilltops, the consciousness of others blazes to life. They know a terrible thing has happened. They feel it. They're sharing in it. You'd think it would be horrible, an awful amplification. It's not. It's a comfort, a sort of tribute.

The chatter around us brings me back to the room.

Officers are making note of Charlie's vast collections. Was this some kind of heist? Others, however, aren't so sure. Reports are coming in of the downed helicopter, and of people climbing over houses and moving cars.

A man with a thick, bulbous nose and a red scalp shining through sparse hair appears. He's got his thumbs tucked into his belt and glares from Ian's face, to mine, to Hunter's.

"I'm taking you three down to the station."

"Fine, but I'd like to make a call first," Hunter tells him.

"I'm sure you would."

"Charlie was my cousin. We're not the criminals here."

The officer nods. "One call. I'm in no rush."

"Great," Ian mutters. "Just what we need. They'll own us after this."

Whoever *they* are, I have no idea. Just like I have no idea how one call is going to help get us out of this mess.

It does, though. Hunter takes the call outside on the back porch. When he comes in again, he hands the phone to the man with the bulbous nose. His expression goes from impatience to surprise. Finally he nods. "Understood," he grunts, and hangs up.

His men shoot him expectant looks.

"This is no longer our job, boys. Head on out. Let's move it."

I stare in awe. I can't believe it. They're leaving. They're clearing out completely. Whoever was on the other end of that line had more power than the police chief. A lot more. Given Ian's simmering rage, I'm not sure I want to know, or the price we'll have to pay for their help.

OUTSIDE, THE RAIN HAS DWINDLED to a dismal trickle. Blurred lines streak Charlie's windows and sliding-glass door. With the men gone, the house has taken on a stunned silence. Ian and Hunter right the kitchen table and overturned chairs. They raise the toppled cabinet and replace it against the wall.

Shattered glass and blood are sprayed across the floor.

Hunter crunches across it, sinks into a chair at the table and presses his forehead to his bloodied knuckles. "I can't believe he's gone."

Ian shoots me a glance. "What I'm wondering is how King found this place." He drills into me. "Any ideas?"

"How would she know?" Hunter snaps.

My hands, however, are fisting at my sides and I'm thinking about Charlie. I'm reliving his resentment toward Hunter. His regret that he called King to hand over my blood. My promise to keep that truth from Hunter. My emotions are clearly streaming right out of me because Ian takes a step closer and Hunter speaks.

"What's going on, Aeris?"

"She called Gage!" Ian says. "Look at her! She's guilty as hell."

"No. I didn't call Gage." I lick my lips.

Ian continues to glare. I sense his disbelief, and he lets me feel the full force of it. It twists into me so that I'm confused. I can't match it with my own convictions. The contrast is physically painful, and I think I'm going to throw up. I struggle to shut him out. For the first time, I see how emotions can be used as a weapon. It's awful.

"Quit that," Hunter says. "Of course she didn't contact him. Right, Aeris?"

"Right." I throw the word out with the force of truth behind it.

Ian's pressure backs off. "Fine." His emotions turn directionless, trailing out into a generalized, fuzzy annoyance. To Hunter, he says, "You should have killed him. This needs to end."

"King? I'm not sure I didn't." Hunter's face is grim.

"Not King—Gage."

"That wasn't Gage," I say. "He was under King's control."

"Great, even worse," Ian sneers. "So now what? King's out of commission and your friend is a maniac drone gone wild?"

"Maybe. But she's right. The guy's a victim."

"We need to find him," I say.

"A little reminder," Ian says. "He's the enemy now. That ship has sailed."

I glance at Hunter.

"She's right," Hunter says. "We have to help him."

"Not happening."

"We need to know what kind of hold King has on him."

"He was lucid for a moment. I know we can turn him back to normal," I say.

"Maybe." Hunter rises. "I need to call Martin Potter back. He's going to want an explanation."

"Who's Martin Potter?" I ask.

"The guy who just saved our asses. I'm afraid this could take some time."

"Yeah. Time isn't what I'm worried about," Ian snarls, rubbing his flaming hair. "It's what we're going to owe him and his people for their help."

"What about King and his men?"

"My guess is they're done for a good while," Hunter says.

Ian starts opening and slamming cupboard doors. "What does a guy need to do to get a decent glass of whiskey around here?"

"Liquor cabinet's in the living room. Near the piano. Potter knows his duty," Hunter says. "King stepped way over the line coming here."

"Want to talk about stepping over the line? What about you? She wasn't supposed to happen."

"Neither were we." His words fall into dead silence.

I want to shrink. So Potter's with the authorities. The ones Hunter mentioned earlier.

"I made the right decision when she was on our operating table," Hunter says. "And if you don't see it, Ian, I hope someday you will."

My heart surges with gratitude.

Ian's face is splotched with suppressed anger. He frightens me, his brash manner, his abrasive attitude. Still, I step over the broken glass and take his hand.

He looks startled.

"What's this?" he demands.

"I'm sorry," I say. "I'm really sorry for everything I've put you through."

From the table, Hunter says, "Don't apologize to him. It's not your fault."

Ian pulls his tense hand free.

"I mean it. You helped me climb houses, leap over cars."

His emotions are gripped to mine, even stronger than if we were still holding hands. He's a good person. I feel that.

"If you hadn't shown up, I'd be dead."

Without meaning to, I've made him see that he made the same decision Hunter did all those weeks ago. In the heat of danger, he chose life. My life. He reached out to me with his powers, shared them with me, and carried me through.

Looking into my face, a faint, chagrined expression fills his pale eyes.

"Damn," he mutters. Then he lets out a short bark of laughter. "Damn."

"Someday I hope it will be my turn to help. If I can, I will. I promise."

He swears again under his breath, gives me a curt nod, and leaves, heading in the direction of the living room and the whiskey.

Hunter looks amused. With a laugh, he says, "Huh! Well, that's a new one. Ian changing his mind about something? I think he actually forgave you a little. Not that this was ever your fault. Amazing. Unheard of!"

"I can hear you perfectly clearly in here," Ian shouts.

"You'd almost think there's a nice guy under all those Irish freckles."

"I heard that, too," Ian shouts.

Hunter laughs again.

I doubt Ian's resentment toward me is gone, but my shoulders relax a little listening to their banter. I pick my way across the glass-strewn floor to the tall broom cupboard next to the fridge. The partially sliced baguette is still on the counter, a startling sight, almost as though Charlie might walk in and resume making lunch. My stomach clenches and I avert my eyes. They go to the floor, right to where Charlie had lain. His blood is still there, a deep crimson stain.

Will it come off? Or will it forever color this favorite room of his, a genetic mark, a ghostly presence, his way of remaining immortal in his house forever?

Then it hits me.

I'd pushed everything to the back of my mind. The chambers beneath the earth. The recasting. The agonizing meltdowns. My anger. His immortality.

Hunter is immortal.

While I'm going to wither and fade and crumble back to the earth.

What had Charlie said? *It happens quicker than you think.*

I do have an idea. The hours fly by with Hunter. The days zoom past. In four or five years, I'll be his age. After that, while he marks time, I'll be growing old. Ancient and curled and turning to dust. And he never told me.

"How are you doing?" Hunter asks, rising from the table.

"Fine."

"Still worried about Gage?"

He might be able to sense my turmoil, but he can't read my mind. I have to give him time to grieve. And then we're going to talk.

THIRTY-NINE

I LEAVE HUNTER TO HIS PHONE call and Ian to his whiskey.

Climbing the same stairs that Gage thundered up in pursuit, I grind my teeth. I blinded his right eye. It's unforgivable. A nightmare. Where did he escape to with King? Back to the training facility Gage told me about? If nothing else, I know now that he's not dead. They won't kill him, either. For now, he's on their side. And in an odd way that gives me hope. It's his insurance policy that will keep him safe until we can get to him and bring him home.

My feet burn and ache, and so do all my muscles. My mind is going way too fast to think about cleaning up just yet. I pad past the bedroom with the crushed blood vials and carry on down the hall to Charlie's study.

It's dark, the sky iron gray through the partially closed shutters. There's a light on the desk. Switching it on suffuses the room with a yellow glow. A laptop lies tucked away on a shelf. I carry it to the desk and crawl into the big leather chair.

The laptop whirs to life. Opening a browser, I type two words into Google: *WINTERBORN SURVIVORS*

It's unlikely to bring up anything. Still, it's worth a try.

Movement downstairs makes me pause, listening hard to see if Ian or Hunter is headed up the stairs. They're not thinking of ensconcing themselves in here, are they?

The hall remains empty.

My attention returns to the screen.

A chill races over me. It surges across my skin like an electrical pulse.

There's a Wikipedia entry.

I click on it and start to read.

Winterborn

From Wikipedia, the free encyclopedia

Winterborn is the name for a mythical laboratory that's said to have been situated in the **Arctic Circle**. According to the story, Winterborn housed a group of scientists who were performing early genetic experiments on human tissue to try to induce a healing response. The research was based on work using genetic code from the immortal scarlet jellyfish (***Turritopsis dohrnii***). Part of its **DNA** was used to mutate a butterfly and create a new, immortal butterfly species called the ***Phoenix recastus***. According to the story, when this new butterfly reaches what would normally be the end of its life stage, it reverts to its **chrysalis phase** and is reborn fourteen days later, fully reformed and perfect. This cycle is thought to repeat several times per year, and/or when the affected specimen is severely injured, thus rendering it **immortal**.

Basis in reality [edit]

It's important to note that while the *Phoenix Recastus* is undocumented, the *Turritopsis dohrnii* is real. This jellyfish has achieved **biological immortality** by reverting to its **polyps stage** rather than dying, from where it grows back to maturity.

Further speculation [edit]

Conjecture states that the scientists experimented on unwitting personnel on the Arctic base. Those personnel unexpectedly achieved immortality and earned the nickname the **Winterborn Survivors**. None have ever been found.

I glance up to see Hunter in the doorway. His gaze, dark and soft, roams over me. Of course he'd come. Of course he'd sense my churning thoughts, my emotions skewing all over the place.

"You look like you've just seen a ghost," he murmurs.

"Do I?"

Not a ghost. A mythical survivor in the flesh.

"I came to check on your toes." His words are light, yet it's clear a part of him has been ripped away. The part that was Charlie. The part that was family.

"My toes?" I stare at him, not really registering his words. Instead I'm clamping down on my emotions, keeping him out, barely holding back my own turmoil. How could he not tell me about my mother? About what he is?

He says, "I was worried your feet might be all cut up."

I close the browser window and shut the laptop. "They're fine. Just a little sore."

He comes closer. It's true my feet are filthy. Dust coats every part of me.

"You do know Charlie would have been mortified to find you barefoot in his study, tracking gravel all over his carpets, right?"

"Yeah. Sorry. I got distracted."

"That's a problem." He rolls my chair back.

"What are you doing?" I say.

He trails a finger down my cheek. Ragged though he is, he sweeps me up into his arms and suppresses a cough. "Someone has to clean up the natives around here."

"Put me down!"

"Never."

My resentment is momentarily softened by the awareness of his skin, of his warmth, of his strong arms.

"Let go." I give him a halfhearted punch, careful not to harm him further.

"Your struggle is futile."

"I give up," I say. "Where are you taking me?"

He kicks open the bathroom door. "The tub."

And for now, I don't want to talk. I just want to be. We survived and I want to live. In this moment. Steamy water is splashing into the oversize basin, and we're stripping our clothes and climbing in, slipping in the water and laughing. His lips are in my hair.

Carefully I touch his wound. "The bullet hole's clean, already starting to heal."

Hunter runs a testing hand over his chest. He winces, clearly in pain, and shakes his head. "Yeah . . . never ceases to amaze me." Freezing, he stares at his watch, then grabs it and takes a closer look. "Five p.m.—" A pulse of panic shoots straight from his heart to mine. His hands fasten onto my shoulders. "Did you take your—"

My medicine. I forgot about my medicine!

Terror slicks through me. I scramble, upright, leaping from the tub and sending soapy water spraying everywhere.

"King came before noon. There was no time! I didn't think. I—"

I'm quaking in fear. Not again. My legs twitch into action and I tear past him, out into the hall, slipping and sliding toward my room. I fumble for the bag; it's where I left it, under the bed. My hands find the bottle. I struggle with the safety cap, tear it off, and spill out a silver pill. Water— there it is, a half-drank glass on the nightstand. I lunge for it.

"Wait!" Hunter says, snatching the pill from my palm.

"What are you doing? Are you crazy?"

"Don't you understand?"

"I told you. I forgot!" I fumble for a new pill.

"Stop, Aeris, stop. It worked." He gets hold of me. "By god, it really worked."

"What worked?" I ask, even as the truth dawns.

"You missed your dose, and nothing happened! Nothing, you're fine!"

"I . . . you're right. But then—that means . . . it's over?"

His eyes are glistening with relief. "Almost. You're going to be fine! You're going to be just like you were."

Fine. Exactly how I was.

My stomach plummets to my toes. It's too soon. I'm not ready. I don't want to go back to being the closed-off person I was before. I no longer care about the threat of recasting. I'd endure anything to stay with him like this forever.

"But I can still sense you," I say, desperate for him to be wrong.

"Yes, yes, you can. It's much weaker, though."

"How do you know that? Maybe I'm getting better at blocking you out. And look at how I survived that fall. How do you explain that?"

"The way you healed must have made you a lot stronger. It's the only explanation. The other effects are on their way out."

"How long until we can't feel each other anymore?"

"I don't know."

I press my face against him. "It doesn't seem fair."

"It's a good thing. The best thing."

We're silent for a long time, gripped together in our own thoughts.

"I don't want to lose you," I whisper. "I don't want to lose this."

He sits down on the bed with me and gently touches my cheek. At the same time, his sadness, his dread of our coming loss pours into me as if the emotion were my own. "I don't, either."

Our magical bond is going to break. We'll just be two people, staring across the vast distance that separates human souls.

We lie down, sinking together into the soft comfort of the deep duvet.

We're here now. I have to grab this moment. Time is already ticking forward. Someday I'm going to find myself like Charlie, gazing at a tattered photo of Hunter and me and aching at how fast the time went. Never again will we be these two people we are today. He pulls me to him and wraps me in his safe arms, and I never want this feeling to end.

FORTY

IT'S LATE WHEN I DIAL Dad's number. The rain has stopped, so I escape onto the back deck. The leaves and grass are black slicks in the dark. The night is heavy with the sorrows of today. I listen to the phone ring, nervous. Hunter assured me Dad's safe.

What if Hunter's wrong? I can't lose him, too. Then he comes on the line.

"Dad?"

"Where are you?" he demands, worry plain in his voice.

I release the aching breath I'd been holding. "It's good to hear you, too."

"Are you all right?"

"Yes. Fine."

"I've been worried out of my mind!"

"I know. I'm sorry. Hunter's taking care of me."

"And you couldn't pick up the phone before now? It's been all over the news. The attack on the house in New Haven. I knew it had to be you and Hunter." I haven't heard him this angry in a long time.

"I'm really, really sorry, Dad. I thought Victoria would call you."

"Yes. She did. But I wasn't about to trust her until I heard your voice."

"Well, I'm here now, and everything's all right."

"Where are you? I'm coming to get you."

"Not yet." My stomach is in knots, knowing how anxious he is. "Not until the . . . effects are all gone. It's safer this way."

"You can recover here." He sounds desperate to keep me on the line.

My fingers tighten around the handset. "I just want you to know that I miss you. I love you, Dad. I'll be home as soon as I can. Promise."

"Wait, is Gage with you?"

An ache fills my lungs. "No."

"Do you know where he is?"

"I—I saw him earlier."

"Is he coming back soon? What should I tell his father? And Ella? They'll be wanting news."

"Tell them . . ." What can I say? That Gage has gone rogue? My fingers start trembling, and I sink down onto the waterlogged wood steps.

"You still there?" Dad asks.

I nod, even though I know he can't see me.

Hunter promised that we'd track him down and remove him from King's influence. In the darkness, a lone cicada sings out. We'll get him back. I have to believe it's true.

"Aeris?"

"I'm here." My voice is thick. "Tell them Gage will be coming home. But right now, he just—"

"Just what?"

"He just needs some time."

Upstairs, I find Hunter pacing in my room. Treading a path in the deep carpet at the foot of that Transylvanian bed. He looks up when I come in.

"We need to talk," I say.

He stops pacing.

"I know about the shed."

"Charlie told you."

"This isn't on Charlie. I found it myself."

"And the code?"

"Yeah. I guessed that one, all right. My mother's name. Really, Hunter? After you said you'd told me everything?"

"Actually, I didn't say that."

"What I didn't learn about was the whole recasting thing. I had to hear that from King. You're immortal? When were you going to tell me?"

He stands and goes to the window. "I don't know. A million times I started to and then . . . I guess I just . . . I wanted you too much. I wanted to pretend we were normal. I knew it had to come out. And when it did, it would all be different. I just wanted a few days."

I stare at his hunched shoulders.

"I asked you about my mom. Straight up."

His shoulders tighten, and he nods. "I know."

"You wanted to be with me, but you kept that from me? She's practically the most important thing in my life. She's dead. I've spent my whole life searching for answers and you . . . you—"

"Stop. I know. It's ripped me apart since the minute I figured out who you were. But your dad didn't want the truth coming from me. He made me give my word. And I was happy to."

Rage flares. "What? You were happy to? So my dad's known all this time? How could he do this to me? Hide this from me?" My god, it's like I don't even know my own father.

Hunter turns and makes a calming motion with one hand. "He hasn't known. He found out because I told him. And then he was worried. He didn't want to see you hurt."

"Well, the secret's out now. So you better start talking."

He gestures at the bed. "Want to sit?"

"No. I'll stand, thank you very much."

"Her name is not Julia Perdu."

"Oh yeah? Then what is it?"

"It's Julia Dryas. Her father, your grandfather, was the lead geneticist on the Winterborn project. We were in the Arctic together. I was twenty-eight, an elite soldier with top secret clearance. It's all I ever wanted to be. I loved my work. I thought I was invincible. It was a Monday morning, just after seven. I spotted several flares several miles out, so Ian and I took snowmobiles to investigate, thinking someone was in trouble. Too late we realized it was a ruse. Russians attacked the facility. We heard the explosions across the ice. When we got back, the place was in ashes. A war zone. Less than twenty survivors. Our radio equipment was destroyed. We had no way to call for help.

"It was my worst nightmare, and I've never forgiven myself. There they were, a group of wounded people, half without even a parka on, standing in the howling ice. Your mother was one of them, only a kid. She was in the lab with your grandfather when he was crushed under a falling beam. He guided her to a case of syringes and told her the stuff in them could keep us alive, but only to use it as a last resort, if help didn't come."

"So you injected yourselves?"

"No. We started walking. People got frostbite. We had no food. But no one wanted to take the drug."

"Why not?"

"Your grandfather was experimenting on himself. We saw what he went through. How sick he got. We knew about the recasting. He told Julia this was a stable version."

"But you didn't believe him?"

He shakes his head. "No, but the temptation was growing stronger. After two people died, things got a lot worse. Julia had a dog. A black Labrador. Phoenix, he was called." He pauses as if caught by some old pain. "A lab tech named Thomas came up with the idea to inject him and see if he died. If he survived, anyone who wanted to take it would. We never saw the results. A white wolf attacked our camp, but Phoenix fought him off for a long time. Until the wolf dragged him away. God, he was such a good dog. The best." Hunter lets out a long breath. "We never saw him again."

My hands squeeze and release at my sides. The dog from the crate, the one Mom had been so protective of. The one on the PRL plaque. They'd named their research lab after him.

"But you injected yourselves eventually."

"That night we lost a third person. We were frozen. Starving. We were eating snow. Still, we were sure help would come. We agreed to wait. We made a depression in the snow and huddled together to sleep. I woke up after your mom had injected me. I was the last one. She was turning the final needle on herself when I caught her and threw it down."

I stare at him in disbelief. "She injected you without your permission?"

"It was forty-six years ago."

I frown.

"She was five, Aeris. She was a child. She wanted us to live. And so we did."

FORTY-ONE

THE ROOM IS DEAD STILL. No sound except my breathing. And I don't know if it's relief or understanding, yet tears are trickling down my cheeks.

"I don't blame her," Hunter says. "I never did. I never will. She was right. We wouldn't have made it. But some of the others still carry a grudge."

"Like Ian?"

Hunter nods.

"And Victoria?"

"Not really. Not so much. I think she changed her mind after meeting you."

"Was she one of the scientists?"

"No. She was your mother's nanny."

My hand goes to my mouth. "Victoria? Are you serious?" Despite my tears, I let out a small laugh.

"Yeah. I know. Go figure. No idea how that happened."

"Why didn't my dad tell me? I still don't understand."

"Maybe he thought you'd feel some unwarranted obligation to right a family wrong. To pay her dues. To drop your music and put your efforts into fixing this. When we got back to civilization, we escaped. But only after they took her and put her in the foster system. They changed her name to erase her past. Perdu . . ." He laughs, rueful. "Someone's sick idea. It means 'lost.' We never saw her again. But I know she dedicated her life to finding a cure for us. Your dad's afraid he's going to lose you, the way he lost her."

Dad knows me too well. Because, as Hunter says it, I know it's true. I do have an obligation. To Mom, and to them. This is my legacy. To find her killer and to know what answers she'd been bringing to Switzerland.

She'd been happy. Overjoyed. She'd found the solution to their suffering. A way to fix them. I'm sure of it. A flash of memory startles me. One I've never had before. Of us peering through a frosty hotel window at the mountain above and her saying that after this trip everything was going to be different. When we got home, we were going to live with Dad. And she wouldn't be busy anymore. It would be the three of us. Together.

That trip was supposed to be her salvation. Our salvation.

And now her crusade would be mine to bear.

As I look at Hunter, my mind is reeling back to that happy day that became a nightmare car crash. I'm hearing her voice when she told me she'd always be with me. I'm feeling her hands thrusting me out the door to safety. I'm seeing the black smoke coiling all the way to the heavens.

Then I recall the man's arms that lifted me screaming and fighting from the bushes and carried me through the blackness to safety.

"That was you," I gasp.

"Yes."

Night air whispers softly over the windowsill.

"Yes, that was me. I saw the flames and came to investigate. I found you there, clinging to the branches, and you wouldn't let go. It just about broke my heart. So you can imagine my shock when I saw you outside the Zenith Club. That's when I should have driven away. Let you be. Instead, I just had to find out if it really was you."

I sink down on the bed beside him. "I'm glad you didn't drive away."

His arm comes around my waist, and my head rests against his chest.

"So who killed my mom?"

"I don't know."

"Well, we're going to find out. And I know how. There was a man who searched our car. I saw his wrist. He had a tattoo. Two letters. *WB*."

"Winterborn."

"Yes. Winterborn."

"I'll find him, Aeris. If it's the last thing I do."

"We'll find him together."

A commotion sounds downstairs.

"Hunter? Ian? You guys here?" It's Victoria.

I hear Edward, too.

We hurry downstairs to meet them.

"We came as soon as we could," Edward says.

"Where's Lucy?" I ask.

"We couldn't leave the horses. Not with the new pony in the barn. She's manning the fort," Edward says.

Blaze. I'll be able to see Blaze again. And then they're offering Hunter their condolences, and we're all gathered in the kitchen, and I'm looking at Victoria and realizing she cared for Mom. She knew her and I'll be able to ask about her, things Dad didn't even know. So I go and sit beside her and we talk.

HOURS LATER, BACK UPSTAIRS, HUNTER puts his arms around me and kisses me.

I have so many questions, still. Like why, of all places, did Hunter set up his research lab in Deep Cove? And was it truly a coincidence that Gage lives so close? And what about Dad, why did he move to the one place where people are living that are connected to Mom's research? There will be time enough for answers. For now, I don't want to think about any of it anymore. Of death and loss. Of Mom and Gage. Of Switzerland and Mom's killers.

I don't want to think about the secret shed in Charlie's backyard and the glass recasting boxes, about the pain that will engulf Hunter. About his immortality and my own mortal life. All I want right now is to burn away the horrors of the past and the challenges that will come.

We go to the bed, pull back the covers, and crawl in together.

In this small world of two, he's everything to me and I'm everything to him.

His kisses are my kisses, mine are his. Ours. Sensations mirrored, echoing back on each other, on and on until infinity. Gentle and then more urgent. We understand everything. We know everything. There can be no uncertainty, no awkwardness. What he wants, I want. What sends fireworks exploding in his mind, sends them exploding in me, too.

Strong fingers and hot skin, soft lips and powerful twining legs. A sea of passion sweeps us aloft. We're a single mind, a single soul, a single body, blending in unbound ecstasy. Trembling and real and surreal. Murmurs melt into groans into cries. We know each other, as neither has ever known a soul before. We are each other.

We are one.

FORTY-TWO

"Aeris?" Victoria calls through the bedroom door.

"Come in. It's open," I call.

She steps inside. I'm standing in a towel, my damp hair pushed behind my ears.

"Hi," I say.

"Thought you might want these." She's holding a familiar suitcase.

"You brought my clothes?"

"I did."

"You're a lifesaver." I go to her and give her a hug.

She freezes, and she's all hard, cold leather and bone and muscle, apart from the soft cascade of hair down her back. I sense her heart melt slightly. After a pause, her arms come around me, and she gives me a hug back.

Downstairs, the others are in the kitchen.

"Can't lie," Hunter tells me. "I liked seeing you in my clothes, but yours are even better."

"Big surprise," Victoria says, and takes a seat across the table from Ian, who's halfway through eating a grilled panino.

"Ham and Gruyère all right for you?" Edward asks, handing me a plate.

"Yes, thank you. This looks great."

We all sit and dig in, and for a while there's silence except for requests to pass the fresh-squeezed orange juice. Despite our sadness, I hope Charlie would approve.

The conversation comes to life, centered around his memory. The funeral needs planning. Hunter's earlier happiness begins to dampen again, tinged with an awful sense of guilt. He blames himself for Charlie's death. For bringing him here. I put down my panino, unable to take another bite.

There's no way to tell him he didn't let Charlie down. My mind roams to Gage, lingering in that sore place that aches and bleeds without end.

"I want Charlie's funeral to celebrate who he was," Hunter says.

"I say we bury him with a case of hundred-year-old Scotch whisky," Ian says.

"You would," Victoria says, shooting him a blast of exasperation. "Let's have fireworks. A whole load of them."

"Might I suggest a reception at the museum that's going to be caretaking a large portion of Charlie's collection?" Edward says.

I, however, am still wresting with the awful truth of Hunter's future and mine. I'm going to be like Charlie one day. I'm going to be the one looking at the photograph of us, wondering where the time went.

I slip away to where I always go when I need to be alone. The piano.

I want to play Mom's song. I need to connect to her. More than anything, I need to feel her there. I sit down, and something awful happens.

I can't remember it.

I can't remember the song. The notes. The words. Any of it. My pulse throbs in my temples, escalating to near panic.

I force my thoughts back through the years, back to the rustic hotel by the sea. I squeeze my eyes shut and grasp for the image of my mother and her navy-blue dress with the white belt. My small size, my four-year-old self on the piano bench, pressing my shoulder into her. Her arm comes around me, her wonderful arm, which smells of lilies and soap. She squeezes me to her and I can hear her fairy-tale voice as she begins to sing.

And suddenly the song comes. It's there, my treasure, my keepsake, my touchstone to her.

I set my fingers on the keys and begin to play.

Land of the white wolf
Home of the reindeer
Where still the mighty bear
Wanders at will

White sea and frozen shore
I will return once more . . .

I shiver as I realize the song reminds me of Winterborn.

"Those aren't the words I know." Hunter has come into the room.

"That's how my mother used to sing it. Maybe she wrote it that way to remember."

"Maybe."

A thought comes to me that I can't quite catch. Then it's gone.

My fingers falter, and I drop them into my lap. "If she found a cure, one has to exist. We'll find it, won't we?"

He's silent for a long time. "I don't know."

"You have to answer."

"I'm trying to."

I rise and go to the front window. Pressing my palms to the cool glass, I look out at the mist-shrouded world.

Hunter's Porsche SUV squats in the driveway, black and powerful as a bulldog. Beside it lies a sleek, low racing vehicle. Hunter's other car. His monster. The beast I first saw him leaning against on that fateful night.

I hadn't realized that was how Victoria and Edward got here.

It's so fitting that Hunter drives a vehicle with butterfly doors that a laugh escapes me.

"What's funny?" Hunter asks.

"Nothing." I swivel to face him. "I want to go for a ride."

"A ride?"

"In your fast car."

"My fast car, huh?" In this light, the green flecks in his amber eyes take on a devilish burn.

FORTY-THREE

Outside Hunter clicks the key fob. The doors glide up to welcome us in. I dart beneath the passenger wing and into the compact, leather-scented interior. A four-point belt harness straps me tight against the molded seat. Hunter slides in and switches on the ignition.

My fingers run along the carbon-fiber door. Then I hold on tight as we shoot out the driveway. The rear-mounted engine growls at my back. It's like we're strapped to the front of a rocket. We roar down the road, the low throttle of the engine a promise of thrills to come.

Hunter guides us out of the neighborhood. Out of town. Down a forgotten country road.

A lone car passes, its headlights catching Hunter's eyes and making them glow with that otherworldly flash in the moment he turns to glance at me. The sight of his eyes, his face, his powerful body in this enclosed, tiny world sends a rush of heat coursing through my veins. It surges along my skin, all the way to my lips, and I smile.

"Faster," I say.

He presses the pedal deeper, and we glide into hyperspeed. I rest my head against the seat and watch the speedometer hit seventy, eighty, one hundred.

My heart thrums in time to Hunter's, in time to the engine.

We're flying fast. Flying away from everything. This butterfly has wings and I'm not sure where it's carrying us, only that in this moment it's enough. Tomorrow I'll worry about the threat of Hunter's recasting. Tomorrow I'll worry about my growing older.

Today it's just the two of us.

He takes my hand and shoots me a thrilling glance.

For now, I feel safe. I feel whole.

I feel alive.

I feel immortal.

Thank you for reading.
There will be more to come!

Drop me a line any time, I can be found at suewyshynski.com.
I'd love to hear from you.